Two Action-Packed Novels
of the American West!

SIGNET BRAND DOUBLE WESTERNS

RIDE TO HELL

and

LONESOME RIVER

SEP 95
JUN 06

SIGNET Double Westerns For Your Library

Ride to Hell

formerly titled *The Highwayman*

and

Lonesome River

By

Frank Gruber

Ⓞ

A SIGNET BOOK

NEW AMERICAN LIBRARY

TIMES MIRROR

PUBLISHER'S NOTE

These novels are works of fiction. Names, characters, places, and incidents are either the product of the author's imagination or are used fictitiously, and any resemblance to actual persons, living or dead, events, or locales is entirely coincidental.

NAL BOOKS ARE AVAILABLE AT QUANTITY DISCOUNTS WHEN USED TO PROMOTE PRODUCTS OR SERVICES. FOR INFORMATION PLEASE WRITE TO PREMIUM MARKETING DIVISION, THE NEW AMERICAN LIBRARY, INC., 1633 BROADWAY, NEW YORK, NEW YORK 10019.

Published by arrangement with Mrs. Lois Gruber. Originally appeared in paperback as separate volumes published by The New American Library.

Ⓢ SIGNET TRADEMARK REG. U.S. PAT. OFF. AND FOREIGN COUNTRIES REGISTERED TRADEMARK—MARCA REGISTRADA HECHO EN CHICAGO, U.S.A.

SIGNET, SIGNET CLASSICS, MENTOR, PLUME, MERIDIAN AND NAL BOOKS *are published by The New American Library, Inc., 1633 Broadway, New York, New York 10019*

First Printing (Double Western Edition), June, 1983

1 2 3 4 5 6 7 8 9

PRINTED IN THE UNITED STATES OF AMERICA

RIDE TO HELL

CHAPTER ONE

~~~~~~

When the fifes are shrilling and the drums are rolling as the regiments go marching by, when grown men and women are cheering themselves hoarse, a boy cannot be blamed for being hypnotized by the crowd hysteria. Of course, a boy of twelve cannot enlist in the army, but he can be enrolled as a drummer boy.

War . . . ?

War is glorious and war is far away and besides, the rebel rabble will disperse at the first whiff of gunpowder.

And then . . . Shiloh.

The band plays, the drummers pound their drums and the regiments swirl past them to the attack . . . and then reel back, defeated . . . decimated. They reform, new regiments join them, new bands and more drummers. Forward, the regiments, louder the drums, louder the gunfire.

The drums falter as bullets and blood spatter among them and then the drums again pick up the beat, faster, louder, as the drummer boys try to drown their panic in a welter of sound and fury.

The dead.

The wounded.

The living.

Night . . . blessed night.

Sleep.

Sleep? Sleep, for the drummer boy who has seen the dead and the wounded and the living on Shiloh

1

battlefield . . . the drummer boy who is not quite thirteen years of age?

Sam Bonner's bed had not been too bad. The space between the two unpainted buildings was fairly narrow and no one had used it as a thoroughfare during the night so he had not been trampled on while sleeping. Of course he had had no blanket, but a man does not really need bed coverings in May, even in Dakota Territory.

He had a splitting headache and there was a taste in his mouth much like that of well-worn buffalo-skin moccasins. He remembered absolutely nothing of the evening before.

Well, this was the morning after. It would have to be lived. He was ravenously hungry, and as he came out of the slot between the two buildings he searched his pockets. His fingers encountered a single coin, a half dollar.

Directly across the street was the DEADWOOD ELITE RESTAURANT. He crossed and was about to enter the restaurant when a sign caught his eye. It read: "BREAKFAST, $1.00."

That was that. But he had to have something to ease his queasy stomach. A good stiff drink might do it.

He recrossed the street and entered the DEADWOOD SALOON. It was a large place which might have as many as a hundred customers in the evening, all anxious to spend their money for drink, gambling or the entertainment provided by the proprietor, one Rufus Chadwick, who was well on the way to becoming the richest man in the community. Right now, however, the only persons in the saloon were a couple of swampers, cleaning up, a bartender polishing brass and a single customer at the far end of the bar.

The sour smell of stale beer assailed Bonner's nostrils and almost caused him to retch. He fought it down and moved up to the bar.

"Whiskey."

The bartender waited, pointedly. Bonner dropped his

half dollar on the bar and the man brought a bottle and glass. Bonner filled the glass to the brim, sloshing over a quantity of whiskey.

"Don't do that," the bartender warned tonelessly.

Bonner gulped down the whiskey and as it burned its way down into his stomach, he refilled the glass. He sent it after the first. The bartender picked up the half dollar.

"That does it."

Bonner felt the whiskey permeate his innards and it was good. His stomach felt easier, a warmth spread through his limbs and the shakiness left his hands.

"How about another?" he asked the bartender. "On credit."

The man shook his head. "No credit."

"My credit isn't good for twenty-five cents? After I spent fifty dollars here yesterday? Or was it a hundred?"

"Yesterday was yesterday and today is today," said the bartender. "Anyway, I'm only the bartender. The boss gives the credit, if any."

A lean, sardonic-faced man came out of a room at the far end of the bar. He wore a Prince Albert with a velvet collar, a frilled white shirt and he smoked a black, twisted stogie.

He smiled thinly as he came forward. "Give the man a drink, Amos. He isn't laughing, so he needs a drink bad."

With a steadying hand, Bonner filled the glass for the third time. But before he carried it to his mouth, he looked sidewards at Rufus Chadwick, the owner of the DEADWOOD SALOON.

"I did some laughing yesterday?"

"Aren't you always laughing, Bonner? You're about the happiest chap in these diggings."

"Sure," said Bonner and downed the whiskey. It did the trick. The last of the queasiness disappeared from his stomach. His hand was steady and he was back to normalcy. Almost.

"Feel better?" Chadwick asked. "Have another."

"I don't mind."

Chadwick nodded as Bonner poured out the fourth drink. "Drink it up, Bonner. You may need it. You did a lot of laughing yesterday after you hooked me for a hundred."

Bonner let the glass of whiskey stand on the bar. "I took you for a hundred?"

"Don't you remember?" He took a sheet of paper from his vest pocket, unfolded it and slipped it along the bar so Bonner could read it. "Man, you must have had a bigger load than I realized, not to remember this."

Without picking it up, Bonner read the text of the document. It was a simple bill of sale whereby he, Sam Bonner, transferred all right and title to a certain mining claim, described, to Rufus Chadwick for the sum of one hundred dollars. The signature, although shaky, was undoubtedly Sam Bonnèr's.

"It's a bill of sale for my claim. A hundred dollars, eh?"

"It's all in the game," Chadwick said easily. "You win today, lose tomorrow. You didn't take out but fifty dollars from this claim in two months of work, including Sundays."

"That's right," Bonner said carefully. "The claim wasn't worth much. But you bought it for a hundred."

"Like I just said, it's a gamble. Win today, lose tomorrow. You laughed when you sold me this claim. You laughed like hell when you were spending the hundred you rooked me out of." Chadwick held up a soft white hand, palm outward. "Your privilege, Bonner. A man has to do his best. *You* did your best. Well, I did *my* best, too. So you can't blame me."

"Go ahead," said Bonner quietly. "Give it to me."

"The worthless claim you sold me, it, ah, wasn't as worthless as you thought."

Chadwick picked up the bill of sale, folded it and stowed it away. In the act of doing so he brushed his Prince Albert aside and revealed a double-barreled derringer protruding from his lower vest pocket.

"As a matter of fact," Chadwick continued, "I've already sold the claim—at a profit."

"How much profit?"

"Really, Bonner!"

"A *fat* profit?"

"A substantial one. Shall we leave it at that?"

"How much profit?" asked Bonner.

"I'm afraid I can't answer that. The Syndicate people asked me not to divulge . . ."

That was as far as Chadwick got when Bonner's fist smashed him full in the face. Chadwick staggered back, caught at the bar to keep from falling. He was sluggish as he reached for the double-barreled derringer and that saved Bonner's life.

A heavy gun thundered and the derringer flew from Chadwick's hand. The man at the far end of the bar, holding a Frontier Model carelessly, came forward.

He was almost a physical twin of Sam Bonner; six feet, within a pound or two of a hundred and sixty-five and the same generally lean features. And the gleam in his eye matched that which was usually in Bonner's when he was cold sober.

He said: "He got twenty thousand for the claim."

Bonner exclaimed softly, "Twenty thousand . . ."

"You were out in the hills," the man with the Frontier Model said, "you didn't know that the Syndicate people were buying up all the claims near their Number One. But Chadwick knew it and he got you drunk as soon as you hit town . . ."

"I'll remember this," Chadwick said thickly.

"Remember my name, too," said the man calmly. "Wendell Morgan."

"I'll remember it," said Chadwick and walked toward his office. He entered, slamming the door behind him.

The man called Wendell Morgan chuckled as he slipped his Frontier Model smoothly back into its holster. "There's nothing you can do, Bonner. The Syndicate owns your claim. Unless you want to sue . . ."

"Me? Sue the Syndicate?"

"That's what I mean. All right, admit you've been a damn fool and let it go. That's what I did . . ."

"You, too?"

Wendell Morgan grinned wryly. "Not exactly the same way. But you see before you the only man who came to a gold camp with a big stake and lost it in said gold camp." He signaled the bartender with a raised forefinger. The bartender quickly brought a second glass. Morgan filled it and nodded to Bonner to refill his own glass.

"My partner Artie Upright and I drove a herd of Longhorns from Texas to Dodge City. We didn't like the prices in Dodge, so we continued on to Ogallala. We sold out for eight thousand, of which more than two thousand was our own money. The other six belonged to the ranchers in Texas from whom we bought the stock. So did we send them their money? Uh-uh. Artie heard about this here Deadwood and talked me into coming here to double our money, our own as well as the six thousand belonging to the Texas men." He took a five dollar gold piece from his pocket and tossed it to the bar to pay for the drinks. "This is what's left of the eight thousand . . ."

Bonner shook his head. "What'll happen when you go back to Texas?"

"I'll let Artie tell you. Oscar, my change!"

The bartender brought the change and the two men left the saloon. They walked a half block to a smaller saloon and in the back room to which Morgan led Bonner, they found Artie Upright and two men named Macdougal and Brown.

"Boys," announced Wendell Morgan, "this is Sam Bonner, the lamb who got clipped by Rufe Chadwick for twenty thousand."

Macdougal, a swarthy man with hair coming down almost to his eyebrows, regarded Bonner sourly.

"Chadwick's still living?"

"Dirty Dave Macdougal," Wendell Morgan said. "He's partial to carving his initials on people he doesn't like."

"Nobody'd cheat me out of twenty thousand and live," sneered Dirty Dave.

"Dave's got a point there," said Artie Upright cheerfully. "However, I happened to be in the DEADWOOD SALOON last night and I'd say you wasn't in a condition to know if it was Wednesday or half-past midnight."

Bonner nodded thoughtfully. "Dirty Dave Macdougal, Artie Upright, mm, you'd be Tommy Brown, I suppose?" He nodded to the still unidentified man in the room.

"From old Missouri," replied Brown. "I rode with Bloody Bill Anderson during the war and I don't care who knows it."

"You'll brag about that once too often," remarked Wendell Morgan.

"I didn't say I rode with the Missouri bunch *since* the war," growled Brown, "but I know them all. Jesse, Cole, Frank . . . Why, I mind the time I slapped young Jess—"

"Yah!" jeered Artie Upright. "You never slapped Jesse James even when he was a kid. Leave that out, Tommy. You're small potatoes."

Wendell Morgan said carefully, "There's talk that Jesse James was in Deadwood a couple weeks ago."

"I saw him," said Brown. "I told you that I seen him."

Sam Bonner made an impatient gesture. "I've heard all that talk. Every time a stage is held up, Jesse James is blamed for it. Nice. Covers up for the lads who really pulled the job."

"Well?" asked Artie Upright boldly.

Bonner looked thoughtfully at Artie Upright, then turned to Wendell Morgan. There was inquiry in Morgan's eyes.

Morgan said, "The bunch of us couldn't scrape up twenty dollars between us."

"What you're suggesting," Bonner said deliberately, "is that we hold up the stagecoach."

CHAPTER TWO

~~~~~~

Eleven miles from Deadwood where the winding road passed through a small clump of cottonwoods, the five men stood waiting for the stagecoach to approach.

All of them had handkerchiefs tied about their throats, which could be quickly raised to become masks. All were armed with revolvers, and five horses were tethered to the trees nearby.

The coach was still around a bend in the road, but it could plainly be heard.

Morgan raised the handkerchief so it covered the lower part of his face. "Remember now, careful with the guns." He picked out Tommy Brown. "We don't want to hurt anyone."

"Nobody's going to put a bullet through me," Brown said belligerently.

Artie Upright chuckled. "They'll be more scared than we are."

Sam Bonner hesitated for one last moment, then drew a deep breath and raised the handkerchief over his face; by doing so he crossed his personal Rubicon. He had been near the river's edge so often in the past ten years, he had even dipped his feet into it now and then, but this was the first time he had plunged into it entirely. From this point on there was no turning back.

He drew the Frontier Model that Wendell Morgan had given him that morning and stepped out into the dust of the road that led to Deadwood.

Wendell Morgan moved up beside him. "The first time is always the hardest," he said in a low tone.

Bonner made no reply. The horses pulling the stage-coach appeared around the bend and then the coach itself came clattering into sight.

Wendell Morgan fired his revolver into the air. "Stop right there, Mister!" he yelled.

The stagecoach driver, an experienced man, began sawing on the lines. Beside the driver, a Wells Fargo guard swore roundly and swung down with a double-barreled shotgun.

A gun on Bonner's right roared and the Wells Fargo man tumbled from his high perch and hit the dust of the Deadwood road. Beside Bonner, Wendell Morgan cursed softly.

Bonner passed the Wells Fargo man on the ground. He was lying on his back, sightless eyes staring at the blue sky, blood welling from a hole in his forehead.

They swarmed about the coach; Upright, Morgan, Dirty Dave Macdougal, the trigger-happy Tommy Brown and Sam Bonner.

"Line up," Macdougal sang out to the passengers who were climbing out of the coach. "Line up with your hands up."

They stumbled out, four pallid-faced passengers. Then one more descended, a girl in her early twenties, a girl wearing a green velvet traveling dress and a green hat with a curled ostrich feather on the left. She was the only one of the five passengers who did not seem frightened. Her face was flushed, her eyes were flashing.

"Hey, lookit this," exclaimed Artie Upright.

"Don't you touch me," the girl cried angrily.

That was a challenge that Upright could not resist. Chuckling wickedly behind his mask, he moved toward the girl. Bonner started forward, but Wendell Morgan moved past him swiftly.

"None of that," he snapped.

Artie Upright hesitated, then shrugged. "You're right, a man shouldn't mix his business with pleasure."

He half whirled, prodded one of the male passengers with the muzzle of his revolver. "All right, Mister, shell out!"

Trembling as if with an ague, the passenger took a cheap silver watch from his vest pocket. "Th-that's all I got!"

"The hell with that," snarled Upright, knocking the watch to the ground. "We want money." He thrust his hand into the man's trousers pocket. He brought out seventy-five cents.

"You ought to be ashamed of yourself," he said bitterly. "Travelin' around the country with seventy-five cents in your pocket."

Tommy Brown had whisked a wallet from another man's pocket. He skimmed out the contents, five one dollar greenbacks. He rocked the man with a back-handed blow on the face. "Where's the rest of your money?"

"That's all I've got," the passenger said tautly.

Dirty Dave Macdougal produced three dollars from one of the men. The fourth passenger voluntarily produced two dollars in bills and two quarters, bringing the cash loot up to eleven dollars and a quarter. The outlaws searched the men thoroughly, found another silver watch which they rejected. Brown then stepped up to the girl.

"It's your turn now," he said coolly. "What've you got in that bag?"

"Uh-uh," said Wendell Morgan promptly. "It's bad enough robbing men . . ."

"—And killing them!" flashed the girl.

Morgan nodded soberly. "I didn't count on that, Ma'am. You're right, we—we killed a man for eleven dollars and twenty-five cents. That's pretty cheap."

"You'll be hanged!"

"They got to catch me first," blustered Tommy Brown. "They been tryin' that for a long time."

A mile from Deadwood the five highwaymen broke up. Wendell Morgan rode in with Artie Upright. Tommy Brown and Dave Macdougal circled the camp to come in from the west and Bonner rode in by himself in the wake of Upright and Morgan.

He tied his horse in front of the ELITE RESTAURANT and went in and had breakfast. He was still eating when the stagecoach clattered past the restaurant and he was aware, a moment later, that people were rushing down the street.

He was paying for the meal when a man burst into the restaurant.

"Jesse James held up the stagecoach!" the man cried out. "Killed the shotgun guard."

Bonner passed the man and went out of the restaurant. He stood on the high wooden sidewalk and looked up the street. A crowd was gathered around the stagecoach in front of the town marshal's office.

Wendell Morgan rode up to the hitchrail in front of the DEADWOOD SALOON and tied his horse. Then he strolled casually up the street toward the crowd in front of the marshal's office. After a moment, Bonner himself cut diagonally across the street.

By that time the body of the shotgun guard had been taken into the marshal's office and a semblance of cohesion of thought was beginning to appear in the comments of the bystanders.

One man said: ". . . A posse's no good. It ain't got no reg'lar leader and everybody wants to get home as quick's possible."

"Vigilantes!" exclaimed a second man. "That's what we need. When the law can't handle the job, it's time the people took over. . . . In Virginia City . . ."

"Whoa!" shouted the marshal, a heavy-set man named Kellems. "We don't want no Vigilantes in Deadwood."

"You said it, Mister," chimed in Wendell Morgan audaciously. "The Vigilantes get rid of the road agents, but who gets rid of the Vigilantes . . . ?"

The eyes of the marshal fell upon Wendell Morgan. Bonner, watching closely, saw suspicion enter them. "I got no authority outside of Deadwood," the marshal said, "but if you boys want me to, I'll lead the posse—and I'll get the men who murdered Lafe Treadway."

A murmur of approval went up. "I'll ride with you!" shouted one man.

"Cound me in!" volunteered a second.

A third man volunteered quickly, then Rufe Chadwick, the owner of the saloon, threw up a detaining hand. "Wait a minute, boys, let's not start chasing all around the hills right off the bat. Where would these road agents hole up?"

"Maybe in your saloon?" jeered Wendell Morgan.

It was the wrong thing to say. There were quick jibes and taunts and a few uncomplimentary remarks about the owner of the DEADWOOD SALOON, but Rufus Chadwick fixed Wendell Morgan with a baleful glare.

"How do *you* make your living, Morgan?" he demanded. "Nobody's ever seen you do a day's work."

Sam Bonner moved easily up beside Wendell Morgan.

"I buy claims from drunken miners," retorted Morgan. "I buy 'em for a hundred dollars and sell 'em for twenty thousand."

The news of Chadwick's *coup* had spread about Deadwood and had not enhanced Chadwick's reputation. Most of the men present were miners and they had a natural antipathy for the saloon-keeper who eventually got most of their hard-earned money.

"Get back to your rotten whiskey, Chadwick," shouted a man. "Your whiskey and your marked cards."

A chorus of similar remarks went up and Chadwick strode off. But the look he gave Wendell Morgan—and Sam Bonner—was not one that either would be likely to forget. If Chadwick had been an enemy before, he was doubly so now.

Wendell Morgan winked at Sam Bonner. "See you in an hour," he whispered out of the side of his mouth.

Bonner left the crowd. He went to the only two-story building in Deadwood, the hotel, and in the lobby sat down in a rocking chair where he could look out upon the street. Twenty minutes later, the town marshal, Kellems, and a half dozen men galloped past. The posse, going out to look for the highwaymen.

Bonner got up and was about to leave the hotel when the door was opened from the street and a rough-looking man brought in two expensive carpetbags. Behind him came the girl from the stagecoach. The man set the bags on the floor and touched his floppy hat.

"Here you are, Miss Thompson."

"Thank you," replied the girl.

The man left the hotel and the proprietor of the hotel hustled out from behind the desk to catch up the carpetbags. "Your room's ready for you, Miss Thompson," he said. "Right next door to your father's. Uh, sorry about that trouble you had out on the road."

"It didn't bother me," Vivian Thompson said coolly. "Not nearly as much as the cracked springs on the coach." She winced. "I didn't mean that. I—I know there was a man killed and—" She stopped, her eyes meeting Sam Bonner's.

Bonner returned her look boldly and she averted her eyes and followed the proprietor of the hotel up the stairs.

CHAPTER THREE

Shiloh . . . the trenches of Vicksburg, Chickamauga, the battle above the clouds, Atlanta and the march to the sea and at last, the end of the carnage.

Home.

A drummer boy at twelve, a cavalry veteran at sixteen.

Home?

A pegger's bench in the shoe factory. Fifty cents a day. A pallet in an attic, the drumming of the rain on the roof. The drumming of Shiloh.

Randolph Thompson had made his ten or fifteen million in the Comstock Lode, some of it from the actual silver in the ground, but most of it from the buying and selling of silver stocks. He knew when to buy Comstock stocks and when to sell them. Believing that the Comstock Lode was about played out, he had withdrawn and gone to Boston where his wealth enabled him to match million for million with men who had torn wealth from the sea and from the earth. When the strike in the Black Hills became known, geologists in the pay of Boston capitalists were soon combing the hills and before Deadwood was a year old, Boston money was buying up mines. Discreetly, a few thousand for a claim here, a few thousand for another a mile away. And then, suddenly, a cool half million for the best mine in the area, which somehow happened to be in the very center of the perimeter of mines that had been bought up gradually by the Syndicate. Their cards were now on the table. They wanted no repetition of what had happened in Nevada, where the Apex Mining Law had been established in the courts. Under this law, a miner could follow a vein or seam of ore in any direction it ran and right into and through adjoining property. All the miner had to prove was that the vein "apexed" or began on his own property. And *that* was a hard thing to disprove. It didn't have to be proved as much as it had to be disproved.

So the Syndicate with its vast capital went out to buy up all the claims which could conceivably cause them trouble later on. They didn't care whether the claims had gold, silver or metal of any kind. All they wanted was the property so they would own every inch of ground within a mile of their central property.

Sam Bonner's had been one of these claims. He had sold it to Rufus Chadwick for a hundred dollars and

Rufus had promptly sold it for twenty thousand to the Syndicate. He had probably already made the deal with them before he had plied Sam Bonner with liquor.

A wire fence had already gone up around the Syndicate's Number One mine and inside the fence, buildings of rough planking were going up rapidly. An armed man stood by the gate leading into the property as Sam Bonner rode up.

"Like to see Mr. Thompson," Bonner said to the guard.

"A lot of people would like to see him," replied the guard. "He's busy."

"Not too busy to buy up claims."

"You got a claim to sell?"

"That depends on what Mr. Thompson's willing to pay."

The guard stepped aside. "You'll find him in the second shack on the right."

Bonner went through the gate to the designated building which had apparently just been completed, for shavings and sawdust were still lying about. He entered and found himself in a small outer office. A man wearing a gun was seated at a rough table working over a ledger.

"I want to see Mr. Thompson," Bonner said, "about a claim."

The man got up. "Just a minute."

He went through a door at the rear of the shack, remained a moment, then came out. He was followed by Randolph Thompson. Thompson was in his early fifties, a rugged outdoor man who had, through the virtue of his millions, become a gentleman. He wore fine Irish linen, broadcloth trousers and a coat of matching material.

He carried a chart mounted on heavy cardboard. "Can you mark your claim on this chart?" he asked. "If it's within our area, we're interested in buying."

The chart was a simple map of Deadwood and the surrounding territory. Claims on it were numbered.

Bonner searched the map a moment, then put his finger on a spot. "This is the claim."

"Number 153." Thompson looked sharply at Bonner. "We already own one hundred and fifty-three."

"You bought it from Rufus Chadwick."

"That's right."

"When did you buy it?"

Steel came into Thompson's tone. "Are you contending that Chadwick did not own the claim?"

"No, no, he bought it all right. From me. When I was drunk."

Thompson frowned. "I see. You're going to claim that the sale was an illegal one inasmuch as you were under the influence of liquor at the time. I warn you that you will lose in a court of law . . ."

"I'm not going to law about it," Bonner interrupted. "That isn't why I'm here at all. I just want to know something for my own information . . . exactly *when* you bought the claim from Rufe Chadwick."

The mine owner hesitated. "May sixteenth, the day before yesterday."

"The day before yesterday?" Bonner nodded. "When did Chadwick start dickering with you?"

Thompson showed sudden annoyance. "I don't see where all this is leading . . ."

"I'd like to know!"

"The only thing that's pertinent is that Mr. Chadwick was the *legal* owner of the claim when he sold it to me . . ."

Vivian Thompson came out of her father's private office. She was wearing a muslin dress that had probably cost as much as the entire building in which she was now wearing it.

Bonner said doggedly to Randolph Thompson, "The only thing I really want to know is whether Chadwick was dickering to sell you the claim before he actually bought it from me."

"Why don't you ask Chadwick?"

"That'd be a waste of time."

Thompson made an impatient gesture. "And you

think you can pump *me* for information? I'm sorry, I'm a busy man."

He turned abruptly and strode past his daughter into the private office. Bonner stared after him for a full second longer than was necessary, because he was quite aware that Vivian's eyes were on him and that the moment he shifted his glance from the private office door, his eyes would have to meet hers.

She spoke, "I've seen you before."

His eyes met hers. "Yes. At the hotel last night."

"Before then."

"I don't believe so."

"Yes."

"Where?" Bonner challenged.

She smiled lazily. "Not too far from Deadwood."

"It's possible," conceded Bonner. "I've been around Deadwood for three or four months."

"But *I* haven't. I only arrived yesterday."

"I hope you enjoy your stay." Bonner bowed stiffly and turned to the door. He went out.

Outside, he strode toward the gate and, nodding shortly to the guard, went through. His horse was tied to a tree some fifty yards away and he was untying it when he heard the rattle of wheels and clatter of hoofs behind him.

As he swung up on his horse, a buckboard rolled past. Vivian Thompson was driving a spirited team, apparently hired from the Deadwood Livery Stable.

"Going to town?" she called cheerfully.

Bonner was not keen on accompanying her on the mile long ride, but there was obviously no other direction for him to take since the rutted trail ran directly to Deadwood.

He rode up beside the buckboard.

"I'm a little nervous driving alone," Vivian said. "They tell me there are road agents operating around here."

"What's a road agent?" Bonner asked cynically.

"You're asking me?"

"I know a man," Bonner went on, "a man who

worked pretty hard all his life. He didn't make much and he didn't have much, but he was swindled out of the little he did have. By so-called honest, respectable citizens . . ."

"So he figured the world owed him a living and turned road agent?"

"Miss Thompson," Bonner said deliberately. "Your father's worth fifty million dollars, more or less. You were born with a gold spoon in your mouth . . ."

"Silver."

"All right, silver. You've had everything you've ever wanted. You're wearing a dress right now that cost as much as the average man in Deadwood earns in a year's hard work. You've come out here from New York because you think it's cute or quaint or exciting. You think you're seeing life in the raw. It's going to be something to tell your friends about back in New York. Your friends who never had to stand in an icy stream all day long shoveling gravel—your friends with their soft white hands who sometimes have to exert themselves by using a pair of scissors to cut the coupons from their bonds . . ."

Vivian Thompson clapped her gloved hands together. "Bravo, Mr. Bonner, bravo. You've told me off properly. I'm blushing. Of course, there are a few things wrong with your facts that you won't mind if I correct. Yes, my father's a rich man. Whether it's fifty million that he's got, or only five, I don't know, but he's rich, you're quite right about that. But twenty-five years ago he crossed the state of Nevada on his bare feet. He met my mother in a California gold camp where she was running a miner's boarding house. *Her* mother was killed by Indians crossing the plains, but her father lived long enough to get to California—and a few months afterwards. I was born in a gold camp and until I was eight years old the dresses I wore were made out of flour sacks. My father, until that time, was using one of those shovels you were talking about. And he was standing in water about ten hours a day. Then he got lucky. He made a strike that netted him all of fifteen hundred dollars. With that he went to Nevada and bought some feet in a Virginia City mine. He lost every cent of his investment and he went down into the shafts of the Ophir mine and used a pick-ax—and shovel—for another two years. My mother took in washing and I—I helped her. They saved another fifteen hundred or two thousand dollars and bought some more feet in a mine. This time they didn't lose it. Inside of a year my father had a million dollars . . . and my mother was dead. She'd worked just a little too hard for just a little too long."

Bonner rode beside the buggy, frowning as the millionaire's daughter recounted her father's experiences. When she concluded, he shook his head.

"There's just one thing I'd like to see . . . you with flour-sack dresses!"

CHAPTER FOUR

Artie Upright and Wendell Morgan had a one room log cabin at the far edge of Deadwood, about a quarter of a mile from the nearest house. They also owned the claim, but the shovels and gold pans were rusted from long disuse.

Tommy Brown was seated on the doorstoop as Sam Bonner rode up and dismounted. Brown shot out a stream of tobacco juice as Bonner tied his horse to a sapling nearby.

"Been sellin' any more claims lately?" he jeered.

Bonner gave him a withering look and, stepping past Brown, entered the cabin. The place was crudely furnished with a double-deck bunk, a plain table and some stools. A rusted, sagging stove provided warmth and cooking facilities. Artie Upright was frying bacon over the stove and Wendell Morgan was sprawled out in the lower half of the double-deck bunk. He sat up as Bonner entered.

"Well?" he asked.

Bonner shook his head. "I didn't get anything out of Thompson."

"Didn't think you would."

Upright looked over his shoulder. "Forget it, Bonner. It's done and there's nothing you can do about it."

". . . Except maybe take it out of Chadwick's hide," suggested Morgan. He paused a moment. "Or his pocket."

Upright turned around. "D'you think he keeps the money in his office after he closes up?"

Morgan grinned. "He doesn't close up. He's open twenty-four hours a day."

"Yeah, but along toward morning there ain't nobody but him and the help in the place."

"I'm way ahead of you, Artie," said Morgan. "Along about one A.M.—when there're still forty or fifty customers in Chadwick's—he takes the bulk of his money over to the bank. They open it up for him special. . . ."

Upright showed disappointment. "Well, it was an idea." He looked at Bonner. "They panning any gold at the Syndicate's Number One?"

"I didn't see any."

Upright carried his bacon to the table and deposited it on a tin plate. "This is the last grub in the house and I've got two bits in my pocket."

"That's two bits more than I've got," said Morgan. "Looks like we'll have to make another collection."

"Tomorrow?" asked Upright eagerly.

"Count me out," Bonner said.

"You've come into money?" Morgan asked.

Bonner took a silver dollar from his pocket and tossed it to the table. "I've been eating lightly. Take this."

"It's all you've got?"

Bonner nodded.

"What're you goin' to do for grub?" Upright asked casually.

"Get a job, I guess."

"Where?" asked Morgan pointedly.

"Plenty of miners hire men."

"Men who've got sticky fingers?" Morgan cocked his head to one side. "Or didn't you know you've got a bad reputation?"

"You been seen in bad company," chuckled Upright. "Those bad *hombres,* Wendell Morgan and Artie Upright."

"Chadwick," said Morgan. "He's been spreading it around."

"I think," Bonner said, "I'll have another little talk with Mr. Rufus Chadwick."

"What good'll that do?" asked Morgan. "It won't put any gold in your pockets."

"Sure," said Upright. "We had bad luck the last time. We held up a stage coming *into* Deadwood. We got eleven dollars. But there're people *leaving* Deadwood with dust in their pokes. We might get a thousand, maybe two."

"A man was killed last time," Bonner said.

"So?"

"It could have been one of us," Morgan said. "That's the chance we take in this business." He smiled thinly. "I don't figure to be buried with a long gray beard."

"A short life, but a happy one," Upright agreed.

"I think I'll give work another try," Bonner said.

Morgan shrugged. "That's your privilege, Sam."

Sam Bonner spent three hours the following morning going from one claim to another. Most of the miners told him that they weren't taking out enough dust to pay for an extra hand, and when Bonner volunteered to wash sand for a percentage of the find, he found them strangely reluctant to accept him even on that basis. One or two claimed that it would exhaust their claims too quickly. Others demurred vaguely and said they would think it over and let him know. Only one

man came out bluntly and told Bonner that he wanted
no part of him.

He returned to Deadwood shortly before noon and
was fully conscious of the fact that he had eaten no
breakfast and was ravenously hungry.

He traveled half the length of the Deadwood street
before he became aware that the town was strangely
quiet. There were horses and wagons on the street and
men too, but all were moving about with a minimum
of noise. A storekeeper stood in the doorway of his
store and regarded Bonner with sober eyes.

Bonner was afoot, since he had returned the horse
he had used for the last couple of days to Wendell
Morgan. He quickened his step as he passed the DEAD-
WOOD SALOON.

A stagecoach was standing in front of the town marshal's office, but there was no one on the stage or in it.
Then, as Bonner approached the marshal's office, men
began to come out; Kellems, the marshal, a man with
a bloodied bandage bound about his forehead, Rufus
Chadwick and several businessmen of the town.

Chadwick saw Bonner and spoke in a quick under-
tone to the marshal. Kellems cleared his throat. "You,
Bonner, I want to ask you some questions. Wendell
Morgan and his pal, Upright, are friends of yours . . ."

"Wendell Morgan," Bonner said clearly, "saved my
life when Rufe Chadwick tried to kill me after he'd
cheated me out of my claim . . ."

"I told you the man's mixed up with that crowd,"
Chadwick cried angrily. "They lie for each other . . ."

"You calling me a liar?" Bonner demanded.

"You see?" Chadwick cried triumphantly. "Now he
wants to gun me!"

"Now wait a minute, Chadwick," said the marshal,
"let's not get mixed up in personal feuds. Bonner,
where were you all morning?"

"Looking for work."

"Work? What kind of work?"

"Panning gold. Digging . . . anything . . ."

"You weren't with Morgan and Upright along about nine o'clock this morning?"

"No."

"Where were you at that time?"

"I told you—looking for work."

"Where were you looking for this work?"

"Along the creek."

A miner who had come up moved forward. "He hit me for a job."

"This morning?" exclaimed the marshal.

The man nodded. "Musta been around nine fifteen, nine thirty."

"The holdup was at nine o'clock," Chadwick said angrily. "He could have made it to the creek by nine thirty."

"Maybe," said the miner, "but before he struck me for a job, he was talkin' to Zeb Flothow who's got the claim right above me. I saw him there. They was arguin' for quite a spell."

Chadwick pounced on that. "Arguing? What were they arguing about?"

"About my reputation," Bonner flashed at Chadwick. "The story you've been spreading around."

"I haven't been spreading any story about you. Nothing that isn't true. You been hangin' around with Morgan and his pals and everybody knows what they are. Road agents . . ."

"You can prove that?" Bonner snapped.

Chadwick chuckled wickedly. "You tell him, Marshal."

"At nine o'clock this morning," Marshal Kellems said, "the eastbound stage was held up. Rather, an attempt was made to hold it up, because the attempt failed and"—the marshal paused significantly—"and Wendell Morgan was wounded and captured." He nodded toward the building. "He's in the lockup right now."

"How bad is he hurt?" Bonner asked.

"Not bad. Just a bullet in his leg. The point is——"

"The point is," sneered Chadwick, "we're going to

string him up. And his friends along with him. As soon
as we catch them . . ."

"Whoa!" cried Kellems. "You can stop that kind of
talk right now. Wendell Morgan may get hung, but it's
going to be after he's had a fair trial and he's been
found guilty."

"There ain't no question of his guilt," snarled Rufus
Chadwick. "He was caught red-handed and I don't
see the use of any trial."

A man in the crowd yelped, "You said it!" and
Rufus Chadwick pounced on that. "I say it's a waste of
time to hold him in jail until a judge gets good and
ready to come around and give him a trial."

"That's lynch talk, Chadwick," said the marshal. "I
don't like it one bit."

"Maybe you don't, Marshal," Chadwick retorted.
"Sheriff Plummer over in Virginia City didn't like it
either."

"Are you accusing me of being in with the road
agents?" challenged Kellems.

A hush had fallen upon the crowd. Rufus Chadwick shot a quick look around, saw no visible support
for himself at the moment, and took the quick way out.
"I'm not accusing you of anything," he mumbled and,
whirling, walked away.

The marshal looked after Chadwick, then made a
gesture of dismissal to the group gathered around him.
"Morgan's in jail—he'll be taken care of. Go about
your business now."

The crowd began dispersing. Bonner walked down
the street. He hesitated in front of Chadwick's saloon,
then continued on to the edge of town.

He looked over his shoulder, saw no one coming up
behind him and then continued on to the cabin where
Artie Upright and Wendell Morgan had lived.

The door hung open and he looked inside. There
was no one in the cabin. Bonner had not expected
there would be. He went around behind the cabin
where Morgan and his friends usually kept their horses.
There were no horses there.

He was turning away when a low whistle reached him. A hundred yards behind the cabin was a clump of heavy brush. Bonner walked easily toward the woods.

As he neared them a voice said: "Duck! Someone's coming up the road . . ."

Bonner darted into the brush and found Artie Upright standing near a saddled horse. He turned and looked through the fringe of shrubbery past the cabin. A miner was strolling along the rutted road, headed for Deadwood.

Upright said, "They got Wendell!"

"I know," Bonner said. "And Chadwick's making lynch talk."

"They wouldn't!" cried Upright quickly.

"I don't know," said Bonner shaking his head. "The marshal's all right, but Chadwick's crowd could stir up something."

"We've got to get him out," Upright declared.

"Out of jail?"

"Of course. . . . How bad is he hurt?"

"They didn't tell me," Bonner said. "In fact, I had a few bad moments myself. Chadwick tried to put me in the holdup."

Upright frowned. "It was Tommy Brown again. He just can't keep his finger off the trigger. Things were going fine, then all of a sudden Tommy got to shooting and first thing you know, everybody was shooting. We were lucky to get away. Dirty Dave got creased, but not bad."

"Where're Brown and Macdougal now?"

Upright made a gesture. "Just as well you don't know. I'm having trouble with Tommy as it is. He thinks you spilled it about the stage."

"That's not true!"

"I don't think it is." Upright hesitated. "Why'd you come out here now?"

"I thought one of you might be around . . ."

"Well, I was."

"I thought you ought to know about the lynch talk."

Upright winced. "Why'd it have to be Wendell? Tommy and Dave——" He shrugged. "We've hung around together up here, but Wendell and me, we go 'way back. . . ."

"After this," Bonner said, "I don't think I ought to get in touch with you again. They may be watching me."

"You're probably right." Upright frowned. "D'you know a man named Fair—Jim Fair?"

"I think I've seen him around . . . tall, heavy-set, about thirty."

"That's him. Fair wasn't ever one of us, but I've done him a couple of favors. If you want to get a message to me, tell Fair to come out here and——" Upright shot a look toward the cabin, "tell him to open the window. It's closed now and I'll see that it's kept closed, but if you want to leave a message, tell Fair to drop it inside the shack and leave the window open."

Bonner nodded. "I'd better get back to town."

"All right, Bonner and—thanks."

Bonner started to turn away and then Upright said, "Oh, how are you fixed for money?"

"I'm not."

"Here——"

Upright held out a handful of gold coins. "We made a strike before the shooting started."

"No," said Bonner bluntly.

"You took a split the other day!"

"That was different." Bonner hesitated. "I guess you think I'm splitting hairs . . ."

"The long way!"

"I'd just as soon not take any of this money."

"Have it your way. And if I don't see you again . . . good luck!"

Bonner nodded and walked off.

By supper time, Sam Bonner could think of nothing but the pangs in his stomach. He hadn't eaten a mouth-

ful of food all day and he saw no immediate prospects
of getting any money to buy food. He toyed with the
idea of going to the restaurant and offering to wash
dishes for a meal and was actually walking toward
the place when he spied Jim Fair going toward the
DEADWOOD SALOON.

Bonner called to him. "Jim!"

Jim Fair stopped and Bonner crossed to him. As he
recognized him, Fair frowned. "You're Sam Bonner."

Bonner nodded. "Artie Upright told me to get in
touch with you . . ."

Fair winced. "I don't know Artie Upright—not to
talk to, I mean."

"I see," said Bonner. "If you don't know him, he
couldn't have done you any favors."

Fair looked covertly over his shoulder. "It ain't
healthy to know Upright and his crowd. Not now it
ain't."

"Wendell Morgan's a friend of mine," Bonner said.

"I know. I—I oughtn't to be seen talkin' to you."

"Well, don't be," Bonner said curtly. He started to
turn away, but Fair caught his arm.

"Here—I heard you was broke!" Fair tendered him
a coin. Bonner, angry, was about to brush aside Fair's
hand, but his anger was not strong enough to overcome
his hunger.

He took the coin, said, "Thanks" and turned away.
He recrossed the street and in the light from the restaurant saw with surprise that the coin was a ten dollar
gold piece.

CHAPTER FIVE

The shoe factory.

Hammer, peg, hammer, peg.

Ten hours a day, six days a week. A working man's life. A life of toil and a full dinner pail.

Memories?

Memories of the blood-drenched earth at Shiloh?

Hammer, peg, hammer, peg.

The march to the sea . . . Sherman's raiders . . . Sherman's robbers.

You there, boy, you're falling behind. Keep that hammer moving!

Hammer, peg, hammer, peg.

Shoes . . . shoes for the gentlemen, shoes for Milady . . . Shoes . . . boots.

Boots for cavalrymen.

Sam Bonner came out of the DEADWOOD ELITE RESTAURANT and saw the clump of men gathered outside the building that housed the office of Marshal Kellems and the little jail at the rear. The men were quiet, but across the street in the DEADWOOD SALOON there was noise that was unusual for even the DEADWOOD SALOON.

Bonner crossed and pushed open the swinging doors of Rufus Chadwick's saloon. The games were operating to full capacity but the men were lined up before the long bar, three and four deep. A hulking, bewhiskered man who was dressed like a miner and looked like a miner, but had strangely soft hands for a miner was belaboring an audience, already roused with liquor that had been poured freely and for which no payment had been asked.

The orator was booming: ". . . Every manjack of you knows what happened in Virginia City. No miner's life was safe, no traveler carried an ounce of dust out of the diggings. Men were murdered in their sleep. The sheriff brought no man to trial unless he was forced to it and always the man brought to trial was acquitted. 'Cause why? 'Cause the sheriff himself was the leader of the road agents . . . !"

A roar went up and as it subsided, a dissenting sharp voice shouted, "You accusing Kellems of being in with the road agents?"

"I'm telling you," roared the man with his back to the bar. "Why should we take any chances? Wendell Morgan was caught red-handed—he's guilty as hell. I say, do what they did in Virginia City. Set an example . . ."

"Lynch him!"

"Lynch him!" roared a score of whiskey-roughened voices.

"Wendell Morgan never worked a day in his life," shouted the spokesman. "He was a road agent in Texas and he's a road agent in Dakota. As long as him and his kind are around here, not one of you working men is safe. You stand in the water all day, you shovel gravel and you pan it . . . hard, backbreaking work, and when you get an ounce of pay, who gets it? Wendell Morgan . . . !"

"Lynch him!" roared two-score voices in the DEAD-WOOD SALOON.

Bottles of whiskey were lined up on the bar. A miner reached for one and there was no protest from the men behind the bar. Another bottle was scooped up, a third . . .

"Lynch the road agents! String them up. Hang Wendell Morgan . . . !"

His stomach threatening to heave up the only food he had eaten that day, Sam Bonner reeled toward the door of the saloon. He went through and stood outside, braced against the hitchrail. Men began to pour out of the saloon. Two or three brushed against Bonner, bruising him on the hitchrail.

Marshal Kellems stood in the doorway of the office that led to the jail at the rear.

"Go home, men," he pleaded earnestly. "Don't do anything for which you'll be sorry the rest of your lives."

"We want Morgan!" yelled a half-drunken miner.

"Lynch him!" screamed a voice at the rear of the crowd.

There was a concerted pushing from the rear and Marshal Kellems was shoved into his office. Men swarmed past him and in a moment or two they had Wendell Morgan and were dragging him out of the jail onto the street.

An addition had been started at the side of the hotel and a heavy beam stuck out some six feet, about eight feet from the ground. One of the would-be lynchers spied the beam and yelled to his cohorts.

"Here's a fine place—just made for hanging!"

The movement toward the hotel promptly began. Wendell Morgan, battered and bruised from cuffing along the way, soon stood in a small cleared spot under the protruding beam. The mob now needed a leader for the final act, but the man who had instigated the movement inside the saloon was oddly missing.

Rufus Chadwick assumed the leadership. "Bring up a horse," he ordered.

A man untied a horse from the hitchrail where Sam Bonner stood, some sixty or seventy feet from the lynching spot. Bonner climbed up on another horse so he could see over the heads of the crowd.

A flash of light blinded him for a moment and he looked upward at the second floor of the hotel. Framed in an open window was Randolph Thompson, and then—the head and shoulders of Vivian Thompson appeared beside her father. Below them, some ten feet to the left, was the beam over which a rope was just being thrown. The hands of Wendell Morgan had been tied behind him and he was forced onto the horse. A man stood beside the horse, a rope in his hand. He was fashioning a noose.

Rufus Chadwick, now the open leader of the lynching mob, stepped up beside the horse.

"You've got one minute left, Morgan," he said. "Name the men in your gang."

"Go to hell," said Wendell Morgan.

Rufus Chadwick whipped out a revolver and was about to reach up to strike Morgan in the face, but he thought better of it.

"He's had his chance," he snapped. "Put the rope around his neck. . . ."

But his previous request of Morgan had struck a note in the minds of some of the would-be lynchers. One of them, soberer than the others, took it up. "Give him a chance—if he names the others, we let him go. . . ."

"We're *not* letting him go!" cried Chadwick. "There's blood on his hands—he's the one who killed the shotgun guard. . . ."

"We don't know that," protested a man. "It might have been one of the others . . ."

"Who was it?" yelled a man somewhere toward the rear. "Name him and you don't hang."

"Yeah, name him!" cried several voices.

"Put the rope around his neck," ordered Chadwick, frantic that the lynching would be frustrated.

The man who had fashioned the noose thrust it into Chadwick's hands. "*You* do it."

Chadwick tried to force the noose back into the other man's hands, but the man backed away. "It's your party."

"It's not," protested Chadwick. "We're all in this. And we're doing the right thing. We've got to warn all road agents in this territory that they can't go robbing and killing honest citizens. . . ."

"Look who's talking?" hooted a man in the crowd. There were one or two yelps of agreement and

Chadwick saw that the temper of the mob was rapidly cooling. Quickly he reached up and tossed the noose over Wendell Morgan's head. With his own hands Chadwick then tied the loose end of the rope around a post. All that remained now was to drive the horse out from under him.

Chadwick wanted someone else to do that job. "Hit the horse!" he ordered.

"It's *your* hanging," a man said.

Cursing softly, Chadwick stepped up to strike the horse's flanks.

Fifty feet away, Sam Bonner rose up in the stirrups of the horse he had commandeered. His revolver was thrust out. He pulled the trigger.

"Goodbye, Wendell!" Bonner cried out softly.

Morgan's body jerked from the impact of the bullet. He was dead a fraction of a second before the horse leaped out from under him.

A dead man dangled from the rope.

Bonner jammed his heels into the flanks of the commandeered horse. It galloped past the mob surrounding the body of Wendell Morgan and was fifty yards or more past it before a single gun was fired.

There was no pursuit. No man, except Chadwick's closest underlings, could be found who were willing to go after the man who had killed Wendell Morgan a fraction of a second before he was hanged.

Chadwick remained in his saloon all that night and the next day. His underlings, heavily armed, remained with him and there were virtually no customers.

CHAPTER SIX

~~~~~~~~~~~~~~~~~~~~~~~~~~~~~~~~~~~

The highways, the roads and the trails, the farmlands and the prairies and the desert . . . the canyons and the mountains. Cow towns and trail towns, boom towns and ghost towns, mining camps and cities. Bad men and peace officers, soldiers and Indians. Sam Bonner, erstwhile shoe pegger, saw them all.

Death on the prairie.

Death in the mountains.

Death on the battlefields.

Life is expendable and death is the end.

Live for the moment—live for all it is worth and enjoy it while you can, if you can. Laugh . . .

Laugh, lest you weep.

Baker Falls, as its name suggested, was located on a river, some forty miles from Boston. It had a population of approximately twelve hundred and was the trading center for a substantial farming area, but this business from the farmers would not have justified its population. Two industries did that; a mill where cotton cloth of a fair quality was woven and a shoe factory. The Tanner Shoe Company.

Before the war, the shoe factory had employed some fifty hands and, moved with patriotism, Joseph Tanner had promised every man who enlisted in the army would find his job awaiting him upon his return. He had not included boys in this promise, but in 1865 a tall, lean youth had come into his office and informed him that he was ready to go back to work. Tanner

scarcely remembered the boy who had run away from
home at the age of twelve to enroll as a drummer boy,
but the business of the shoe factory had prospered during the war, so that three hundred hands were now
employed. A shoe pegger could always be used and
Tanner sent the ex-drummer boy to a shoe-pegger's
bench.

He had completely forgotten the matter when, some
weeks later, one of his supervisors came into his office.
"I know how you feel about veterans, Mr. Tanner," the
supervisor said. "You promised them jobs when they
came back from the war, but that boy, Bonner, isn't
giving us a full day's work . . ."

"Bonner? Isn't that the name of the man who——?"

"This is his son. He was a pegger before the
war. . . ."

"What's he doing now?"

"Still pegging. He's only sixteen or so. But he isn't
doing as much work as a boy of twelve. His mind's not
on his work. I catch him dreaming . . ."

"We can't have that. We pay good wages and we
expect good work from our employees. The matter's in
your hands, sir. If the boy doesn't work . . ." Mr.
Tanner shrugged.

At the end of the week, Sam Bonner was discharged.

Eleven years, within a month, after his dismissal
from the shoe factory, Sam Bonner swung down from
the Boston train and looked down the main street of
Baker Falls.

It had changed scarcely at all. The shade trees that
lined both sides of the street had not grown. They had
been old trees when Sam Bonner, as a young boy,
walked barefooted along the dusty street because his
father was a drinking man and there was never enough
money in the family to buy shoes for Sam. Only in winter did he wear shoes and then they were frequently his
father's overgrown castoffs.

Baker Falls.

Why had he returned? To start all over again? With
the memories of the past sixteen years tugging at him?

No, it wasn't that. It was just . . . well, where else could he go? California? He'd seen it. Chicago was an alien city. New York was a jungle of buildings and people. The prairies? He'd been in Kansas and Nebraska. Dakota . . .

. . . He could never again go to Dakota.

He swung down the streets carrying a small carpetbag which contained a change of clothes and—a revolver wrapped up in an old shirt.

He wore a modest sack suit and a pair of blackened shoes. Two months of work in Cincinnati and rigid economy had enabled him to save enough money to outfit himself and finance the trip to Baker Falls. He had enough money in his pocket to carry him for two or three weeks, provided the price of room and board had not greatly increased in Baker Falls.

A block from the railroad depot he turned in to the hotel. Lem Stufflebeam, the proprietor, greeted him courteously.

"Good morning, sir," he said.

"Good morning, Mr. Stufflebeam," Bonner said casually.

"Ah, you're an old guest?" He watched closely as Bonner signed the register, then swung it around to read it again. "Sam Bonner," he said slowly. "You're not——?"

"Yes, I am, Mr. Stufflebeam."

"Well, wouldn't have recognized you. Been away quite a spell."

"Eleven years."

"Is it that long?" The hotel man surveyed Bonner, noting the cut and material of the suit he wore. "Been in business?"

Bonner shrugged, indicating an affirmation. "Things haven't changed much in Baker Falls."

"Why, there've been quite a few changes. How long've you been gone—eleven years? Mmm, the shoe factory's built a new wing since then. Yes sir, Mr. Tanner employs three hundred and fifty people there now."

"Has he raised his wages any?"

The hotel proprietor frowned. "Why, I don't know that there's been any complaint about wages. Mr. Tanner pays just about what any other shoe factory does. Mmm, let's see, you used to work there yourself, didn't you?"

"I was a pegger."

"Of course. And if I'm not mistaken, your father also, ahem, did he not also work there—at times?"

"Rarely," said Bonner deliberately. "My father was the village drunkard."

"Aren't you a little, ah, harsh regarding your, ah, father?"

"My father was a good customer of your saloon," Bonner said, "when he could pay for it and sometimes when he couldn't. In fact, I wouldn't be surprised if he died owing you money."

"Well, yes, there was an amount due me, but . . ." The full implications of that statement suddenly brought back the memories to the hotel man and he cleared his throat. "No sir, that's a thing of the past, sir. I, ah, forgive me for going into the matter. The subject is a painful one to you, I'm sure."

"Not at all," Bonner said. "Everybody in Baker Falls knew the facts. My mother starved to death and——"

"Starved? Oh, no, please—" cried Stufflebeam, throwing up his hands in horror.

"The verdict was that she killed herself. I know that," Bonner said coldly. "When I was in the army, my mother had to work at the shoe factory. My father managed to get most of her pay which he spent for liquor. My mother killed herself in the winter of '64. What else could she do? It was that or starve. My father then sobered up long enough to hang himself."

A shudder went through Lem Stufflebeam. "I, ah, I'm sorry," he mumbled. "Were you, ah, planning to stay long in Baker Falls?"

"That depends. How much do you ask for a week's room and board?"

"Sev . . . I mean, eight dollars."

Bonner laid a twenty dollar greenback on the desk. "Take out a week's room and board."

Stufflebeam gave him twelve dollars in change, consulted the key slots and dropped a key on the desk. "Room seven, Mr., uh, Sam. It's at the front. A very fine room."

Bonner nodded and climbed the stairs to the second floor. He found Room Number Seven. It was a tiny room, scarcely larger than a closet. It contained a small bed, a chest of drawers and a stand on which stood a pitcher and bowl.

He slipped the valise under the cot and washed his hands and face, then descended to the lobby. Stufflebeam was not behind the desk, but voices were chattering in the bar off the lobby, and Bonner assumed that the hotel man was in there discussing with the bartender and the town loafers the return of Sam Bonner to the place of his birth.

It was an event for Baker Falls.

Bonner stepped out upon the street and strolled the length of Main Street, down one side of the street and back on the other. He met numerous people he recalled from his youth, but none recognized him, although one or two of them gave him sharp glances.

On his return trip, he paused on the far side of the street, across from the hotel, then decided to continue on to the depot. On the other side, perhaps an eighth of a mile from the depot, was a sprawling red brick building. Over it was a large sign that could be read from the railroad tracks: TANNER SHOE CORP.

Bonner looked thoughtfully at the sign. One word had been changed since he had been employed in the factory. The "Corp." was new; in the old days it had been "Co."

To the right of the railroad tracks, almost opposite the shoe factory, was a small pond covering perhaps ten acres. Sam Bonner had gone swimming in that pond in summer and had skated on it in winter.

The pond was actually an overflow from the river that gave the power to the shoe factory, and the falls

shortly above it had been the original inspiration for
the name of the village.

It was a peaceful summer scene. Baker Falls was a
quiet village. Yet, there was turmoil in this town underneath the apparent quietness. Sam Bonner had
known it in his youth. He had run away from it once
and he had returned and a second time he had left it.

A strange uneasiness filled him. There was nothing
for him in Baker Falls. They did not forget. He was
the Bonner boy who had run away from home, the son
of Sam Bonner who . . .

Bonner turned back to the town, half decided to ask
for a refund of the room and board money he had paid
at the hotel.

Entering the hotel he found that it was the noon
hour. The dining room on the right side of the lobby,
across from the saloon, was open and a whiff of fried
chicken assailed Bonner's nostrils. Fried chicken and
hot biscuits.

He entered the dining room. A waitress nodded to a
table near the door. "Will this table do?"

Then Stufflebeam, the hotel man, came bustling up.
"This way, Sam!" He led the way through the pattern-
work of tables to a small one at the very rear that was
partly concealed by the open kitchen door. In going to
it, Sam passed at least four small tables at which no
one sat.

He seated himself at the table. "I'd like the chicken."

"The girl will take your order," replied Stufflebeam.
"But I, uh, I've got to tell you the chicken's twenty-five
cents extra. The corned beef is on the regular dinner."

"All right," said Bonner. "I'll pay the extra."

Stufflebeam went off and a waitress came up. Bonner
ordered the chicken, then looked around. He gave a
sudden, violent start. Three tables away, looking at
him, was Vivian Thompson whom he had last seen in
Deadwood.

She beckoned to him. Bonner hesitated, then pushed
back his chair and walked over to Vivian's table.

"I've just ordered myself," Vivian said. "Won't you join me?"

"You're sure you want me to?"

"Of course."

Bonner's eyes met those of the hotel proprietor. Stufflebeam's face registered horror. He came dashing forward. "Please, Sam . . ."

"Miss Thompson asked me to join her," Bonner retorted testily.

"That's right, Mr. Stufflebeam," said Vivian, smiling. "Mr. Bonner and I are old friends."

"You—you know him?" gulped Stufflebeam.

"Do you think I would ask a complete stranger to join me for dinner?"

"N-no," said Stufflebeam. He went off, breathing heavily.

As Bonner sat down, Vivian said, "It's fantastic, meeting you like this!"

"This is my home town."

"Why, we're practically neighbors. *We* live at Natick; that's less than twenty miles from here."

"You came here just for dinner?"

She laughed. "Of course not. Father's here on business."

"Business in Baker Falls?"

"The shoe factory," Vivian explained. "Father owns it."

Bonner leaned back. "Since when?"

"I'm not sure. Two years, perhaps there. I know what you're going to say, shoes and gold mines. The truth of the matter is, Father has invested in a number of enterprises. He keeps telling me that it isn't wise to put all your eggs into one business. As I understand it, the local shoe factory got into financial difficulties a few years ago and needed further capital. Father furnished it."

"He's here with you?"

"No—I'm with him."

Bonner shook his head in bewilderment. "I may as well tell you right now, for I'm sure our fine hotel proprietor will tell you the moment he gets an opportunity. I used to work at the shoe factory. I started there at the age of eleven. My father before me . . ." He stopped.

"Your family lives here?"

"My family's dead."

"I'm sorry." She looked at him closely. "There was something in your tone a moment ago, a—a hardness . . ."

"In Baker Falls," Bonner said, "you couldn't have invited a worse person to join you at dinner than Sam Bonner."

She sobered for just an instant, then forced a smile back to her face. "Oh, come now, you're not going to tell me that you were the local bad boy?" She suddenly lowered her voice. "They—they don't know about Dakota?"

"No. I don't believe there was anyone in Deadwood who even knew that I once lived in Massachusetts." He paused. "You *saw* what happened there?"

Her eyes dropped as she nodded.

A waitress came with a tray of food and both Vivian and Bonner had time to compose themselves. When the food was set out and the waitress had moved off, Vivian said, "You're going to stay here now?"

He shook his head. "I don't even know why I came."

"That's simple enough. A person's home always has a pull. Of course I was raised in the West, but Father's from Natick originally, and he always talks of it as home. He—he was a clerk in a grocery store before he went West. You were, what did you say? A shoe pegger?"

"Your father's rich now. They've forgotten that he was once a grocery clerk. They haven't forgotten that I was a shoe pegger and that my father . . . my father was the village drunkard." The harshness came again into Bonner's voice. "I don't want to tell you the rest of it, but I'm sure you'll hear it within ten minutes after I've left this table."

Vivian reached impulsively across the table to lay

her hand on Bonner's, then caught herself and withdrew the hand. "Perhaps you shouldn't have come back."

"I *know* it, now."

"You're going then?"

"As soon as I can."

A cloud came over her face. "Where?"

"I suppose I can still get a job as a shoe pegger . . ."

"You, a shoe pegger? After——" She winced. "I mean, after the active life you've led out West."

"You don't know what kind of a life I led out West. You only saw me in Deadwood."

"And you were there just two months."

"Two months? How do you know it was two months?"

She looked at him without fluster. "I asked about you."

"Why should you ask about me?" Bonner asked in surprise.

"I was interested." This time she did drop her eyes. "Indirectly, I suppose, my father is responsible for—for what happened. He bought the mining claim out of which you were cheated."

"Was I really cheated? I've been thinking about it. I sold if for a hundred dollars. It wasn't worth more."

"But the man who bought it from you sold it to Father for twenty thousand dollars. If *you* had received that twenty thousand . . ."

Bonner frowned. "I'm not sure. I'm not sure any more . . ."

Two men stopped at the table; Randolph Thompson and Joseph Tanner who had once been the sole owner of the Tanner Shoe Company.

Thompson's face was dark with suppressed anger. Tanner did not recognize Bonner and was beaming in the expectation of being introduced to a young man who was having lunch with the daughter of Randolph Thompson.

Thompson said, "You're Sam Bonner!"

Vivian exclaimed, "Father, you're late."

Bonner pushed back his chair, rose. "I believe I'm through."

"No, you're not," Vivian said quickly. "Father, you remember Mr. Bonner. This is his home town. . . ."

Joseph Tanner exclaimed, "Bonner? Seems to me I remember an employee named Bonner, some years ago." He frowned. "But he was an older man."

"My father," Bonner said stiffly. "But I also worked for you. I was a pegger. . . ."

"A pegger? Of course—I remember now. Didn't you run away from home and enlist in the army as a drummer boy? I seem to recall . . ."

Bonner bowed to Vivian. "Excuse me, Miss Thompson." He stepped past Joseph Tanner, then Randolph Thompson and walked stiffly out of the dining room.

CHAPTER SEVEN

Heavy feet came clumping along the threadbare carpeting in the corridor on the second floor. Then knuckles rapped on the door of Bonner's room.

Bonner, sprawled on the bed with his hands locked under his head, called out, "Yes?"

"Sam? Lem Stufflebeam. Got a letter here for you."

Bonner swung his feet to the floor and stepped to the door. He opened it. The hotel proprietor extended a sealed envelope. "Miss Thompson asked me to give it to you."

Bonner nodded, but Stufflebeam did not turn away. He cleared his throat. "Met them out west, didn't you?"

"Mr. Stufflebeam, don't waste your time."

Stufflebeam cocked his head to one side. "Eh?"

"You'll get nothing out of me."

Stufflebeam bristled. "Why, I was only tryin' to be neighborly. . . ."

"Is that why you charged me eight dollars for this room and board, when your regular price is only seven?"

"I—I guess I made a mistake. It's Number Eight that costs more . . ." Stufflebeam fished in his pocket and reluctantly held out a silver dollar.

Bonner brushed it away. "Keep it. I may be eating the chicken again instead of the corned-beef dinner."

"You always were a bit strange, Sam," the hotel man whined. "Folks used to say . . ."

"I know what they said!"

"All right, Sam, all right." Stufflebeam turned and clumped toward the stairs.

Bonner closed the door and looked at the envelope. Then he ripped it open. The note inside was written in a fine backhand. It read:

> Sam——
> Father's business keeps him here until evening. It's too hot to wait in the hotel, so I'll be on Tanner's Pond most of the afternoon.
>
> Vivian Thompson.

Bonner started to tear the note in half, then refolded it and put it in his pocket. He took a quick turn about the narrow room. Vivian had not been discreet. She had given the note to Lem Stufflebeam to deliver and if Bonner left the hotel immediately upon receiving it, he would suspect a tryst . . . and everyone in Baker Falls would know before nightfall that the daughter of the multimillionaire, Randolph Thompson, was having a rendezvous with—with Sam Bonner, the son of Sam Bonner, Sr.

He exhaled heavily and sat down on the bed. He remained seated for approximately twenty minutes, then got up and walked down to the lobby of the hotel.

Stufflebeam was behind the desk and cast a covert glance at him.

Bonner strolled to the door leading to the saloon, hesitated as if trying to make up his mind, then turned and sauntered to the front door. He stopped a moment, looking out upon the street, then finally went through the door.

Outside he turned right, walking aimlessly to the next corner. He stopped there, turned right and began to walk more quickly. He circled the complete block, coming back to Main Street, near the railroad tracks. There he looked carefully around, saw no one on Main Street in particular who seemed to be watching him and cut swiftly across the field to the pond. He saw a boat on its placid waters long before he reached the pond. It was some fifty feet from the shore.

Vivian Thompson was rowing idly. She saw him and called, "Sam!"

He pointed along the shore to the right, continued walking. Vivian began to ply the oars and followed him, rowing diagonally toward the shore.

After a while Bonner stopped and waited until the rowboat lightly touched the grassy bank. He stepped aboard.

"I thought you were never coming," Vivian said.

"If I'd come right away, everybody in town would have known it," Bonner said. "Stufflebeam's a big blabbermouth." He took the oars from Vivian. "This is a rather public place, as it is."

"Afraid to be seen with me?" Vivian asked mockingly.

"What did your father say after I left this noon?"

"Father's inclined to be stuffy at times."

Bonner said earnestly: "I'm an outlaw. I've——"

"Oh, bosh!" interrupted Vivian. "To quote my stuffy father, an honest man in the West is one who's got a job. If he loses his job, he becomes an outlaw. A sheriff today, an outlaw tomorrow."

"I'm sure your father made that observation at some time previous to today." Bonner shook his head.

"I didn't just hold up a stagecoach in Deadwood. You —you saw what happened that last night."

"I saw," Vivian said, sobering. "I've had nightmares because of it." She looked at him, her eyes clouded. "I think what you did for your friend was the bravest thing I ever saw any man do."

Bonner jerked back, staring at her. "You think that . . . was *bravery?*"

"Wasn't it?"

"I don't know," Bonner said slowly. "At the time the thought of Wendell Morgan being hanged was unbearable. It's not the way *I* would want to die. Wendell had befriended me—he'd saved my life. I was drawn to him and I did what *I* would have wanted him to do for me in a situation like that. But . . . did I have the *right* to do it?"

"What does your conscience tell you?"

"Conscience?" A wave of sudden anger shot through Bonner. Anger, not at Vivian, but at the circumstances of his life. "I've seen too much of death. I was a drummer boy at the Battle of Shiloh . . . I was at Vicksburg, at Chattanooga and Chickamauga. I was a cavalryman before Atlanta and when Johnston surrendered to Sherman in North Carolina, I was just sixteen years of age. I came home, then, a veteran . . . and I found that my mother was dead because I hadn't been home to protect her against my drunken father. And then my father couldn't die quietly. He had to kill himself. . . . After all that I went to work over there in the shoe factory, pegging shoes. . . ."

The words came out in a passionate torrent, as Bonner sat facing Vivian in the rowboat. He was unaware that her hand had reached out and was gripping his own in sympathy.

He stopped talking as suddenly as he had begun. He looked at the girl facing him and there was a vast hunger in him that he knew could never be satisfied.

He said quietly, drained of emotion, "I've never talked like this to anyone."

"I know. I—I'm glad you told me."

A sudden flash of light struck Bonner's eyes and he looked across the pond toward the shoe factory. Sunlight reflected from a mirror, or . . .

He said, "I think your father's watching us from the shoe factory. With a telescope."

Vivian gasped. "He wouldn't!" She looked over her shoulder, saw a streak of light reflected. "It's just the sun shining on the windows." She turned back to face Bonner.

"You'll come to Natick?"

"I don't know. I came here to—to rest and think things out. I had a memory of Baker Falls being a quiet, peaceful place and I thought if I had a couple of weeks of doing absolutely nothing. I could work things out in my own mind. The future . . ."

"You're twenty-seven, aren't you?"

"Not quite—twenty-six."

"Five years older than I. But I think yours have been harder years."

He nodded. "I've been in California, all over the West. I worked on the Union Pacific in '68 and '69. I drove cattle to Kansas from Texas and I hunted buffalo in the Panhandle. I've dug for silver and for gold. I've seen it all and—and none of it's been good. Not for me, it hasn't."

"That's because you're too old. Too old for your years. You had no youth."

"A lot of other men didn't have any. Your father, I imagine."

"That's right. He's told me over and over how he went to work when he was scarcely twelve."

"Yet he became a millionaire and I—I became a highwayman."

"Don't say that. You made a mistake. It isn't too late to rectify."

"A man was killed in that holdup."

"And a man paid for it. I don't think society has the right to expect more than a life for a life." Vivian leaned toward Bonner. "Take your two weeks, Sam. Do your thinking and then . . . come to Natick."

CHAPTER EIGHT

Bonner left Vivian at the pond shortly after three thirty. He strolled back up Main Street and went to his room at the hotel. He stretched himself out on the narrow bed and tried to sleep but could not.

An hour went by, two. The dining room would be opening downstairs, but Bonner was not hungry. He did, however, finally get up from the bed and wash his face and hands. The late afternoon sun had made the room sticky with dead, warm heat.

The clumping of feet in the corridor came to Bonner's ears. Stufflebeam again . . . and another pair of feet.

Knuckles rapped on the door.

"Yes?" Bonner called.

"I've got a message for you, Sam," replied the voice of Stufflebeam. "An important one."

Bonner unlocked the door and pulled it open. A giant dragoon pistol was thrust in his face by the man who accompanied Stufflebeam.

"Throw up your hands!" the man ordered. "You're under arrest."

Bonner took a quick involuntary backward step. "What the devil are you talking about?"

"I'm Deputy Sheriff Burnside," the man with the gun said. "You oughta remember me, Sam. We worked at the same bench when we was kids."

"I see," Bonner said grimly. "And this is your idea of a joke?"

"No joke, Sam," Burnside said doggedly. "I got

orders to arrest you and I warn you not to try anythin'
fancy because I'm a awful good shot with this here old
popgun."

"He means it," Stufflebeam said. He had taken a
quick step behind Burnside after knocking on the door
and enticing Bonner to open it. "We understand you're
wanted out in Dakota and we're holdin' you until
they come to take you back. You . . . you got a gun in
that carpetbag under the bed . . ."

"You've searched it?" Bonner's lips twisted in con-
tempt. He said to Burnside. "Who told you I was
wanted out in Dakota?"

"Mr . . ." began Burnside, then caught himself.
"That's neither here nor there. A complaint's been
made and it's my duty to take you down to the county
jail and hold you there."

"All right," Bonner said wearily, "let's go down to
this jail of yours."

There wasn't a single diner in the dining room when
Bonner and the deputy sheriff reached the lobby. All
were in the lobby, although a few stood in the door-
ways leading to the saloon and the dining room into
which they could dart in case there was sudden, unexpected violence. They had all known that an arrest
was about to be made and they wanted to see the prisoner taken off to the local jail.

The courthouse was a two-story red brick building
that had been built shortly after the War of 1812. Its
corridors were dark and lightless. The deputy sheriff's
office was at the rear of the first floor. From there, a
flight of stairs led to the basement of the courthouse
where old furniture and files were kept. A corner of
the basement had been walled off into a fairly large
cell which contained two bunks and a wooden stool. A
barred window high up on the outer hall furnished
the only illumination for the cell.

Stufflebeam, the hotel man, did not accompany
Bonner and the deputy to the courthouse, but the deputy marched a few paces behind Bonner on the block
and a half walk, the dragoon pistol thrust out ahead of

him. More than half of the townspeople saw Bonner on that march and he heard, on no less than three occasions, the same phrase, "like father, like son!"

Then, with Bonner in the big cell and the door locked between him and the deputy, the latter made the remark that Bonner was already dreading to hear: "Your old man spent quite a lot of time in this here place."

"Andy," Bonner said, "you reminded me that we used to work at the same pegging bench over at the factory. You remember then, that we also went to school together and that we once shared the same desk."

"Sure, I remember," admitted Andy Burnside. "That was under Old Sprowl. He was awfully handy with the switch . . ."

"And once I took a switching that was yours . . ."

"I don't remember that."

"You will if you'll think back. I could have told Sprowl you were the one who threw the eraser, not me. You'd have got the switching. And it was a good one that time."

"I dunno," said Burnside. He looked suspiciously at Bonner. "What're you drivin' at?"

"Where's the sheriff?"

"Jess Tatum? He just had himself an operation in Boston for kidney stones. He won't be back for a week or so. You might say I'm the sheriff while he's gone."

"That's what I wanted to know. Then how did you come to arrest me?"

"Well, I heard that you was wanted out in Dakota for robbin' and killin' somebody. . . ."

"You took it upon yourself to arrest me? Without a warrant?"

"I got a warrant. Judge Peckham wrote it out."

"Who got him to issue it?"

"I didn't say anybody *got* him to do it."

"Peckham wouldn't tell you the time of the day without witnesses. He's the most cautious man in Baker Falls."

"I got to go now," said Burnside. "My supper's ready."

"Wait a minute, Andy . . ."

"I can't . . ."

"Andy!" Bonner said sharply. "Unless you want to find yourself up in front of Judge Peckham, you'll listen to me. How long have you had this job of deputy?"

"Five-six months."

"How many people have you arrested in that time?"

"What's that got to do with it? You know there ain't much crime in Baker Falls. Right now, as you can see for yourself, you're the only prisoner we got. We had a fella in here two weeks ago, though."

"A tramp?"

"Worse'n that. A burglar. He tried to get a handout from Mrs. Watson, old Sarah Watson, and when she wouldn't give him anything, he went around behind her house and stole a whole pie she had settin' there to cool. Judge Peckham gave him three days to cool off and then I run him out of town."

"You're a new deputy," Bonner said. "You don't know the law very well. A prisoner has a right to see the warrant that he's arrested on and he has a right to demand an appearance before a judge. . . ."

"Oh, you'll get that, all right. Judge Peckham said he'd listen to you tomorrow mornin' at ten o'clock. . . ."

"At that time you'll have to prove that you had sufficient evidence to arrest me. And if you can't prove it, Andy, I'll swear out a warrant against you for your false arrest. Understand that? I can do it."

"You can't arrest me, I'm a deputy sheriff!" cried Andy Burnside.

"False arrest is a crime in every state and territory of the United States. Believe me, Andy, I've been around. I know *that* much about the law. . . ."

Andy Burnside whirled away. He rushed up the stairs to the first floor of the courthouse.

He returned inside of an hour. "T'aint so," he growled. "Judge Peckham says I was only the—the instrument—in makin' the arrest. I ain't guilty of nothin'."

"Did he also tell you that I had the right to know the name of my accuser?"

Burnside hesitated. "We talked about it."

"Who was it?"

"Mr. Thompson."

"Randolph Thompson?"

"That's all I got to tell you. If you want to charge anyone with false arrest, that's your party. Mr. Randolph Thompson . . ." Burnside smirked. "Mr. Thompson only happens to be the richest man in this part of the state. He says you held up a stagecoach out in Dakota and killed a man. And we'll get proof of that by tomorrow morning. Judge Peckham's already sent the telegram."

That was what Sam Bonner had wanted to know and he resigned himself to his fate.

The following morning after a poor breakfast brought to him by Andy Burnside, Bonner was taken upstairs to the courtroom. Judge Peckham, who was actually only a justice of the peace, was a man past seventy. He had served the township as a justice for half of those years. He peered at Bonner over steel-rimmed spectacles.

"You're beginning to look just like your father," he observed. "Many's the time I had him right here before me."

"Am I being held for my father's misdemeanors?" Bonner asked testily.

"Got a tongue like your father, too," snapped Judge Peckham. He held up a sheet of paper and studied it. "This here's a telegram I just got from Deadwood in Dakota Territory. Let me read it: *'Judge O.S. Peckham, Baker Falls, Massachusetts. Sam Bonner is wanted in Deadwood on a charge of highway robbery and murder. Will obtain extradition papers from governor and come to your city to bring prisoner back to Deadwood. Signed: Kellems, Marshal.'"* He put down the sheet of paper. "Well, Sam, this is a very serious charge and there's nothing I can do but hold you here in the local jail until this Marshal Kellems arrives to take you back to Deadwood. Have you anything to say?"

Bonner shook his head.

The judge hesitated, then picked up a wooden gavel and banged it on his desk.

"Andy, remove the prisoner to his cell."

CHAPTER NINE

On the fifth day of Bonner's incarceration, Andy Burnside came to the cell in the basement of the courthouse. "Fella says he's your lawyer, wants to see you."

"I sent for no lawyer."

Burnside shrugged. "I asked Judge Peckham and he says I got to let you talk to him."

"All right," Bonner said indifferently.

Burnside clumped back upstairs and then returned, accompanied by a man wearing a black Prince Albert, a silk hat and gray-striped trousers. Bonner could scarcely conceal a violent start.

The man was Artie Upright!

"How are you, Mr. Bonner?" Upright asked cheerfully. Without waiting for a reply he turned to Burnside. "Now, if you will open the door . . ."

"The judge didn't tell me to do that," protested Burnside. "Here—here's a chair. You just set it down right there and you can talk to him through the bars."

"A lawyer and his client have the right to privacy," protested Upright.

"You got privacy," declared Burnside. "I'm going upstairs and you'll be all alone down here."

He retreated to the stairs and went up.

Upright watched until Burnside was out of sight, then thrust his hand through the bars to grip Bonner's. "Sam!"

"How'd you know I was here?" exclaimed Bonner.

Upright grinned. "Damnedest thing happened." He shot a covert glance over his shoulder at the stairs, then lowered his voice. "Me and the boys held up a stage. It was going to Bismarck and there was a sack of mail on it. I wasn't even going to bother with the mail, but you know Tommy Brown. He thought there might be money in the letters. So he came across one from Marshal Kellems of Deadwood to the territorial governor. Kellems couldn't leave Deadwood right away, so he wrote a letter to the governor asking for extradition papers for you. He figured the papers would be all ready for him when he got to Bismarck two days later. That was three days ago. We were only sixty or seventy miles from Bismarck at the time, so we rode there, got on the train and we been traveling ever since. Got to Boston late last night and I got this outfit this morning and came out here."

"Three days ago?" Bonner asked. "That means Kellems got to Bismarck yesterday. He learned then that his letter hadn't reached the governor."

"Probably," said Upright carelessly. "I forgot to mention, however, that Dirty Dave Macdougal stayed in Bismarck. I have an idea that Kellems hasn't gotten to see the governor."

Bonner exclaimed, "But why, Artie? Why've you gone to all this? I scarcely knew you in Dakota."

"You did something for Wendell Morgan, Sam," Upright said gruffly. "You risked your own life to—to do what you did." He cleared his throat. "Only one thing in all his life bothered Wendell. Hanging. He talked to me about it and I imagine he talked to you about it."

"No, he didn't. But it was what *I* would have wanted in his place."

Upright nodded. "The thing now is to get you out of here. What's the law situation?"

"You saw it."

"The baboon who brought me down here? That's all the law there is?"

"He's only the deputy. The sheriff's in Boston in the hospital. He won't be back for another three or four days."

"By that time you'll be west of Chicago."

Bonner hesitated. "What's the feeling about me in Deadwood?"

"We haven't been there much. After Wendell—after what happened to Wendell, we moved. Up around Bismarck. We've been doing a little better. Still nothing to brag about, but I've got a little money in my pocket, even after paying the railroad fare for all three of us."

"Three? You said Dirty Dave stayed in Bismarck."

"That's right. Tommy's with me . . . and Leo Basgall, who joined up with us. A very good man with horses. He talks their language."

"Brown and Basgall are with you here in Baker Falls?"

"Not exactly. They got off one station back and I think they're looking over the horse situation there. We're going to need some horses tonight." Upright frowned. "The deputy told me this was your home town."

"I suppose he also told you about—my family?"

"He did say something about it. He also mentioned that Randolph Thompson swore out the warrant for your arrest. That was a new one. I hadn't any idea that he was anywhere in this part of the country."

"He lives just about twenty miles from here," Bonner said, "and he also happens to own the local shoe factory."

"But why should he go out of his way to make trouble for you? Is Rufe Chadwick behind it?"

Bonner shook his head. "Thompson happened to see me talking to his daughter. . . ."

"Oh-oh!" said Upright. "I think I catch on." He nodded. "Saw her in Deadwood. A very handsome filly!"

Bonner made an impatient gesture. "The cards are stacked against me. I've had a lot of time for thinking these last four days. My mind's made up."

"Yeah?"

"I've got the name, I'm going to have the game."

Upright brightened. "Now you're talkin', Sam. I know your heart wasn't in it out there in Dakota, but now you've made up your mind, things are going to be all right. We can use another good man . . ."

"The shoe factory here in town," Bonner said, "employs three hundred and fifty people. Unless they've changed their system, they pay the employees on Saturday. That's tomorrow. There ought to be about ten thousand dollars in cash at the bank tomorrow morning."

Artie Upright whistled softly. "We never got more than five hundred off any stagecoach."

"The risk isn't worth it," said Bonner. "If I'm going into this business, I want to be paid well enough."

"I've no objections," Artie Upright said. "Tomorrow, you said? We were figuring on getting you out of here tonight."

"No. That'd create too much of a fuss and might put them on their guard. The bank opens at eight o'clock. The Boston train arrives here at eight thirty. The payroll money comes on that. Give them ten minutes to get the money to the bank . . . eight thirty's the time and I don't think I ought to get out of here before eight twenty-five."

"You know the roads around here?"

"I used to know them. I don't think there are any new ones since I lived here ten years ago. We'll head southwest out of town, cut across to the east and scatter. A couple of us can take the New York train and a couple can keep on east and get the boat at Fall River. That'll have us in New York almost as soon as the train."

Upright's face showed approval. "I guess maybe we didn't make any mistake coming East."

"You'll have good horses?"

"The best we can steal."

"I wish you didn't have to steal them."

"We don't have enough money to buy horses."

"It's all right this time, Artie. But that's one thing we ought to watch in the future. It's too risky riding around on a stolen horse."

Heavy footsteps sounded at the head of the stairs, then began descending to the cellar. "You fellows about through?" Deputy Sheriff Burnside called.

"For the time being," Upright replied. "I'll want to see my client again tomorrow." To Bonner: "Don't worry about a thing, Mr. Bonner. The charges are obviously false and I'll have you free in no time at all."

"Oh yeah?" asked Burnside cynically.

CHAPTER TEN

The people of Baker Falls were early risers. Deputy Sheriff Burnside brought Sam Bonner his breakfast at six thirty and came to get the tin plate and cup a few minutes before seven.

"Sheriff Tatum'll be back on the job Monday," he told Bonner cheerfully. Then he added wickedly, "It'll seem like old times to him having a Sam Bonner in here."

Bonner held back a retort. He had an hour and a half more in the Baker Falls jail. And a little more than an hour and a half in the town of his birth where the name of Bonner was a byword, an epithet.

He paced the rather large cell. He had no watch and could not tell the time, but at last he heard the *whoo-*

hooing of the train as it approached the depot. Five minutes more.

No . . . !

Boots scuffled suddenly over Bonner's head and a man cried out sharply, in pain. A heavy thud of a body falling to the floor punctuated the cry.

Then Artie Upright came running down the stairs carrying the key to Bonner's cell.

"Here we go, Sam!"

"You're five minutes early."

"What's five minutes more or less?" cried Upright, fumbling for the lock with the large iron key.

"These things have to be timed exactly," said Bonner frowning. "What happened upstairs?"

"The big deputy went for his gun. Tommy Brown buffaloed him. He's out. Come on . . ."

He turned the key, pulled open the door. Bonner ran out past Upright to the stairs. He burst into the sheriff's office to find Tommy Brown, with drawn gun, watching Andy Burnside, who lay on the floor, semiconscious. Burnside was groaning.

"Hi, Bonner," Brown greeted him casually.

"Hello, Tommy," replied Bonner. "Where are the horses?"

"Outside. Basgall's holding them."

"I need a gun," said Bonner.

"Take the sheriff's," suggested Brown, pointing to the huge dragoon pistol on the floor.

"Not that blunderbuss." Bonner's eyes darted to a rack which contained an army rifle and a rather good Navy Colt that hung from the trigger guard. He sprang across the room, took down the Navy Colt. "My own gun!"

"Let's go," said Upright a bit nervously. "The sheriff's coming around."

"This'll put him back to sleep," said Brown casually. He stopped and smashed his gun barrel across the skull of Andy Burnside. He raised it for a second blow, but Bonner caught his arm.

"That's enough."

"Still chicken?" sneered Brown. "I thought by now . . ."

"There's no time for that, Tommy," snapped Upright. He headed for the door.

Outside, under a huge shade tree, a squat, swarthy man sat astride a big bay and held the reins of three other horses. Upright, Brown and Bonner mounted swiftly.

A moment later they burst around the corner onto Main Street. The bank was a half block away. They bore down on it. "Brown," Bonner snapped, "you and Basgall stay outside with the horses. Artie and I'll go inside."

He sprang from the horse, throwing the reins to Basgall. He strode quickly across the sidewalk and heard Upright at his heels.

The bank was a rather small one with only two tellers and an enclosure in which sat the president of the bank, old Jonas Wheelwright. There were three customers in the bank, one of them an elderly man who had been paymaster of the shoe factory when Sam Bonner had first gone to work there at the age of twelve.

"Don't anyone make a wrong move," Bonner said savagely as he strode toward the enclosure of the president.

Old Jonas Wheelwright gulped. "Why, it's Sam Bonner!"

"The factory payroll," snapped Bonner, "and everything else you've got here . . ."

"Robbery!" cried Wheelwright. "You've stooped to robbery now. I always said . . ."

"The devil with what you always said . . . !" snarled Bonner. He lunged forward and snatched a small Boston bag from the paymaster's hand. He whisked it open. It was already filled with stacks of greenbacks and a considerable amount of silver.

Bonner gestured to the vault which stood open. "Get the rest of what you've got in there," he ordered Wheelwright.

"Sam," said the old banker, too shocked to move. "You're making a mistake. Why, I've known you since you were a small boy. This—this is your home town. . . ."

"Move!"

Artie Upright thrust out his revolver, aiming so he would miss the old banker's head by inches. He pulled the trigger. "You heard the man!"

Wheelwright collapsed completely. His body began to quake and saliva drooled from his lips over his chin. Bonner whirled away from him, strode into the vault. He took a quick glance around, saw a metal chest and tore it open. It was partly filled with stacks of greenbacks. He stuffed them rapidly into the Boston bag.

"Hurry!" called Artie from the main part of the bank.

Bonner closed the leather bag and stepped out of the vault.

"Ready!"

"I'm warning you, now," Upright said to the tellers and the customers. "Don't nobody make a move for two minutes. Anybody comes rushing out of the bank's liable to get a bullet in his head. . . ." He backed toward the door, stood in the doorway until Sam Bonner had gone through.

A bank holdup was completely unknown in the village of Baker Falls. But the sound of the gun fired inside the bank had brought several of the neighboring merchants out upon the sidewalk and they were standing there when Bonner and Upright burst out of the bank and rushed for their horses.

Tommy Brown calmly sent a bullet crashing through the glass of the bank window, whirled his horse and sent two quick shots at windows across the street. He wound up with a wild whoop.

They were off, then, past the hotel where Stufflebeam, the proprietor, stood pop-eyed in the open doorway, past the street on which the courthouse was located and a block away, out upon the open highway.

There was no pursuit, for there was no one in Baker

Falls to organize one. After a while someone would think to go to the railroad depot and send out telegrams to Boston, to towns in the vicinity. By that time Bonner and the other bank robbers would be miles from Baker Falls.

They followed the road that led to the south and west for a fast three miles or so of riding, then Bonner, seeing a clump of woods ahead on the right, signaled to the others.

They reached the woods and after entering them a short distance, pulled up.

"How much did we get?" Brown asked.

"I don't know," Bonner replied.

"Let's see!"

Upright exclaimed, "This is no time to stop and count the money."

"I can ride a lot faster and harder if I know how much my take is," retorted Brown.

Bonner dismounted and tossed the leather Boston bag to the ground. "Might as well split it now, then we can separate."

The others climbed down from their horses with alacrity and the leather bag was turned upside down.

Tommy Brown chortled. "This looks mighty good to me. One-fourth of this'll keep me in clover for quite a while."

"One-fifth," corrected Bonner. "Dave Macdougal gets a split."

"That's right," Upright agreed. "He did his part of the job by staying in Dakota."

Brown did not protest, but he eyed Bonner sourly. "Seems to me for a fella we come a long ways to help, that you been givin' orders kinda free like."

"Good orders," said Upright quickly. "We wouldn't have this money if it hadn't been for Sam."

Bonner signaled to Upright. "You count."

Five minutes later the bank loot had been roughly sorted out into five piles, each amounting to a little over nineteen hundred dollars.

"Now, about breaking up," Upright said. "I'll go with Sam, heading east."

"Suits me," agreed Brown. "Me and Leo'll head west." He looked at the fifth share of the money. "Who takes Dave's share?"

Upright looked at Bonner. The latter nodded to Brown. "You take it with you." He paused. "This money isn't going to last forever and if we want to get together again . . ."

"How about Ogallala?" suggested Upright. "It's a pretty good town and I don't think any of us are known there. Besides, I told Dave to go there if we missed him in Dakota."

"A month from now?" asked Bonner.

Upright looked inquiringly at Brown and Basgall. "Suits me," growled Brown.

"A month from today then, give or take a day."

That was agreed upon and the four men again mounted their horses. Their pockets stuffed with packets of greenbacks and quantities of silver, they waved to each other and Brown and Basgall quickly headed westward.

Upright and Bonner turned their horses to the east.

They rode through the patch of woods, coming out upon a rocky pasture in which several cows were grazing. They cut across this to a wooden fence and followed it to a gate. This, in turn, led them down a lane to a farmhouse.

A farmer, harrowing a small field, watched them in surprise, but Bonner and Upright paid no attention to him. They rode out of the farmyard onto a winding dirt road and followed it, two miles, to a wider and better traveled road. Upright was for turning right on the road, but Bonner stopped him.

"Artie, I know I said we could catch the night boat at Fall River and I'll go with you if you insist, but I'd like to go north a ways."

"Not back to Baker Falls?"

"No—Natick."

"That's pretty close to Baker Falls."

"Perhaps too close, but still—I think they'll be expecting us to travel as fast as we can. South and west. North might be better."

Upright hesitated. "Sam, I like the way you handled this business. Reminded me of Wendell. He never lost his head when the going was rough. And he could handle Tommy Brown and Dirty Dave. Mind you, I'm not afraid of them, but . . ." he shrugged. "We need them on these jobs, but they've got to be kept in line. It was Tommy's quick trigger that got us in trouble at Deadwood."

"I'll handle Brown," Bonner said confidently.

"I'll back you." Upright paused. "All the way." He turned his horse northward.

Within an hour the two men rode into a tiny hamlet. They rode through it, then dismounted from their horses and headed them into an open field.

They walked back into the hamlet and approached the blacksmith. A rig was standing outside the shop.

"Nice little rig you've got there," said Bonner.

The blacksmith, a Yankee, regarded Bonner shrewdly. "Gets me around, right smart."

"You've got a good horse to go with it?"

"Got a gelding out back. Pretty fair animal. Raised him from a colt." The smith put down his sledge. "Like to see him?"

"Wouldn't mind," said Bonner. "Matter of fact, Tom and I had a little accident yesterday afternoon. Our horse broke a leg and we took to walking. Gettin' tired."

The blacksmith led the way to a small corral behind the blacksmith shop. A gelding, some five or six years old, stood in the small enclosure.

"Kinda tired looking," Upright remarked.

"This here horse?" asked the blacksmith. "I ain't a braggin' man, but he c'n outrun any horse in ten miles and he c'n do it on less fodder'n any horse you ever saw."

"How much for him and the rig?" Bonner asked.

"You mean you want to buy this horse?" asked the

blacksmith with assumed surprise. "Couldn't sell him nohow. Like I said, he's practically one of the family. Raised him from a colt . . ."

"A hundred dollars," suggested Bonner.

"Couldn't think of it," gulped the smith, then added, "And forty for the rig?"

Bonner took out a packet of bills and counted off seven twenties. The blacksmith showed disappointment. "You ain't gonna dicker?"

"Too tired. Let's hitch up."

Inside of five minutes, Upright and Bonner were in the rig riding smartly out of the hamlet.

Some three hours later, they drove the rig into a dense patch of woods near a fair-sized village, unhitched the gelding and turned him loose.

They walked into the village and in ten minutes purchased a pair of saddle horses which they rode northward.

Artie Upright, carrying a market basket covered with a cloth, walked up the circular drive to the huge white colonial house. He pulled the knob of the doorbell and heard the jangle inside the house.

A heavy-set Irishwoman opened the door. "We do all our marketin' at the store," she said tartly and tried to close the door.

Upright put his foot in the door. "This is something special, Ma'am, something the lady of the house ought to see."

"The lady of the house don't talk to peddlers," snapped the domestic. "If you don't take your foot out of the door, I'm going to break it off."

"Sure and you wouldn't be doing that, Ma'am," exclaimed Artie Upright in an assumed Irish brogue that had a touch of Texas drawl in it. "Miss Thompson'd be awful mad if you sent me away." He raised his voice. "I know Miss Thompson would want to talk to me."

Inside the house, a voice called, "Who's asking for me, Nora?"

"It's just a peddler, Ma'am," replied Nora, the house-keeper.

"With something you'd like to see, Miss Thompson," Upright called. "And maybe hear . . ."

The door was pulled open wider and Vivian Thompson looked inquiringly at Artie Upright. "What is it?"

Artie flicked the cloth back from over the basket. "I'm selling a special kind of apple, Miss Thompson." He caught Vivian's eye and made a quick gesture, a signal to her to get rid of the housekeeper.

Vivian inhaled sharply, then said to Nora, "All right, Nora, I'll talk to the man." She waited a moment until the housekeeper started off, then asked tautly:

"What is it?"

"I'm a friend of Sam Bonner . . ."

Vivian stepped out upon the veranda, pulling the door shut behind her. "Where is he?"

"Could you be riding in a buggy out on the south road around sundown?"

"Yes!"

"Then you'll see Sam—if there's nobody else around."

The Thompson surrey was the finest in Natick and the team of horses that pulled it had cost in the neighborhood of five hundred dollars and was reputed to be the fastest team in the county. Vivian Thompson sent the surrey rolling smoothly out of Natick as the sun was sinking over the western horizon. She wore a frilly white dress, without a hat, for it had been a warm day and she wanted to give the impression of taking a ride in the evening to cool off.

A mile out of town, Sam Bonner stepped out from behind a wide spreading maple tree.

Vivian pulled up the team and Sam climbed into the surrey beside her.

"Why did you do it?" Vivian cried.

"You don't know what happened in Baker Falls?" Bonner asked. "Right after you told me to think things over for a couple of weeks?"

"I learned today. They—they arrested you . . ."

"You didn't hear who swore out the warrant?"

Vivian faltered. "N-not . . . father?"

Bonner nodded and Vivian groaned.

"They were going to take me back to Dakota and hang me."

"But robbing the bank, Sam! You didn't have to do that!"

"I'm going to be a hunted man the rest of my life," Bonner said. "I won't have time to get jobs and earn money. I'll have to steal it from here on."

"No, Sam, no!"

"The cards were stacked against me. I've got to play them the best I can."

Vivian's tone showed abject despair. "I—I was counting on seeing you at the end of the two weeks. I thought you would think things over and start all over . . ." Her voice became bitter. "I'll never forgive father for what he did."

A quarter of a mile up the road, Artie Upright waited with two saddled horses. Bonner saw the horses and Upright and he said:

"I think I would have come to you next week. But now . . . well, this is goodbye."

"There's no . . . chance?"

"I can't think of any."

"Tell me just one thing, Sam . . . why . . . today, after what happened this morning . . . did you risk coming here?"

Bonner took the reins from Vivian's hands, pulled the horses to a full stop and took Vivian into his arms. He kissed her gently and she was limp, unresponsive. He started to release her and she gripped him tightly. This time her kiss was firm, almost . . . desperate.

He released her and handed the reins back to her.

"There's someone coming up ahead. You'd better turn back before they recognize you." Quickly he sprang to the road, half saluted her.

"Goodbye, Vivian!"

"Goodbye!" she cried softly.

He started walking toward Artie Upright. He did not look back.

A hundred yards down the road he encountered a farmer driving to town in a rickety buggy. The man nodded to him. "Evenin'," he said gruffly.

"Good evening," Bonner replied politely.

CHAPTER ELEVEN

By 1876 the big boom in Dodge City, Kansas, had passed its peak. Plenty of cattle were still coming up the shifting Chisholm Trail but cattle prices had become soft. The grazing was scarce and the steers were lean and stringy. Buyers were particular, wanted fatter beef. And they wanted it for a lower price.

The supply in Dodge City exceeded the demand. Smart cattle drovers skirted Dodge City and continued through the state of Kansas, into Nebraska. Wyoming and Montana cattlemen bought entire herds of Texas longhorns in Ogallala and drove them to their home ranges.

The packing houses sent buyers to Nebraska. The grass was lush in the more northerly state and the drovers who traveled the extra distance were in no hurry to sell their beef. They gazed the steers for some weeks on the nourishing buffalo grass and put from one hundred and fifty to two hundred pounds of extra beef onto a steer. The beef was better, the steers weighed more and with the Wyoming and Montana cattlemen buying entire trail herds, the supply did not exceed the demand.

So Ogallala became the metropolis of the Northwest.

The year before, Artie Upright and Wendell Morgan had brought a small Texas herd to Ogallala and had sold it at a good profit. Had they returned to Texas with the money they had received, Wendell Morgan would have been alive in 1876. But there was that trait in the character of the two men that had led them to risk the money that was not rightly theirs. To retrieve what they lost, they continued on to Deadwood, lost everything and became what they became. Wendell Morgan was buried in Deadwood.

Artie Upright and Sam Bonner got off the Union Pacific at the depot in Ogallala and Upright looked down the wide street that was packed with seething humanity and shook his head. "This is where it started."

"They know you here?" Bonner asked.

Upright shrugged. "A tinhorn or two may remember a prize sucker, a girl or two may remember the money she got from me, but . . ." He paused. "You mean do they know me by name? No. Nobody cares about anyone's name in Ogallala."

At Omaha the two men had bought Levis and woollen shirts, flat-crowned Stetsons and Justin boots. Both men wore black cloth coats, but they were like the coats of a hundred men in Ogallala, rough woollen cloth with very little shape or style. They were dressed like three hundred other men they would encounter in Ogallala. Each man carried a blanket roll in which was a cartridge belt, holster and a revolver.

In the pockets of each man remained something over nine hundred dollars. It was three weeks since the affair in Baker Falls.

They walked down the street to the OGALLALA HOTEL, a two-story building that had been the first wooden structure in Ogallala, built when the town had been railhead for the Union Pacific. Originally, the lumber of which it had been built was green lumber and it had shrunk, so that now there were cracks a half inch wide here and there.

They rented a double room at the hotel for five

dollars a day, took the holsters and revolvers from their blanket rolls and strapped them about their waists. When they descended to the lobby, they looked like almost every other man in Ogallala.

The hotel clerk looked quickly over his shoulder and called to them, "Gents, you're new in town. Just to welcome you to Ogallala, take this card over to the GRAND PRAIRIE. It's good for one free drink . . ."

Artie Upright took the printed card. "This is a fine welcome, Mister, and we appreciate it. And so will you, after you get a commission on what we spend after the free drink."

The clerk looked discomfited. "A man's got to make a dollar when he can."

"How's the action at the GRAND PRAIRIE?" asked Upright.

"Fastest in town, straightest games. Ben Tutt's dealing faro and you've heard of him."

"That we have," retorted Upright. "I also know about that trick box of his."

The clerk shuddered. "Don't say that! Ben don't like people to make remarks like that. He, ah, planted a man on'y last week."

"And you're trying to steer us to his game? Who do you get a cut from—the undertaker?"

Disdainfully, Artie Upright turned away. As they passed through the door he growled at Bonner, "This Ben Tutt took Wendell and me for over two thousand last year. That's why we couldn't go home to Texas. I think I'll just see if I can't set some of it back."

"Will it be a fight?" Bonner asked somewhat anxiously.

Upright winked at Bonner. "I've learned some things since last year. Ben Tutt carries a gun in a shoulder holster under his left arm. But he also has a derringer up his sleeve; works with some kind of a spring. His left arm. If you watch his left, I'll take care of the right and I think I can promise you a fat dividend."

They had reached the GRAND PRAIRIE, which was only two doors from the OGALLALA HOTEL. Frowning,

Bonner followed Upright into the rather large saloon and gambling hall. Although it was still only mid-morning, there were a score or more of customers, about half of whom stood around a faro game.

"That's Ben," said Upright, pleased. "Slip me your money. I'll double it for you."

Bonner swore under his breath, but he had come this far and could not retreat. He took a fat packet of bills from his pocket and passed the money to Upright. Jauntily, Upright approached the faro game.

"Ben Tutt," he said, "long time!"

Tutt, a cold-eyed man of about forty, looked sharply at Upright. "You're the Texas man went north with some money that was supposed to go south."

"You've got a good memory for faces, Ben," said Upright pleasantly. "I got a fresh roll. Think you can take it from me?"

"If I don't, someone else will. Name it."

Upright took Bonner's packet of money from his pocket, added his own roll. Ben Tutt regarded the money with satisfaction. "Make your bets, gentlemen."

Upright peeled a twenty dollar bill from one of his rolls and placed it on an eight. Tutt grunted. "I thought you wanted to gamble."

"I like to get wet gradually," retorted Upright.

Smoothly, Tutt slipped the top card from the left side of his card case to the right. "Ten wins, eight loses.

"You're wet," he said to Upright, gathering in the twenty dollar bill and a couple of other bets. He paid out one.

Upright placed two twenties on a queen. "I'm gettin' wetter."

The queen did not come up in the next deal and Upright added two twenties to his bet.

"Ace wins, queen loses," droned Tutt as he dealt.

"I'm wet now," said Upright. "You're getting near the bottom of the deal."

"Two kings, a nine, two jacks and a trey are still out," said Tutt. "The nine has lost three times."

"Chances are it won't lose a fourth time then," observed Upright. He began to count out bills. Players at the table piled money on the nine.

"I suppose you've got a limit?" Upright asked "Something around two hundred?"

"Your wad's the limit, Texas," Tutt replied coolly.

"Is it?" Upright seemed to hesitate, then put down his entire roll along with Bonner's. "Eighteen hundred, more or less."

"You've got a bet, Texas . . . eighteen hundred, more or less."

Tutt raised his hands to deal the remaining cards in his card case, but Upright threw out his left hand, his right remaining at his side.

"Just a sec, Tutt," he said. "I'm superstitious. Sam," nodding to Bonner who had walked around the table and stood at Tutt's left hand, "you deal 'em this time."

"Not in my game," Ben Tutt snarled. His left hand shot out over the table . . . and Bonner chopped down on it savagely.

Tutt yelped in pain. A double-barreled .41 derringer skittered out from his sleeve, flew across the table. Tutt swore savagely and his right hand went under the left lapel of his coat . . . and froze there . . . as Upright thrust a Frontier Model at him.

"Bring it out, Tutt," Upright cried. "Bring it out!"

Slowly, his face white, Tutt brought his right hand out from under his coat. It was empty.

"Step back," ordered Upright.

Tutt pushed back his chair, got to his feet. His eyes burned as they bored into Upright's.

"You can't get away with this," Tutt warned ominously.

"Of course not," said Upright quite cheerfully. His eyes never leaving Tutt's face, he walked completely around the table, nodding to Bonner as he came to Tutt's place at the table.

With his left hand, Upright took the cover off the card box and with a fingernail pried out the remaining few cards that were to have been dealt.

"Look at this," he invited the former players at the table. One card dropped off, leaving the balance in Upright's hand. He laid the thin packet gently on the table. "Take a good look!"

Several men leaned forward to examine the cards. One cried out angrily, "There's a hole through the edge with a horsehair tying the cards together."

"Right," said Upright. "Gambler up in Deadwood got shot and he showed this to me after I promised I'd see he was buried without his boots on. . . . These cards don't get shuffled, he double-cuts and they stay on the bottom. You watch the sequence, the nine's lost three times, chances are the nine'll win this time. The suckers bet big . . . and the nine's tied down. . . ."

"Yeah, but he deals them—there ain't no horsehair on the cards," exclaimed one of the players.

"Look at the inside of the box. It's got a sharp ridge. When he deals these last cards, he rubs them against the ridge, hard. It cuts the horsehair . . ."

A roar went up around the table and Ben Tutt blanched. "I'll pay all bets," he bleated.

"I lost four hundred in this game this week," shouted a player. "You'll pay me that."

"I lost two-fifty," another man cried.

"I'll pay—all I've got . . ."

"My eighteen hundred first," Upright snapped.

"Adam!" cried Tutt, "bring my cash box. . . ."

A man wearing a flowered vest darted into an office, came out with a tin box. He brought it to the table. "You can pay up and get out of town, Tutt," he said curtly. "I want no crooked gamblers in my place."

A man grabbed the tin box from the saloonkeeper and dumped its contents onto the faro layout. There were bills and gold coins. A dozen hands reached for the money. Upright raised his revolver, fired a bullet into the ceiling.

"My eighteen hundred first," he yelled. "Then you can fight over the rest."

"He's right," said a man. "If it hadn't been for him, we wouldn't be getting anything back."

Upright counted out eighteen hundred dollars that he had bet on the nine, added eighteen hundred from Tutt's money and pocketed the huge wad of bills. He signaled to Bonner and they left the GRAND PRAIRIE. "Easiest money I ever made," chuckled Upright.

"And Ben Tutt?" asked Bonner. "You proved him a crook in public."

"He's through in Ogallala. He'll put his tail between his legs and run."

"I hope so," said Bonner soberly.

"Let's get some grub," Upright suggested.

CHAPTER TWELVE

The TRAIL DRIVERS' CAFE was across the street and Bonner and Upright went in and sat down at a table. Upright brought out all the money he had pocketed at the GRAND PRAIRIE and began to divide it up. A waitress came to the table.

"You want food or a bank for that?" she asked.

"I want the best Texas steak in the house," replied Upright. "And here's ten dollars if you cook it yourself." He thrust a bill at the waitress, a rather attractive girl in her mid-twenties.

"For ten dollars more, I'll eat it, too," the girl retorted, stowing away the bill in a pocket. She looked inquiringly at Bonner. "You want me to cook your steak, too?"

"Not for ten dollars."

Upright winked at the girl. "He's got a girl in Texas and he promised her he wouldn't look at a Kansas girl. Or is this Nebraska?"

"It's Nebraska and it's Tuesday."

Upright guffawed. "Sister, you and me are going to hit it off, all right. What time do you get through work here?"

"At nine o'clock, but my husband usually calls for me about ten minutes before nine."

"Your husband?" cried Upright.

"Deputy Marshal Cooley."

"Goodbye, ten dollars," exclaimed Upright.

The waitress went off into the kitchen.

A man came into the cafe and sat down at the counter. The waitress remained in the kitchen and after a moment or two the man got up and went out. Two minutes later Leo Basgall entered and came to the table.

"Heard you was in town," he said quietly.

"Tommy and Dave are here, too?" asked Upright. Basgall shook his head. "I left Tommy in Chicago. Said he was havin' a good time and he was goin' to stay there until—until he had to go to work."

"Damn!" swore Upright. "He'll shoot off his mouth there." He leaned across the table. "What about Dave?"

"I went to Bismarck." Basgall hesitated. "Dave gunned Kellems. According to the way I got it, he stopped the stage just a mile from town. The marshal opened up on him and Dave got him. But Dave stopped one himself . . ."

"He isn't . . . ?"

"Uh-uh, he got away all right. But the marshal named him before he cashed in. They was offerin' five hundred dollars reward for Dave . . ."

Upright groaned. "What this outfit needs is a boss." He looked at Bonner.

Bonner said, "If a man doesn't do what he's told, he doesn't ride with us."

Upright's eyes narrowed. "You mean that?"

"I think you know me by now."

"I think I do." Upright looked at Basgall. "Any objections?"

"Me?" shrugged Basgall. "You shoulda slapped down Brown back there in Massachusetts."

"I was new then," said Bonner grimly. "But I'm ramrodding from here on." He paused. "We're going into this for big money and our organization's going to be solid. You brought this up, Artie. That means no more business like with Ben Tutt."

"Eighteen hundred dollars wasn't a bad haul for a five minute job."

"But it wasn't a safe job." He nodded to Basgall. "You heard about it pretty quick."

"It's up and down the street."

"My name, too?" asked Upright.

"Sure."

Bonner groaned. "This is a long way from Massachusetts, but it's on the main line. Your name's being tossed around Ogallala. . . ."

"Yours, too," said Upright quickly.

Bonner looked at Basgall. The latter nodded.

"All the more reason," said Bonner. He pushed back his chair. "Let's travel."

"My steak!" cried Upright.

"Let's go!"

Upright got to his feet. The three men started for the door. Before they reached it, the waitress popped out of the kitchen. "Your steaks . . . !"

Upright tossed a crumpled bill to the nearest table. "You eat them, sister. You and your husband."

Outside, Bonner turned to Basgall. "You've got a horse?"

"Bought one yesterday."

"Meet us north of town."

Basgall walked away. Bonner searched the other side of the street, saw the sign of a livery stable a block away. He signaled to Upright and they walked in silence to the stable, Upright getting gloomier with every step.

The livery had a corral full of horses and a few in some stalls.

"Cowboys," the livery man explained laconically. "Lose their money, sell their horses."

Bonner and Upright picked out a horse apiece, bought a saddle. They gave the livery man a hundred dollars and received ten dollars change. As they walked the horses to the street, a lean man wearing a star on the pocket of his white shirt came up.

"Howdy, strangers. Leavin' us already?"

"The town's too tame," Upright said flippantly, but watched the marshal narrowly.

"Tame?" asked the marshal. "Ain't you the fellows called Ben Tutt?"

"Tutt, the tinhorn?" sneered Upright.

"Mmm," said the marshal thoughtfully. "Upright. Name's familiar."

"It's more familiar in Texas."

The marshal hesitated, then nodded. "Just thought I'd warn you. Tutt's got a partner, Martindale. They're having a pow-wow at the OMAHA SALOON. Tutt's drinkin'."

"He wants a fight, he'll get it," snapped Upright.

Bonner said smoothly, "There won't be any fight. We're riding on."

"Good," said the marshal. "I told Tutt last week I'd get him the next time he pulled his gun. I'd have to make good on that promise. I'd have to *try* to make good."

"I'm not running out on any fight," Upright declared.

Bonner looked at him steadily. "I'm riding now."

He mounted the newly purchased horse and turned it into the street. Before he had gone twenty yards, Artie Upright was galloping his horse to catch up to him.

"All right, Sam," he said as he came up.

Bonner nodded. "Good."

They crossed the Union Pacific tracks at a trot and rode out of town. They picked their way through a Texas herd grazing on the rich buffalo grass and a mile beyond, caught up with Leo Basgall, who was loping along easily on a bay gelding.

"You know the marshal?" Bonner asked Basgall.

"Good man. Name of Dietrich."

"Does he know you?"

"Ain't much he misses."

Bonner frowned. "We need Dave and Tommy, but we've got to hole up."

"There's a fella in town I knew in Cheyenne," Basgall said thoughtfully. "He's one-quarter Crow, like me."

"Can you trust him?"

"Me," said Basgall, "I don't trust anyone. Not where money's concerned."

Bonner looked at Upright thoughtfully. "This Dietrich, he didn't place us, but I've got a feeling that he's going through his reward notices right now."

"Reward notices from where? Deadwood—or Massachusetts?"

"Either place. It doesn't matter. We can't let Tommy Brown and Dave Macdougal walk into Ogallala."

"If we don't know where they are, how're we going to stop them?"

"Tommy'll come by train from Omaha. Leo, you can be in Omaha by tonight. You can wait around the depot until he shows up."

Basgall nodded agreement. "Whatever you say. I'll ride to the next depot east and get the train there at five o'clock."

"That's fine, Leo. Nobody knows you in Omaha and you ought to be all right. How badly was Dave Macdougal wounded at Bismarck?"

"I dunno. He stopped one all right, because there was blood. They lost him when he crossed the Missouri, but as nearly as I could find out, there was quite a lot of blood."

"That was three weeks ago," said Upright. "If he could travel at all, he shoulda been here." He hesitated. "I think we ought to cross him off."

"Not if there's a chance," Bonner said. "You fellows came all the way to Massachusetts for me. I think every man in the group ought to have the feeling that he can count on the rest of us."

"Up to a point," said Upright.

Bonner shook his head. "Past that point."

Basgall regarded Bonner thoughtfully. "It's a good feeling." He pointed ahead. "There's a canyon, 'bout five miles ahead there. They don't graze any cattle in it and there's quite a bit of cover. Might be a good place to wait."

"Look for us there."

Basgall gave Upright and Bonner a half salute and wheeled his horse to the right to ride to the first depot east of Ogallala where he could board an east bound train that afternoon.

"I think he's going to be a good man," Bonner said.

"A safe man," agreed Upright. "Which is more'n you can say for Tommy. Tommy'll fight anything on two legs or four, which is sometimes a good thing, but you've got to ride herd on him all the time."

"He'll obey orders," Bonner said firmly, "or he won't ride with us. What about Dave? You know him better than I do."

Upright hesitated. "All right, I guess, if someone tells him what to do, but not much on his own."

"I'll tell him what to do!"

"And me, Sam? You'll tell *me* what to do?"

"Who made the decisions between Wendell and you?"

"One of us'd suggest something and if the other thought it was all right, we'd do it. We never had but one or two fights in all the years we were together."

"We can't afford to have *any* fights, Artie," Bonner said. "We're going into a different business."

"What's so different about it? Wendell and me and the boys were holding up stages before we met you . . ."

"We're never going to hold up a stage."

Upright's eyes narrowed. "That bank in Massachusetts, Sam, that was all right. But remember, it was your home town. You knew all about the place. . . ."

"We'll know all about every place we tackle, Artie. That's what I've been getting at. Everything will be worked out to the finest point. We're not going to take any chances. I've made up my mind to get a hundred thousand dollars and since there are five of us, that means we'll have to get a half a million. We're not going to get that much all at one time. We can't count on luck, not the number of times we're going to have to pull these jobs. That's why we've got to play things safe—not take the slightest chance ever, not trust to luck one bit. The Baker Falls thing was luck. We're never again going to trust to luck."

"And when you get this hundred thousand for yourself?" Upright asked. "What then?"

"Then I quit."

Upright nodded thoughtfully and was silent for a few minutes. Then he said, "Texas is a big place; there's a lot of the state they don't know me. With a hundred thousand and a new name . . ." He grinned. "Yeah, they'll call me a colonel with that much money. Sounds all right. A few thousand acres in East Texas— I'm from West Texas—some horses and steers, that's the life."

CHAPTER THIRTEEN

They slept in a grove of cottonwoods in a ragged canyon that night. In the morning, Upright shot a scrawny jackrabbit and they roasted it over a fire of dry wood. Upright wrinkled his nose in disgust.

"With eighteen hundred dollars in my pocket, I eat jackrabbit!"

"It's filling," said Bonner.

"And it gets damn cold out here at night," Upright complained. "We shoulda picked up our blanket rolls at least."

"I'd rather be cold than face Dietrich," said Bonner. "You, me and Basgall are known in Ogallala. Tommy Brown isn't. So we'll wait here until Tommy comes and then he can go into town and see if Dave's showed up. He'll know enough by then not to shoot off his mouth."

"At least we can cut out a steer and have some beef," Upright said.

Bonner shook his head. "Let's not get the Texas men trailing us in here."

Upright groaned. "I can't live on jackrabbits."

"You can get fat on them."

They shot two more jackrabbits that afternoon and ate them. The next day Upright sulked and would not eat at all. But on the third day his hunger got him up at daybreak and when Bonner himself got up, Upright was roasting a rabbit over a meager fire.

Six days went by and Bonner was worried. Tommy Brown, living it up in Chicago, might decide not to rendezvous with his former friends. He might prefer city life for a while. He might also have run afoul of the law in Chicago and could even now be sitting in a Chicago jail.

Upright suggested as much on the sixth day. "We can't wait here forever. If Dave's ever coming, he'll be in Ogallala by now. And Tommy—you remember he didn't quite like the way you took over back there in Massachusetts."

"We'll wait three more days," said Bonner.

The next day, the seventh since Basgall had left them, Bonner, alone in the little grove of cottonwoods, heard the clatter of iron shoes on rocky ground. Upright was out, searching for the inevitable jackrabbit.

Bonner moved quietly to the edge of the cottonwoods and peered out. A hundred yards away, coming toward him, were two riders. They were Leo Basgall . . . and Dirty Dave Macdougal!

Bonner stepped out into the open and held up his hands. Basgall and Macdougal put their horses into a trot.

"Look who I picked up in Omaha," Basgall said, indicating Macdougal.

Dave Macdougal grinned sheepishly. "I got winged up in Dakota and the thing wouldn't heal, so I went down to Omaha and got doctored up in a hospital. Last night I run into Leo at the depot."

"Tommy Brown?" Bonner asked.

Basgall shook his head. "He never showed. I didn't think you'd want me to wait any more."

"I guess he isn't coming."

Dirty Dave looked around. "Where's Artie?"

In the distance, to the north, a gun sounded. "He's just gotten our lunch. We've been living on jack-rabbits . . ."

"Artie?" exclaimed Dirty Dave. "Him that was so finicky about his grub in Deadwood?"

"How do you feel, Dave?" Bonner asked.

"Like silk. The rest in Omaha did me good. On'y I'm mad. Leo tells me you gave me a split on the Massachusetts bank and Tommy's got that money. Spendin' it in Chicago."

"You'll get your cut of that, Dave," Bonner said, "even if we never see Tommy Brown again." He reached into a pocket and brought out a packet of banknotes. He counted off a thousand dollars. "Here's half of it."

Dave accepted the money with jubilation. "Sam, you're all right. Leo told me you'd made yourself ramrod of this outfit and I'll admit I wasn't so sure of that, but if this is the way you do business, I'm back of you all the way."

"I'm counting on you," Bonner nodded. "Here comes Upright."

Upright came loping around a bend in the canyon,

carrying a jackrabbit. When he saw Basgall and Macdougal he let out a whoop.

"Now we'll get out of here." Then he looked quickly around. "Where's Tommy?"

"He never showed," said Basgall, "but I ran into Dave in Omaha."

Upright appealed to Bonner. "We can't wait any longer for Tommy."

"You're right," agreed Bonner. "I'd rather there were five of us for what I've got in mind, but if we plan it right, I think four are enough."

"I knew something was cooking in that skull of yours," said Upright. "You haven't said hardly a word the last two days."

Bonner picked up a stick and drew a straight line on the ground. "This is the Union Pacific. Here's Ogallala," he slashed the straight line with a quick cut, "and here's Omaha . . ."

"A train!" cried Upright. "That's the scheme."

Bonner nodded. "The James boys have done all right with trains. They've never operated this far west, but I figure the Union Pacific is as good a line as any . . ."

"Maybe we'll get some of that Deadwood or California gold," said Upright enthusiastically.

"We'll be ready for it if there is any," said Bonner. "Now, this is all pretty open country and we can expect to be chased by a couple or three posses. I've given that a lot of thought and I know we've got to make a run for it and we can't count on a start of more than three or four hours, to be absolutely safe, only two hours. Like I told you, Artie, I want to play this safe. Absolutely safe."

"Go ahead, Sam!"

CHAPTER FOURTEEN

Sand Springs was a hamlet consisting of a half dozen houses and three stores. It existed chiefly because there were a few ranches in the vicinity and it had a depot for the same reason. The ranches bought supplies from the east and they were dropped off at the depot. And, in return, they shipped cattle from Sand Springs.

The east bound Union Pacific roared through Sand Springs at eight ten in the evening. It stopped only for passengers, which was about once or twice a month.

At ten minutes to eight the station agent and telegraph operator who also ran the SAND SPRINGS EMPORIUM, a general store some fifty yards from the depot, sent his last telegraph message for the day, announcing to the operator west of him that he was closing for the night, that there were no passengers and the train had a clear run through Sand Springs.

The agent came out of the depot then and was about to cross the tracks to throw the all-clear semaphore signal. Sam Bonner who had come around the depot and stopped on the platform, stepped forward.

"Put the signal on stop."

"You want a ticket east?"

"No, I just want you to stop the train, that's all."

"I can only stop it for passengers."

Leo Basgall appeared at the other end of the platform. The agent looked at him, then back at Bonner.

Bonner said, "You're right, it's going to be a hold-up."

The station agent swore softly. "I always thought this might happen sometime . . ."

"It's happened."

The agent shrugged. "You're the boss." He crossed the tracks to the semaphore signal and flipped it over to *Stop*.

Bonner, who had followed the man, nodded approval. "Now, you've got a couple of red lamps."

"Certainly."

"Let's go in and light them up."

"You're the boss."

Leo Basgall remained on the platform while Bonner entered the little depot with the agent. The latter got two red lanterns, lighted them.

"All right?"

"The telegraph—you'd be at it the moment we left."

The agent grimaced. "You don't miss much."

Bonner crossed to the telegraph instrument and tore it loose. He threw it to the floor, stamped on it two or three times, then, drawing his revolver, smashed the barrel on the part remaining on the desk.

"We need the extra time," he said.

"And me? What about me?"

"You'll stay in here nice and quiet until it's over. You won't get hurt if you do."

"That suits me," said the agent. "This is only a part-time job and the company can't expect me to risk my life for forty dollars a month." He pulled up a chair and seated himself, crossing his legs comfortably.

Bonner looked at the clock on the wall. It said: 8:03. Basgall rapped on the window.

Bonner left the depot. The headlights of the approaching east bound were coming around a wide curve. Bonner shaded his eyes to cut down the glare and saw two swinging red lights, some two hundred yards down the track.

Upright and Macdougal.

He handed one of the red lanterns to Basgall.

"Let's go."

Basgall crossed the tracks, took up a position near the semaphore signal and began swinging his red lantern back and forth. Bonner remained on the station platform for another minute or two until the approaching engine signaled with its steam whistle, two short blasts.

Then Bonner stepped off the platform and began swinging his lantern.

Brakes were squealing long before the engine came to a full halt opposite the station. A fireman started to lean out and drew back quickly as Bonner's revolver almost touched his face.

"Holdup!" cried the fireman. He scurried to the far side of the cab, started to clamber down and ran into Basgall's gun.

"Down!" ordered Basgall.

Bonner climbed up to the cab and gestured to the engineer. The engineer, white-faced, followed his fireman down on the other side. Bonner descended.

The conductor came running forward, closely followed by Artie Upright. "This is an outrage," the conductor protested. "We're not carrying any money on this train."

"*You* may not be," Bonner said calmly, "but we'll take a look at the express car." He signaled for the conductor to start back.

The express-car door had been partly open, but as Bonner and the conductor approached it was suddenly slammed shut.

"Tell him to open," Bonner ordered.

"Carlisle," called the conductor. "The train's being held up. They—they want you to open up."

A gun exploded inside the express car and a bullet tore through the wooden door. Bonner moved to the side of the door, pounded on it with the muzzle of his revolver.

"You're going to get hurt," he called out.

"So're you," came the defiant yell from inside the express car.

"All right," Bonner said loudly, "put the dynamite

under the car." He gestured to Upright. The latter, chuckling, got underneath the express car, crunching the crushed rock of the railbed with his boots. The listening agent inside the car sent a bullet through the floor.

Upright crawled out from under the express car.

"You've got ten seconds," Bonner called out. "One, two . . ."

"All right," came the muffled reply. "Pull out the fuse . . ."

Upright again crouched and crunched gravel underneath the express car.

The door was whipped open a foot, another, two feet. The frightened face of the expressman appeared in the opening.

"Throw out your gun," cried Upright.

A rifle was thrown out. Bonner nodded to Basgall. "You stay out here."

He clambered into the express car, followed by Artie Upright.

The car was dimly lighted at one end with a lantern, brightly with a reflector lamp at the other side. A safe was directly underneath the bright lamp.

Crowding the expressman ahead of them, Upright and Bonner headed for the lighted side.

"Open it up," Bonner ordered.

The expressman groaned, "If I do, you'll get the Pinkertons after you."

"Fine," said Upright. "Now, open it up."

Reluctantly, the agent took a key from his pocket. He unlocked the iron safe door, pulled it open. Upright pushed him aside and reached into the safe. He brought out several paper-wrapped parcels, tore them open. Two contained consignments of jewelry. "Throw them aside, Artie," Bonner ordered.

"We could get some money on them."

"Too risky. We just want cash."

"There's none here," said the unhappy expressman.

None of the parcels contained money. But there was a fat manila envelope in the safe. Upright tore it open, yelped in glee. "Money—nice and new." He looked at the address on the envelope. "Hey, they got a bank in Deadwood now. This is for them."

"Put it in your pocket," said Bonner. To the agent, "What else have you got?"

"Regular express. Stuff going to stores in Omaha, Chicago. Machinery . . ."

"Machinery going east?"

The expressman was perspiring. "That's what it's marked." His eyes went to the dimmed end of the car. Bonner strode past him.

At the far end of the car were three wooden boxes, reinforced with strap iron. The boxes were quite small, not over a foot in size each way. They were stenciled *Machinery*, but bore no name of consignee.

Bonner pointed his revolver at one of the straps of iron, pulled the trigger. The bullet split the iron strap, tore into the box, splintered the wood. Stooping, Bonner attacked the splintered wood with the muzzle of his revolver, enlarging the opening.

The twenty dollar gold pieces spilled out.

"This is it, Artie!" he cried. Artie Upright ran over, scooped up the coins.

"Wow! We're rich."

The expressman shuffled over. "Sixty thousand in double eagles," he moaned. "From the San Francisco mint, going to Chicago . . . I'll lose my job over this."

"Why should you?" asked Bonner.

"I wasn't supposed to say anything about this . . ."

"You didn't. We just happened to find it." Bonner picked up one of the small heavy boxes and carried it to the door. He set it down on the edge of the floor. Artie Upright piled up the two remaining boxes, one on top of the other, and panting, got them to the door.

Bonner leaned out and fired three quick shots into the air.

Far down the side of the train, four horses came galloping. Dirty Dave Macdougal was riding one of the horses, leading the others by the bridle reins.

Bonner and Upright dropped to the ground, waited for the horses.

Macdougal pulled up with the horses. Bonner picked up one of the wooden boxes, handed it up to Macdougal. Basgall mounted and Bonner gave him a second box. Upright mounted with difficulty, clutching the third wooden box to his bosom. "This is the kind of weight I don't mind carrying," he chortled.

Bonner took the bridle reins of the fourth horse. "Go ahead, boys," he told the others.

The three outlaws started their horses at a dead run. Bonner swung into the saddle, waited until the others had a start of a hundred feet or more.

Then he said to the conductor, "So far nobody's been hurt. Let's keep it that way."

He kicked his mount's flanks with his heels and the animal sprang away. Bending low in the saddle, Bonner followed his friends.

Ahead of the train, they cut the tracks and headed north from Sand Springs.

They rode a swift two miles, then pulled up.

Saddlebags were thrown to the ground and the wooden boxes were hacked open. "Fifteen thousand apiece," said Bonner.

"Plus this." Upright threw down the manila envelope he had extracted from the expressman's safe. It contained five thousand dollars in twenty dollar bills, all new and crisp.

The money was quickly divided and the four men remounted their horses. "You know the plan now. There's just one place they won't be looking for us tomorrow morning. . . ."

"The train," chuckled Upright. "I like that."

"Stick to the plan," Bonner said earnestly. "No matter how it looks, stick to the plan. Leo, ready?"

"Ready, chief!"

Bonner and Basgall wheeled their horses, took off to the east. Upright and Macdougal headed west.

The weight of the saddlebags bothered the mounts somewhat, but Bonner and Basgall continued through the darkness at as swift a pace as the horses could manage with continual prodding.

Bonner's horse was heaving and in considerable distress, when they finally splashed through a shallow stream and pulled up in a clump of cottonwoods. Horses whickered in the darkness and Basgall, who had a way with horses, leaped from his exhausted mount and ran into the cottonwoods. He reappeared in a moment leading two saddled horses.

Carpetbags of heavy material were tied to the saddles. Basgall threw them to the ground. Quickly the two men emptied the contents of the saddlebags into the carpetbags and then hooked the weighted bags over their saddle pommels.

Bonner held out his hand to Basgall. "Remember now, you'll probably see me on the train, but don't even look at me. We're strangers, no matter what happens."

"I won't know you," said Basgall.

"Right!"

They mounted the fresh horses and each man rode off, one to the east, one to the south. Basgall was headed for a small town some twenty miles east of Sand Springs, on the Union Pacific. Bonner had a longer ride.

There was a small town eight miles east of the town where Basgall would board the train, but Bonner would pass it up and go to a town twelve miles beyond, thirty-eight from Sand Springs.

Upright and Macdougal would be repeating a somewhat similar routine during the next morning, with one exception. Upright would ride the Union Pacific to Cheyenne, Macdougal to Ogden, Utah.

CHAPTER FIFTEEN

Bonner rode through the night, alternately pressing his horse, then walking it. Two or three times he stopped and allowed the horse to rest for ten minutes. He was still in the saddle when the sun rose over the eastern horizon, but by its light he could see a cluster of buildings ahead and on his right, the shimmering rails of the Union Pacific.

A half mile from the town, Bonner dismounted from his horse. He unsaddled it, took off the bridle and turned the animal loose. He picked up his weighted carpetbag then and walked to the village.

Carrying his bag he entered the village, which consisted of a block and a half of stores and saloons, and finding a restaurant, had a substantial meal. He took his time eating and when he left the restaurant, he walked to the depot. Several people were on the platform and two men were ahead of him at the window buying tickets.

When Bonner's turn came, he thrust a ragged greenback under the wicket.

"Ticket for Grand Island."

The agent gave him a ticket and the change. Bonner went out upon the platform. The timing was nice. The east bound morning train was just pulling into the depot.

One or two passengers got off the train and about seven or eight boarded it. The coach Bonner stepped into was fairly filled, but just ahead was an empty seat. Bonner started toward it, then winced.

The man by the window was Leo Basgall.

Bonner continued past him and went into the next car. He found a seat there beside a tobacco-chewing cattleman. The man looked at Bonner as the latter sat down beside him, stooped and shot out a mouthful of tobacco juice upon the floor of the coach.

"Goin' to Omaha?" the tobacco chewer asked.

"Grand Island."

"That's only a hop and a jump. Me, I'm going all the way. Chicago. Hear about the holdup last night?"

"Where?"

"Sand Springs. Old Jesse got himself a hatful— sixty-five thousand in gold."

"You mean Jesse James?"

"Who else?" The cattleman made an impatient gesture. "I know, they say Jesse's blamed for everything, but this one's got Jesse's trademark. Couldn't a been anyone else."

"What's Jesse's trademark?"

"Smooth getaway, nobody hurt. That's Jesse every time."

"I never heard of Jesse operating this far west," said Bonner.

"He's been in Iowa, hasn't he? And Illinois. Why shouldn't he try Nebraska for a change?"

"No reason I guess."

The conductor came along and took Bonner's ticket. "Grand Island," he observed.

"Just a hop and a jump," repeated Bonner's seat companion. "That far I'd ride a horse."

The conductor punched the ticket, wrote a number on a slip and stuck it in Bonner's hatband. He went on. Bonner breathed a little more freely.

Shortly after noon the train pulled into Grand Island, the largest town between Ogallala and Omaha. Bonner shook hands with the cattleman who had helped him while away the time on the train.

Finding a livery stable, he bought a horse, and mounting, crossed the Platte and headed south. He rode in a southerly direction until late afternoon, then headed eastward.

He slept under the stars that night without food, and rising early the next morning, continued eastward. In midmorning he entered a town and had a good meal, then resumed his eastward progress. He rode until an hour after darkness, when he saw lights ahead. Many lights.

In a little while he reached the edge of Lincoln and, unsaddling his horse, turned it loose. He hid the saddle in a clump of brush, then carried the heavy valise into Lincoln.

He found the railroad depot and discovered that a train left for Omaha in a little over an hour. He had a dinner at the railroad depot restaurant, then boarded the train.

Shortly before midnight, he checked into the best hotel in Omaha and went to bed.

In the morning he bought a complete change of clothes which he carried in a newly purchased valise to the hotel. He changed, made a bundle of his outdoor costume and stowed it away in the carpetbag, transferring the contents of the carpetbag to the valise. He concealed the carpetbag under the bed, then checked out of the hotel and went to the Omaha depot where he boarded a Chicago bound train a few minutes later.

The train rolled across Iowa, crossed the Mississippi sometime during the night, and by early morning pulled into the Chicago Depot.

Bonner became completely relaxed now, for the first time since he had boarded the Union Pacific train at Sand Springs. Chicago was a bustling city. The Big Fire of five years before had given the western metropolis a civic pride and every merchant and shop owner in Chicago seemed to be trying to strain his resources to build larger and more modern quarters. Fashionable homes had sprung up on the near North side and the city was stretching out to the north, to the west and the south. Its progress was blocked only to the east by Lake Michigan.

Bonner registered at the Potter House, the finest hostelry west of New York. He got a large, beautifully furnished room with windows facing the lake.

A few minutes after entering his room, a newspaper was slipped under the door. Bonner was somewhat perturbed, then realized that this was simply an additional service of a luxury hotel. But he received a shock when he picked up the newspaper and bold headlines leaped at him. They covered three columns of a story. The headlines read:

Sam Bonner Isn't Jesse James
Declares Allan Pinkerton
He Has No Confederate
Army to Help Him
I'll Get Him
in One
Week

The article was an interview the famous detective had given out the day before as he departed on a trip to Nebraska. A reporter had chided Pinkerton about his inability to apprehend any members of the Jesse James confederation of Missouri, and the detective pointed out that Jesse James was a former member of Quantrill's band of guerrillas, a close friend of many former high-ranking army men in Western Missouri who, because they were former Confederates, not only sheltered the members of the James confederation, but gave them aid and comfort. Pinkerton went on to relate some of his own experiences in the stronghold of the Jameses. Clay County, Missouri, he declared, was James territory; those of the citizens who were not sympathetic to Jesse James were afraid of him. All were spies and informers to the Jameses. Pinkerton had lost three men in Clay County and he frankly admitted that his far-flung detective organization could never apprehend Jesse James until the law enforcement officials of the State of Missouri themselves were willing for Jesse James to be brought to trial.

But Sam Bonner, Pinkerton declared, was another matter. He was a two-bit highwayman whose background in crime consisted of stopping stagecoaches in the Black Hills country. One of his men had already been hanged and Bonner himself had been captured with ease in his home town of Baker Falls, Massachusetts. True, he had made his escape from the antiquated jail in Massachusetts, but he was no Jesse James. He had stumbled upon a rich haul in his holdup of the Union Pacific at Sand Springs, Nebraska, but he had no Clay County, Missouri, to hide in. Apprehending him was a matter of time only and he, Allan Pinkerton, and his son, William, were taking the field in person. With the single exception of Jesse James, the Pinkerton Agency had never failed to get its man.

Bonner remained in his room all that day, having his meals brought up and tipping well for the service. In the evening, a newspaper was brought to him and when the waiter left the room, Bonner read it.

Only a small article on the bottom of page one referred to the affair at Sand Springs. A telegraphic dispatch reported the arrival of Allan Pinkerton in Ogallala, Nebraska. There, he had already learned that Sam Bonner and his chief lieutenant, Artie Upright, had spent a few days in Ogallala, some three weeks ago. Their trail had been followed for some distance out of Ogallala, but the trailers gave up when it was apparent that Bonner and his gang were headed back for their old stamping grounds in the Black Hills.

Bonner turned the page and a name brought a gasp from him. "*Randolph Thompson in Chicago. Financier Denies That He Seeks Control of the New York Central Railroad.*" The article was a brief one.

The financier had been recognized getting off the New York Central train and the reporter had questioned him as to his business in Chicago, but had obtained little information. The Eastern capitalist refused to answer questions put to him. The reporter, however, made mention of his traveling companion, Ran-

dolph Thompson's daughter, reported engaged to a
Back Bay Bostonian.

Bonner slept uneasily that night. The next morning
he went down to the lobby and stepped to the desk.

"I saw by the paper that Randolph Thompson's staying at this hotel," he said to the clerk.

The man shook his head. "Not any more he isn't.
He checked in yesterday morning and took the train
to St. Paul late in the afternoon." The clerk smirked
importantly. "Understand he's going to buy the Northwestern Railroad."

"I thought it was the New York Central."

The clerk winked. "Trying to throw the stockholders off. That's the way these capitalists work. Say
they're going to buy something, let the stock run up,
then turn around and snap up something entirely different. Staying with us long, Mr . . . uh . . . ?"

"Conger. I'm in the shoe business."

"Ought to be a good business since everybody wears
shoes."

Bonner nodded and turned away.

Outside the hotel he signaled to a hack and when it
approached, he climbed in. "North Wells Street," he
said. "Number 314."

The hack driver touched the brim of his high sil
hat and the hack rolled smoothly away from the hotel
After a moment or two it turned into the wide thor
oughfare that divided Chicago's north side and south
side. Madison Street.

Some ten minutes later the hack pulled up before
a new five-story brick building. "Here you are, sir!"

Bonner gave the man a dollar and signaled to him
to keep the change. The hack driver exclaimed grate-
fully. "Want me to wait for you, sir?"

"No, I may be here quite a while."

Bonner entered the building and consulted a direc-
tory. He found an entry: *Chicago Home Weekly, 304.*
He climbed the stairs to the third floor and found a
ground-glass door with the inscription on it: CHICAGO

HOME WEEKLY, MALCOLM NEDDERCUTT, EDITOR &
PUBLISHER.

He entered and found himself in a tiny room containing two desks, heaped high with newspapers,
magazines and paper of all sizes and colors. A tired-
looking man wearing thick eyeglasses looked up
from the desk.

"Yes?"

"I'd like to see Mr. Neddercutt," Bonner said.

The man looked toward a door not quite closed.
"What's it about?"

"An advertisement he had in the paper."

"Oh, that." The man got up, walked to the door and
stuck in his head. "Man here about the ad," he said
into the room.

He turned and signaled to Bonner to go into the other
office. Bonner entered and found himself in a room
about the same size as the first and just as littered with
newspapers and magazines. A bright-eyed little man of
about thirty popped up behind the littered desk.

"You want to see me?"

"About your ad in the *Tribune* . . ."

"Yes, sir," said Mr. Neddercutt enthusiastically. He
covered his mouth, coughed twice, then removed his
hand. "You understand the ad, I take it?"

"It said, *'young man wanted for national magazine,
no experience necessary.'* "

Neddercutt showed fleeting disappointment. "That
wasn't all it said."

" *'Small investment required,'* " Bonner finished.

"Right. As long as you understand. You see, our
business is largely by mail and a considerable amount
of money comes in. Since you, I mean, ah, our employees, are handling large amounts of money, I think
it only fair that I, as the employer, should have financial assurance of the, ah, honesty of our employees."

"I quite agree with you, Mr. Neddercutt," Bonner
said. "It is possible, however, that I am not qualified
for this position. What does the work consist of?"

Neddercutt picked a newspaper from his desk. He

handed it to Bonner. "That's our publication, Mr., ah . . ."

"Conger. Ralph Conger."

"Mr. Conger, the *Chicago Home Weekly* is one of the foremost publications in its field. At the rate it is going, we hope soon to equal our leading New York competitors, the *New York Ledger* and *The New York Weekly*. Are you aware of the tremendous profits that those magazines are earning?"

"I've seen them on the newsstands, but I know nothing of them."

"The *New York Ledger* enjoys a circulation of three hundred thousand copies per issue and earns its owner some two millions of dollars a year."

Bonner sent a quick look around the small, untidy office. Neddercutt noted the look and chuckled. "We're not quite in the class of our worthy competitors, Mr. Conger, but we'll get there, Mr. Conger, we'll get there. After all, we are only six months old. How much circulation would you say we now enjoy?"

"Two hundred thousand?"

"In time, Mr. Conger, in time. With a little more capital and, ah, a more vigorous editorial policy, we'll soon be there. Since we are new and do not have the great profits of the *New York Ledger,* we are compelled to reprint English serials in our little publication. While these are all right, we have learned that our midwestern reading audiences prefer more typically American, more, ah, vigorous stories. If we could afford to pay the price, a fine serial by Mrs. E.D.E.N. Southworth might boost our circulation by as much as a hundred thousand copies. Or perhaps a rousing tale of the West by Colonel Prentiss Ingraham or Ned Buntline might do the trick. . . ."

"These stories cost considerable money?"

"My dear Mr. Conger! The authors I have mentioned are in great demand. The eastern magazines are bidding for them. Yet for a paltry four thousand dollars I could purchase a smashing tale by Ned Buntline that he discussed with me only last week. A story of Jesse James, no less."

"Ned Buntline knows Jesse James?"

"He knows them all. Jesse James, Wild Bill Hickok, Buffalo Bill. My dear Mr. Conger, Ned Buntline spends a considerable amount of time on our western prairies gathering material for his fascinating stories. He writes only of what he knows and that is why he enjoys such amazing popularity."

Bonner nodded thoughtfully. "You intend to use the —the investment I make to purchase a Ned Buntline story?"

Mr. Neddercutt had to cover his mouth again as he went into a fit of coughing. When he finally cleared his throat, he blinked rapidly and said, "Precisely, Mr. Conger. You, ah, have four thousand dollars?"

"Yes."

"You might even have a . . . a little more?"

"Yes."

Neddercutt drew a deep breath. "Mr. Conger, I am about to give you the opportunity of a lifetime, the opportunity to make an investment in the fastest growing business venture in the city of Chicago, a business that has such great potentials that I—that I—" He floundered, then gulped. "A twenty-five percent interest in this firm for five thousand dollars."

"I would draw a salary also?"

"A salary? Uh, of course you'd draw a salary. Naturally, the amount would depend on how much of an interest you have in the firm. I draw only a modest salary myself, mmm, a hundred dollars a week. That is not unreasonable, considering that I am three-quarters owner of this company. As a one-quarter owner, I should think you would be entitled to a salary of, ah, shall we say twenty-five dollars a week?"

"Let's say fifty."

"My dear Mr. Conger, isn't that a—a bit high?"

"Mr. Neddercutt," said Bonner, "just what is the real condition of this business right now? How much circulation do you actually have?"

"Why, I couldn't say offhand. We—we have been printing fifty thousand copies a week."

"You sell them all?"

"Well, no. You see, we turn the entire edition over to the news company. They pay us four cents for every copy sold. . . ."

"How many are sold?"

Neddercutt gulped. "In excess of twelve thousand a week."

"Less than one-fourth. And how much do you owe the printer?"

Neddercutt wiped his perspiring brow. "Why, ah, not very much. Just for one or two issues . . ."

"How much?"

"Fourteen hundred dollars. Of course, there's the previous printer."

"How much?"

"Six thousand dollars. He's—he's the one who's been threatening me. But I'm sure I can keep him from foreclosing with a substantial payment on account. Say, two thousand to him, one thousand to the present printer. That would leave a considerable operating capital."

"It wouldn't enable you to buy that rousing tale from Ned Buntline."

"We wouldn't actually have to put out the money at once. We could pay him upon publication, or slightly after publication. . . ."

Bonner came to a sudden decision. Then he nodded briskly. "All right, Neddercutt, I'll bail you out. But it's fifty percent of the business and we each draw fifty dollars a week salary. And I'll put up six thousand in new capital."

Neddercutt thrust out a shaking hand. "Mr. Conger, welcome to the firm!"

Bonner indicated the outer office. "Where does he come in?"

"Olcott? He's my—*our*—editor. He gets eighteen dollars a week and he's worth every penny of it."

"We might even give him a raise."

"He's been asking for it. I think it'd be good policy to keep him happy. Suppose we increase his salary to . . . uh, twenty dollars a week? On the first of next month. By which time, I hope," Mr. Neddercutt coughed gently, "you'll be able to put up the—the six thousand."

"I can put it up today."

"Mr. Conger!" cried Neddercutt happily.

CHAPTER SIXTEEN

Bonner walked briskly all the way back to the Potter House. Entering the hotel he went up to his room. He unlocked his valise and counted out six thousand dollars in double eagles. He made a neat parcel of the money, then tied it with a bit of string. He descended to the lobby and was crossing to the door when a voice sent a shock through his entire body.

"Sam!"

He stopped, rooted to the floor. He wanted to turn and could not. Vivian Thompson came up from behind, circled to get in front of him. Vivian Thompson, wearing a dress that could have been created only for her.

Bonner said, "I—I thought you'd gone to St. Paul with your father."

"Oh no, he went alone. He'll be back here the day after tomorrow." She looked around. "Where can we talk?"

"You can't be seen with me!"

"You're staying here at the hotel?"

He hesitated, then nodded. "I—I didn't know you were here until I read it in the papers."

"What's your room number?"

"You can't come there!"

"Who says I can't?"

Bonner groaned inwardly. "Four-twelve."

"Five minutes," she said, turning away from him.

Bonner walked to the door, then turned and climbed the stairs to the fourth floor. He entered his room and dropped the parcel of gold coins on the bed.

There was a discreet knock at the door. He opened it and let Vivian into the room. She went into his arms. "Oh, Sam!" she sobbed. "It's been terrible. Every night I thought tomorrow . . . tomorrow I'll hear that he's dead."

He released her. "The paper said you were engaged to a Boston man."

"Father gave that out. I scarcely know the man."

"Who is it?"

"Peter Nichols. He—he's involved with Father in some business dealings." She frowned. "Father wanted that to get out just in case . . ."

"In case someone tied your name to mine?"

She did not answer which was an affirmation. She walked to the window, looked out over the lake a moment, then turned. "Is it true . . . that story the papers have been carrying . . . about the train in Nebraska?"

"I told you there wasn't anything else I could do."

Her lips trembled. "I know, but I—I hoped against hope . . ."

"They'd hang me in Deadwood if they got me back there and I think your father would leave no stone unturned to have me taken back to Deadwood . . ."

"Should you be here in Chicago?"

Bonner hesitated. "I thought it would be the safest place for me—a big city where nobody pays any attention to anyone else . . . the city where Allan Pinkerton also happens to have his headquarters." Bonner almost smiled. "He's out in Nebraska right now looking for me and I'm here within a mile of his office."

Vivian regarded him soberly. "You've changed,

Sam. You—you sound almost triumphant, as if you'd won a—a victory."

"I've made my peace with myself. I've never done anything right in my life. But it's always bothered me. Now it doesn't any more. I've made my choice, finally and definitely."

"And me, Sam?" Vivian asked desperately. "What about *my* choice?"

"Your father forced me into this."

"Does that make it any easier for me?"

He walked to her and took her into his arms. She clung to him. "What're we going to do, Sam? What're we going to do?"

"There's nothing for us," he said dully.

"Jesse James is married," she said after a moment.

He stepped away from her roughly. "And what kind of a life has she got? Hiding, chased, afraid every time he leaves her for a day, an hour, that she'll hear he's been killed." His eyes became steely. "She was one of his own kind, his kin. You . . . you're the daughter of Randolph Thompson . . ."

"——Who used to wear dresses made of flour sacks!"

"You don't wear them now and you're not going to wear them again." He shook his head violently.

"You said it, not I."

"We said goodbye in Massachusetts."

Vivian strolled toward the bed, reached down idly and picked up the little parcel that lay on the bed. For a moment she was unaware of its extremely heavy weight. Then she whirled. "What's in here?"

"Gold," Bonner said harshly. "Gold from the Union Pacific!"

Vivian threw the parcel back upon the bed as if it had suddenly turned to fire.

Bonner said gently, "Don't you see, Vivian? You can't even touch it."

She went to the door. With her hand on the knob, she turned. "Tonight, Sam. I've got to see some people now and—and I must think."

She went out.

Bonner waited a half hour, then got his valise. He put the parcel of gold into it and walked down to the lobby. He paid his bill at the desk, and outside climbed into a hack.

He had himself driven to the Northwestern Depot and there carried his valise into the Madison Street door. He walked through the depot and came out on Canal Street. He accosted a hack driver.

"Do you know of a good boardinghouse somewhere on the North Side?" he asked the man. "I've just come to Chicago to take a job in a dry goods store and I can't spend too much for room and board."

"How high can you go for room and board?" the hack man asked.

"Not over eight dollars a week."

"Get in," said the hack man. "There're a dozen good places you can find for that over on Ohio Street."

The hack rolled smartly down to Wells Street, crossed the bridge to the north side and some twenty minutes later stopped before a brownstone house which had a small sign outside: ROOMS FOR GENTLEMEN ——BOARD.

"Try this place," said the hack man.

"It looks fine to me," said Bonner. "Here . . ." He gave the man a dollar. "You won't have to wait."

"Thank you, sir. . . ."

The hackman drove off. Bonner waited for a moment, then walked in the opposite direction. He walked swiftly down Rush Street for two blocks, then turned east on another street. The houses were quite similar to those on Ohio Street and several of them had signs outside, stating that they took in boarders. Bonner picked out one of the better houses and, going in, soon engaged room and board for ten dollars a week. He was given a quietly furnished, rather large room on the second floor overlooking the street.

Again, he took the parcel of gold from the valise and locking his valise in the closet and pocketing the key, he left the boardinghouse. He boarded a horse streetcar and a few minutes later dropped off across the street from 314 N. Wells Street.

He climbed to the offices of the *Chicago Home Weekly* and discovered that Olcott, the editor, was alone in the offices.

"Where's Mr. Neddercutt?" Bonner asked.

"He had to go over to the printer's," replied the editor. He leaned back in his chair and regarded Bonner owlishly. "Mr. Neddercutt tells me that you're buying a half interest in this business."

"That's right."

"Could I ask you for some of my back pay?" Olcott went on. "My landlady's given me until tonight to pay my back rent."

"How much pay have you got coming?"

"Three weeks. It'll be four on Saturday."

Bonner took a roll of bills from his pocket and peeled off four twenties. "You've been raised to twenty dollars a week."

Olcott picked up the bills reverently. "Manna from heaven," he said softly. "I never thought I'd see anything like this again."

"Things are going to improve, Olcott," Bonner said. "I know that the paper's had a hard time of it . . ."

"Mr. Conger," Olcott said fervently. "I'm only the editor here, but you've just saved my life. I don't care if I lose my job for it, because even if I do, I've got more money right now than I ever had at one time in my life. I want to tell you just one thing—don't give Mr. Neddercutt the money to pay the bills he owes. Pay them yourself."

Bonner smiled. "I was intending to do that very thing. In fact, if you'll tell me where to find the printer Mr. Neddercutt's gone to see, I'll go over right now and pay him."

"It's the Bixby Printing Company on South Dearborn. They sent over a letter by messenger telling Mr. Neddercutt that they were going to file a petition for bankruptcy unless he paid something on account at once."

"That's the printer he owes the fourteen hundred to? Or the six thousand one?"

"No. Bixby's the twenty-two hundred dollar printer."

"Neddercutt mentioned only two printers."

"There are four; the amounts total ten thousand and fifty-four dollars. Mr. Neddercutt hasn't paid a dollar on his printing bill in something like five months."

"I see," said Bonner. "What other bills are there?"

"My salary you just paid. Of course, there's the rent for the office, but that's only three months at thirty a month. Nothing to speak of. We haven't used any art work or engravings in the past three months, but I believe there's a little engraving bill of around three hundred dollars. A man comes here about twice a week dunning for it. Oh—I almost forgot, there's a man named Dunning. Neddercutt hired him about a month ago to work here. He put up five hundred dollars for security . . . He walked out two weeks ago and he wants his five hundred dollars back. He had a lawyer in yesterday about it."

"In other words," said Bonner, "the business is bankrupt . . . and Neddercutt's a crook?"

Olcott shrugged. "If he wasn't a crook, he'd have been shut down three months ago. He's kept going by hook and crook."

"Suppose," Bonner said, "suppose the bills were all paid? Is there a chance of a business like this making a go of it?"

"Yes, these story papers sometimes become tremendously successful. But I don't think it can be done the way we're operating, reprinting stories from English magazines, just because there's no international copyright and we don't have to pay for the stories."

"Well, Neddercutt's aware of that. He said if he had the money he could buy a story from a Mrs. Southworth . . ."

Olcott laughed. "Mrs. Southworth writes exclusively for the *New York Ledger* and she gets around seven thousand dollars for a story."

"Well, how about Ned Buntline? I've read some of his stories and Neddercutt tells me that he could have bought one from Buntline when he was here just the other day."

"Buntline was here?"

Bonner winced. "Damn Neddercutt for a liar. But you *could* get a Buntline story?"

"For cash on the line, yes."

"How much cash?"

"Three thousand, four at the outside."

The hall door was slammed open and a truculent-looking man wearing a derby came in. "Where's Neddercutt?" he demanded.

Olcott shot a quick look at Bonner. "Mr. Neddercutt's stepped out for the moment."

"Good," said the truculent-looking man. "Then he won't step in here again." He took a folded document from his pocket. "I'll just nail this up on the door outside and seal the door."

"What is it?" asked Bonner.

"A notice of creditors' foreclosure. I'm from the sheriff's office."

"How much money is needed?"

The man from the sheriff's office shrugged. "Three of the creditors got this up. It says they want eight thousand, five hundred and twenty-four dollars and thirty-five cents."

"Tell the creditors to come and get their money," Bonner snapped.

"What?"

Bonner broke the string on the gold parcel and unwrapped it. "I've just bought into the business here. All debts will be paid in full . . ."

The man with the derby looked at the money, then at Bonner. "I don't know anything about this. My job's to take these notices around and nail them up."

"Well, take it back with you and tell the creditors to come and get their money."

"I can't do that."

Bonner took two of the gold pieces and handed them

to the man from the sheriff's office. "Can you do it now?"

The man hesitated and Bonner added another gold piece. "Yes sir," said the man, "I think I can do it."

He went out, passing Neddercutt coming in.

"You're through," Bonner said. "That was the man from the sheriff's office with the creditors' foreclosure notice."

Neddercutt winced. "I was afraid of that." His eyes went to the gold. "What—what did you say about me being through?"

"You told me you owed only two printers. There are four."

"I—I may have overlooked a bill or two."

"Two fat printers' bills—and a few other things."

Neddercutt gulped. "Things are bad. Let's face it. Uh, could you come into my office and talk it over?"

Bonner shook his head. "Write out a bill of sale."

"I couldn't do that. The *Weekly's* my baby. I started her and I——"

"You can start another."

"It takes a while to get going."

"I'm paying up all your bills. Your credit rating's all cleared up."

Neddercutt brightened. "That's right." But his eyes went again to the stacks of gold. He licked his lips. "Mr. Conger, why, uh, couldn't you just let the creditors have this business. With that much money you and I could start all over and . . ."

"Write out the bill of sale," Bonner snapped. "Here——" he scooped a handful of coins and thrust them at Neddercutt. "That'll pay your board for a few weeks while you hatch up something new."

After Neddercutt had taken his personal effects from his office and departed, Bonner sat down with Olcott and made up a list of the creditors. Then they closed the offices and went around to the creditors. Bonner had to return to his boardinghouse and get more gold.

By evening he was sole owner of the *Chicago*

Home Weekly . . . at an expenditure of twelve thousand and two hundred dollars.

He had left a little over two thousand dollars in gold and eight hundred in greenbacks. That night, at his room in the boardinghouse, Bonner reviewed the events of the day.

The more he thought of his business venture, the more satisfied he became. Sam Bonner of Deadwood and Sand Springs, Nebraska, was the owner and publisher of a story paper in the city of Chicago. He lived in a boardinghouse on the north side and every day he would go to his office on North Wells Street . . . less than a mile from the offices of Pinkerton's International Detective Agency.

Pinkerton and his son, William, returned to Chicago. They issued no statements as to their failure to apprehend Sam Bonner who had robbed the Union Pacific of sixty-five thousand dollars.

Randolph Thompson returned to Chicago. He, too, made no statements to the newspapers, but one of them reported that he was considering the purchase of the Nickel Plate Railroad. Thompson, himself, accompanied by his daughter, entrained for New York.

Bonner read about that in the paper. He did not again return to the Potter House or go anywhere within four blocks of it.

CHAPTER SEVENTEEN

A month after his arrival in Chicago, Bonner walked to the main post office on South Clark Street and inquired at the general delivery window for mail for

Julius V. Schlager. Three letters were handed to him.

One was postmarked San Francisco, one St. Louis and the third New Orleans.

The first was a badly spelled scrawl. It read simply: *"I am havving a fin time hear in New Orlens. My adress is 715 Bellfonte Street."* It was signed: *"Leo."*

The San Francisco letter was from Artie Upright and the final letter, also a scrawl, was from Dave Macdougal. Bonner walked slowly back to the offices on North Wells Street.

Olcott now worked in the inner office at the old desk. A young man named Rucker worked in the outer office. A second desk had been installed in the inner office for Bonner and as he entered, Olcott pointed to some mail on Bonner's desk.

"You'll be interesetd in the top letter," he said, "from the news company. It's got a check in it for the sale of the first issue since you took over."

Bonner picked up the letter and check. "Nineteen thousand, three hundred and forty-four copies sold," he exclaimed.

"That's a gain of over eight thousand," said Olcott. "Five thousand copies a week more and you'll be breaking even. And here's something I want to show you—a letter from Ned Buntline—he's written that Jesse James story and he's bringing it with him."

"He's coming here?"

"Tomorrow. He's on his way west again, but he intends to stop off in Chicago for a couple of days. I've never met him but I've heard that he's quite a character."

"I'm sorry I won't be able to meet him," Bonner said. "I've got to go out of town for a week or so."

"But what about the Buntline story? He won't sell except for cash."

"Here's part of it," Bonner said, handing the check from the news company to Olcott. "I'll give you enough more to bring it to two thousand. Pay him that and tell him he'll have the other two thousand in thirty days. That's one of the reasons I'm going out of town

—to raise more money. I've got some property in Connecticut that I'm going to have to sell."

"You'll leave my pay before you go?" Olcott asked. "And Rucker's?"

Bonner nodded. "I'm catching a train at three o'clock to New York. But I'll go out now and get the money."

He left the offices and took a hack to his boarding place. There he took the last of the gold from his valise. He counted what he had in his pocket and discovered that he would have a little over four hundred dollars left when he gave the money he had promised Olcott at the office.

His Chicago venture had been an expensive one. He packed his valise and carried it with him when he left his room.

Shortly before two thirty, Bonner walked into the Northwestern Depot and bought a ticket for St. Paul. He was turning away from the ticket window when a ragged, bewhiskered man, whose breath smelled strongly of whiskey, accosted him.

"Mister," whined the man, "can you spare a hungry man a dime for a bite of food? I ain't eaten since . . ." The man stopped, reacting violently.

"Sam Bonner?" he cried out.

Bonner stared at the man. "Tommy Brown . . ."

"Bonner!" croaked Brown. "You're the last man in the world I expected to see in Chicago . . ." He gripped Bonner's arm. "Never was so glad to see a man in all my life." He suddenly lowered his voice and looked furtively over his shoulder. "Almost forgot, you're a big man now. Hey—Old Pinkerton would like to set eyes on you. This is his town, you know . . ."

"Easy," warned Bonner.

"Sure, sure," said Brown furtively. "I ain't forgot. What . . . where you going?"

"To meet the boys," Bonner replied.

"How—how are they?"

"All right."

"Dave made it?"

"Yes, but he was plenty sore because you never showed up with his share of the money from Massachusetts . . ."

"I did show up. I went up to Bismarck and I looked all around for him but he was gone. I—I figured maybe he'd died. There was some story going around that he'd been shot . . ."

"He was, but he's as good as new."

"Sam," Brown said earnestly, "I've had an awful time here in Chicago. I—I was robbed of my money and half the time these last few weeks I ain't had enough to eat. You . . . you s'pose the boys would want me with them again?"

"They'll do what I tell them to do," Bonner said. He hesitated. "We could use you for something I have in mind . . ."

"Anything, Sam. I know the business. Give me another chance, that's all I ask . . ."

Bonner took out some bills, counted out five twenties and gave them to Brown. "Get yourself cleaned up, buy some new clothes and come to St. Louis. Saturday. The Planters Hotel Bar, but don't get drunk . . . I've got to run now, my train's ready to leave . . ."

"I'll be there, Sam!" Brown said fervently.

With a hundred dollars in his pocket, Tommy Brown left the Northwestern Depot and crossing the street, entered a saloon. He smacked a twenty dollar bill onto the bar and shouted to the bartender, "The bottle!"

The bartender took up the twenty dollar bill and eyed Brown suspiciously. "Who'd you steal this from?"

"I didn't steal it," retorted Brown. "Just ran into an old friend of mine and he gave it to me, plenty more, too."

"Who'd give *you* money?"

"You tryin' to insult me," cried Brown angrily. "Gimme back my money and I'll take my business where it's appreciated."

The bartender held onto the bill. "I think this is

counterfeit. That's the only kind of twenty dollar bill a bum like you would be likely to have."

"That money's good," roared Brown. "You give it back to me." The bartender moved away and Brown, screaming frantically, started clambering over the bar to get after the man. A uniformed policeman came into the saloon at that moment and ten minutes later Brown found himself in the Madison Street Police Station.

The remaining twenty dollar bills were found on Brown.

The next morning Brown, sobered, but even filthier than he had been the day before, was brought before a judge. The judge took one look at him and wrinkled his nose in disgust.

"Vagrancy, thirty days!"

"No!" shouted Brown. "You can't jail me for thirty days. I got to be in St. Louis Saturday."

"Is the St. Louis jail any better?" asked the judge sarcastically. A soberly dressed man, wearing a derby, came up and whispered to the judge. The latter shrugged. "Talk to him if you like."

The man stepped up to Brown. "What's your name?"

"White," said Brown promptly. "Tom, I mean, Ted White."

"How about a different color. Say . . . Brown?"

"My name's White," Brown said loudly. "Ted White."

"What's your occupation?"

"I—I'm a carpenter, but I been out of work lately."

The man with the derby caught one of Brown's hands and turned up the palm. "Seems to me you've been out of work quite a long time."

"I been sick."

The man with the derby nodded thoughtfully and moved away. Brown was taken to the county jail and put in a large room with a score of other prisoners, half of them vagrants.

Later in the afternoon a turnkey came to the door of the cell and called out, "White!"

Brown, seated at the far end of the room, on the floor, made no move. The turnkey called out again, "White—Ted White!"

Brown got quickly to his feet. "Hey—that's me!"

The turnkey crooked his finger at him. He led the way up a corridor into a small room furnished simply with a table and a bench on each side of the table.

A hulking man in his early thirties sat at the far side of the table. The turnkey shoved Brown into the room and closed the door on him.

"Sit down, Brown," said the big man.

"You got the wrong man," protested Brown. "My name's White."

"White, Brown, what's the difference?" The big man studied Brown. "Feeney was right, you fit the description."

"I don't know anybody named Feeney."

"This morning, in the courtroom, Feeney spoke to you." The big man nodded. "My name's Pinkerton . . ."

Brown, starting to sit down, rose up in sheer horror. "Allan Pinkerton!" he cried.

"My father," said the big man, "I'm William Pinkerton." He took a sheet of paper from his pocket and began to read: "Member of Wendell Morgan's gang, operating in and around Deadwood, Dakota Territory . . . broke Sam Bonner out of jail in Baker Falls, Massachusetts, held up the Baker Falls bank . . . mmm, quite a record . . . with Sam Bonner robbed the Union Pacific Railroad of sixty-five thousand dollars at Sand Springs, Neb . . ."

"No!" shouted Brown, unable to contain himself longer. "It's a lie. I didn't—I ain't Tommy Brown. My name's White. Ted White."

"Don't be a fool, Brown," Pinkerton said calmly. "I can get a dozen men here from Deadwood to identify you. I can bring a dozen more from Baker Falls and it so happens that the conductor of the Union Pacific is in Chicago right now. . . ."

"I wasn't there! That's one thing you can't prove on me."

"No? Well, maybe you weren't at Sand Springs, but how about Baker Falls?"

"I don't know what you're talking about." The fire in Brown began to dwindle and the detective was quick to note it.

"I'm not after you, Brown," Pinkerton said. "You're just one of the gang. Oh, we'll hang you, but that's unimportant . . ."

"It ain't to me!"

"——It's Bonner we want. Our agency represents the Union Pacific Railroad and we don't like our trains to be held up."

"I wasn't with Bonner on that."

"I said a minute ago, maybe you weren't. I'm willing to give you the benefit of the doubt. But there's still Baker Falls, Massachusetts. Ten thousand dollars was taken there." Pinkerton paused. "And there's a thousand dollars reward for the arrest of Sam Bonner. Sam, I said. No reward for Tommy Brown. Get that, Tommy? No reward for you. In fact, they don't even care if they get you or not, as long as they get Sam Bonner."

The panic was high in Brown. He snatched at the straw that was being tendered to him. "It's just Sam they want?"

"That's right. Of course, there's still the Deadwood business. A man was killed in one of your holdups and that's hanging." The detective's voice became a smooth purr. "On the other hand, we don't represent anyone in Deadwood and there's no reward, so I wouldn't be inclined to press the Deadwood thing . . . unless you force me to do it."

"Me force you?"

"By not telling me where Sam Bonner is."

"I don't know."

"Come now, Tommy. I've got a complete report on you. You've been hanging around Madison Street for a month, cadging drinks, panhandling nickels and dimes. Then all of a sudden you're found with a hundred dollars in your pocket. Where did you get the money?"

"I—I found it."

"Nobody reported losing a hundred dollars. And nobody reported being robbed of five twenty dollar bills . . . Who gave you the money? Sam Bonner?"

Brown made one last denial, but there was no conviction in his tone.

"I don't know any Sam Bonner."

Pinkerton got to his feet. "All right, Brown, I wasted my time. Go back to your cell now. Think things over —think hard. And when you get ready to talk, tell the turnkey to send for me."

William Pinkerton left the county jail smiling.

CHAPTER EIGHTEEN

Sam Bonner reached St. Paul and an hour later went aboard a train for Des Moines. He reached St. Louis on the following afternoon, Friday.

He obtained a room at a modest hotel near the river, at least a half mile from the Planters Hotel. Dave Macdougal, wearing a wrinkled white suit and a two days' growth of beard, sat in a rocking chair on the veranda as Bonner entered the hotel. He did not even look at Bonner, but twenty minutes after Bonner entered his room, Dave opened the door without knocking.

"Am I glad to see you!" Macdougal said as they shook hands. "You got something lined up? I'm down to my last dollar."

"You spent over fifteen thousand dollars since we parted?" Bonner exclaimed.

Macdougal groaned. "I got into a game over in Green River, Wyoming, that took me for most of it. I had a straight flush, queen high. What do you think beat me?"

"A straight flush, king high."

Macdougal winced. "You think it was rigged?"

"The odds against two such hands in a single, high-stake game are too great, Dave."

"That's what I figured," Macdougal agreed. "And the fella who held that hand against me ain't playin' poker no more. On'y trouble was, I had to make a fast ride for it and I didn't have no time to get the money. Uh, can you lend me a couple of hundred, chief?"

Bonner grinned wryly. "You lost your money in a poker game, Dave. I lost mine in—in something else. I've got a hundred and eighty-two dollars, that's all. But here——" He took out a twenty dollar bill and handed it to Dirty Dave. "Go easy with it. We'll have to wait until the rest of the boys get here and that may be a few days." He paused. "By the way, Tommy Brown's coming. . . ."

"That dirty, double-crossin' thief!" cried Macdougal. "I lay my hands on him . . ."

"You got your money, Dave," said Bonner. "We need five good men for the job I've got lined up and we can't fight among ourselves."

"Whatever you say, boss, but I never was very keen on Tommy. And back there in Deadwood he used to talk about you . . ."

"Never mind, Dave. Now, listen carefully. Tommy's going to be in the bar of the Planters Hotel tomorrow. Talk to him, but don't tell him where I'm staying, or where you are, for that matter."

"You mean you don't trust him?"

"It's not that. I don't want too much contact between any of us, at least not regular contacts. The Pinkertons are after us, I guess you know that."

"I've heard talk."

"They've got a big organization and a lot of people. I think none of us ought to see the others until we're ready for a move. And then we move quick. Find out where Tommy's staying, but keep away from him. We'll send him word when we're ready. And Dave, the same for you. Don't talk to me and don't come to my room again. Don't talk to Leo Basgall and Artie Upright when you see them. Understand?"

Macdougal nodded, but did not seem very happy. "This twenty's all you can spare now?"

"For the moment. Until I find out how the others are fixed. It'll take a considerable amount of money for what we're going to do."

Macdougal hesitated, then nodded agreement. "You're the boss, Sam."

He left the room.

Bonner waited a half hour, then left the room and the hotel. He walked to Market Street and took a stage-coach to the Missouri Pacific depot, where he bought a round-trip ticket to Kirkwood, a dozen miles out of the city.

An hour later he got off the train at Kirkwood and strolled casually down the street. He passed a bank, turned back and entered. At one of the teller's windows he tendered a twenty dollar bill and asked for five dollars in ones and three fives. He left the bank and spent an hour strolling about the town. Finally, he returned to the Kirkwood Depot and waited forty-five minutes for a train that took him back to St. Louis.

The next day, Saturday, Bonner again went to Kirkwood. Arriving there he went to the livery stable and rented a rig, telling the liveryman that he was looking at some farm property out in the country.

It was late in the day when he returned to St. Louis.

A note was under his door. It read: "I got to see you. Dave."

Bonner exclaimed angrily, then struck a match and burned the paper, crushing the ash between his fingers. He sat down in a chair facing the door.

Fifteen minutes later someone tried the door tentatively. Bonner called out: "Yes?"

The door opened and Dirty Dave Macdougal entered. His suit was more wrinkled, he still had not shaved.

"This is important, boss," Dave said quickly.

"Close the door," Bonner snapped.

Macdougal closed the door and came forward. "This couldn't wait, Sam. I saw Tommy Brown. He was stinkin' drunk and makin' a lot of noise. They was just about to throw him out when I come along."

Bonner swore softly. "Where is he?"

"I got him a room at the Mississippi Tavern—that's two blocks up the street. When I left him an hour and a half ago, he was sleepin'."

"I'll see him," Bonner said grimly. "But you keep away from him now. What name is he using?"

Macdougal showed discomfiture. "The way he was actin' I was afraid to register him under a different name. He might have said somethin'——"

"Never mind," said Bonner, striving to contain his anger. "Here—wait here in the room for at least ten minutes. . . ."

He got up and left the room.

Outside, he walked down the street to the MISSISSIPPI TAVERN. It was a dingy, two-story building whose paint had peeled and cracked. A long veranda ran down the front. A saloon seemed to occupy most of the first floor.

Several guests sat on the veranda as Bonner passed. He walked another block or two, then turned back and without hesitation, climbed the short flight of stairs to the veranda.

The lobby was a small one, crowded in between a restaurant on the left and over-size saloon on the right. The saloon seemed to be enjoying a good patronage, judging from the loud talk and boisterousness that emanated from it.

A weary-looking man, wearing a battered steamboat captain's hat, sat behind the desk.

"What room has Mr. Brown got?" Bonner asked.

"Brown?" The man consulted the register. "That's right, the drunk. Mmm, try Room Nine . . ." He pointed toward a flight of stairs that led to the second floor.

Seething inwardly, Bonner climbed the stairs. The door of Room Nine stood partly open. Inside, Tommy Brown, wearing an ill-fitting second-hand suit of black material and a pair of battered boots, sat in a rocking chair with his feet upon the bed. He was bleary-eyed and had a bottle in his fist as Bonner pushed open the door.

He looked stupidly at Bonner a moment, then delayed reaction overtook him. He swung his feet to the floor.

"Sam!" he croaked.

He got up, lost his balance and fell back into the chair. Bonner closed the door, strode across the room and rocked Brown's head with a sharp right-handed slap, then a backhand.

"You drunken fool," Bonner said savagely. "I should have let you rot in Chicago."

"I been sick," Brown whined. "I—my stomach's awful. Got to take somethin' to settle it . . ."

"I'll give you until Monday to sober up," Bonner said. "If your stomach hasn't settled by then, or I even smell whiskey you'll stay right here. Wait a minute . . ."

He caught hold of Brown's arm and jerked him to his feet. Quickly he searched the drunken man and emptied his pockets of money. He fished out a crumpled five dollar bill from the handful and threw it to the bed. "That'll buy you your food until Monday."

He shoved Brown back into the chair. "This is your last chance!"

He jerked open the door and went out. He was a block from the hotel when something seeped back into his angry consciousness. Something he had been too angry to note a few minutes ago. He thrust his hand into the pocket where he had stowed Brown's money, counted it. Sixty-seven dollars . . . and he had left a five dollar bill with Brown.

Three days ago, in Chicago, Bonner had given Brown a hundred dollars. True, the clothes Brown had bought were second-hand, still they must have cost him fifteen, possibly as much as twenty-five dollars. The railroad fare from Chicago to St. Louis would account for another ten dollars.

Yet Brown looked as if he had been on a prolonged binge. Even if he had bought no food to speak of for three days, the cost of the whiskey alone would be considerable. And Brown was a convivial spirit. He couldn't drink quietly in a barroom. He had to talk and a man who talks loudly and drinks freely usually finds plenty of friends who will listen to him talk and brag if the drinks are forthcoming frequently enough—and paid for by the talker.

Bonner thrust the money back into his pocket, wheeled and walked back in the direction of the MISSISSIPPI TAVERN. He looked sharply at the pedestrians he passed, continued on past the hotel and went another two blocks.

He went into a cigar store, then, and bought a long, thin cheroot. He left the shop and stood outside a moment, lighting the cheroot. His eyes flickered off to the right. A man stood fifty feet away, apparently idly reading a folded newspaper. Bonner had passed the man after he had turned beyond the hotel to come in this direction.

Bonner abruptly turned down the side street, walked swiftly two blocks without looking back, then turned right and walked to Market Street. He threw away his cheroot and went into another cigar store. Again he bought a cheroot and waited until he was outside before he lit it.

Again, under the cover of cupping his hands about the cheroot, to light it, he darted a glance to the right. The same man stood sixty or seventy feet away, reading a newspaper.

That settled it.

Bonner walked a block to where a couple of hacks stood at the curb. He climbed into the first, said, "The Planters Hotel."

Five minutes later he climbed out of the hack in front of the Planters Hotel. He gave the driver a half dollar and said loudly, "Wait, I'll only be a minute or two."

He did not look back, but knew that a hack had pulled up a short distance away. He strode into the hotel, wheeled to the barroom and walked to the rear of it, where there was a swinging door. He pushed through it and found himself in a kitchen.

"Excuse me," he said to a couple of startled cooks and continued to a door at the rear.

He stepped out into an alley and with long strides walked quickly to the next street. He whirled to the right, walked to the next corner and stepped into a hack. "Union Depot," he curtly told the driver, "and whip up the horses, I've got to meet my aunt who's coming to town."

The hackman put the whip to his horses and Bonner leaned back in his seat, although he did not relax. He looked back after a few minutes. There were hacks on the street behind him, but as nearly as he could tell none of them contained a passenger who looked like the man who had followed him from the MISSISSIPPI TAVERN to the Planters Hotel.

He continued on to the depot, paid the fare, then stood outside the depot for five minutes, studying the people who descended from other hacks. Reasonably satisfied, he went in and consulted the big blackboard which announced the arrival and departure of trains. One entry caught his eye. He strolled away from the bulletin board, started off to the right, then wheeled and went left to a ticket window.

"Ticket for Granite City," he said.

He paid the small amount requested, then hurried out to the platform and boarded a train just as it was beginning to move.

The train rolled slowly out of the depot, through

downtown St. Louis and crossed the bridge over the Mississippi.

"East St. Louis," called the conductor, coming into the car.

Bonner rose and left the car as the train pulled into the East St. Louis Depot. His ticket called for him to continue to the next town, Granite City, but this was as far as he wanted to go at the moment.

Quite a number of passengers boarded the train at St. Louis, but only three, as well as he could tell, got off. One was a woman. The two men did not remotely resemble the man Bonner sought.

Exhaling heavily, he walked into the town. He found a small rooming house and engaged a room for a week, giving the name of Pincus.

CHAPTER NINETEEN

He slept late the next morning, then had breakfast at a small restaurant near the rooming house. He picked up a St. Louis Sunday newspaper from the counter and leafed through it, scanning the headlines of all the articles. On page five he came across a two-inch article that he read twice. It bore a Chicago dateline and was to the effect that William Pinkerton, son of Allan Pinkerton, was leaving Chicago on Friday to make an investigation in Winnipeg, Canada, at the instigation of the Canadian government.

Late in the afternoon, Bonner rode across the Mississippi in a horse-drawn streetcar. When they reached the Missouri side he remained in the car until they reached Twelfth Street. There he transferred to a Ma-

plewood stagecoach and an hour later got off in front
of a small brick hotel. He crossed the street to an ice-
cream parlor and taking a seat near the window had a
dish of vanilla ice cream.

"This is good stuff," he told the waitress. "Wonder
if you could put up a quart and send it to some friends
of mine who are staying at the hotel across the street."

"I think we can do that," said the waitress. "What's
the name?"

"Arthur, Mr. Sam Arthur."

Bonner paid for the ice cream, then left the shop
and walked to a combination news and shoe-shine
stand a few yards away. He looked over the magazines and newspapers for a few moments, then climbed
up on the high stool to have his shoes shined.

The colored man was still at work when Bonner
saw Artie Upright come out of the hotel and cross
the street to the ice-cream parlor. He peered through
the window, then looked up and down the street. For a
moment his eyes stopped on Bonner, but gave no sign
of recognition. He did, however, begin to stroll in
that direction. He passed Bonner and turned right at
the next corner.

Bonner paid for his shine, stood for a moment idly
looking in either direction, then followed Upright. Two
blocks away, on a shaded street, the two men met
and shook hands warmly.

"This careful business is getting me down," Upright
declared, after the greetings were over. "I got in last
night and every time I'd hear a step in the hotel corridor, I'd think it was Allan Pinkerton. . . ."

"William Pinkerton," Bonner corrected. "He knows
we're in St. Louis."

Upright regarded Bonner skeptically. "Oh, come
now, how would *you* know that?"

"I read in the paper this morning that he was supposed to have left Friday for Winnipeg, Canada."

"This is a long ways from Winnipeg."

Bonner shook his head. "The Pinkerton Agency
never talks about what they're really doing. So when

I see something in the paper, some little piece of information that there's no point really in their releasing to the papers, I look in the other direction. Anyway, I have other reasons to know that they're here. Tommy Brown . . ."

"Brown!" cried Upright. "What's he got to do with the Pinkertons?"

Bonner related the circumstances of his meeting with Brown in the depot in Chicago. When he concluded his recital of the events of the preceding day Upright's face creased into a frown.

"That's not proof, Sam. Dave told you he was blowing off in the Planters Hotel. It might be a city detective who got interested in Tommy . . ."

"The money . . . more than he should have had."

"I know, but you also know Tommy—if he saw a man flashing a roll he'd follow him into an alley."

"How are *you* fixed for money, Artie?"

Upright grinned wryly. "Not too well. I don't mind saying I was awfully glad to get your telegram. . . . I've got about eleven hundred left, that's all."

"That's more than I've got, Artie."

"You? I would have said you had nine-tenths of your roll left. After what you said about getting that hundred thousand . . ."

"I invested my money, Artie."

"In what?"

Bonner shook his head.

Upright looked at him sharply. "Still don't trust anyone?"

"Anyone can make a slip. I've made a couple myself. . . . Can you ride out to Webster Groves tonight?"

"That's the next town, isn't it?"

"Yes. Leo Basgall ought to be there now. Here's what I want you to do . . ."

The two men walked about the shaded streets of Maplewood for almost an hour. Finally they parted a block from the hotel where Upright was registered.

Bonner strolled around Maplewood for a few minutes more, then came out upon a dusty road. He turned west on it and walked for an hour. A cross-road had a sign and arrow pointing to the left which read: Webster Groves, 1 mile.

Bonner continued on for another mile. By that time it was fairly dark, but he plodded on along the wind-ing road until he saw lights ahead on the right.

It was a rather large building, well lighted inside and lanterns hanging out front. There were numerous rigs, buggies and surreys standing around. A large sign over the building read: MANCHESTER POST TAVERN.

Bonner entered and found a huge room off the en-trance. It contained some twenty tables. Half of them were occupied by convivial groups. Bonner went in and got a small table and ordered a supper of knock-wurst and sauerkraut. He washed it down with a huge stein of beer. As he paid for the repast, he said to the waiter, "You have rooms here?"

"Just rooms," the waiter said, frowning.

"Exactly what I want—a place to sleep for the night."

"Well," said the waiter, "you may not get much sleep. It's Sunday night and we don't close until two A.M."

"A little singing and music won't keep me awake."

The waiter went into the lobby and returned in a moment with a bloated German, the proprietor.

"A room you want so early?" he asked Bonner.

"I'm tired. I didn't get much sleep last night."

"*Ach, ja*, Saturday, sure." He winked at Bonner. "Is a cool night for sleeping today. You want maybe some extra blankets . . . or something?"

"No," said Bonner firmly. "I just want to sleep."

The proprietor of the inn seemed disappointed, but finally accepted three dollars from Bonner and led him to a room on the second floor.

Bonner was up at five o'clock in the morning and tightening his belt, started walking down the dusty Manchester Road. Shortly before seven he reached a crossroads village and found a blacksmith who had a horse he was willing to sell for forty dollars. Not a very good horse.

After twelve o'clock, Bonner traded the horse for one with a sounder wind. A saddle was added and he paid sixty dollars to boot.

By this time Bonner was some forty miles from St. Louis and in the distance he saw rolling hills. He made a wide circle on his fresh horse, cut across fields and at four o'clock in the afternoon came to a large field that was only three miles out of Kirkwood. He skirted the field until he came to a grove of maples and there dismounted and tied his horse to a tree, safely inside the woods.

Bonner moved to the edge of the trees, where he had a clear view of the field and there threw himself upon the ground.

A half hour passed and then Bonner saw a figure appear at the far end of the field, the side closest to the village of Kirkwood. He watched the figure grow larger until it reached the approximate center of the field. Then it stopped.

A faint voice came to Bonner's ears, but he paid no attention to it. Ten minutes went by and a second figure appeared at the far end of the field. The first man saw it and moved toward it. They met, then turned together and came to the center of the field.

The two men stood in the center of the field for a good ten minutes, then moved toward Bonner. He waited until they were fifty feet away, then got to his feet. Still remaining in the shelter of the trees, he called out, "Tommy, this way. Leo, get back and keep watch."

The two men separated. Tommy Brown came to the edge of the maples, saw Bonner and came toward him. He was cold sober and red of face. "Anything you say, Sam, I got coming to me. I started hitting the bottle in Chicago and couldn't seem to taper off. I don't even know how I got to St. Louis." He added ruefully, "You shouldn't have given me the hundred in Chicago. I'd had a long, dry spell."

"All right, Tommy, I'm not going to lecture you,"

Bonner said. "I'm just going to tell you this. One step out of line and you're through. Now go with Leo and let me warn you again, don't get out of his sight for a single minute. If you do, he's got orders to cut you loose."

"That's a little rough, Sam," growled Brown. "But I admit I got it coming to me. Uh, when's the job?"

"You'll find out."

"I ought to have time to get ready."

"You're as ready now as you'll ever be."

Brown hesitated a moment, then shrugged. "You're in the driver's seat."

"Remember it, Tommy!"

Bonner turned and got his horse. Untying it from the tree and mounting, he continued on through the woods. He did not look back to see Brown rejoin Basgall.

In a coulee between Webster Groves and Kirkwood, Bonner found Artie Upright and Dave Macdougal, some two hours after his talk with Tommy Brown. It had been dark for an hour.

"You saw Brown and Basgall?" Upright asked.

"Yes, but I only talked to Brown."

"And?"

"I don't know. I didn't see anyone." He turned to Macdougal. "How about you, Dave?"

"Not that I know of, Sam. But I did all the things Artie told me to do."

"Artie? Since you met Dave this morning?"

"Nobody followed us," Upright said flatly. "We bought the horses and they're all staked out."

"And the steamboat tickets?"

"Dave has them."

Macdougal touched his pocket. "Safe and sound."

"How's the money holding out, Artie?" Bonner asked.

Upright chuckled. "Fine. What do you think of that Injun, Basgall? He had six thousand dollars with him and he says he's got eight thousand salted away. The guy must have been living on beans and bacon ever since Sand Springs."

"He may be the smartest of us all."

"Me," said Macdougal, "I got six-bits in my jeans."

"What do you figure this one'll bring?" Upright asked.

"I wouldn't be surprised if it went bigger than the Union Pacific one."

Upright whistled softly and Macdougal exclaimed, "They won't deal me no queen-high straight flushes this time!"

"Let's get some sleep," suggested Bonner. "I'll take the first watch, Artie."

"You and those watches," grunted Upright. "A fella'd think you'd been in the army."

"I have been."

"Uh? Since the war?"

"During the war."

"You were too young!"

"I was too young," Bonner said, "but I was there."

"Shows how little anyone gets to know about his friends," Upright grunted. "Me, I was seventeen in '64 and when I wanted to join up with Kirby Smith, my ma said I was too young. Then, in early sixty-five I was eighteen and they wanted to draft me and I said, the hell with it, there wasn't any point in it, any more and I hid out in the caney-brakes. There was quite a bunch hidin' out there."

CHAPTER TWENTY

Bonner slept little that night. He remained alert until around midnight, then wakened Upright, who was sleeping soundly, but even with Upright on guard, Bonner scarcely closed his eyes. He relieved a drowsy Upright around two in the morning and in an hour or so finally awakened Dave Macdougal.

Bonner slept then until daylight.

They ate a cold breakfast that Upright and Macdougal had brought along with them the day before, then Bonner got a stick and scratched the final details of the *coup* on a smooth piece of bare earth.

"Got it now?" he asked after a half hour's explanation.

Both Upright and Macdougal nodded, but Bonner was not satisfied. He rubbed out his diagrams on the earth and handed a stick to Macdougal. "Explain it to me."

Macdougal fumbled on one detail and again Bonner drew an outline map and talked earnestly. Finally, a few minutes after seven, Bonner mounted his horse.

"Do you feel right about it?" he asked.

Upright swore roundly. "I feel like hell!"

"That's good," said Bonner. He looked at Macdougal. Dave nodded.

Bonner rode off at a trot. He did not tire his horse but he rode five miles to traverse what could have been only three miles had he taken a more direct route. Finally, at ten minutes to eight he entered Kirkwood from the west.

Business men were opening stores, townspeople were going back and forth. Some farmers had come into town early and had their wagons already standing at the hitchrails. Bonner rode easily up to the bank and some ten feet beyond to the front of a millinery shop. There he dismounted and tied his horse to the hitchrail with a slip-knot.

The clock in the window told him that it was four minutes to eight. A business man with a sack of currency came and stood in front of the bank door, waiting for the bank to open.

Upright rode up from the east and tied his horse beside Bonner's. He looked at Bonner standing idly in front of the millinery shop and passing him, went to join the business man in front of the bank.

"Two minutes," he said casually to the business man.

The man nodded. A farmer joined Upright and the other man. He consulted a large key-winding watch. "Clock's thirty seconds fast," he observed.

Dirty Dave Macdougal, his white linen suit none the better for having slept in it, trotted up on a horse. He rode up to the hitchrail, but remained in the saddle. From his vantage point he could see in all directions.

Inside the bank, a man appeared and unlocked the door. The man with the sack of currency crowded past Upright into the bank. Upright followed him, then the farmer.

Bonner turned, looked at the bank and past it. Leo Basgall, mounted on a rangy horse, turned into Main Street and approached at an easy lope.

Bonner drew a deep breath and strode toward the bank.

Inside the bank, Artie Upright stood at a stand, scribbling on a bank slip. He kept one eye on the door. Bonner came in, drawing a revolver from under his coat.

"All right," he announced loudly, "this is a hold-up!"

Outside the bank, Leo Basgall, having dismounted in front of the bank, slipped under the hitchrail and crossed the sidewalk to take up a stand at the door of the bank.

A block and a half away, Tommy Brown came around a corner, put spurs to his horse and drawing a revolver, began firing wildly.

In front of the bank, Leo Basgall cried out in panic. He drew a revolver, sent a wild shot down the street in the direction of Tommy Brown.

"Sold out!" he cried.

Across the street from the bank, a window went up and a rifle was thrust out. It roared and Basgall, across the street, reeled sidewards. He didn't go down, but he was badly hit. Another bullet, coming from a gun in the doorway of a store, missed Basgall by inches and crashed through the plate glass window of the bank.

Dirty Dave Macdougal, wheeling his horse, sent a shot at the man in the upper window, across the street. He missed and the rifle cracked again. Dirty Dave pitched from his horse into the dust of the Kirkwood street.

In the bank, there was wild commotion. At the report of the first gun fired by Tommy Brown, Bonner cried out to Artie Upright: "Let it go!"

Upright, however, was already going into one of the tellers' cages.

Then the front window crashed and a bullet cut a bar of the first teller's cage and ricocheted into the wall. "Artie," cried Bonner, "come on!"

Upright saw stacks of bills only feet from him. He lunged into the cage, grabbed up two huge handfuls of bills and then turned. At the rear of the bank, a man stepped out of a room with a shotgun in his hands.

He thrust it toward Upright. In an instant, Upright would have been cut in two at the short range, but Bonner, crying out, threw down on the man with the shotgun. His gun thundered and the shotgun clattered to the floor. It went off, but the blast went into the ceiling. The man who had held the shotgun pitched to the floor.

Suddenly sobered, Upright dropped the money he had scooped up and came rushing out from the cages. Bonner, standing by the open doorway, was coolly exchanging shots with a man across the street.

Upright came running, plunged through the door. He yelped as a rifle bullet fired by the man on the second floor, across the street, ploughed through his left arm.

Bonner sprang through the door. In one wild glance around, he saw Leo Basgall, down in a huddle beside the bank door. Dave Macdougal's riderless horse was plunging and kicking because Dave's booted foot, twisted in the stirrup, caused a drag. Macdougal's lifeless body was stamped and whipped about as the horse fought to get free of the entanglement.

Bonner and Upright, side by side, covered the short distance to their horses in front of the millinery shop.

The rifle banged across the street once more and Upright stumbled and fell to his knees. Bonner skidded to a stop, grabbed him about the waist and half-dragged, half-led him to his horse. Reaching it, he lifted Upright into the saddle.

Bonner himself pulled the slip-knot that tied Upright's horse to the rail, forced the reins into Upright's hands and turned the animal west. Not until then did Bonner untie his own horse and vault into the saddle.

Upright was badly hit, but quite conscious. Bonner, riding behind him, sent a quick look to the left. The rifleman was drawing a bead on him. Bonner sent a quick shot at the window and the glass shattered over the rifleman's head, causing him to duck inside.

He was the most dangerous of Bonner's and Upright's antagonists. Shots were still fired at them, but they went wild. The two men galloped to the first corner, continued straight ahead. Then a man stepped out of a doorway and whipping up a revolver fired at them.

It was Tommy Brown.

The bullet missed both Bonner and Upright, but Upright began to saw at his reins. "Get that dirty traitor . . ." he mumbled. His horse came to a halt, but the sudden stop was too much for Upright. He fell from the saddle and hit the dusty street.

Bonner whirled his horse to go back to Upright. He was too late. Brown fired a second time and Upright, trying to pick himself up from the road, collapsed. Bonner knew by the way he fell that he was through.

Cursing wildly, Bonner emptied his revolver in the direction of Brown, but the traitor, having felled Upright and finding his revolver suddenly empty, pitched headlong behind the shelter of a wooden water trough. Bonner's bullets smashed into the trough, but the wood and the water in the trough saved Brown. Bonner could not stop.

Already horses were being mounted in the next block.

Bonner turned and galloped away.

Across the street from the bank, William Pinkerton came dashing down the stairs and still carrying his rifle, rushed for a horse. Two Pinkerton men came dashing from adjoining buildings. Across the street in the bank, a fourth Pinkerton man was dead. But there were three of them after Sam Bonner and they were led by William Pinkerton, a more ruthless, a more remorseless man-hunter than even his distinguished father.

A mile out of Kirkwood, Bonner turned left at a crossroads. He leaned forward as he rode, urged his horse to greater speed and prodded it by kicking his heels into the animal's flanks, finally its belly.

Another crossroad and he turned left. Two miles from Kirkwood. Ahead, a half mile, was a patch of woods. Two fresh horses were supposed to be there, left by Leo Basgall. Two other horses were north of Kirkwood, but those had been in charge of Tommy Brown.

According to plan, Brown had not been told anything until the very last possible moment. He had not been told in what town the "job" was to be pulled. He had not been left alone for a moment until five minutes to eight that morning. Then Leo Basgall had left him with two horses at the edge of Kirkwood and told him where to go with them. But Brown had not gone.

Brown had not been left alone for a single moment . . . yet the Pinkertons were waiting in Kirkwood.

Bonner was nearing the woods now. Three hundred yards behind him, a cloud of dust told him that the Pinkertons were following. It would be close. He'd have to find the horses quickly, he'd have to make a quick change. The pursuers would close up on him fifty yards, possibly a hundred, but he would then be on a fresh horse . . . and theirs would be winded.

He saw the horses now. Exultantly, he left the road. And then a man stepped out from behind a tree, with a leveled rifle. Bonner threw himself flat over his horse's neck and the bullet whined over his head.

A cry was torn from his throat as he whipped his jaded mount back onto the road. Another bullet sang over his head, but he was riding again, riding for his life. He kicked his tired horse savagely and it responded with a last burst of speed.

The Pinkertons lost a precious half minute leaving the road, pulling up their horses, dismounting and climbing on the fresh horses. In that half minute Bonner gained distance.

He whipped around a crossroad, pulled his wearied horse to an abrupt half and jumped to the ground. Then slashing at the horse's flank with the barrel of his revolver, Bonner, afoot, plunged for the shelter of some shrubs beside the road.

Crouched behind the shrubs he looked intently to the right, where his horse was cresting a low rise in the road. Would it make it before the Pinkertons came around the corner.

It did. With not a second to spare. The Pinkertons, on their fresh horses, came around the corner, continued on down the road, after the dust cloud they saw on the far side of the low rise. A quarter mile . . . could it be a half? If so, Bonner had a chance.

Bent low, he ran back toward the road and turning left, ran with every last ounce of effort he could muster. Back, back toward the place where the Pinkertons had changed their mounts.

It was a quarter mile or more and Bonner had never run so fast in his life.

He saw them, four horses, too wearied to scatter.

He had no trouble catching one and he mounted and turned it back to the west road that cut across to the one that led back to Kirkwood.

The three or four minutes of rest had refreshed the horse somewhat. If he did not have to press it too hard for a few minutes it might carry him safely to . . . the railroad tracks that he knew were a mile or less away.

The horse made the Missouri Pacific tracks and there Bonner turned it loose. Bonner himself found concealment behind a gravel pile, along the right-of-way. He lay there at full length.

Three minutes, four . . . It was coming. He could feel the vibration of the earth. Five minutes. A puffing engine came around a curve, bore down toward Bonner. It was a freight train, a rather long one. There was a slight upward grade and the engine was having heavy going of it.

Six minutes. The engine came up to the gravel pile behind which Bonner lay, roared past. Bonner waited, counting twenty. Then suddenly he sprang up from the ground and ran alongside the train. A coal car passed him, a box-car, then another coal car. Bonner made a desperate leap, caught the iron ladder rung and was slammed violently against the side of the coal car. But he was playing for his life; his grip on the rung was like a steel claw. He recovered, found a footing and crawled up and into the empty coal car.

CHAPTER TWENTY-ONE

The attempt to rob the Kirkwood, Missouri, bank was made on Saturday. The following Wednesday, shortly after ten in the evening, a grimy, wearied man dropped off a freight train in the town of Independence, on the other side of the state.

It was Sam Bonner, but this was not the freight train he had boarded outside of Kirkwood. It was not even the dozenth he had traveled on. He rode ten miles on a train, dropped off when he saw cover nearby and waited there, letting one and sometimes two trains go by before he hopped another.

Only once in those four days had he eaten and the food had been raw potatoes that he had dug out of the ground with his bare hands.

Independence was ten miles from Kansas City, via a straight, wide road that saw much travel. Bonner walked the ten miles but he did not travel on the road. He crossed fields, went through patches of woods. He tried to keep a hundred yards distant from the road. It took him five and a half hours to negotiate the ten miles.

In Kansas City he slunk through alleys until he came out upon a street near the depot, where he saw a sign over the door of a rambling two-story building: BEDS, 20 CENTS. It was almost four o'clock in the morning, but Bonner entered.

A clerk dozed in a cubicle just inside the door. Bonner awakened him and tendered two dimes. "Like a bed."

The clerk yawned and looked at the door. "Why bother this late?"

"I'm tired."

"Rules of the house, get out by eight in the morning."

"I'll be up."

The clerk took the money and led Bonner into a large room which contained about twenty unkempt cots. Most of them were occupied, but Bonner found an empty one between two snoring ruffians, one of whom smelled strongly of whiskey.

He dropped on the bunk and was asleep in an instant.

"Rise and shine!" yelled a raucous voice.

It penetrated Bonner's sleep and he blinked open his eyes. A club tapped the soles of his feet. "Come on, come on, get up."

A heavy-set man with a stout club stood over Bonner. He got up, saw that virtually all of the bunks around him were empty.

"This ain't the Eldridge House, you know," the big man went on. "What do you want for twenty cents?"

Bonner got up, rubbed his eyes and started for the door. Outside, bright sunlight caused him to blink. Next door to the flophouse was a small cafe. Ragged and unshaven as he was, Bonner noted through the window that some of the patrons looked no better than he. He went in and had a breakfast of eggs, coffee and ham for twenty cents.

Refreshed, Bonner left the cafe and started down the broad avenue. He went less than a hundred feet before he came to a second-hand clothing store. Entering, he bought a fairly respectable pair of trousers for a dollar. He had them wrapped up in a newspaper, then about to leave the store, stopped to look at a flannel shirt. He wound up by buying it for thirty-five cents.

A block further up the street he came to a barber shop which had a small card in the window: BATHS, 25 CENTS.

He entered and enjoyed the luxury of a bath. When he was finished he put on the trousers and flannel shirt he had bought. He wrapped his old clothes around his revolver and finished by rolling the bundle into the newspaper he had brought with him.

In the barbershop he had a shave and haircut.

Four blocks up the street, he bought a suit of black serge and a white shirt and string tie. He put them on in the store, purchased a carpetbag and depositing the old clothes, along with the bundle containing his revolver, left the store and continued up the long incline to the heart of Kansas City. A Stetson hat bought at a store completed his dress and he finally mustered up courage to enter the Eldridge House, where he engaged a room.

Without taking off his newly purchased clothing, he stretched out on the bed and slept until two o'clock. Then, washing his face, he went down to the lobby of the hotel and purchased two Kansas City newspapers and one from St. Louis that had come in on the morning train.

He carried them back to his room, went carefully through the Kansas City papers, but found no mention of his name . . . or that of Pinkerton. The St. Louis paper, however, mentioned Sam Bonner in two articles. The body of Arthur Upright had been claimed that afternoon by a middle-aged woman from Texas who said that the dead man was her son whom she hadn't seen in two years. "He was a good boy," she told reporters, "but that Bonner fellow, he's the one that led him astray."

The second item in the St. Louis paper bore a New Orleans dateline. William Pinkerton, vice-president of the great detective agency, had arrived in New Orleans in the search for Sam Bonner. Two Mississippi River steamboat tickets had been found on the body of the outlaw identified as Leo Basgall, and because of them Pinkerton was now in New Orleans. He expected to make an arrest at an early date.

New Orleans. The last time it had been Winnipeg and on the very day William Pinkerton was supposed to be in Winnipeg he had been in St. Louis.

He picked up the Kansas City papers, scanned them again closely, hoping to find a clue in them. On the back page of one of the papers he found something that jolted him.

Noted Author Visits K.C. (read the item) *Ned Buntline, one of America's most popular and prolific authors, is again a visitor in K.C. Interviewed in his suite at the Eldridge House . . .*

That was as far as Bonner read. He put down the paper, stared at the wall for a long moment. Then slowly he began to nod. He got up, went to the door and descended to the lobby.

"I understand Mr. Ned Buntline is at the hotel," he said to the man behind the desk.

"Yes, sir," was the reply. "He always stays here when he is in K.C."

"What room is he in?"

"He's occupying Suite 201-A . . ."

"Thank you." Bonner started to turn away, but the clerk called to him, "Please—Mr. Buntline never sees anyone except by appointment . . ." but Bonner pretended not to hear. He was already climbing the carpeted steps to the second floor.

On the second floor he knocked on the door marked 201-A. A deep voice called out: "Come!"

Bonner opened the door. A huge, florid-faced man in his mid-fifties stood facing the door, twirling in each hand a gigantic revolver. Bonner started to back away, then saw that there was another man in the room and that four revolvers similar to the ones being twirled by Mr. Buntline were spread out on the sofa.

"Who're you?" boomed the big author.

Bonner advanced into the room. "My name is Ralph Conger. I happened to be staying here at the hotel and learned that you also were here, so I thought I'd just drop in——"

"Of course, of course. One of my readers . . ."

"Not exactly," replied Bonner. "One of your publishers."

Buntline looked at him sharply. "Publisher? I don't believe I recall . . ." Then suddenly he beamed. "Of course, my dear sir, Mr. Conger, the proprietor of the *Chicago Home Weekly*. This is indeed a pleasure . . ." He shifted both guns to his left hand and thrust out a meaty hand that enveloped Bonner's.

"Yes sir, a great pleasure. I saw your editor, Mr. Olcott, in Chicago. He told me that you were out of town at the moment . . . I beg your pardon, I want you to meet an old friend of mine . . . Chief of Police Spier, of Kansas City . . ."

The other man, who had been sitting in an armchair, rose to his feet. He shook hands with Bonner.

"A pleasure, Mr. Conger."

Bonner had to fight down a rising panic. Chief of Police . . .

"How are you, sir?"

"A drink, Mr. Conger," boomed Buntline.

He put down the revolvers and reached for a bottle and tumbler. He poured it about half full of whiskey, then refilled his own glass. He reached for that of Chief of Police Spier, but the latter covered it.

"No more for me today, Ned."

"Ha, you Westerners don't know how to drink," cried the famous author. "Mr. Conger, your health!"

He downed his whiskey in two huge gulps. Bonner barely tasted his own. Then Buntline was picking up the guns again. He thrust one into Bonner's hand.

"What do you think of that, Mr. Conger? The Buntline Special . . . the Colt people made them up for me special. Hand-tooled, twelve-inch barrels . . ."

"Rather long, aren't they?" Bonner observed.

"Accuracy, Mr. Conger, accuracy, the longer the barrel the better the accuracy. Right, Chief?"

Chief of Police Spier shrugged. "Every man to his taste, Ned. I personally like a shorter gun. . . ."

"But does Wild Bill or Buffalo Bill?" cried Buntline. "You've seen Wild Bill shoot, Mr. Spier . . ."

"Yes, I have."

"He's incredibly accurate at long ranges and the secret of it is simply this—a longer barrel. A light powder charge and a long barrel. . . . I'm taking these to Dodge City with me, Mr. Conger. Had them made up special for Wyatt Earp and some of the boys. Ahem," he cleared his throat. "Indeed, I'm glad to see you here in Kansas City, Mr. Conger, because the reason I'm going to Dodge City is on your behalf. Mr. Olcott liked the Jesse James story so well that he wanted another at once—from the other side of the fence, so to speak. The law side. That's why I'm going to Dodge. A little story for you in the Buntline style . . ." He beamed. "Wyatt Earp is to be the hero. What do you think of that?"

"Why, it sounds all right to me, Mr. Buntline."

"Ned, Mr. Conger, Ned to my friends. Yes, sir, I'm certainly glad you're here. Your Mr. Olcott wanted the Wyatt Earp story, but I was of half a mind to do a quick switch as a result of the Sam Bonner business and do a story about old Sam, but if it's the Earp story *you* want, that's it. Perhaps we can work in the Bonner story after this . . ."

"He may not be around that long," observed the Chief of Police.

"Don't you believe it! If I know Old Sam he'll give Billy Pinkerton the slip, as he's always done in the past."

"You know Sam Bonner?" Bonner asked cautiously.

Buntline winked. "That would be telling, Mr. Conger . . . in the presence of a Chief of Police."

The Chief of Police looked thoughtfully at Ned Buntline. "Speaking as John Spier, Ned, *do* you know Sam Bonner?"

"Speaking as Colonel Edward Judson, which is my real name, I've met the gentleman. Although I'll admit that I never expected him to become as famous as he has. Well, for that matter, I never thought it of Frank and Jesse. Why, the first time I met them . . ."

An hour passed, during which Ned Buntline regaled his audience of two with accounts of the famous and infamous men of the West, outlaws, bad men and peace officers. He was an entertaining speaker and a braggart, Bonner thought, as he listened.

He did not know that Ned Buntline himself had led a life of astonishing adventure. At the age of fifteen, as a midshipman, he had fought seven duels in two days and won them all. He did not know that Buntline could outfight, outshoot most of the Western men he had glorified in his vivid fiction.

He did not know that Buntline himself had once been lynched by a mob in Nashville, Tennessee, and hanged . . . and cut down nearer dead than alive.

But as Bonner listened to the spinner of tales a plan formed in his mind. Buntline was above suspicion. He knew every law enforcement officer in the

West, he knew . . . the Pinkertons. A traveling companion of Buntline's—Buntline's publisher—would also be above suspicion.

CHAPTER TWENTY-TWO

The biggest Texas trail herd of the season arrived in Dodge City the same day that Ned Buntline and Sam Bonner stepped off the train, but the arrival of the famous writer caused more of a stir in the trail town than did the big herd, which would mean some thousands of dollars in the tills of the numerous saloons on Front Street.

Wyatt Earp, a rawboned man of indeterminate age, met them at the depot. As they proceeded down the street, Bat Masterson came out of a saloon and pumped the hand of the famous writer. Billy Tilghman, another deputy marshal, joined the entourage a few steps down the street and in the hotel lobby they added another man, Billy Mason, also a deputy marshal of Dodge. Buntline invited them all to his newly rented suite on the second floor of the hotel, where he opened up his suitcases and presented the four law enforcement officers with the Buntline Specials. The presentation required a libation, of course, and Bonner, who was of the party, yet somewhat aloof, had to fake his drinking, but even so he took a sip now and then and after two hours of the party he quietly left it and went to his own room, adjoining the Buntline suite.

Whiskey, away back in Deadwood—how long ago had that been?—had started it all and Bonner had sworn to himself that he would never again have a hazy brain.

He poured cold water into a pitcher and laved his face in it. As he was drying it with a rough towel, there was a knock on the door.

Bonner looked toward his valise on the bed, hesitated, then strode to the door and opened it. Wyatt Earp stood in the doorway. "Quite a man, Buntline," he observed.

"Quite a writer," said Bonner.

"That's what I want to ask you about, Mr. Conger," said Earp. "Ned wrote me that he was coming out here to write a book about me. I ain't much for that sort of thing and it's been bothering me. I've read some of the things he's written about Cody and Hickok, and, well, I hate to say this, but Ned gets a little, shall we say, enthusiastic at times. I've got a job here in Dodge and I'd kind of hate to have people, well, make remarks about what they'd read about me." Earp opened his coat and drew out the long-barreled Buntline Special that he had stuck into the waistband of his trousers. "What can you say to a man who'll have a gun like this made up for you? It must have cost him a lot of money. Still——" Earp frowned. "What I'm getting at, Mr. Conger, is how can I tell Buntline that I'd just as soon he wouldn't write a story about me?"

Bonner smiled faintly. "I've been with Ned for three days now, and I don't think I've had a chance to say ten sentences in that time."

"That's what I mean," Earp hesitated. "He said you were his publisher, that he was writing this story for you."

"That's right. I'm the owner of the *Chicago Home Weekly*."

"That's even worse. There's a lot of those papers sold here in Dodge, although I don't see many people with books. What I was going to say, what if you don't happen to like the story Ned writes?"

"Our readers like everything that Ned Buntline writes."

Earp showed concern. "If I don't talk to him, he'll write the story anyway, and then he'll use his imagination, and it'll be all the worse. Some of the things he's written about Bill Cody . . . ! You couldn't switch him onto writing about somebody else?" Earp looked hopefully at Bonner. "He said somethin' about doing a story on Sam Bonner. Seems to me that'd be of interest right now and Billy Pinkerton's right here in Dodge and could give him a lot of stuff about Bonner . . ."

The trap had sprung on Sam Bonner. He had tried to play it safe, so very, very safe, and he had walked right into the trap. Earp was talking, but Bonner did not hear him, not until Earp said, sharply: "What do you think, Mr. Conger?"

"Eh? I—I was thinking about . . . Sam Bonner . . ."

"That's what I said, if you could get him to do the Bonner story I'd appreciate it a lot. I know I shouldn't be talking to you like this, behind Buntline's back, but I—I just couldn't stand for Ned to print a story about me."

"You say . . . William Pinkerton's in Dodge?"

"He's got a notion that Bonner's headed this way. I know Billy don't like to talk, but he owes me a couple of favors and if you'd kind of, uh, turn Buntline loose on him, I think he might tell him some things about Bonner that'd make good smart reading."

Bonner said: "But does he *know* anything about Bonner?"

"What Billy Pinkerton don't know about Bonner, or any other crook or killer, ain't worth knowing," Earp said fervently. "What do you say we go over and have a talk with him? He's staying at the Dodge House across the street. . . ."

Panic almost caused Bonner to shiver. "Tomorrow, Mr. Earp. The trip and—and the drinking have been too much for me. I don't feel up to it." He stopped as Earp regarded him curiously. "I'll do it— I'll get Ned off you and—and write the Bonner story. But I've got to get a good night's sleep first. . . ."

Earp nodded. "All right, Mr. Conger, you do look

a little peaked. I'll talk to Bill meanwhile and . . . Well, thanks. Thanks a lot."

He went out and then Bonner did shake. He fought to control the panic to the extent that he was able to open his valise and take from it his revolver, but then he had to sit down on the bed and fight to compose himself.

He had no time. Even now Wyatt Earp might be across the street talking to William Pinkerton. Or Pinkerton might be on the street, down in the lobby.

Bonner had lost. He had played it safe and he had lost.

A loud shout came through the thin panels. Ned Buntline roaring at one of his own jokes. Ned Buntline, who knew William Pinkerton, who knew Wyatt Earp and Bat Masterson and all the law officers in the West. And all the bad men.

"Damn, damn, damn!" Bonner swore softly.

He got up, stuck the revolver into the waistband of his trousers and reached for the door. And couldn't open it. As thin as the door was, it shielded him from reality. Yet it also brought the moment of reckoning closer.

He had to open the door. He had to go through it . . . and run.

Run as he had never run before.

He opened the door, walked past the partly opened door of Ned Buntline's suite. At the head of the stairs, leading down to the lobby, he paused. He did not know who was in the lobby . . . Pinkerton could be in it.

But he had to descend the stairs and walk out to the street. There again he had to take a chance. Pinkerton might be outside the hotel, he might be any man he would meet. Pinkerton had seen him in Kirkwood. At a distance, in the heat of battle, but nevertheless he had seen him . . . over the sight of a rifle.

Bonner walked stiffly down the stairs and if anyone had made a sudden move or spoken abruptly to him he would have torn the revolver from under his coat and fired it.

No one spoke to him, no one made any sudden noises.

Bonner walked through the lobby, out upon the street. The sidewalks were seething with humanity, honky-tonk girls, business men, Texas trail drivers, cattle buyers from the Eastern packing houses, buffalo-hunters, Indians.

Bonner walked through them, his right hand gripping the lapel of his coat. He walked to the edge of town and there stole the first horse he had ever stolen.

It was a rangy horse, somewhat larger than the Texas cow ponies. It stood, saddled and ready, outside a barbershop. Bonner untied it, mounted and sent the horse at a slow trot toward the narrow bridge that spanned the Arkansas River.

He paid his toll of twenty-five cents to the bridge tender, crossed the bridge and let out the stolen horse at a mile-eating pace. He fought down the panic that almost caused him to press the horse to its limit. He had a little time, how much he did not know. It might even be twelve or fourteen hours. He couldn't count on it, though, because it might only be twelve or fourteen minutes. But he had time.

There were no relay stations along the road he was traveling. His pursuers had to ride horses, as he rode. They could obtain no more fresh horses along the way than Bonner could himself get. The flight and the chase was an even one. It was a matter of endurance.

Bonner trotted the horse, he walked it. Sometimes he even let it out into a steady lope. When the horse showed signs of tiredness he dismounted and holding it by the reins, let it rest and even graze for a few minutes.

Night came and he continued. Bonner was weary, his horse was tired. They continued on. The moon came up and still Bonner pressed along. The trail was a well-churned one, made by millions of hoofs coming for four years up from Texas.

Close to midnight, when Bonner's mount was heaving mightily, he saw a flicker of light ahead. He could skirt it, he knew, but he would only be losing distance by it. His flight had to be direct and straight; for the pursuit would be that way.

He rode toward the light and as he approached he discovered that it was a campfire beside a chuckwagon. It was a group of Texas trail drivers returning to Texas. There would be other such groups. Men were wrapped in blankets sleeping but there was a sentry near the horse cavvy.

Bonner rode up to him. "How about trading horses?"

"You've got to travel fast?"

"That's right. A—a little trouble in Dodge." That was the right appeal to a Texas man. Virtually all of them had trouble in Dodge. Many of them received broken heads in Dodge, some remained in Dodge to be buried in Boot Hill. Dodge City was Yankee land and the marshals of Dodge were Yankee marshals.

"Just a minute," said the horse sentry. "I've got to talk to the foreman, but I'm pretty sure it'll be all right with him."

He walked to the campfire and roused a sleeping man. "Stranger wants to trade horses," he said to the man. "Trouble in Dodge and I guess they're after him."

The foreman threw back his blanket and got to his feet. He regarded Bonner sleepily. "Texas?"

"Somebody'll be along and ask you about me. Just as well you don't know."

The foreman nodded. "See what you mean. Sure, we got plenty of horses. Take your pick and change your saddle while we rustle you up a little grub."

"I'll eat riding," said Bonner.

The foreman laughed. "Must be Wyatt himself after you."

Bonner made no comment. He approached the horse cavvy and picked out a horse in the darkness that seemed to have plenty of spirit. He shifted the saddle from the spent horse, put it on the Texas horse.

When he was mounting, the foreman came up with a parcel of food.

"I never saw you," he said. "Luck!"

"Thanks."

Bonner rode on into the darkness.

Trail herds were going north. Pinkerton would get information from the Texas men. He would know from day to day how far he was behind Bonner. Bonner passed chuckwagons and trail crews riding south. Pinkerton, too, would overtake them and hear of Bonner.

It was open and straight. It was simply a matter of speed. Bonner covered the ground. He slept a half hour, an hour when he could stand it no longer, two and even three hours. He ate when he could get food, never taking time to sit down.

He lost weight and Pinkerton would lose weight. Bonner crossed the Red River, he traversed the *Llano Estacado,* or Staked Plains. He rode across the flat, treeless Texas Panhandle. He changed horses seven times. Pinkerton could do scarcely better.

He traveled seven hundred miles in less than six days.

From Dodge City to the Texas Panhandle he rode as straight as a crow would have flown. But now the Chisholm Trail petered out. It became a myriad of trails spreading east, south, west and various subdivisions of the compass.

It was still a matter of traveling the shortest distance in the quickest time. Bonner left the trails and headed east by south. Days later he entered Dallas and remained there long enough to buy a little food and ask a single question: "How long since the east stage left?"

Nine hours, he was told.

He hit the rutted trail, sent his wearying horse along it as fast as he could. The horse almost foundered and then Bonner committed a crime that was unpardonable in Texas. He saw two horses grazing a mile from a miserable shack and he stole one of the horses. He sent it galloping along the rotted trail of the stagecoach line.

He stole another horse late that evening and continued with it almost through the night, when he fell asleep riding and hit the ground with a violent thud. He slept three hours then and his horse, hobbled nearby, was fully rested.

He rode into the morning and stopped at a stage relay station. The man who ran the station had a horse of his own. He was dubious about the brand on the horse Bonner rode, but twenty dollars boot money caused him to make a deal. The stage, the agent also told Bonner, was less than two hours ahead.

Bonner caught up with the stage in the early afternoon.

He simply turned his last horse loose and boarded the stage, paying for his fare to Galveston.

Bonner knew how hard it was to catch a stagecoach. He had caught this one himself. They kept the horses moving and they changed them frequently at relay stations.

There were four passengers in the stagecoach. Bonner scarcely exchanged a word with any of them that first day. In spite of the jolting and bouncing, he slept. Slept the sleep of the utterly weary.

He slept through most of the night and so he was awake the next morning when they rolled up to a relay station and the passengers got out of the stagecoach to stretch and to have breakfast.

Every muscle, every bone in his body seemed to ache, but his senses were once more alert. He saw the two men standing in front of the stage station as he walked toward it with the other passengers.

Both men picked him out. "Your name Bonner?" one of them asked.

Bonner stopped. "It isn't, but what if it was?"

"Texas Rangers," said the second man. "We'll still ask you to raise your hands . . . steady . . . !"

Bonner raised his hands slightly above waist level, held them palms turned outward. A quick reach . . . and a slug would blast him. He knew it. These men were experts.

He said: "My name isn't Bonner."

The talking Texas Ranger shook his head. "If it

isn't, there's no use getting yourself killed. But we're taking you to Denton. It's just a matter of *how* we take you."

"Where's Denton?" Bonner asked.

"Fifty miles," was the reply. "Big place. Telegraph wire direct to Austin. And a tight jail."

"I suppose," Bonner said slowly, "I can ask *why* you want this—this Bonner?"

"Oh, you can ask all right. The Bonner we want is *Sam* Bonner."

"I'm supposed to know who he is?"

"Not if you've been living west of the Pecos. But you come from Dallas and maybe up north. You'd know who Sam Bonner was. We've got a good horse for you. Shall we get moving?"

"Can't I eat breakfast?"

"We've got grub."

CHAPTER TWENTY-THREE

Denton.

The biggest small town in a hundred miles. A small courthouse and a small jail. And twenty-four prisoners crowded into the jail, four and five to a cell.

A troop of Texas Rangers was stationed in Denton and the canebrakes were not too far from Denton. Artie Upright had once told Bonner about the canebrakes. There were a lot of men in them, men wanted in Texas and some not wanted in Texas, but in other places.

Unfortunately, they had to come out of the canebrakes now and then. That was when the Rangers got them. And sometimes they went into the canebrakes to get them.

Denton was a busy place. Two stages a day came from the east, two went east. The telegraph wire hummed all day and much of the night.

It was from the sheriff, who had charge of the jail, that Bonner learned the answer to the riddle.

Yes, William Pinkerton had followed him down the Chisholm Trail. But not at the tremendous speed that Bonner had credited him with. There was no need of that. There was only one direction for Bonner to go, straight south and then south by east to hit the coast where he could conceivably get on a boat that would take him to New Orleans or Mobile.

Pinkerton had understood all that. He was an experienced man in such things . . . and the Pinkerton Agency had vast resources. A telegraph wire ran from Dodge City to the East, to Chicago. Telegrams could be sent all the way to New Orleans, then to Galveston, to Austin . . . to Denton.

The Texas Rangers at Denton had known days before Bonner ever entered North Texas that he was heading their way. All they had to do was pick up Bonner and hold him. A Pinkerton man was on the way from New Orleans. He would reach Denton a few days before William Pinkerton would arrive from the north. Time was not too important. The jail in Denton was good and strong.

Bonner was in the Denton jail three days and three nights and then during the morning of the fourth day the sheriff summoned him from his cell and led him to a small room adjoining his office.

"Pinkerton?" Bonner asked as he entered the little room.

The sheriff smirked and left the room. The door remained open and a moment later Bonner heard a quick step . . . and she came into the room.

"Sam!" she sobbed.

"Why?" he cried. "Why, Vivian, would you come here?"

"What else? What else could I do when my father paid them to track you down? You didn't know that? You didn't know that my father had engaged the Pinkerton Detective Agency to—to catch you?"

Bonner stared at her. "The Pinkerton Agency represents a lot of the railroads, the—the bankers' association . . ."

"They also represent my father. *He* employed them to find you. He—he heard that we met in Chicago and that was when he employed the agency. They came across this man who knew you . . . Brown . . ."

"Tommy Brown."

"Father talked to Brown in Chicago and he went to St. Louis with him and Mr. Pinkerton. They almost caught you there. Later, when the message came in Chicago that they were expecting to catch you here in Texas, I had it out with Father. We broke—definitely. I'm with *you* now, Sam . . . to the end."

Bonner backed to the far wall. A harsh laugh came from his throat. "Vivian, I've tried to tell you this before. I tried to tell you in Baker Falls that day. I've destroyed everyone I've ever known who—who meant anything to me. I destroyed *you*. . . ."

"You haven't, darling, you haven't."

He raised a hand quickly to ward her off. "The only peace I've ever known was when I thought that I would never see you again. I thought that way . . . I couldn't hurt you. This—this is the worst thing that you could have done. Showing me, like this, that you—you *had* to come to me." He groaned in anguish. "If you'd only stayed away . . . if you'd written me, denouncing me for ruining our life, then—then I could have gone out."

"Like Wendell Morgan?" she flashed at him. "Is . . . that . . . what you want? Because they're here, they came on the same stage with me. They want to take you back to St. Louis. They can hang you there and I —I can watch . . ." There were no tears in her eyes for she had no more to shed, but dry sobs wracked her body.

Bonner said: *"Go, Vivian, go!"*

The sheriff appeared in the doorway. "Sorry, Miss Thompson, I—I can't let you stay here any longer now."

She did not even hear the sheriff. The law officer touched her arm, took hold of it and led her from the room. Bonner remained rooted to the floor, against the wall, where he had retreated from Vivian.

Then in sheer anti-climax, Tommy Brown entered. He was sleek and prosperous, cheerful. "Hi, Sam!" he greeted Bonner flippantly. "What's the matter, didn't the little lady cheer you up? Hey, I rode with her all the way from Austin and she's all right. Don't blame you a bit. It was worth the try what with her looks and not even to mention her old man's money . . ."

"I can't kill you, Brown," said Bonner tonelessly. "They'd stop me before I could do it."

"Hey!" cried Brown mockingly. "Is that a way to talk to an old pardner? A man who's come to——" He looked quickly over his shoulder, "to *help* you!"

"How're you going to help me, Tommy . . . up the scaffold?"

Brown chuckled. "We never did hit it off, did we, Sam? And in St. Louis you slapped me around and made me crawl on my knees. Well, that's all right, Sam. I don't hold a grudge. I got money in my pocket and no sheriff's looking for me. I never had it so good. So, go ahead, say all the dirty things about me that you want to say. And then when you get all finished up, I'll talk . . . and you'll listen . . ."

"Talk!"

"Don't you want to call me names first?"

"It'd be a waste of breath."

"It sure would, Sam, it sure would. All right, I'll let you have the good news. You ain't going to hang. You ain't even going to go back to St. Louis and go to the penitentiary. Hang on—this is really going to jolt you. You're going to walk out of here and you're going to ride down to Galveston nice and easy and there you're going to get on a boat and go to South America. Or Europe, if that's where you'd rather go. You get your choice and all the whole thing costs you is one little tiny promise. A promise that you won't never come back to the United States."

Tommy Brown rocked back on his heels and smirked. "Ain't that something, Sam, old boy? Ain't you glad now that you didn't call me names? Or don't you believe it?"

"Tommy," said Bonner wearily, "if you fell over dead this moment I wouldn't believe it, because I know you'd pop up somewhere again to betray me."

For just an instant the good humor flitted from Brown's features, but then he forced it back. "All right, maybe I polished it up a little. You know damn well I hated your guts from the first time I ever saw you, up in Deadwood. So I'll give it to you straight this time. It's all true what I said, except that it ain't my doing. If I had my way you'd be hung today and I'd be the one that would put the rope around your neck. But Thompson wants it that way. South America or Europe!"

"Thompson?" asked Bonner, finally roused.

"Who else? She was here just a minute ago, wasn't she? Thompson don't want you hung and he don't want you in the pen. He wants you out of the country, somewhere where his girl can't find you. That's it, straight."

Bonner stared at Tommy Brown. "Or is it that he doesn't want the scandal of a trial . . . with his daughter's name perhaps brought into it. . . . Is that it . . . ?"

"What difference does it make?" snarled Brown. "You're getting out of here. I've paid the sheriff five thousand dollars—yeah, Thompson's money—you get a horse and you ride to Galveston. Your passage on the boat is already paid for. All you got to do is ride there and get on the boat . . . and never come back . . ."

"Bring in the sheriff," said Bonner.

The sheriff had been listening just outside the door. He stepped into the room. "I get sixty dollars a month," he said. "I've saved eighty-four dollars in twelve years.

Yes, I took the five thousand and there's a horse out front. Nobody's going to bother you . . ."

"The Pinkertons?"

"Just the fellow who came with him," the sheriff nodded to Brown. "He's in the hotel across the street. The Rangers—there ain't a one in town. Some kind of inspection out at the camp."

"Right now? I go right now . . . ?"

"The sooner, the better," growled Brown. "You go straight to Galveston and the ship's the *Boston Clipper*. You go right on her when you get to Galveston. Understand that?"

Bonner drew a deep breath. "All right."

The sheriff indicated the door. Bonner followed him, with Brown on his heels. They went down a narrow corridor into an office which had a door leading out to the street.

CHAPTER TWENTY-FOUR

The sheriff pulled open the door leading to the street. He stepped out, pointed to a saddled horse standing some twenty feet away.

"There's your horse!"

Across the street, Vivian Thompson stood on the veranda of the hotel. A man came from the interior of the hotel behind her, stepped past her. His hand was in the pocket of a sagging sack coat.

Tommy Brown crowded through the sheriff's office door, behind Bonner.

He said nastily: "Ride, Bonner, ride . . . *to hell!*"

Bonner half turned, smashed Brown a terrific blow

in the stomach with his right fist and with his left tore the revolver from Tommy Brown's hand.

He took two tremendous leaps and cleared the wooden sidewalk. He went down to his knees, came up and fired at the man springing past Vivian Thompson across the street, the man who wasn't a Pinkerton man at all, but who was Tommy Brown's assistant murderer.

For of course it was a lie. Bonner wasn't meant to go to South America or Europe. True, they didn't want him to hang, they didn't want him to go on trial, back in Missouri. They didn't want any of that.

They wanted only one thing . . . they wanted Sam Bonner dead.

Randolph Thompson wanted Sam Bonner dead.

Killed while attempting to escape.

The man across the street cried out and pitched to the ground on his face. Bonner whirled back, sent a shot at the sheriff, but missed. The sheriff stumbled back into his office. Brown . . . Brown was down on his hands and knees, scurrying after the sheriff.

Bonner ran for the horse, mounted it.

"Sam!" cried Vivian Thompson. "Wait—Sam . . . !"

She ran out into the street. Bonner, whirling his horse, had to swerve it suddenly to keep from running her down. A gun inside the sheriff's office roared.

Vivian cried out, stumbled.

Bonner yelled hoarsely, jerked on the reins so savagely that his horse reared up on its hind legs. He slid over the back of the horse, hit the ground and threw himself at Vivian. She was kneeling, kneeling and sobbing.

And blood was staining her dress under her heart.

Tommy Brown, with one of the sheriff's guns in his fist, sprang out upon the sidewalk in front of the sheriff's office. He sent a quick bullet at Sam Bonner . . . and missed.

Then Tommy Brown died from Bonner's return bullet.

Bonner dropped his gun into the dust of the Denton

street and gently took the kneeling Vivian into his arms. She went limp and he settled her down onto the ground.

"Goodbye, my darling," he said softly.

He straightened. The sheriff stood in the open door-way of his office, his gun in his hand. His eyes went to Bonner and beyond, to Vivian Thompson. He did not try to shoot at Bonner.

Bonner stooped, picked up his gun and deliberately walked to the horse that had stopped rearing. He mounted, looked at the sheriff and at some people who were on the sidewalk.

Then he turned the horse and started out of Denton at an easy canter.

He rode for the canebrakes. The Texas Rangers would find him in the canebrakes for he would not make himself hard to find.

They would kill him.

They would kill a dead man, for Sam Bonner had died when Vivian Thompson had died.

LONESOME RIVER

ABOUT THE AUTHOR

FRANK GRUBER was an eminently successful professional writer, who wrote some 400 stories that have been widely published in magazines and reprinted in anthologies. His first book, *Peace Marshal*, appeared in 1939. The next year, his first mystery novel, *The French Key*, was voted the best mystery of 1940. His 58 books include 22 Westerns, 33 mystery and suspense novels, and 3 biographies. His TV scripts include such successful series as "Tales of Wells Fargo," "The Texan," and "Shotgun Slade." Total sales for Mr. Gruber's books now exceed 12 million copies in the United States and 75 million in foreign countries. Among those titles published by Signet are *Broken Lance*, *The Bushwhackers*, *Quantrell's Raiders*, and *Town Tamer*.

1

In the living room of Lobo ranch house, in a plain pine coffin, lay the mortal remains of Sam Barker, soon to be interred in the barren soil that he had loved so fiercely.

On Lobo range, the blight of fourteen months of drought had taken its toll. There was no grass, there was no water. Steers and cows lowed pitifully as they stood in the waterless bed of Lobo River.

Lily Barker rode across the vast domain that Sam Barker had wrested from the wilderness. She saw the signs of the drought everywhere, but was only vaguely aware of their significance. Lily was sixteen and for two, almost three, years had not known this country. Four days ago a telegram had come to her aunt's home in Massachusetts and she had hurried more than halfway across the country to the home she had not seen in almost three years, to the father from whom she had been parted; the father in whom life flickered so feebly that he did not even recognize her.

Lily saw death that evening and now, the following day, she rode across Lobo to get the smell of death from her nostrils, to think . . . to think. . . .

She sent the mustang tearing across the stricken range two miles, three, into the mouth of Lobo Canyon where the sands of Lobo River were still slightly damp, where sickly tufts of grass still clung to the sandy, rocky soil.

A wolf, a giant lobo, darted across her mustang's path, causing the horse to shy so that Lily was almost thrown from the saddle. By the time she brought the horse back under control the lobo was gone, having bounded into a rocky draw that led off from the main canyon.

A gun banged in the canyon and the sharp, anguished cry of the wolf told of his fate. Startled, Lily turned her mustang into the draw.

She saw the man and the dead wolf. The man was as lean and hungry-looking as the wolf he had just killed. He wore torn, patched Levi's, a floppy, shapeless black Stetson and a woolen shirt that, while clean, had long months ago outworn its usefulness. The revolver in the man's hand, however, was well-oiled.

He was stooping over the carcass of the lobo as Lily rode into the draw. Hearing the clatter of her horse's hoofs, he whirled. His revolver started to come up but when he saw that the rider was a girl he lowered the gun and slipped it smoothly into a worn leather holster.

A stubble of two or three days' growth was on his face, Lily noted. She saw, too, that he was young, probably only four or five years older than herself. She knew, of course, that he was the person who had just killed the wolf, but the first words that came from her were inane.

"You've killed him!"

He looked at her with hostility in his eyes. "You're Lily Barker," he said flatly, almost accusingly.

Her eyes went from the man to the wolf, back to the man. "Isn't—isn't this Barker land?"

"It's all Barker land." He paused a moment, then added quietly, "I'm Tom Weber."

The name meant nothing to her. She had come from a house of death, had traversed a land of death and now saw death once more, a dead lobo, but still death.

She said petulantly, "What right have you to trespass on this land? And kill on it!"

He stared at her, surprise in his hostile eyes. He touched the dead wolf with the toe of his battered boot. "This is a lobo——"

"What of it?"

"Everybody kills a lobo. It's the thing to . . ." It was not a proper answer and he gave it up. "I forgot, you've been away. What is it—three years?"

She started to nod automatically, then caught herself. "Are you one of our hired hands?"

"I told you," he said, becoming angry, "I'm Tom Weber."

"That's what you said, but . . ." She paused, as memory tugged at her. "Weber . . . ?"

"My Dad and yours came to this country together!"

She winced. "Of course. I—I remember now. Tom . . . you're Tom, the boy whom I . . ." She was going to say, "The boy whom I idolized," and then she recalled that she was no longer a child. She said, "How is your father?"

"Drunk," he said flatly, "as usual."

Having just come from seeing her father stretched out, pale in death, the callous, irreverent comment on his father somehow shocked Lily. A little shudder ran through her figure, stiffening it. "Thank God," she said, "that I don't have to

2

live in this Godforsaken country. If this is what it does to people——"

"No," Tom Weber interrupted, "you don't *have* to live in it. You can go back to the East where it's nice and soft and comfortable. Where you don't have to see cattle and people dying, where you don't have to cry over the death of a lobo wolf, where——"

"Stop it!" Lily cried, suddenly angry. "I've had just about all I can take for today. I only left the house because of——"

"You don't even have to go back," Tom Weber retorted. "They're plenty of people on Lobo. They'll bury your dead. They'll take care of everything. Fred Case and his crowd can handle everything for you. You can go back and they'll send you your money every year——"

"Not for long," she flared. "I'm going to sell the ranch as soon as I can."

"Sell?" he cried. "You'd *sell* Lobo?"

"Why not? As you just said, it's nice and comfortable in the East. I don't *have* to live in this country."

"But your father spent his life building up Lobo and you—you'd sell it?"

"Just as quickly as I can. It's nothing but sand and rock, the bleakest and most desolate land I saw coming across the country. I—I remembered it as green and beautiful, but this—this is nothing!"

"We've had a drought," Tom Weber said, "the worst since your father and mine came out here. But it'll rain again and then you'll see this country spring to life——"

"I hate it!" Lily cried passionately. "It makes people hard and ruthless."

"The land doesn't do that," Tom Weber said soberly. "Besides, this country can be changed." He pointed to the main canyon. "Your father was going to build a dam across the mouth of Lobo Canyon. Then when it rained the water would be stored up and fed out as it was needed. A dam would make all of the valley outside a worthwhile place, a good land. Your father thought so; he was going to do it. Only . . . he didn't have time."

"He didn't have time for me," Lily burst out. "He sent me East because he was too busy buying land, raising cattle, buying more land. He wanted to be a cattle king. That's all he was interested in."

"He was doing it for you," Weber said quietly. "He was thinking of your future."

"He should have thought of—of my mother. This land

3

killed her and—and then he sent me away. He didn't want me around to remind me of what he'd done to my mother. . . ."

"You fool!"

Lily reacted violently. "What—what did you call me?"

"A fool, a blind, stupid fool."

"How dare you?" gasped Lily. "How dare you?"

"*You* complain!" raged Tom Weber. "You, whose father left you a million acres of land? You, who were raised in the East with all the luxury that money could buy? You complain? Do you know why I shot that wolf? Why, I was *hunting* a wolf? Because I haven't eaten in two days, because my drunken father has drunk away everything he ever had—and because I can get ten dollars for that wolfskin over in Barkerville, which'll buy us enough food for another week—and maybe a bottle of whiskey, thrown in, for my father."

Lily stared at Tom Weber, incredulity in her eyes.

"Sell your ranch," he went on remorselessly. "Sell it and get out of this country. It's no place for you. You might get those soft white hands of yours soiled. You might——"

"Stop!" she cried. "Stop, or . . ."

She half raised the riding crop, not to strike him, but to defend herself—against the lashing of his words. Tom Weber misunderstood the instinctive gesture. He saw the raised whip—and a whip meant something else to him.

He cried out, "You'd whip me? Like a dog who's dared to snap at you?"

Rage overcame him and he leaped forward, lunging for the whip. And then she did strike him. She lashed him across the face with the whip and struck him with it once again.

Weber's hands tore her from the saddle. She fell against him—and then, suddenly, his face was against hers and he was kissing her savagely, brutally—contemptuously.

"Go back to your East," he snarled, shoving her away. "Go back and tell your friends that you were kissed by a—a lobo wolf." He whirled away from her and strode out of the rocky draw.

Lily remained, staring after him. After a moment her eyes fell to the whip at her feet, to the dead lobo.

When Charlie Weber and Sam Barker came to Lobo Valley and decided that this land was as good as any other they had found so far, they divided the long valley roughly between them. A river came out of the canyon and meandered back and forth across the valley and it did not seem to make

4

any difference to either which side of the valley he occupied. The two men were the closest of friends and remained so for some years.

Then Weber's wife—Tom's mother—died, and Charlie Weber began to spend more and more time in the tiny hamlet that had sprung up at the lower end of the valley. And more and more he neglected things at his ranch. People began to move into the valley. Weber sold off a bit of land, a thousand acres here, two thousand there. His cowhands robbed him blind and by the time Tom Weber was fourteen the ranch was but a hollow shell. A ramshackle house, sagging corrals, a dilapidated barn and a few hundred head of cattle roaming wild, mostly unbranded. Charlie Weber drank them away gradually, and by the time his son, Tom, was twenty-one, there were no steers on Weber land at all. Had there been, their grazing area would have been greatly curtailed, for a paltry 320 acres remained legally in the name of Charlie Weber.

Tom Weber thought of all this as he rode from his encounter with Lily Barker, across the dry lands to the place he still called home. He tightened his belt once, for the pangs of hunger gnawed at him.

He reached the tumbledown shack and inside found his father asleep on the messy cot. An empty whiskey bottle lay on the floor beside the bed. Savagely, Tom Weber kicked it across the room, where it hit a wall and crashed to splinters.

He caught his father by his unwashed shirt, shook him violently.

"Wake up," he cried. "Wake up, you drunken sot!"

Charlie Weber groaned. He tried to open his eyes, could not quite do so. Tom Weber shoved him back to the bed and stared down at him. "Sleep," he said savagely. "Maybe you'll never even wake up. That'd be the best thing you ever did in your life."

He looked around the untidy place, saw nothing that he believed worth taking and whirled, stepped out of the door. Without once looking back he started walking toward Barkerville twelve miles away. Reaching Barkerville, he continued walking over more of the dry lands and finally, sometime during the night, over the pass that led to the world beyond.

He was through with Lobo Valley.

Tom Weber had been gone from the only home he had ever known more than an hour when Lily Barker rode up on her mustang. Charlie Weber was drawing a bucketful of

5

muddy water from the shallow well near the house. He sloshed the water over his head and then, groaning, faced Lily.

"You're Sam's daughter," he said heavily.

Lily shoved the carcass of the lobo wolf from her saddle pommel. It fell at Weber's feet. His eyes went down to it, held for a moment, then came up to meet the steady blue eyes of the girl.

"Tom forgot this," Lily said coldly. "He shot it so he could sell it to buy food for you and him to eat. And perhaps a bottle of whiskey for you."

Contemptuously, she turned her horse away and put it into a gallop.

For a long moment, Charlie Weber looked after her. Then a groan was torn from his lips and he turned and stumbled toward the house.

2

It had been a chilly night and the hoboes in the boxcar had huddled together as the train banged and jolted over the grades and screeched around the hairpin turns. Now chinks of daylight were showing through the cracks of the doors and the hoboes were stirring.

"Man's a fool to travel at night," shivered one of them as he flailed his arms to warm himself. He began kicking refuse together. The car had recently hauled a shipment of machinery and there was a quantity of oiled paper scattered about, which the hoboes had not seen during the night.

Weber, his back braced against the far side of the car, his legs stretched out before him, opened his eyes. A chill was in his bones and he thought that he had never been so numb in his entire life, but he was a man who didn't complain about the bad days and didn't exult over the good ones.

The nights . . . when he slept . . . they were all right.

The hobo got together a huge pile of oiled paper and refuse and struck a match to it. A chatter of approval went up as the hoboes gathered around the fire to warm themselves.

"This is all right!" one of them cried.

"Yeah, but we got to watch it," another cautioned. "The

6

shacks on this run are a rough bunch. Throw a man off in the middle of the dry lands."

The flames roared high and the oily smoke caused the hoboes to cough and choke. One of them opened the door and as the smoke billowed out the atmosphere cleared inside the boxcar.

Back in the caboose, a brakeman looked out of his elevated window and saw the smoke shooting out of the boxcar.

"Train's afire!" he cried to his teammates.

He gave the signal to the engineer and the three brakemen began to gather up their paraphernalia, a couple of fire extinguishers, some buckets with sand and, of course, their pickax handles, without which no railroad shack is fully equipped.

The brakes began to squeal and screech and, as the train slackened speed, the brakemen jumped out of the caboose and ran ahead to the boxcar from which the smoke was pouring.

Weber knew what was coming when the train began slowing up. He clambered to his feet and caught up his newspaper-wrapped bundle, which contained an extra pair of Levi's, a flannel shirt—and a well-oiled Frontier Model.

He edged toward the door and before the train was fully stopped, leaped out. He landed, running, on the traveled right of way.

The brakemen saw him. "Hobo!" one of them cried.

They came forward at a dead run, but the shout had been heard inside the boxcar. Other hoboes began pouring out, a half dozen, a dozen. The trainmen charged into them and began flailing right and left with their pickax handles.

Some of the hoboes got away unhurt, some carried aching flesh with them, one or two, broken bones. Three hoboes remained sprawled on the ground near the boxcar.

Weber ran. He cut away from the roadbed, crossed a rutted dirt road and headed for a clump of cottonwoods. He heard feet pounding behind him, but did not even bother to look over his shoulder. He ran as swiftly as he could. He ran because it was the thing to do. When you were a hobo you ran from the railroad shacks. Hoboes did not fight against railroad men. There was no profit in it. Hoboes who fought trainmen were sought up and down the line by both trainmen and peace officers. They could never travel that road again.

So hoboes ran.

Weber reached the cottonwoods and pulled up.

A lean man with a two days' growth of beard on his face came up, panting.

"This is one way of working up an appetite," he chuckled.

"It was a fool trick, starting that fire," Weber said.

"Sure, but who said hoboes were smart?" The man regarded Weber sharply. Like Weber, he also carried a bundle wrapped up in a newspaper. "Going far?"

Weber shrugged.

The other man chuckled. "You kept to yourself. I thought maybe you weren't a regular."

"I've traveled other ways."

"You look like a man who's been on a horse."

Weber nodded.

"My name," the hobo said carefully, "is Paul Partridge."

"Paul Partridge?"

"I thought you'd know the name."

"I've heard it, but I didn't think Paul Partridge would be riding in a boxcar."

Partridge grinned. "Sometimes it's a good way to travel." He looked inquiringly at Weber. "You've been around."

"Some."

"You look like a fella I once saw in Ogallala."

"I've been there. But I've also been in Cheyenne and in Denver, in Salt Lake and Flagstaff. My name is Tom Weber."

"Weber?" Partridge's face screwed up in thought. "I guess I never knew anyone named Weber." He looked out of the cottonwoods, toward the road that paralleled the railroad right of way. "Wonder how far it is to Barkerville?"

"About eighteen or twenty miles."

"How would *you* know?"

"Barkerville's my home town."

Partridge whistled softly. "Been away, eh?"

"For a spell."

"How long?"

Weber made an impatient gesture of dismissal. "What difference does it make?"

"None, I guess. Only I'm going to Barkerville and I'd kinda like to get a rundown on the place."

"Nothing to run down. It's cow country. All right, when there's rain and grass, the country's fine. Most of the time, though, it's a dry land and things aren't so good. The town of Barkerville's a few houses and stores."

"How big?"

"Fifty-six people, maybe. Probably a little bigger, now that there's a railroad running through. I guess they've put in a depot and maybe some loading pens."

"You've been away quite a spell," Partridge said.

"You've been there?"

"No, but a fella who wrote me a letter said Barkerville was a kinda busy place. County seat."

"It was a county seat when I left. If it hadn't been for that there wouldn't have been more than one store and saloon in Barkerville. It's a poor country."

"Who's a fella name of Alderton?"

"A rancher?"

"How about Denver?"

"Mike Denver used to own the saloon, although I guess he also ran some cattle on a little place he had." Weber frowned. Denver was the man who had sold the whiskey to his father. "Denver sent for you?"

"Uh-uh."

"It wouldn't be Walter Alderton," Weber went on, "although, come to think of it, Alderton would be pretty old by now. His son, Jeff, might be——"

"Yeah, Jeff, that's right. The fella who's running for governor."

Jeff Alderton running for governor?

Tom Weber had been away from Lobo Valley for a long time!

Eleven years.

3

It was early evening when Weber and Partridge dropped off a freight a hundred yards from the depot in Barkerville.

Partridge said, "See you," and with a wave, disappeared into the darkness.

Weber looked toward the blaze of lights ahead. Barkerville had grown . . . a lot.

He continued on toward the depot, noting loading pens, freight cars on a siding. The depot . . . it couldn't be the depot of a hamlet; it had a telegraph office, a waiting room and a large shed attached that was apparently an express and freight office.

A man stood on the platform regarding Weber as he came up. He was a lean, sardonic-eyed man with a star pinned to his shirt pocket.

"You get off that freight?" he asked of Weber.

"Make any difference?"

"We got a jail here for hoboes!"

"I'm just passing through."

"Then pass. Don't figure on spending the night here."

Weber turned into Barkerville's Main Street. Eleven years ago it had contained a saloon, a blacksmith shop, a general store and a half-dozen houses. Now both sides of the street, for two blocks, were lined with buildings, most of them business establishments.

A restaurant caught Weber's eye. He fingered the two coins in his pocket, a quarter and a dime. It was thirty-five cents more than he had had when he had left Barkerville; he was returning richer than he had left. And eleven years older.

He entered the restaurant. There were four or five patrons at tables, but the counter was deserted. Weber took a stool near the front and consulted the menu scrawled on a blackboard. *"Roast beef, 50 cents. Steak, 50 cents. Coffee and pie included."*

"Coffee and pie," Weber said to the waiter, a bleary-eyed man of about fifty.

"Care for the dinner? Got to charge you fifteen cents for on'y coffee and pie."

"Just the pie and coffee," Weber repeated, then felt it necessary to add, "I'm not hungry."

He ate the pie and drank the coffee and left the restaurant. Outside, he stopped to look down the street.

The man with the star, who had cautioned him not to spend the night in town, came up.

"I told you," he said grimly, "git movin'."

Weber was conscious of the weight of the parcel under his arm. In jail they would probably open it up and discover the revolver—a revolver that hoboes do not carry.

"All right," he said, "I'm going."

A man came walking along the sidewalk, a heavy-set man, well in his fifties. Weber started to pass him and, as he did, the man suddenly threw out his arm.

"Wait—I know you!"

"Mr. Eads," said Weber.

"Tom—Tom Weber!" cried Marshall Eads. One hand gripped Weber's shoulder, the other caught his hand and pumped it. "It's good to see you, boy. I was beginning to think you'd never come home."

"You know this man, Mr. Eads?" asked the man with the star.

10

"Know him?" cried Eads. "He wet me when he was only two-three weeks old." Then suddenly he snorted. "Why, his dad and Sam Barker were the first settlers in this valley. The name of this town couldda been Weberville as easy as Barkerville."

"Weber," mused the deputy sheriff. "I don't seem to recall the name."

"Of course you don't. You're a Johnny-Come-Lately. Why, there was a time when . . ." Eads winced and his words trailed off, but he caught Weber's arm. "Tom, I've got to talk to you." He began to propel Weber along the sidewalk.

"Mr. Eads," protested Weber, "I'm just passing through."

"Nonsense, this is your home. You've *come* home." He stopped before a two-story brick building. Huge lettering on the window read: *Barkerville State Bank.*

Eads took a key from his pocket, unlocked the door, then, throwing it open, stood aside for Weber to enter. "Yes," he said, "I'm the banker." He chuckled. "Not bad for a man who came to Lobo Valley with just a wagonload of groceries."

He bustled in behind Weber, struck a match and lit a lamp. He led Weber to an enclosure at the front of the bank and pushed him into a big chair.

"Now, what's this nonsense about just passing through?"

"Barkerville means nothing to me," Weber said tonelessly.

"Don't it, boy? You lived here most of your life, your Ma died here and your Pa . . ." He paused, then continued, "Your Pa still lives here."

So Charlie Weber was still alive. In eleven years Weber had not written to him, had not heard from or of his father. Eleven years more of boozing . . . he must be something to see.

"Besides," Eads was saying, "there's your ranch. What am I going to do about it?"

"*My* ranch?"

"Your ranch. Three hundred and twenty acres of the best land in the valley."

"My father's ranch," said Weber.

"Uh-uh, your'n. It was deeded to you eleven years ago. Mmm, a day or two after you disappeared. It's your land. You can sell it——"

"With eleven years' back taxes against it?"

"The land's free and clear. The taxes have been paid."

"By—my father?"

Eads hesitated, then shrugged. "They been paid. Jeff Alder-

11

ton'll buy it from you. He's asked me about it several times. I even tried to locate you a couple of years ago. That was when he was spreading out, right after he married Lily Barker——"

"Jeff married Lily Barker!" exclaimed Weber softly. "Didn't—didn't she go back East after her father died?"

"You *have* been out of touch, Tom. Didn't you even know that Lily Barker built a dam across Lobo Canyon, that she brought water—and prosperity—to all of Lobo Valley? Why, if it hadn't been for Lily Barker, I'd still be running a general store and Mike Denver would be running a saloon. And Lobo River would be a dry coulee, ten months of the year!"

Lily Barker married to Jeff Alderton. Lily Alderton, the wife of *Governor* Alderton.

"Go out to your place," Eads said, "look it over and if you still decide that you don't want it, I'll sell it for you." He suddenly grimaced. "Mmm, I almost forgot. You may have a little trouble with the squatter who moved into your old house awhile ago. But maybe it's just as well to get him off the place before he gets any ideas of preempting or such." The banker thrust a hand into his pocket. "Would I be insulting you if I asked if you had any money?"

"The deputy sheriff told you I came in on a freight."

"A—a loan?"

"No."

"All right, Tom, all right. But remember I'm a banker. My business is lending money. If you decide you want to stay and fix up the ranch, come and see me."

"That won't be likely," said Weber.

He got up, hesitated, then nodded to the old banker and left.

4

The road, as Weber remembered it, ran west and north out of Barkerville. It cut directly across Lobo land, barely touched a tip of the old Alderton ranch, crossed the first of the several bends of Lobo River and continued on toward the Weber ranch, an island, surrounded by Lobo. At least that was the way it had been.

It was twelve miles. An easy two hours' jog for a horse, three hours and a little more afoot.

Leaving Barkerville, Weber trudged along the road for an hour, then came to the first crossing of Lobo River. A bridge had been built across it. In the old days, even during the spring rains, it had been possible to ford the river on horseback. In the dry season you didn't even get a horse's feet wet. It should have been a dry season now, yet Weber could hear the gurgling water under the bridge.

Old Sam Barker had been right. All Lobo needed was a dam across the mouth of Lobo Canyon.

And Lily Barker had put up the dam.

After another hour of walking, Weber crossed the river again, also over a bridge. He had scarcely traversed it than he heard the pounding of horses' hooves coming from the direction of Barkerville. He ran swiftly back to the bridge, got out of sight beside it before the horsemen crossed.

There were two and they were riding swiftly. It was getting on toward eleven o'clock and the moon was high, almost full. One of the riders, now wearing a flat-crowned Stetson, was Paul Partridge, with whom Weber had come into Barkerville.

Weber stood in the road, waiting until the hoofbeats died in the distance. Then he continued on. Another mile and he passed the river for the third time. On the right, a hundred yards back from the road, was a block of shadow.

The house in which Tom Weber had been born, in which he had lived for twenty-one years.

It wasn't much of a house; it contained only three rooms. A barn and shed, not too far from the house, had fallen, at least one side of it had collapsed, so that it was now a misshapen huddle.

The house was dark, but Weber heard a horse moving in a pole corral near the barn and, having been forewarned, knew that someone was in the house.

He stopped a hundred yards away, unrolled his bundle and took out a revolver. He spun the cylinder carefully, tested the action and thrust the gun behind the waistband of his Levi's. Rewrapping what remained of the bundle, he moved cautiously to the house.

The door was closed, but Weber, listening, heard deep breathing inside.

He called out, "You, inside!"

The heavy breathing stopped and rusted bedsprings squeaked. Weber stepped back to one side and called again.

"Put on a light!"

13

A voice inside grumbled, "Let me alone, I ain't botherin' nobody."

"Put on a light," Weber repeated. "I'm coming in."

There was more grumbling inside, but feet slithered on the floor and after a moment a match was struck. Weber waited until it was put to a lamp, then shoved open the door.

He entered his own home for the first time in eleven years.

A man faced him, scowling. He was about thirty-five, tall, heavy and filthy. He hadn't shaved in a week and he had certainly made no pretense of cleaning up the room for more than a month. A cot stood to one side. The man was fully dressed except for boots and hat and apparently slept that way. A few pieces of dirty clothing were scattered over the bed and on a rickety chair nearby. A kitchen table was heaped with food, dirty utensils and a few odds and ends, including a rather surprisingly clean Frontier Model. A shotgun leaned against the wall near the bed.

"Who're you?" the squatter demanded. He seemed rather surprised at seeing a stranger; he had possibly expected his midnight caller to be someone he knew.

"This place," said Weber, "looks like a pigpen."

"Oh, yeah?" sneered the man facing Weber. "You don't look so good yourself." His hand reached out casually for the table. Weber raised his foot and knocked the table over against the man.

The squatter scrambled clear of the debris, saw that he could not immediately locate his revolver and, whirling, headed for the shotgun.

"Let the gun alone!" snapped Weber.

The man stopped, hesitated, then turned. "You got a crust comin' in here and knockin' my things around."

"*Your* things?" Weber snapped. "Well, get together whatever's yours and clear out."

"Now, wait a minute," the man growled. "Maybe you got the drop on me right now, but you can't get away with chasin' a man out of his own house——"

"This," said Weber, "happens to be *my* house."

The squatter stared at Weber. "Ain't no one lived here in years. . . ."

"I'm Tom Weber. I've been away."

"How do I know you're Tom Weber?" the man demanded. "All I got's your say-so. Ain't no one ever seen Tom Weber. I found this place deserted and fallin' to pieces. I fixed it up——"

"You fixed up, hell!" snarled Weber.

14

"I took care of it. I got rights."

"Sue me."

"You think I won't? This country ain't like it was when you was here. There's things shapin' up that you don't know a thing about and I happen to know some people . . ." The squatter suddenly stopped, squinting at Weber.

Weber made a small gesture with his hand. "Go ahead."

The man shook his head. "Just because I'm a squatter don't mean I ain't got friends."

"Well, *I* haven't got friends," Weber said, "but this is my property and you're leaving it."

"You're making a mistake. A big mistake. My name happens to be Tate Hopkins——"

"And mine's Tom Weber."

The man who called himself Tate Hopkins glowered at Weber. "My name don't mean nothin' to you? Well, how about Paul Partridge? *That* mean anythin'?"

"I've heard it."

"Then I guess you've been around a little. You know what kind of a man Partridge is. . . ."

"A gunfighter."

"Just about the best there is. Some think mebbe Tom Fargo's the best, but I don't hold with that. I happen to know that Partridge once backed down Fargo."

"You *saw* him back down Tom Fargo?"

Hopkins hesitated for an instant. "Partridge is on his way here. What do you say to that?"

"I say you're not Paul Partridge," retorted Weber. "And you're still getting out of here."

Hopkins made an abrupt capitulation. "All right, but don't say I didn't warn you. I'll just get my duds and——"

He turned and moved toward the bed. His too-quick surrender, his casualness did not fool Weber. As Hopkins stepped up to the bed and lunged for the shotgun, Weber was springing forward. His fist caught Hopkins on the jaw as the squatter caught up the shotgun and turned.

Hopkins cried out in sudden pain. The shotgun dropped from his hands and he reeled back against the wall. Weber caught him coming off the wall with a short chopping blow on the side of the head. Hopkins went down to his hands and knees. He remained there a moment, then shaking his head, got slowly to his feet.

"I'm going," he mumbled, "soon's I get my boots on, I'm goin'."

He stepped wobblingly to the side of the bed, sat down and

15

began drawing on his boots. Weber, meanwhile, caught up the double-barreled shotgun, broke it and extracted the shells. He also found Hopkins' revolver and took the cartridges out of it.

He thrust both weapons at the squatter. "You can get the rest of your stuff tomorrow."

Hopkins took the two weapons, stood up and shuffled to the door. There he turned for a parting shot. "You ain't seen the last of me, bub!"

He went out.

Weber followed the man to the door and stood there until Hopkins saddled his mount in the corral and rode off.

He turned back into the house then. He picked up the lamp and went into what had been the "front room" of the house. A wave of nostalgia shot through him.

He had left it hastily eleven years ago, left everything as it had always been since he remembered, the table with its old-fashioned ornate lamp, two leather armchairs, a sofa. Pictures . . . a picture of his father and mother taken on their wedding day still hung on the wall. The glass was broken, the picture was dusty and smeared from age, but it was still recognizable.

He went on into the room that had been a bedroom. A sagging bed, from which the mattress had been stripped, was against the wall. A chair that had been whole eleven years ago lay on the floor, two legs broken. A cheap dresser had one drawer removed and another sagging. Before he had moved into the kitchen for convenience, the squatter, Hopkins, had been hard on the furniture. It wasn't just the dust and dirt of eleven years; the man had treated everything roughly.

Angrily, Weber returned to the kitchen. He gathered up whatever clothing there was of Hopkins' and dumped it in a pile just outside the kitchen door. He found a well-filled cartridge belt with holster attached and threw that out with the other things.

A broom stood in one corner, but the straws had long ago rotted away. Hopkins had apparently not favored sweeping, and Weber was unable to find another broom. He did, however, get a bucket of water from the shallow well outside and sloshed water over the floor, then used a pair of cast-off Levi's as a mop to clean up the water and dirt.

About two o'clock in the morning he began to feel tired, but the thought of sleeping in Hopkins' filthy bed was not an appetizing one and he went out to the barn where he found a pile of moldy hay and threw himself upon it.

5

Lily Barker Alderton came out of Lobo ranch house wearing a brown linen suit and a straw hat with a bright feather stuck in it. At twenty-seven Lily had reached the full flower of womanhood. Her skin, only lightly tanned, was as smooth as it had been eleven years ago, but then when she had been scarcely more than a child, she had known only impatience, a petulance that was attributed to childhood. Now she was a calm woman, a woman whose face was a mask, which brightened frequently and made her a truly beautiful woman. Yet something was missing in that beauty. It was a spark, a light in her veiled eyes that Jeff Alderton knew *should* be there and could never quite kindle. It had not been there even on their wedding day.

As he drove the buckboard around to the house, he was thinking of that. So much, perhaps, that he did not remember to get down from the buckboard and help her step up on the hub of the wheel. Lily climbed in beside him and he flicked the whip at the rumps of the horses.

The animals started off at a swift trot and a slight frown creased Alderton's smooth forehead. It was not missed by Lily.

She said, "What's the problem?"

He gave a slight start. "No problem. Why?"

"Something's bothering you."

"I've a lot on my mind these days. This business of campaigning, glad-handing people I wouldn't even talk to another time . . ."

"You like it, Jeff, you know you do."

He grinned wryly. "Maybe I do, at that." He was silent for a moment, then, "It's rustlers."

"Rustling—on Lobo?" Lily was surprised. This was something that had never been mentioned during her tenure on the ranch.

"Fred Case tells me that our calf crop north of the river is the smallest he's ever known it."

"That's lobo country. They've always killed stock up there."

"I haven't seen three loboes this past year. Neither have

17

the boys. Besides—it's more than that. Fred says between six and eight hundred. Maybe more."

"But where could the rustlers—if it *is* rustlers—drive the stock? Into the mountains?"

"Rawlins touches us on the north and east. There's about three miles of common border between us and Rawlins."

"Surely you're not accusing Rawlins!"

"No," replied Alderton glumly, "you don't accuse a rustler—until you catch him." He paused. "And I'm sure it isn't Rawlins himself. He's put on some salty characters lately and I wouldn't put it past any of them to sweeten up their pay a bit."

"Would it help any to talk to Mike Denver? After all, he's Rawlins' brother-in-law."

"But he's hardly his brother-in-law's keeper!"

The sun shining through the broken barn roof awakened Weber. He got up, brushed hay from his clothing and walked out of the barn. The sun was at least two hours high. He walked to the well, drew a bucket of water and washed his face and hands and became aware then that he had eaten almost nothing the day before.

He went into the house where he found a chunk of mildewed bacon and a sack of hominy grits. He cooked some of the hominy on the dirty stove, drank a cup of strong coffee and gnawed a piece of the bacon. It was poor food and did nothing to return the nostalgia he had felt during the night when he had explored his old home.

Finished with the breakfast, Weber went outside and looked around. Across the road, where Lobo range began, fat steers were grazing; others were drinking water in the shallow flow of Lobo River. Well, that at least was better. Grass grew and cattle drank from the river.

He walked to the bridge where the river crossed to wind its way through a corner of the 320 acre ranch. There was a good six inches of water in the river. He turned and surveyed the Weber ranch. It would take some back-breaking work, but it could be done. A continual flow of water would turn the arid waste into a prosperous land.

Weber returned to his house. He circled it, saw it was in poor shape. The barn was a complete wreck. Everything was rundown, shabby . . . like Weber himself.

A sudden anger shot through him. What was he thinking about? This was not for him!

He found his few belongings, wrapped them about his

revolver and rolled the whole into the torn newspaper in which he had carried them for the past two weeks. Without a backward glance at the house, he started for the road and turned left to head for Barkerville.

After about fifteen minutes of walking, he became aware of something he had not seen the night before, a neat little farmhouse on his left, a fenced garden and a few head of cattle. Another few minutes' walk brought him to still another farm, this one with a field of wheat fenced in. He passed a third and fourth farm, then went along a mile of open range and made the third river crossing. It was open range country from here on.

He was walking steadily, his eyes on the road, when he rounded a turn in the road and saw a rig ahead. It stood on three wheels. A man was trying to lift up the side of the buckboard so his companion, a woman, could move the fourth wheel onto the axle. The buckboard was apparently too heavy for the man, for as Weber approached he suddenly cried out and let go. The buckboard sagged.

The woman saw Weber and spoke to the man. He turned as Weber came up.

"Here, stranger," he said, "can you give us a hand?"

The man was Jeff Alderton, two years older than Weber. At fifteen, Alderton had fought the younger Tom Weber, had mauled him badly but had been unable to make him quit.

The woman was Lily Barker Alderton.

She was smiling at Tom Weber, but she did not recognize him. Nor did Jeff Alderton.

Weber stepped to the buckboard, braced himself and easily lifted up the side. Alderton took the wheel from Lily, moved it smoothly into place. He got a wrench and tightened the axle nut.

"Nothing to it when you've got the muscle."

"Thank you," Lily Alderton said to Weber. "Can we give you a lift to town?"

"I can walk," Weber said shortly.

"You probably can," she replied calmly, "but *we'd* be walking too if you hadn't helped, so the least we can do is give you a lift."

"Climb in, man," exclaimed Alderton testily.

Weber got into the rear of the buckboard.

In a moment the team was trotting along easily. Weber's presence—rather the presence of a disreputable-looking character to whom they were obligated—caused an awkward silence between the Aldertons. Jeff clucked to the horses,

19

bringing them from a trot to a swift run. Obviously, he wanted the journey to end as quickly as possible.

Somewhat embarrassed by her husband's attitude, Lily half turned in the buckboard seat. "You're new in Lobo," she remarked to Weber.

"I'm just passing through," he replied shortly.

She was rebuffed for a moment, then turned back. "Are you looking for work?"

Jeff Alderton exclaimed, "We're letting hands go now."

Weber said evenly, "I'm not looking for a job."

That ended it for Lily. She turned back to the road and the rest of the trip to Barkerville was completed without further conversation.

As they rolled into town, Alderton pulled up the horses.

"This all right?" he asked grimly, then added sourly, "You want a free feed, go out to the picnic grove. There's enough for everyone."

Weber jumped out of the buckboard. He was about to turn away when Alderton called out to him.

"Here!"

Alderton threw a piece of silver at him and Weber's hands, going up instinctively, caught it. It was a silver dollar. Before he could return it, Alderton was cracking his whip over the team and the buckboard was bounding away.

A crooked grin twisted Weber's lips as he stowed away the dollar in his pocket.

A short walk brought him to the restaurant near the depot. It was closed, a sign on the door reading: CLOSED FOR THE GOVERNOR'S BARBECUE.

His breakfast had been a meager one and the long trip to Barkerville had made Weber even hungrier. Besides, he had Alderton's own left-handed invitation. He rubbed a hand over the growth of whiskers on his face and shaking his head, started past the depot. Ahead, he saw a mass of horses and buckboards and beyond a grove in which were gathered several hundred people.

As he walked down the street, Weber noted a huge banner that hung completely across the street. Lettering on it read:

ALDERTON
FOR GOVERNOR

The cottonwood grove was about five acres in extent. A huge pit had been dug in the center of it and here two steers were being barbecued by a battery of cooks. Long tables had

20

been set up nearby, and possibly fifty or sixty people were eating at them. Others were gathered in clumps here and there. Children played furious games among the cottonwoods.

Weber joined a short line of cowboys near the barbecue pit. As his turn came, one of the cooks cut off a slab of beef, put it on a plate and handed it to Weber. "Put your ribs outside that."

Coffee, bread and vegetables were on the tables. Weber seated himself and for ten minutes devoted his attention to putting away the food. When he finally looked up he saw a heavy-set man across the table regarding him speculatively.

"Behind the whiskers," the man said, "you look like Tom Weber."

Weber nodded. "I am, Mr. Sampson."

"Remember me, eh?"

"You were my father's friend."

"Charlie sold me most of my range," grunted Lou Sampson. "Never figured I paid him enough."

"You paid him all he asked."

"You seen your paw?"

"No."

"You will." Sampson frowned. "Marsh Eads said you was back. That's how come I recognized you. Wouldn't have expected to see you here, otherwise. Goin' to stay?"

"No, Mr. Sampson."

"Lou, call me Lou. You're old enough now." Sampson suddenly made a vague sweeping gesture with his hand. "What do you think of Jeff Alderton running for governor?"

"I'm not a voter."

"Why not? You live here, don't you?" Sampson chuckled. "But I think I know what you mean. You and Jeff never hit it off, did you?"

"We weren't exactly pards."

"Didn't think you was. Well, Jeff's become a big man. He had two hundred thousand acres of range country and ran ten thousand head of steers when he married the Barker girl." Sampson paused. "Never thought they'd hit it off, them two. Jeff likes to be boss and Lily's a girl who's used to having things her own way." He suddenly chuckled. " 'Member talkin' to your paw once when you was a squirt. Guess it was the time, yeah, that's how come he said it, when he sold me that land. Said you wouldn't be needin' so much when you grew up, since you'd probably marry the Barker girl and Sam Barker was a cinch to leave enough land, since he was so hungry for it."

21

"My father must have been in his usual condition," said Weber. "Drunk." He got up, nodded coolly to the rancher and walked away from the table.

Sampson stared after him in astonishment.

"Now what'd I say?" he exclaimed.

6

Leaving the table near the barbecue pit, Weber made a wide circle and came upon a group of thirty or forty men gathered under a huge cottonwood. An air of excitement prevailed and Weber discovered that a dice game was going on. A voice he recognized was chanting above the yammering of the other players.

It was the voice of Paul Partridge, the gunfighter with whom Weber had arrived in Barkerville.

"Twenty dollars open!" Partridge was chortling. "Fade it, boys, and go home broke."

"I'll take two dollars of that," said a cowboy.

"I got five!" cried another.

"I'll fade fifty cents," chimed in a third man.

"That's really splittin' me up," protested Partridge. "What chance has a man got cut up nineteen ways?"

"What's open?" demanded a cool voice.

"Twelve-fifty," replied Paul Partridge, then recognized the speaker. "Hello, Governor."

"Not yet, boys, not yet," beamed Jeff Alderton. He was a handsome man, tall, muscular. He wore fancy boots, whipcord riding breeches and a fine broadcloth shirt with a red silk bandana about his throat. A gray Stetson was pushed back from his forehead.

He had a huge roll of bills in his fist, from which he peeled off a ten. "I'll take ten," he announced. "You boys cover the chicken feed."

A cowboy threw down a dollar, another tossed in fifty cents.

"Dollar still open," cried Paul Partridge peevishly. "How long does it take to get faded around here?"

"Shoot!" Weber said suddenly, throwing down the silver dollar Jeff Alderton had given him less than an hour before.

"Hey, Weber!" cried Paul Partridge. "Where'd *you* get the money?"

"Shoot," Weber repeated.

He kept his eyes on Paul Partridge but was aware that Jeff Alderton was regarding him sharply.

"You asked for it," chortled Paul Partridge. He rattled the dice in his fist and rolled them out.

"Boxcars!" roared a dozen throats.

There was a mad scramble for the money on the ground. Weber waited until there was elbow room, then stepped forward to pick up two dollars. As he stooped his eyes met those of Alderton, also reaching for his winnings.

"Well, well, Tom Weber!"

Weber nodded carelessly. "Hello, Jeff."

"So you've finally come home."

"It's still my dice and I shoot ten," snapped Paul Partridge. He threw a gold piece into the dust before Weber.

Alderton promptly covered it with a ten dollar bill. "I've got it."

Alderton moved back, his eyes still on Weber. Partridge rattled his dice and rolled them out.

"Eight."

His next roll was a seven and Partridge exclaimed peevishly, "Never saw such a piker game. Cut a man up and expect him to make a point."

"You want action?" Alderton asked. "Fade the twenty that's on the line."

Partridge threw a double eagle to the ground and Alderton rolled out the dice.

"Seven," he announced, "and forty dollars is open."

"I got twenty of it," Partridge said sourly.

"That leaves twenty still open."

Money began to shower down in small amounts, the largest single bill being a five. After a moment or two there was still three dollars and fifty cents open. Partridge tossed in another dollar and a cowboy came up with fifty cents.

"Two dollars more sees me go," Alderton announced. "How about it, Weber? You haven't faded anything."

Weber threw down his two dollars. Alderton chuckled and rolled out the dice. They came up eight.

"Who's got ten dollars says I can't eight?" Alderton challenged. He waited a moment, but there were no takers and he threw out the dice. They came up ten and he threw them out again.

"Seven!" went up the shout.

A cowboy took the dice, played a dollar and lost it. A second cowboy, already broke, passed the dice. A man played fifty cents, lost and the dice were handed to Weber. He laid out his four dollars. A cowboy promptly covered a dollar.

Partridge threw down three silver dollars. "Go ahead, Weber."

The dice came up eleven.

"I got it all," snapped Partridge.

Weber threw a seven.

"Mine," snarled Partridge.

Weber got five for a point, made two inconsequential throws, then made the five.

"Thirty-two dollars," Alderton said, then mockingly to Partridge, "Still yours?"

Partridge counted out his money. "I got eighteen dollars—all I've got left."

Alderton promptly counted out fourteen dollars. Weber shook up the dice, rolled them out.

"Seven!" cried Partridge in consternation. "How many passes can a man make?"

"I've got it all," Alderton said crisply. "Unless you're dragging down?"

"I'm not," said Weber.

Alderton counted out sixty-four dollars. Weber promptly threw another seven.

"Still shooting?" sneered Alderton.

"Once more."

Alderton put out a hundred and twenty-eight dollars. Weber rattled the dice, rolled them out at least twelve feet. They came up three-one.

"I'll lay you a hundred to fifty," Alderton snapped.

Weber shook his head. "Twenty to ten?" persisted Alderton.

"I got a dollar of that," cried a cowboy.

Alderton made an impatient gesture of dismissal. Weber rolled out the dice. They stopped two-two.

A roar went up among the dice players.

"How lucky can a man be?" Alderton snapped.

Weber began to gather up the money, then suddenly looked up at Alderton. "Care to fade the two fifty-six, Governor?"

Alderton had not objected to anyone else calling him Governor, but the inflection of Weber's tone made it a taunt.

"I don't believe I have that much with me," he said testily. He counted out money. "Two-ten's all I've got left."

"That's good enough."

The dice came up six-one.

"I guess the game's over," Weber said, when the roar died down. He gathered up the money, stowed it away in his pocket. He turned away, but Alderton followed him.

"Wait, Weber!"

Weber stopped.

"What're your plans?"

"I have no plans," Weber said.

"You're staying in Lobo Valley?"

"I haven't given it any thought."

"That little farm of yours . . . I think the house has fallen down by now. Not worth anything, but you've just won a stake. A little more might help you get a start somewhere, so I don't mind helping you out. I'll take the farm off your hands."

"For how much?"

Alderton shrugged. "The land's no good and the sodbusters are in between your place and mine, but . . . a dollar an acre, maybe?"

"Three hundred and twenty dollars?"

"Is that all? I thought you had a full section. All right, I'll give you five hundred. More'n it's worth, but for old times' sake."

"For old times' sake," said Weber, "I'm going to turn you down."

"Have it your way," Alderton said curtly and turned away.

Weber waited a moment, then started off in a somewhat different direction. He had gone only a dozen paces when he stopped abruptly. Lily Alderton was coming toward him. Her color, he saw as she approached, was somewhat high.

"You're Tom Weber," she accused. "I suppose I should have recognized you on the road, but it's been such a long time and—" Suddenly flustered, she exclaimed, "*You* knew me though!"

Weber nodded.

"Then why didn't you say who you were?"

"We didn't exactly part friends the last time we met."

She looked at him, her forehead creased. "That—*that's* how you remembered me all these years?"

"No," he said evenly. He made a flickering gesture of dismissal. "As you can see, the prodigal didn't return fat and prosperous."

"What difference does that make? You're home, that's all

that matters." She stopped suddenly. "You know about Jeff and me?"

"Congratulations."

There was an awkward pause, then, "You're not as I remember you."

"As you said, it's been a long time."

She made one more attempt to draw him out. "Where have you been all these years?"

"It would be easier to say where I haven't been."

"Tom!" called Marshall Eads from a distance. He came up, half trotting. "I've been looking for you. I see you found him, Lily."

"I found him on the way to town," Lily said. "Jeff gave him a dollar for helping him replace the wheel on the buckboard."

"That's more than he'd take from me," Eads said quickly to cover her embarrassment. Then, to Weber, "Understand you threw Tate Hopkins off your place last night. He's been bending Pete Rawlins' ear about it."

"Why should he go to Rawlins?" Lily asked.

"He used to work for Rawlins." The banker grunted. "Wouldn't be surprised if it was Rawlins who got him to squat on Tom's ranch."

"Who's Rawlins?" Weber asked.

"Man who owns everything to the north, east and south of you. He's also Mike Denver's brother-in-law."

Weber looked curiously at Lily. "I thought that range was part of Lobo."

"It was at one time," Lily replied. "I sold it years ago."

"When she built the dam across Lobo Canyon," Eads amplified. "Mike Denver bought the land, brought in the farmers and sold what was left to Pete Rawlins."

Weber nodded thoughtfully. "He's still running a saloon?"

Eads grimaced. "To bring you up to date, he still *owns* a saloon, but he owns a lot of other things and he's quite a politician these days. In fact, he's managing Jeff's campaign for governor." He paused. "What do you think of that, Tom? Jeff Alderton, Governor!"

"I guess he can afford it," Weber said bluntly.

Lily Alderton said stiffly, "I think Jeff's looking for me." She started to turn away. "I'm glad you're home, Mr. Weber."

After she had gone away, Eads said softly, "Kinda rough, weren't you?"

"Those papers you want me to sign to sell the ranch,"

Weber said bluntly. "Would it be possible to go over to your place and sign them now?"

"There's no hurry, is there?"

"I'd like to catch the evening train. The freight train."

Ead's eyes went past Weber, returned to him. "Come to the bank in a half hour." He walked off abruptly.

Weber heard the footsteps behind him. He did not turn. A man came up, came completely around Weber and stopped a half dozen feet away, facing him. He was a grizzled, ruddy-faced man in his late fifties. For a moment Weber and the other man looked steadily at each other, then Charlie Weber said, "Hello, Tom."

"I suppose there are words for an occasion like this," Weber said slowly, "but I never learned them."

The clear blue eyes that looked at him did not falter. Charlie Weber said, "You've changed, son. I wish I could say it was for the better."

"I left with an empty stomach," Weber said, "and I came back the same way. But *you're* different. You're sober."

The eyes of Charlie Weber showed pain. "You're my son, Tom," he said poignantly, "and I've thought of you through the years. I've thought of you a lot. Maybe I've thought of you too much." His face became bleak, his voice almost toneless as he went on, "Certainly I never thought the first words you'd say to me, if I ever saw you again, would be—'You're sober.' "

"Well, we agree on that," Weber said. "I never was able to say those words before I went away . . . because you were never sober."

There was a long pause, then Charlie Weber slowly nodded. "You're quite right." He turned and walked stiffly away from his son.

Weber remained where he was, but his eyes did not follow his father.

7

There was very little emotion left in Tom Weber. It had gone from him through the years. Somewhere deep within him there was perhaps a small reservoir that was not quite drained off, but if there was it went now.

27

In a little while he started to leave the picnic grove. Marshall Eads materialized and fell in step beside him.

"Give the ranch back to my father," Weber said.

"Very well, we'll stop in at the bank and you can sign a transfer. What about the tax money? You want to pay that back to Lily Alderton?"

"*She* paid the taxes?" exclaimed Weber.

"Your father was unable to those first few years. The county put a lien on the ranch and when she heard about it, Lily paid it off and continued to pay the taxes every year. She also paid the road and bridge assessments."

"I'll pay it," said Weber. "I've got four hundred and seventy-six dollars."

"It comes to over seven hundred."

"Why?" exclaimed Weber. "*Why* did she pay the taxes?"

"Why did she build the dam? Why did she sell a hundred thousand acres of Lobo? Why didn't she sell *all* of Lobo and go back East after her father died?" Eads looked steadily at Weber. "Maybe it's because a boy she grew up with had to shoot a lobo wolf so he could buy food." Weber inhaled sharply. "She told me about it, Tom. She told me how she ran into you, how she whipped you, and—how you kissed her!"

"I haven't thought of Lily Barker in over ten years," Weber said harshly. "I ran into her this morning and she thinks I recognized her. I didn't."

The banker nodded. "Well, this is all to the good. You've come back and she can forget you now. And *you've* been back and you can forget her—and your father."

"I didn't come back because of Lily Barker—or my father." Weber drew a grimy, folded envelope from his pocket. He handed it to Marshall Eads.

The banker looked at the inscription on the envelope. "Tom Fargo?"

"It's a name I've used for ten years. . . ."

"I've heard of it." Eads extracted a folded sheet of notepaper from the envelope. He read aloud:

"*Dear Tom Fargo: Come to Barkerville if you are interested in a job at one hundred dollars a month and a thousand dollar bonus at the end of six months.*" Eads hesitated. "*Signed, Pete Rawlins.*"

"A man named Paul Partridge came in on the train with me last night," said Weber. "He got a letter from someone too."

"Does he know you're Tom Fargo?"

"No."

28

Eads put the letter back into the grimy envelope. "*This* is why you came back to Barkerville?"

"I didn't answer the letter," Weber said testily, "and I didn't come here to take the job. Nobody—nobody except you now knows that Tom Weber and Tom Fargo are the same man. Rawlins didn't know it when he wrote that letter. I'm sure he wouldn't have written it had he known."

"Well," said Eads, "if the letter didn't bring you back, what did?"

"One place is the same as another." Weber paused. "All right, I was curious. What's up? A range war?"

"I don't know," Eads said worriedly. "Rawlins has a lot of men on his ranch, but he has plenty of land of his own, plenty of cattle. He's Mike Denver's brother-in-law and Denver is thicker'n thieves with Jeff Alderton." He hesitated. "Jeff Alderton had two hundred and thirty thousand acres of his own land when he married Lily Barker. Between them they now have over six hundred thousand. But Jeff wasn't exactly starving when he married Lily. And he's going to be the next governor of this state. Certainly *he's* not in trouble!"

The barbecue was a free and easy affair, but like goes to like and soon the businessmen of Barkerville found themselves gathered in one group, the big ranchers, Lou Sampson, Homer Quayle, Rawlins and Jeff Alderton, in another. But there was a third group, the largest of all, assembled in a thinned-out grove of cottonwoods.

These were the farmers, the sodbusters. It was to them Mike Denver drifted after passing the time of day with the businessmen and then the ranchers.

Mike Denver knew the farmers. He had sold them their land and kept up his contacts with them.

"Well, boys," he said to a group of the farmers, "it's going to be awfully nice having one of our own people down at the state capitol."

His cheerful words left the farmers unenthusiastic and the smile became a little frozen on Mike Denver's florid face. "Jeff's a good man and he's our friend and neighbor."

"Neighbor, maybe," said a Bohemian, named Leo Blatnik, "friend? I dunno. A rich man is a friend of another rich man."

"That don't go for Jeff," Denver said expansively. "Jeff's pa was as poor as anyone when he first came here. Why, I remember Jeff when he only had one pair of pants to his name and them cut down from his pa's."

"Mr. Alderton is a cattleman," Blatnik went on. "Cattleman is never friend of farmer."

Charlie Weber materialized out of the group. "Nor is a lobo wolf ever the friend of a tame house dog," he said to Denver. "All the votes you'll get out of *us* farmers you can stick in your eye and not even have to rub it."

"But you're eating Jeff's food!"

"Why not? It's free and he invited us. There wasn't anything said about having to vote for Jeff in return for this food."

"Charlie," Mike Denver said, "I'd like to talk to you a moment."

"Talk."

Denver inclined his head in a signal that he wanted the talk to be private. Charlie Weber hesitated, then followed the politician.

"Hard to believe you're one of the farmers," Denver said then. "Why, you and old Sam Barker were the first settlers in Lobo Valley."

"That's right, Mike," Charlie Weber said cheerfully. "I ran my brand over six or seven hundred thousand acres once." He shook his head. "This land you sold the farmers, Mike, it was mine once."

"And now you're farming, what is it? Eighty acres?"

"Forty, Mike. About all a man can handle by himself."

"Your son's back, Charlie," Denver said. "I haven't seen him, but I heard he's here at the grove somewhere."

"I saw him."

Mike Denver studied the old settler thoughtfully a moment. "Three-four hundred votes, Charlie, aren't going to elect or defeat Jeff Alderton, but these are what you might say hometown votes. It wouldn't help us to have it get around the state that Jeff's hometown folks voted against him. I'd like to carry Lobo Valley a hundred per cent."

"You won't. I can tell you that right now. The farmers aren't for Alderton."

"They *can* be. You're one of them these days. You can swing them to Jeff. A lot of them, anyway."

Charlie Weber regarded Denver sharply. "You'll pay me if I do?"

Denver missed the faint note of mockery in Weber's voice. "I'll make it worth your while."

"How much, Mike, how much?"

"We can work out a deal. . . ."

Weber shook his head. "All this land you sold the

Bohunks, Mike, it was mine once. And most of the land that Jeff Alderton's brand now grazes over. You got *that* from me, Mike."

Denver now saw the trend of Charlie Weber's words. "You drank it away," he snapped.

"That's right, I did. But if you hadn't been there, standing with the bottle at all times, I might not have been able to drink it all away. You're a politician now, Mike, but to me you're still a saloonkeeper——"

"And you're still the swamper who worked in my saloon after you drank away everything. When you were starving I gave you a job. And the booze——"

"No," said Weber, "when I became a swamper in your saloon, I drank no more. It was there all the time, all around me, but I never tasted a drop again. Not——after I sank low enough to become your swamper."

Mike Denver said grimly, "All right, you've spoken plainly, Charlie. You've told me where you stand. Just hope that you don't get in my way, because if you do, I'll step on you!"

Pete Rawlins was a scar-faced man in his late forties. He was big, heavy-jowled, heavy-fisted. The woman who had made him Denver's brother-in-law had long since passed away, but his kinship with Denver had endured. In ways the two men were much alike.

He said to Denver, shortly after the latter's scene with Charlie Weber, "Weber's cub is back. He threw Hopkins off his place last night."

"He was able to do that?"

"Hopkins says he got the drop on him."

"All right," snapped Denver, "buy him out. If he won't sell, drive him off. There's going to be enough trouble without him squatting there across the river." He paused. "The farmers, Pete, they're not going along."

"Didn't think they would."

Denver nodded. "Get started."

Rawlins nodded.

8

When Tom Weber left Barkerville, he was driving a buckboard loaded high with lumber, paint, food and supplies. A saddle was on the seat beside him. In his pocket was less than a hundred dollars from the four hundred and seventy-six he had won from Jeff Alderton.

It was late afternoon when he reached the ramshackle house on the old Weber farm. He climbed down from the buckboard and saw that Tate Hopkins' belongings still were outside the door where he had dumped them during the night.

He unhitched the team of horses and turned them into the pole corral attached to the caved-in barn. As he walked back to the house he heard the clopping of horses' hooves and looking toward the road, saw four riders coming along.

He lifted his saddle from the seat of the buckboard and then, reaching for a box of groceries, saw that the riders had turned in toward the house. He carried the groceries to the door, set down the box and turned.

Tate Hopkins was climbing down from his horse. Paul Partridge sat a black gelding easily.

"Hi, boy," Partridge called.

"So you're Weber," said a third man. "I'm your neighbor, Pete Rawlins. This is my foreman, Ches Mainwaring." He pronounced it Mannerin'. "You know Paul and Tate." He grinned wolfishly. "Tate tells me you threw him out in the middle of the night."

"He got the drop on me!" Hopkins growled.

Weber said carefully, "Is this a visit or a fight?"

"You had no call to treat me like you did," Hopkins snarled.

Rawlins leaned heavily on his saddle pommel. "Paul tells me you and him came to town together."

"You might say we bummed together," Partridge chuckled. "Which reminds me, you won all my money today. That wasn't very friendly-like, Weber."

"You've got a gun," Weber said pointedly. "You can take it away from me." He raised his hands a few inches, palms outward, to show that he was not wearing a gun.

32

Hopkins scowled. "He had a gun last night."

"Everybody's got a gun," Rawlins said, "only sometimes they don't wear them."

"Let's see your gun, Weber," Partridge said with a touch of malice.

Weber shook his head. "Four to one?"

"You've got a rough tongue for a man who doesn't carry a gun," Rawlins observed.

Weber made no reply to that. Hopkins, assuming that Weber was properly cowed, moved forward to get his possessions lying beside the door. "This is a helluva way to treat a man's clothes," he complained. He picked up the bundle, saw the clothes were loose and would be awkward to carry. Then he saw the box of groceries. Grinning, he grabbed the box, upended it so that the groceries spilled into the house, on the doorstoop and onto the ground. He dumped his clothes into the box.

"All right if I take this box?" he sneered to Weber.

"Help yourself," said Weber. He walked forward carelessly and without warning smashed Hopkins in the face with his fist. Hopkins cried out, tried to recover his balance but was unable to do so. He fell heavily, the carton of clothes spilling over him.

For a moment he lay stunned, then he let out a roar and struggled to his feet.

"I'll kill you for that!"

He threw himself at Weber, who sidestepped easily and hit him high on the side of the head. Hopkins gasped in agony, reeled forward and almost fell. He turned, shook his head and moved in on Weber once more.

He feinted with his right, jumped in, swinging with his left. Weber took the blow on his arm and crossed with his right. He caught Hopkins squarely on the jaw and the squatter went down flat on his back. He wasn't unconscious, but the will to fight was gone from him.

"Not bad," conceded Paul Partridge.

Mainwaring, Rawlins' foreman, started to climb down from his horse, but Rawlins stopped him with a quick gesture. "It was a fair fight." He smiled thinly at Weber. "You're in the way here. With Tate squatting it didn't make any difference, but you might get a crazy notion to put a fence around this place and I wouldn't like that. I'd better buy you out. What do you say to a couple of hundred?"

"Alderton's already offered five."

"He's a rich man, I'm not." Rawlins scowled. "I'll meet his offer."

"I turned him down."

"How much do you think you can squeeze out of me? Mind you, I still think Hopkins has a claim to this place. It was deserted and he squatted on it. He can take you into court and cause you all sorts of trouble."

"He could do the same to you."

Rawlins shot a contemptuous glance at Hopkins, who was climbing groggily to his feet. "I can handle him. My last offer, a thousand."

"That's good money," Partridge advised.

"It's a long time since I've had a thousand dollars," Weber said wearily. "I don't think I'd know what to do with that much money."

"This may be the biggest mistake you've ever made in your life," Rawlins said ominously. "I'm laying it out for you so you can see it nice and clear. I don't want you here. Do you want it plainer than that? All right, you know Paul Partridge."

"He knows me," Partridge said wickedly.

"I've done a lot of traveling," Weber said doggedly. "I'd like to stay in one place awhile. And this just happens to be my home."

Rawlins turned his horse and rode back to the road. Hopkins, still wobbly, scrambled for his own mount, leaving his rags of clothing scattered about on the ground. He rode off with Mainwaring.

Partridge remained a moment.

"If you've got a gun, Weber," he said, "it might be a good idea to start wearing it. Rawlins means business."

He gave Weber a half salute and rode off.

Weber slept in the house that night, but shortly after midnight he was awakened by an odd roaring noise. The flickering light that lit up the kitchen of the house told him instantly what was happening.

The barn was an inferno when he got outside, but he was able to save his two horses, who were in the corral attached to the barn.

Rawlins had wasted no time.

9

For years, a face had haunted Lily Barker; a lean, hungry-looking face, with cold blue eyes staring from it. The face had been with her much during those years when she had stayed on at Lobo, when she had forced herself to do things she had not really wanted to do, the building of the dam, the selling of so much of Lobo to finance the dam, the days when she had become a cattle queen.

The face had receded into memory. Jeff Alderton had come into her life. The face of Tom Weber became a blur—and yesterday, eleven years after she had last seen it, she had not remembered it at all. He was older, of course, but he had not changed greatly. He still had the lean face, the cold, bleak eyes of a—a lobo?

Wearing Levi's, boots and a soft white shirt, she rode across Lobo, fording the river once with her legs thrust straight out ahead of her to keep from getting them wet. She was riding aimlessly for the sheer enjoyment of riding—yet she found herself, after some time, turning in from the road toward the shack that had been deserted for so long. She sniffed pungent smoke, saw that the barn was a pile of smoldering ashes.

Then she saw Tom Weber near the house. He was crouched low, scratching the ground with a stick.

He looked over his shoulder as she came up, nodded, but did not speak. Lily dismounted, throwing the reins over her filly's head.

The thing he was scratching in the earth, she saw, was a map of Lobo Valley. She watched him a moment in silence as he traced a rectangular section in the north of the valley.

"No," she said then, "the farms don't run all through. Pete Rawlins' ranch divides the north farms from the south. Like this. . . ." She quickly found a twig, stooped beside him and made the correction on the map. Finished, she touched a tiny square in the north farm section.

"That's your father's place." He did not look at her and she added, "You saw him yesterday?"

"I saw him," Weber replied. "He was sober."

She stared down at him, her eyes clouding. "Don't you know?" she said finally.

He exhaled lightly and half turned his head so he could look at her. "Know what?"

"That your father hasn't taken a drink in eleven years. Since—since the day you went away." She hesitated. "Did you meet Helga?" When he made no reply, she gave him the answer to his unspoken question. "Your father's wife."

Weber got slowly to his feet. "Mrs. Alderton, when I left here eleven years ago, I put my father out of my mind. As far as I was concerned, he was already dead. I met a man yesterday whose name happens to be Weber. You tell me he hasn't had a drink in eleven years and that he is married to a woman named Helga. You know what that means to me? Nothing. Nothing whatsoever."

A gasp was torn from Lily's throat. "You don't mean that!"

"Why," asked Weber, "*why* did you pay the taxes on this place?"

She winced. "Mr. Eads shouldn't have told you." A frown creased her forehead. "Your father and mine were friends. We—we grew up together. I couldn't stand the thought of your old home being sold for taxes."

"I'll pay you back," Weber said, "as soon as I get the money . . ." He paused. "Why is Pete Rawlins bringing gunfighters into the valley?"

"Gunfighters?"

"A man named Paul Partridge. And Tate Hopkins, who squatted here, fancies himself as a gunhand."

The frown on her face grew. "You're sure of that? About Rawlins hiring this man Partridge?"

"He also wrote to a—a man named Fargo."

"Tom Fargo?"

"You've heard the name before?"

She nodded. "I've also heard of Paul Partridge. You say Partridge is here now?"

"He was at the picnic grove yesterday and he stopped here with Rawlins on the way home. Rawlins wants to buy me out. For that matter, so does your husband."

"Why would Jeff want to buy this—this place?"

"*You'd* know that better than I."

She looked at him thoughtfully. "You never liked Jeff, did you?"

"My not liking him isn't going to make the Governor lose much sleep, is it?"

"I'm sorry," she said. She walked to her horse, caught up the reins, then turned to him. There was regret in her eyes. "You're not . . . as I remembered you."

He made no reply and she mounted her horse. Even then she hesitated, but when she looked at him he was again crouched over his map of Lobo Valley, scratching in a landmark.

She put her filly into a furious gallop from a standing start.

Jeff Alderton, wearing whipcord riding breeches, was in the office of Lobo, going over accounts with Fred Case, the foreman. He saw Lily ride into the ranch yard and turn her filly over to one of the hands. He got up and leaving the office, met her going to the house.

"I was looking for you about an hour ago," he said.

"I went for a ride."

"Obviously. I meant to tell you that I don't think you should ride too far—for a while."

She looked at him in surprise. "Why not?"

"I told you yesterday that we're losing a lot of stock. I don't think it would be a good idea for you to run into some of the—the rustlers."

"You're sure there *are* rustlers? Have you talked to Sheriff Moon about it?"

"Lobo can take care of its own," he said shortly.

"Lobo always has taken care of—" Then Lily caught herself. "I'm Lobo, too. But you're forgetting something. You're running for public office, Jeff. It's up to you to set an example. If there are rustlers operating in Lobo, we should tell the Sheriff."

He hesitated, annoyed. "I suppose you're right." Then, "You didn't happen to ride by Tom Weber's?"

"Yes," she said, "I did. Why?"

"I made him a price for his half-section. He seems to want more than it's worth."

"I don't think he plans to sell, no matter what the price."

"He say so?"

"No, I just gathered that."

Jeff's eyes did not meet hers. "I can't make him out. There's something—mysterious—about him." He frowned. "I don't think we ought to have anything to do with him."

Lily regarded her husband sharply.

10

The lamp in the Weber house was burning, but Weber himself was not sleeping in the house. He lay, rolled in a blanket, in a small clump of cottonwoods beside Lobo River, a good hundred yards from the house. He slept, as he always slept, lightly, restlessly.

The clop-clopping of horses' hooves awakened him. He sat up, turned toward his house and saw the shadowy figures of three or four mounted men. They rode up to within a few yards of the Weber house and stopped. One of them dismounted and moved to the house.

Weber picked up his gun, aimed in the general direction of the house and pulled the trigger. He fired two quick shots, made a complete turn and crouched low, sped off a distance of a dozen feet. Halting, he fired twice more at the house.

The moon was almost full; it lighted up the clearing around the house and Weber could see the horsemen scattering. One or two fired wildly in Weber's general direction, but none had the stomach to try to charge and locate a man who might be hidden anywhere within a hundred yards and might drill them as they came up blindly.

Each took off from the house in a different direction, but they assembled westward of the house and rode off in a clump. Weber went cautiously toward the house, searched and listened carefully for a few moments, then went to the corral and saddled his own mount.

He was off within five minutes after the marauders had gone, but they were out of sight. He suspected, however, that they would head in a westerly direction and after a few minutes when he reached a clear open spot, he got down from his horse and searched the ground. He found the trail easily enough, made out that there were four horses and, remounting his horse, continued on.

He rode cautiously, knowing that he was in the territory of the enemy. He made no attempt to catch up with the raiders, and when he finally reached a low knoll and looked down upon the headquarters of the Rawlins ranch, he guessed that he was at least ten minutes behind the men he was following.

In the bright moonlight he could make out the Rawlins

spread, a sprawling one-story ranch house, cookhouse nearby, a large bunkhouse and several sheds and barns to which there were attached a pair of corrals. The place was completely dark, however, which surprised Weber.

The four raiders could scarcely have unsaddled their horses and turned in to the bunkhouse. After the abortive raid from which they had just returned, it was only natural that they have coffee, smoke a cigarette or two and rehash the failure of their mission—and perhaps make plans anew for another.

The fact that there was no light on the ranch could, of course, mean that the raid upon Weber's place had been an unofficial one, without the sanction of Rawlins himself. That might account for the quiet return of the four men.

Sitting his horse, Weber watched the buildings below for several moments, then shaking his head, he turned his horse and started back for his own place.

He had traveled perhaps two miles when the head of his mount suddenly came up. Weber, with an instinct for such things, dismounted quickly and stepping forward caught the nose of the horse and pressed together the nostrils, a deterrent to neighing. He led the animal to one side into a small clump of cottonwoods and stopped with his hand on the nose of the horse.

After a moment, his ears made out the clop-clopping of horses' hooves. He nodded grimly. The raiders had not returned immediately to their home base as Weber had assumed. They had left his place, headed straight west, then circled away, to ride in another direction. They were only now returning.

There were four, all right, and as they passed within yards of Weber, he made out two of them. Paul Partridge and Tate Hopkins. He had never seen the others.

11

Charles Weber, who had once owned a half million acres of land and horses and cattle running into the thousands, was currying down one of the two horses in his barn when Leo Blatnik, his brother-in-law, came into the barn.

Blatnik had a forty-acre farm a half mile from Weber's and he had walked over from his place.

"Morning, Charlie," he greeted Weber.

Weber nodded soberly. "Hello, Leo."

"Your wheat looks good. Be ready for cutting in a week."

"If I still have wheat in a week."

"You, too? That's why I came over. My fence was cut last night." Blatnik frowned and shook his head. "And somebody took a shot at the house."

"It had to come to that, sooner or later."

"I think it is time to go to the Sheriff."

"You think that'll do any good? Moon is Mike Denver's man. And Mike Denver is Pete Rawlins' brother-in-law."

"You are sure that it is Rawlins who is making this trouble for us?"

"Who else?"

"I don't know, Charlie. I guess it *has* to be Rawlins. But why? He has plenty of land——"

"No man ever has enough land."

Blatnik seated himself on a nearby upended keg and watched Weber finish with the horse. Weber was aware that something else was on Blatnik's mind and he guessed what it was.

He said finally, "You've heard that my son has returned."

"Yes, Charlie."

"He does not intend to stay. He has never forgiven me."

"He was the stranger at the barbecue yesterday?"

"Yes."

"What sort of a man has he become?"

"I don't know, Leo. I didn't talk to him long enough." Weber was silent a moment. "He is a bitter man—dangerous. . . ."

"Dangerous?"

"He was completely self-sufficient even as a boy. I never seemed to be able to talk to him. Although"—Weber's brow furrowed—"I wasn't in condition very often to talk to him. I guess his life has not been a happy one."

"And yours, Charlie?"

"Helga is a good woman," Weber said. "I think she is happy."

Leo Blatnik's eyes went beyond Weber through the barn door to where Helga was coming from the house to the barn. He waited until she appeared in the doorway, then he said, "We were just talking about Charlie's son, Helga."

Helga Weber was forty-three, a strong woman with tawny blonde hair and a perfectly smooth skin. She had been married once before, her husband dying within a year of their marriage, and after that she had remained unmarried until nine years ago when she had, after her brother's insistence that he preferred to live by himself, gone to share her lot with Charlie Weber, a man making a tremendous effort to rehabilitate himself.

Weber had told her of his former life; he kept nothing from Helga and did not spare himself. If anything, he gave himself the worst of it. Helga, in marrying him, had also come into the union with no reservations. What had been Charles Weber's would be hers. For years she had looked at her husband, in odd moments, when he was wrapped in thought, his eyes looking sightlessly at a wall, or object, or just the distance. She knew that he wondered about the son whom he had treated so badly, wondered if he would ever see him again, and perhaps make amends.

The night before he had told her of seeing his son after eleven years, had told her the words that had been exchanged between them. He had not told her of his own feelings after the bitter interview. That Helga sensed.

She said now, "I want to meet him. Charles, do you think he would come here if you asked him?"

"No, he would not."

"What if I asked him?"

A cloud flitted across his face. He shook his head. "I would prefer that you did not do that, Helga."

"Because you think he would—insult me?"

"Helga," Weber said slowly, "Leo, you are both trying to be kind, to do the right thing. But there is nothing right between my son and me. It was never right. I—I know that now."

He turned and walked out of the barn, leaving his wife and her brother to exchange worried looks.

12

Those who knew of the arrangements in the household of Lobo knew that Lily Alderton and her husband had separate rooms. Early in the marriage Jeff Alderton had told Lily, "I'm up half the night with business and paperwork. I don't think it is fair that I should keep you awake, or wake you every night when I come to bed. I'll move into the adjoining room."

On this morning, Alderton was awake and dressed at five o'clock. Shortly before six o'clock Mike Denver pulled up in a buckboard and came into the house. He joined Alderton for a second breakfast and they discussed some confidential matters that did not pertain at all to Alderton's forthcoming trip.

They were still at it when Lily entered the room. She was surprised to find Denver with her husband.

"You must have gotten up before daylight," she said, then could not resist adding with a touch of tartness, "or you're still up from last night."

Denver chuckled expansively. "Me, I live a clean life. I go to bed early and get up early."

"Mike's driving me to town," Alderton said coolly. "Some matters we have to talk about before I take the train."

"You're going on a trip?" Lily asked, surprised.

"Didn't I tell you? I'm aking the nine-thirty to the capitol. I'll be gone three days."

"Better count on four," suggested Denver. "Some of the boys may want you to give a little talk before the businessmen's clubs."

"I'll see how it goes." Alderton regarded Denver thoughtfully. "I still can't understand why you won't come along on the trip."

"No need to, Jeff. The boys know I'm behind you, but I think it's best they get the idea that I'm quite a ways behind you. They wouldn't like to have it made too plain that I was breathing down your neck."

"All right, you know best about these things, Mike." Alderton got up from the table. "We might as well start for town."

He nodded to Lily and left the dining room to get his bags that he had already packed. Lily waited until Alderton was out of the room, then said, "You're sure he'll make it?"

"Money'll buy anything, Lily," chuckled Denver.

"And Jeff has the money to buy the governor's mansion!"

"Whoa now, Lily girl," exclaimed Denver. "You're putting that kinda blunt——"

"*You* said it, Mike—that money could buy *anything*."

"It can, in a way, but you don't exactly *buy* the governor's job. It's not that raw. You do favors for people, spend a little money here, a little there. Of course, some of it might stick to politicians' hands, but they'd be the first to holler that they weren't bought. And you couldn't prove it."

"What if it turns out that you *can't* buy everything?"

"Eh?"

"I mean, what if Jeff doesn't win?"

"No chance of that," declared Denver promptly.

"But just suppose you've overestimated things, that you've made a mistake somewhere. Like right here in Lobo Valley——"

"Mistake?" growled Denver. "I've made no mistake in Lobo."

"Weren't you counting on the votes of the farmers?"

"No," snapped Denver, becoming angry, "I never counted on a single sodbuster. I made my plans without them. I don't give a damn if we don't get one sodbuster vote. We'll win without them. . . ."

Alderton returned carrying two bags. He shot a quick look from Denver to Lily. "You two have words?"

Denver forced a quick laugh. "Uh-uh, not us, Jeff. Lily was just a little worried that maybe you'd have a tough time winning the election. I assured her that there wasn't anything to it."

"Jeff," said Lily, "I'd like to talk to you a moment."

"Haven't got time. Mike and I have a lot of things to cover."

"There are matters here that need discussing."

"Take them up with Case." Alderton stepped to Lily, gave her a quick peck on the cheek and turned back to Denver. "All right, Mike."

" 'Mornin', Mrs. Alderton," said Denver. He headed for the door, not volunteering to take one of Alderton's bags.

They left the house and Lily, more angry than she wanted to admit to herself, stepped to the window and watched them climb into the buckboard and drive off.

She turned back to the table to have her breakfast, but found that she could not eat. She left the house and went to the ranch office where Fred Case was working on the tally books.

"Jeff tells me we're losing stock," she said, coming directly to the point.

Fred Case was in his early sixties. He had been Sam Barker's foreman, but his duties had become less and less since Jeff Alderton had taken over. He was still foreman in name, but it was Alderton who issued the orders.

He said now, "Yes, Miss Lily, we've lost some head."

"How many?"

43

Case's forehead creased worriedly. "I don't rightly know. Mister Jeff——"

"How many?"

The sharpness of her voice caused him to wince. "Close to a thousand head."

Lily exclaimed, "But that's serious!"

"Yes, Miss Lily."

"What are we doing about it?"

"Miss Lily," the foreman said slowly, "I don't rightly know. Mister Jeff has been pretty busy with the politickin' lately and I"—He hesitated a moment, then went on—"I'm not allowed to make such decisions."

Lily stepped to a wall map of Lobo Valley, on which Lobo was indicated in red and the former Alderton ranch in yellow. "From which range are we losing the stock, Fred?"

Case got up and, crossing to the map, promptly put his finger on the west and north range, the area adjoining the Rawlins land. "Here."

"How many men do we have on our payroll?"

"It varies. Cowboys come and go all the time. Roughly sixty."

"That's a pretty full crew, isn't it?"

"We used to run the old Lobo with less'n thirty. 'Course, some of the men are over in Mister Jeff's old range——"

"How many? What percentage?"

The frown, momentarily erased from Case's features, returned. "That's a little hard to say, Miss Lily." Then Case exclaimed angrily, "No, it ain't. Most sixty per cent of our boys are over that way. Mister Jeff shifted ten men over there only yesterday."

"Why would he do that when we're losing stock up here?"

"I can't answer that. I got my suspicions . . ."

"Suspicions?"

Fred Case gulped. "I guess I've said more'n I should."

"You've said just enough that I think you should say more."

Case drew a deep breath and exhaled heavily. "I've been on Lobo a long time, Miss Lily. I was the first man who ever drew pay from Sam Barker. I've done my job the best I could, the best I knew how; but you're married now, and I'm the last man in the world to make trouble between husband and wife . . ."

He returned to the desk and seated himself heavily before the tally books, his face averted from Lily's probing eyes. Lily looked at him a long moment, then said gently, "Thanks,

Fred, but don't you see, Lobo is still mine. It was mine before—before I married and it's still mine. What you were about to say is that Jeff shifted the men over to the Alderton part of the ranch because he wanted to protect that area first. . . ."

Case made no reply and after a moment, Lily left the ranch office.

Outside, she crossed to the bunkhouse. A cowboy came out as she approached.

"Will you saddle my bay filly, please?" Lily asked.

The cowboy bobbed his head and ran to the corrals. Lily returned to the house and changed to her riding outfit.

13

The team of matched blacks, which were the best harness horses in Lobo Valley, had cost Mike Denver eight hundred dollars. He carried a whip but it was seldom necessary to use it for the blacks liked nothing better than a good run every day. They had already trotted the sixteen miles from Barkerville out to Lobo headquarters, but they had had a half hour rest at Lobo and they would make the return trip to Barkerville in an easy two hours, walking part of the way, trotting the rest.

For an hour after leaving Lobo, Denver and Jeff Alderton talked about Alderton's trip. Denver gave the names of men Alderton was to see, told who they were, what each could do for Alderton. Alderton had a good memory for names, but Denver's acquaintanceship was so extensive that Alderton found it necessary to make notes.

They were more than halfway to Barkerville when Denver suddenly said, "By the way, I'll need another twenty thousand."

Alderton exclaimed, "I just gave you twenty thousand two weeks ago——"

"That's why you're making this trip now. It costs money to swing the right people behind you."

"It's cost me a hundred and twenty thousand already."

"It's going to run you more than that. The boys've come high. They didn't want you."

"I sometimes wish I hadn't gone into it."

45

"You're in too deep to back out."

Alderton said bitterly, "You told me thirty, forty thousand at the most."

Denver shrugged. "I didn't know old Samuelson was going to try for another term. He's had four years to entrench himself. But don't worry, we're knocking the props out from under him. Only it's cost a lot more money than I'd counted on." Denver cleared his throat. "You're going to have to let Pete take another five hundred head. . . ."

Alderton was aghast. "I can't, Mike. I've already had to tell my wife that we're losing stock. She isn't blind and even if she didn't see the shortage, one of the hands would tell her. Fred Case, probably."

"You've got to take that chance, Jeff," Denver said earnestly. "Pete's carrying a big load and he's got to move against those blasted farmers. We need the rancher-squatter fight. How would it look to the voters over in the western part of the state, if it got out that two-thirds of the voters in Lobo Valley were against the gubernatorial candidate just on general principles? A little rancher-squatter fight, that's fine. People can understand that."

"It's a high price to pay. That beef runs about forty dollars a head. Forty thousand in addition to the money I've given you . . ." Alderton groaned.

"It's Lobo money," Denver said quietly.

"What?"

"You were broke when you married Lily Barker," Denver said.

"That's not true!"

"You were land poor," Denver said patiently. "Give me credit for that much, Jeff. It's my business. I have to know how much a man is worth. Otherwise, how would I know how much pressure he can stand? How much it takes to buy him."

"Damn it, Denver," snapped Alderton, "you've got a crude way of putting things."

"I never was one for the spit and polish. You've been taking money from your wife and Rawlins has been taking Lobo stock—not Alderton. You've been careful about that. If worse comes to worst, you're in pretty fair shape. It's your wife who's paid the way. All right, what if your wife doesn't like it? What if she decides you're too expensive a husband?"

"No chance of that," growled Alderton.

"No? What about this Weber lad who's come back? Seems

to me I heard a long time ago that they were pretty thick in the old days."

"When they were children!" snapped Alderton.

"There's none of it hanging over?"

"How could there be? The man's an utter, complete failure. A hobo. No woman in her right senses could see anything in him."

"Women make some strange choices of husbands," Denver said cryptically.

Alderton gave him a quick, sideward glance, but Denver was suddenly interested in the blacks. Barkerville was in sight and he flicked the whip gently over the rumps of the trotting animals. They broke into a gallop.

In Barkerville, Lily tied her horse to the hitchrail in front of the courthouse and went through the building to the rear, where Sheriff Moon's offices were located.

Moon was a heavy-set cherubic-looking man of about forty-five. His eyes were a washed-out blue and his lids were habitually slitted, so that when he was seated and in repose people frequently thought he was asleep.

He was seated in a big armchair, relaxed, when Lily entered the office. A deputy sat on the other side of the desk reading a dime novel.

The slits of Moon's eyes opened a fraction. "Howdy, Mrs. Alderton," he said.

"I came to make a complaint," Lily said bluntly.

"That so?"

The deputy got up and, coming around the desk, pulled up a chair. "Won't you sit?"

Lily ignored the chair. "Sheriff," she said sharply, "are you aware that rustlers have been operating on our ranch?"

"Why, no, ma'am," Moon said mildly, then: "Rustlers?"

"We've lost a thousand head of stock in the last two weeks."

"Well, now, ain't that somethin'." Moon's tone was still casual, sleepy almost, and Lily became angry.

"That doesn't seem to interest you!"

"Oh, sure, ma'am, I'm interested, all right, but this is the first I've heard of it. Rustlers, mmm. Guess I'll have to talk to Mr. Alderton about that."

"My husband's gone out of town for a few days."

"All right, when he gets back——"

"When he gets back isn't soon enough. I want something done about it *now!*"

Moon's eyes closed for a moment, then opened and a little sigh escaped his lips. "I only got two deputies, Mrs. Alderton. On'y so much a man can do."

"It doesn't seem to me that either you or this deputy seem to be doing very much right now."

"Now, Mrs. Alderton," Moon chided gently, "we got lots of things to do all the time. Paperwork. Why, I got a letter in the mail on'y yesterday from the Sheriff of Tuloca County in Arizona, asking me to look for a man he thinks held up the bank there, might be over here. And a couple of weeks ago we had another letter from——"

"Sheriff Moon," Lily said angrily, "I'm not interested in your other matters. I'm interested in what's happening on my ranch *now*. We've lost a thousand head of cattle, and I don't want to lose any more. I came here to ask your help. If I don't get it, I'll have to take care of the matter myself." Then she added, "As we used to do on Lobo."

"You got a right to take care of your own business, Mrs. Alderton," Sheriff Moon said, "long as you don't do anything illegal."

Lily opened her mouth to blast him, then changed her mind. Abruptly, she turned away and stormed out of the Sheriff's office. She went through the courthouse again, crossed the street and headed for Marshall Eads' bank.

She found the banker shaking hands with Leo Blatnik, a farmer Lily had met a number of times.

"Lily," Eads exclaimed, "you're lookin' prettier'n I ever saw you. Got a new color in your cheeks."

"Sheriff Moon just gave me that," said Lily.

"Oh?" The banker opened the gate of his enclosure. "Come in and tell me about it."

She entered the enclosure and seated herself beside Eads' desk. "It's rustlers!" she exclaimed. "I tried to talk to the Sheriff about it, but he isn't interested. Said he'd talk about it to Jeff when Jeff got back. . . ."

"Yeah, that's right. I saw Jeff at the depot, gettin' on the train." Eads gave her a sharp look, quickly dropping his eyes again. "Things all right between you and Jeff?"

"What makes you think they aren't?"

"Oh, I wasn't thinkin' anythin' like that. Just askin'. I know he's away a lot lately. But that's politickin'. I guess Jeff wants to be governor real bad. Mmm . . ." He leaned back in his swivel chair and regarded her thoughtfully.

"Mr. Eads," Lily said, "I want to have a heart-to-heart talk with you."

"Sure thing, Lily, but you can't have a heart-to-heart talk with me if you begin by calling me Mister. It's always been Uncle Marsh . . ."

"Of course—Uncle!"

"That's better. Now tell me again—things are all right between you and Jeff?"

She bit her lower lip. "As you said, Jeff is busy. He *wants* to be governor." She hesitated. "Uncle Marsh, can you give me my bank balance as of this moment?"

"Yes," he said, "I can do that." Yet he made no move to rise from his chair.

She looked at him, puzzled. "I'd like it now."

"Of course. You mean your regular joint account, don't you?"

"It's the only account I have." A little shiver suddenly ran through her. "You mean Jeff has an account of *his* own?"

"Now, Lily, I didn't say that. I ain't allowed to say what people have accounts here."

"Uncle Marsh," Lily said earnestly, "I want to know—the worst. I think it's time I did. I've let things run along too carelessly for quite a while."

"Lily, I've been in Lobo a long time. I came here twenty-some years ago with a wagonload of groceries an'———"

"Please!" interrupted Lily.

"I'll give it to you. You've got about two thousand dollars in the joint account."

"That's impossible!"

"Uh-uh, I looked at it just about an hour ago—when Jeff stopped in to draw out some money. The account's a joint one, either you or Jeff can write checks and draw out money. Jeff's been spending a lot of money lately. I guess maybe he figured he ought to have a separate account—to keep a straighter record of what this politics business is costing him. He drew money out of the joint account———"

"How much? How much has he in his *own* account?"

"Twenty-one thousand dollars."

Lily stared at the banker. "The last beef shipment brought in over a hundred and fifty thousand. Our payroll and operating expenses couldn't have been more than one-third of that in the past four months———"

"Like I said, politickin' costs money, Lily."

The flush that had been on Lily's cheeks when she entered the bank was now deeper. "What is the salary of a governor?"

"In this state, four thousand a year. . . ."

"And Jeff has spent what? Twenty-five—fifty thousand?"

"More than that."

"That's ridiculous. To get a four thousand dollar a year job . . . !"

"Bein' governor ain't just a four thousand dollar job, Lily. The governor's the biggest man in the state. There's a lot of prestige to the job."

Lily said bitterly, "Jeff's neglected the ranch. We've lost a thousand head of cattle to rustlers in the past few weeks——"

"Rustlers? I thought rustling went out of style some years ago."

"It's back. The latest thing. Along with a lot of other things." Lily drew a deep breath. "Uncle Marsh, how does one go about hiring gunfighters?"

Eads blinked. "Now, wait a minute, Lily. You're not thinkin'——"

"Pete Rawlins has been bringing in gunfighters," she said tartly. "He's brought in a man named Paul Partridge, some others probably."

"You've been hearing some things, I can see."

"I have. I've also heard the name of a gunfighter, someone who's supposed to be as good as Paul Partridge. A man named Tom Fargo. I want to send for him."

"You want to hire Tom Fargo, Lily?"

"If possible. If I knew where to reach him, I'd write him a letter. Make him an offer that he couldn't refuse. . . ."

Eads began to drum on the top of his desk with his fingers. A frown twisted his features.

"Gunfighters are a little out of my line, Lily," he finally said. "But——"

She looked at him eagerly. "Yes?"

"It just happens that I *have* heard of this Tom Fargo. I think I even know where to reach him . . ."

"Then tell me, Uncle Marsh! I want to write to him right away."

"You're sure? You've thought it over?"

"I have. My mind's made up."

"Don't you think it'd be better to wait until Jeff gets back, talk it over with him?"

"No!" Her chin came up. "Lobo is mine, Uncle Marsh. I'm going to fight for it. Give me this gunfighter's address."

Eads was sorely tempted, but resisted the inclination to confide in her. "It escapes my mind right now. But I've got some papers at home—newspapers. Saw this Fargo mentioned in one of them. I'll look through them. Tell you what,

50

write the letter and give it to me. I'll address it and mail it——"

"That'll just take more time. I want to get off a letter today."

"It'll go today. Mmm, I'm almost certain that Fargo doesn't live too far from Barkerville. He'll get the letter soon enough. Here . . ." Eads opened a drawer and took out some stationery. "Write your letter now."

14

Weber, his face smudged from soot and charred wood, was working over the ruins of the burned-out barn when Lily Alderton rode up to his house and dismounted.

"You're going to rebuild?" she asked.

"If I decide to stay."

"But you *are* staying?"

"I haven't made up my mind yet. Somebody's trying to drive me out of Lobo."

"You're not going, though?"

"I may not have to. I may get bushwhacked instead. They made a try last night."

She showed alarm. "Why should they be after you? You haven't done anything to anyone."

"I've come back. They want this place and I've refused to sell it."

"Rawlins?"

"Or someone else."

"Please," Lily said worriedly. "Let's not quarrel again."

"I'm not trying to quarrel," Weber said patiently. "Pete Rawlins has tried to buy this place from me and so has your husband. I don't know if there's a connection——"

"There isn't, believe me there isn't. Lobo has lost a thousand head of steers in the past two weeks. I'm almost certain that they went to the Rawlins place. What you said about—about Rawlins getting in gunfighters bears me out. There's no connection between Jeff and Rawlins, I can assure you of that."

"Rawlins is Denver's brother-in-law and Jeff is being managed by Denver."

"You don't think highly of Mike Denver?"

"Does anyone?"

She winced. "You remember him as the saloonkeeper of the old days. He was that, and still is, for that matter. But he's an important man. He's made a fortune out of real estate, is deeply in politics——"

"He's still a saloonkeeper."

"All right, Tom," conceded Lily. "To tell you the truth, I'm not overly fond of him myself. But I don't think he's in league with his brother-in-law. Cattle rustling is not his style—not these days. It fits Rawlins, however, and what you've told me about his bringing in gunfighters indicates that. Well, I've decided that two can play at that game and I—*I've* sent for a gunfighter."

He stared at her.

"The man we talked about yesterday. Tom Fargo. I've written to him."

"You've written to Tom Fargo?" exclaimed Weber. "Where—where did you write him?"

"Mr. Eads has his address. He's mailing the letter to him. He said he wasn't too far from here and I ought to get a reply from him in a few days."

"Unless he's already hired himself out to Rawlins."

"He may switch even then. I—I made him a very good offer. In the meantime"—She paused—"the real reason I stopped by is—I want to offer you a job."

He looked at her steadily. "Doing what?"

"Jeff's away a lot and he's going to be gone a great deal from now on. Fred Case is old. I—I thought perhaps you'd be interested in being foreman of Lobo?"

"You're offering me this job? Not Jeff?"

"I haven't discussed it with him, no. But I don't think he'd object. Why should he?"

"Jeff and I weren't exactly friends in the old days."

"That's a long time ago. He doesn't hold grudges. We need a foreman and . . ." Her voice failed and then she blurted out, "I want you to take the job!"

"You know nothing about me. I've never run a ranch before—not one as big as Lobo. I can't handle the job."

"You'll work with Fred. Fred's old, but he knows ranching—and he knows Lobo. You'll work well together. I *know* you will."

He shook his head. "No."

"But why? You're not doing anything here. You said you didn't even know if you'd stay. You said that you had no money—not enough to pay the back taxes." She winced as she threw that in.

"It's not a matter of money."

"I shouldn't have said that, Tom. I'm sorry."

"If I live, I'll pay you the money."

"If you live?"

"I said somebody's trying to bushwhack me. I can't keep my eyes open every minute of the day and night. Sooner or later, they'll get me."

"You'd be safe on Lobo. There are never less than twenty men at the home ranch."

"It's not a matter of sleeping. They'll hardly get me while I'm sleeping. I know enough for that. It's when I move around. The bullet may come from behind a rock, a tree, any house or shack that I pass. I might get it in Barkerville."

Lily looked at him in disappointment, then a thought occurred to her and her eyes lit up. "You said Rawlins—*they* wanted this ranch. They're after you because of it. All right, suppose you *didn't* own the ranch? They wouldn't want to kill you then."

"I don't figure on being forced to sell."

"Sell to *me!* I'll give you whatever you ask. Then you can come to work for me."

"But I've already refused to sell to your husband——"

"Lobo doesn't belong to my husband. It's mine. We made an agreement before we were married. His ranch was to remain in his name and mine in mine. He wanted it that way. So people couldn't say he was marrying me for Lobo."

Weber shook his head. "I'm sorry, Mrs. Alderton. . . ."

"Don't call me Mrs. Alderton!" The violence of her outburst shook even Lily. Her hand flew to her mouth and she inhaled sharply.

Weber said stiffly, "Your name's Alderton, isn't it?"

"Of course, but . . ." she floundered. "We've known each other for so—so long. You used to call me Lily."

"That was a long time ago, like you said."

She looked at him for a long moment, saw the bleakness in his eyes, the bitter lines in his face and knew that she could not fight him; it was too long, too late. The years had been too hard on him.

She turned back to her horse, mounted and as she turned the animal she was aware that he was following her.

He said, "I think you meant well, but I've got to play out the game. I'm sorry—Lily."

She had ridden a dozen feet before the name "Lily" penetrated. She swiveled in the saddle then, looked back. But he had already turned away.

She rode on, back to Lobo.

15

Pete Rawlins entered the real estate office of Mike Denver and, ignoring the clerk who sat in an outer room, pushed open a door that led into Denver's well-furnished private office. He found Denver standing before a large wall map of Lobo Valley.

Denver looked over his shoulder. "Hello, Pete," he said carelessly.

Rawlins grinned wolfishly. "What dirty job are you scheming out now?"

Denver regarded his brother-in-law impassively. "How many Lobo cattle have you run off?"

"Just what you told me, five hundred."

"Five hundred plus what?"

Rawlins remained unabashed. "Oh, maybe a few more."

"A few hundred more?"

"If you say so."

"Pete," said Denver patiently, "don't try any petty larceny on me, will you? The stakes are big enough for both of us."

"All right, Mike," Rawlins agreed cheerfully. "The count was eight hundred and fifty."

"Where've you got them?"

"In a couple of box canyons on the north end. It's going to take some time to fix the brands and age them a little. I need a few more good men."

"I thought you'd sent for them?"

"I have. I expect a couple in any day." He frowned. "I haven't heard from one I've been counting on—Tom Fargo."

"The gunfighter?"

"The best!"

"Write him again. Offer him more money. I don't like the way things are going. The farmers are getting more difficult all the time. That damn Blatnik's stirred them up."

"You want me to take care of him?"

Denver hesitated. "I don't know if we're ready for that yet. It wouldn't hurt to scare him a little, though."

54

"Might do that right now. He's in town."

Denver nodded. "I had a talk with Alderton this morning. You can take five hundred more Lobo steers."

"Five hundred, plus?"

Denver glanced at the wall map. "Alderton's going to be away for four days." He bobbed his head. "Make it a thousand head, Pete."

Rawlins chuckled. "Just how far do you figure on going, Mike? What's your goal?"

Denver gave his brother-in-law a cold look, then suddenly swept his hand over the entire map. Rawlins whistled. "The whole business, eh?"

"An empire, Pete!"

Weber entered the bank and found Marshall Eads busy with a prospective borrower, but the banker saw him, excused himself and came over to the rail.

"I understand you've got a letter for Tom Fargo," Weber said.

Eads shot a quick look over his shoulder and said in a low tone, "She told you?"

"Yes."

"I didn't tell her you were Tom Fargo."

"Neither did I. But I'd like to have the letter."

Eads frowned. "I tore it up, Tom."

"Give me the letter!"

Eads groaned, hesitated, then took a folded envelope from his pocket. "Here—read it, but don't go away. I want to talk to you."

Weber tore open the letter as Eads went back to the bank customer.

Weber read:

Dear Mr. Fargo:—
I understand you are the best gunfighter in the country. I can use your services and even if you have already taken another job, I will double what you are now getting. Do not take time to write me, but come at once, as your services are urgently needed.
                    Sincerely yours,
                    Lily Barker Alderton
                    Owner of Lobo Ranch
                    Barkerville

Weber refolded the letter, put it back in the envelope and stowed it away in his pocket. Marshall Eads, standing up to hasten the departure of the customer, shot a glance at him.

"Tom—wait!"

"I'll see you later," Weber replied.

Eads started toward him, but Weber walked quickly out of the bank. Outside, he looked up and down the street. A sign across the street caught his eye.

The Lobo

Weber hesitated, then crossed the street.

16

The building housing The Lobo was one of the oldest in Barkerville, also one of the smallest. It was Mike Denver's original saloon. The place was not more than twenty feet wide and some thirty feet deep. A bar ran down the length of one side and was attended by three bartenders, one of whom managed The Lobo for Mike Denver.

One change had been made in the interior. A balcony had been added at the rear of the room, with a narrow flight of stairs leading up to it. On this balcony was a scuffed, ancient desk that was Mike Denver's office when he felt like spending some time at The Lobo.

There were larger saloons in Barkerville, but none did as much business as The Lobo.

Although it was midmorning when Weber entered, there was scarcely room at the bar and several card games were in progress at the tables that filled up the rest of the room.

Two men made room for him at the bar and as he stepped into the opening a bartender looked at him inquiringly.

"Beer," Weber said.

At Weber's right was a mild-looking, tawny-skinned man of about forty-five, Leo Blatnik. Blatnik gave him a covert look or two, hesitated, then as Weber finished his glass of beer, he said in a slightly accented voice, "Can I buy you another beer, Mr. Weber?"

"Why?"

Blatnik was discomfited by Weber's bluntness. "We are related by marriage, I believe. My name is Leo Blatnik and my sister is your father's wife."

"In that case," Weber said, "get my father to drink with you."

Blatnik winced as if struck by Weber's fist. "You are wrong about your father. He does not drink."

"In his time he drank enough to pickle a herd of Longhorns."

"But he has not taken a drink in ten years now."

"He quit drinking—after he drank away everything he ever owned."

"You are a hard man, Mr. Weber . . ."

Weber started to leave the bar, then stopped. During his altercation with Blatnik, two men had entered the saloon and were sizing up the line along the bar. Paul Partridge and Tate Hopkins. Hopkins said something to Partridge out of the side of his mouth and the two men advanced.

Weber expected them to accost him but they ignored him and faced Leo Blatnik.

Paul Partridge took the aggressive. "Your name's Blabnik, isn't it?"

"Blatnik."

"All right, Blatnik. You've been sounding off about the cattlemen, they tell me. Claim we been cutting your wire."

"You have," declared Blatnik. "Two times this week."

"And *you* haven't been doing anything? Then how come we find a Rawlins steer butchered near your place and the hide in your woodshed?"

"If you find a hide in my woodshed you put it there," cried Blatnik.

"You calling me a liar, Bohunk?"

Blatnik realized suddenly that he had been led into a trap and tried to extricate himself. "I do not want any trouble."

"You got trouble, Mister," snapped Tate Hawkins. "Big trouble."

Partridge struck Blatnik in the face with the back of his open hand. "Nobody calls me a liar." He rocked Blatnik's face again. Blatnik cried out and struck blindly at the gunfighter. Partridge took the blow on his raised forearm, grunted and stepped back.

"Well, well!" he rasped. "The little man wants to fight."

He chuckled wickedly, stepped foreward suddenly and struck Blatnik a savage blow in the face. Blatnik staggered back against the bar and recoiled from it, into the flailing fist of Partridge. Blood spurted from his nose and mouth as he dropped to the floor. He landed on his knees, fell forward, but braced himself upon the palms of his hands. In that posi-

57

tion he shook his head to clear away the haze, then raised his face.

It met the boot of Tate Hopkins.

Blatnik's head hit the floor with a thud.

Partridge looked down at Blatnik, then stepped over him.

"Whiskey," he said to the bartender.

He was pouring out a glassful when a sudden hush fell upon the crowd at the bar. Partridge, starting to raise the whiskey to his mouth, looked toward the door:

Sheriff Moon was coming forward. Partridge tossed off his whiskey, made a signal to Hopkins and faced the Sheriff.

The Sheriff looked down at Blatnik, who was trying to roll over on his stomach so he could raise himself to his knees and then to his feet.

"What happened?"

Partridge shrugged. "Man called me a liar."

The Sheriff looked about seeking confirmation. Hopkins said promptly, "That's right, Sheriff. He called Paul a liar, and then he hit him."

Blatnik made it to his stomach and putting his hands under him, got to his knees. "That's a lie, Sheriff——"

"See?" exclaimed Partridge. "He's calling me a liar again."

"He beat me," cried Blatnik. "He slapped me and then he hit me with his fist." He got to his feet, swayed and reeled against Weber, who moved away so that Blatnik almost fell.

The Sheriff rubbed his chin with the back of his fist. "Man can't hold his liquor shouldn't drink. You, Blatnik, I've had complaints about your drinking——"

"Me?" cried Blatnik, aghast. "I—I do not drink."

"You're drunk now," said the Sheriff.

"I am not drunk. I have on'y two beers. That is all I drink—beer."

"With a whiskey chaser," grinned Partridge. "Then you go around trying to beat up people. You ask me, Sheriff, you oughtta throw him in jail until he sobers up."

"Sheriff Moon!" cried Leo Blatnik. "This is a game you are playing. You know I do not look for trouble. I am a peaceful man——"

"That's not what I hear," said the Sheriff. "You've been stirring up your sodbuster friends——"

"That's right, Sheriff," said Tate Hopkins, "and that ain't all. They been rustlin' our cattle, too."

"That's a lie!" screamed Blatnik.

"Now he's calling *me* a liar," grunted Hopkins.

Weber said suddenly, "Well, you *are* a liar, aren't you?"

58

The eyes of Hopkins, Partridge and the Sheriff went to Weber.

"Who're you?" the Sheriff asked truculently.

"My name's Weber, Tom Weber."

Sheriff Moon's eyes narrowed. "I've heard of you. You're Charlie Weber's son. Just returned to Lobo——"

"From ridin' the rods, Sheriff," interposed Paul Partridge. "A bum."

"He's as bad as Blatnik," declared Tate Hopkins. "I was sound asleep night two-three nights ago when he broke in on me and knocked me around. Yesterday, he lit into me again for no reason at all——"

Weber's fist smashed into Hopkin's face. "*That's* for no reason!"

Sheriff Moon whipped out his Frontier Model. "All right, Weber, you've done it! You're under arrest."

"That's the spirit, Sheriff," chortled Paul Partridge. "Ain't nobody can say you don't do your duty. Man makes trouble, he oughtta be locked up." He grinned. "You takin' the Bohunk along, too?"

The Sheriff's face showed perplexity. "I didn't *see* him attack you."

"But I'm tellin' you he did. That's good enough, ain't it?"

"If you'll sign a complaint . . ."

"Oh, sure, I'll do that, all right." Paul Partridge smirked. "I'm a man that believes in the law all the way."

Ten minutes later the cell door was locked on Tom Weber and Leo Blatnik and the two men looked at one another.

"I can't believe it," Blatnik whispered. "*I* am the innocent party, yet *I* find myself in jail."

"You've got company," Weber said.

"But this cannot happen," Blatnik went on. "It is impossible. The Sheriff is supposed to be on the side of the right and I—I *know* I was right. That Partridge man is a bad man."

"He's a killer. If you'd been wearing a gun, he'd have killed you. He might even kill you without your wearing a gun. You're better off in here."

"But you, Mr. Weber, *you* shouldn't be here. You only tried to help me. . . ."

"No," said Weber quickly. "I was fighting my own fight. Hopkins squatted on my land, took over my house. I threw him out and night before last he set fire to my barn. I hit him for *that*."

59

"Something is happening. I do not know exactly what, but I have got a strange feeling. Something evil and terrible is going on. I have heard riders at night. Horses galloping. There—there have been shots. A bullet hit my house only last night. Someone is trying to frighten me and I do not know who it is."

A key rattled in the recently locked door. Sheriff Moon opened the door. "All right," he said testily, "come out."

Blatnik hesitated worriedly, but Weber walked out of the cell into the Sheriff's office. Mike Denver was seated in an armchair, his fingers locked across his expansive waist.

"Sheriff made a little mistake," he said.

Blatnik came out of the cell, saw Denver and stopped. "Mr. Denver," he cried, "I want to tell you what the Sheriff did——"

"Beat it," said Denver. "You're free. You can go. But next time you get drunk, watch yourself."

"I am not drunk. That is what I want to tell you——"

"Later."

"I take only a minute——"

"Can't you see I'm busy?" snapped Denver testily. "I'm talking to Mr. Weber."

"Oh, are you?" asked Weber.

"Why do you think I'm here?" Denver made a flickering gesture in Blatnik's direction and the farmer headed for the door. He went out. Sheriff Moon looked frowningly at Weber and Denver, then followed Blatnik outside.

"Not much you don't own these days," said Weber.

"You're very observing," Denver shrugged. "Just as well. I won't have to waste time. Weber, you're not wanted in Lobo Valley."

"Who doesn't want me here?"

"*I* don't. That's the long and the short of it."

"What about my ranch? Aren't you going to make me an offer for it?"

"I've got more land than I can use now."

"So has Alderton—and Rawlins. Yet both of them have tried to buy me out in the last two days. I thought maybe *you'd* like to make me an offer."

"All right, if that's all that's keeping you here, I'll buy your damn ranch. What do you want for it?"

"You want to buy. You make the offer."

"How big is it? A thousand acres? Two thousand?"

"Don't you know, Mike? You've been in the real estate

business these past ten years. Don't you know my ranch is a half section—three hundred and twenty acres?"

"Hardly worth bothering about. But I don't want you around messing into things that don't concern you. It's worth two thousand to me to get rid of you."

"That's not a bad offer, Mike. Beats those of Alderton and Rawlins."

"I've got some blank deeds at the office." Denver got to his feet. "Let's get it over and you can be gone by tonight."

"Uh-uh, not yet. I'll think about it."

"What's there to think?" Denver snapped. "I'm offering you four times what your dinky little place is worth."

"That's why I want to think it over. Your offer is too good and you were never a generous man."

Denver's eyes became slits. "You're crowding me, Weber!"

"Your brother-in-law's killers are crowding me, Denver," snapped Weber. "You tell them the next man comes to my place at night gets buried there."

"I don't know what you're talking about!"

"No? Then ask your brother-in-law."

"Pete Rawlins can take care of himself," grunted Denver. "I'll give you a friendly warning, though. Don't get tough with him. He'll slap your ears down."

"My ears may take some slapping."

"This game's too big for you, Weber. I'm not going to warn you again. Take my advice, get on the northbound freight this evening and disappear."

Weber gave Denver a quizzical look and walked out of the Sheriff's office. Across the street from the courthouse he entered a hardware store and bought a Winchester and a box of cartridges. Carrying his purchases, he continued down the street to the bank, where his horse was still tied to the rail.

He mounted and rode out of Barkerville.

17

It was early evening when Weber returned to his place. He went into the house and cooked a quick supper. By the time he had eaten it was getting dark outside.

He lighted a lamp, set it on the table and then, loading the Winchester, left the house.

He saddled his horse, mounted and rode out to the road. He crossed the bridge and turned onto Lobo land. He rode his horse at a steady walk, following the river as well as he could.

He rode deep into Lobo land passing, in the dark, grazing cattle and now and then stopping to let a Lobo range rider go by. Each time he kept well out of hailing distance of the rider and was not challenged by any of them.

After an hour's riding, he came to his destination, the dam that now spanned the entrance to what had once been Lobo Canyon.

The dam was an earthen one, some three hundred yards in length; it was reinforced at each end where it became part of the original canyon wall with heavy concrete buttresses. The sluice gates were of wood, reinforced with great straps of iron.

There was a little shack on top of the dam, on the south end. A light shone through a window.

Weber looked at the light for long moments, then dismounted and tied the reins of his horse to a stout bush that grew on the side of the canyon wall.

He started toward the dam and as he approached, discovered that concrete steps had been built alongside the concrete reinforcement. He climbed the stairs, expecting to be challenged by the watchman, but was not.

He reached the top of the stairs after some exertion, and found that he was a dozen feet from the little one-room cabin.

"Hello, the house!" he called.

After a moment the door was opened and a man stepped out. "Come on in," he called to Weber. "C'mon in and have a cup of coffee. I was just makin' some."

Weber entered the cabin and found the watchman to be a man in his late sixties, a grizzled old-timer who had once been a cowboy on Lobo. His name was Shallcross.

"Lonesomest job in the world," he complained to Weber as he set out an extra tin cup. "Ain't had no visitor in over a month."

"Who pays you your salary?"

"Lobo, who else? That's the only time I ever get a visitor and last time Fred wasn't feelin' well and sent out one of the hands with my pay. Poor Fred, he's gettin' old."

He poured out coffee from a steaming, blackened pot. "Hope you like it without sugar," he apologized. "I like sugar myself, but I forgot to order last time I sent in my order."

"This is fine," said Weber. He tasted the scalding liquid and found it palatable enough. It was better than the coffee that he had had in the hobo jungles.

"New on Lobo, ain't you?" Shallcross continued.

"I used to hunt loboes in the canyon."

"Eh? Why, I was ridin' for Lobo then and I don't remember . . ." Shallcross peered across the table into Weber's face. "Come to think of it, your face does look kinda familiar."

"My name's Weber."

" 'Course! Charlie Weber's boy!" Shallcross blinked. "But young Weber lit out years ago, and nobody's ever heard of him."

"I returned a few days ago."

"Bet your pa was surprised. He took it kinda hard when you run out"—Shallcross grimaced—"I get so doggone lonesome here when I do see someone, I can't keep my mouth shut. Sorry—Ben, isn't it?"

"Tom."

"Yeah, Tom. Why, I remember when your pa and old Sam Barker"—Shallcross grimaced again—"No, I can't talk about that neither. Damn us old coots, all we can talk about is the past. Well, I won't do it again, Tom. We'll talk about *now*. When'd you get back to Lobo?"

"Just a few days ago."

"Sure found things different, didn't you? Like this here dam. And Jeff Alderton running the old Lobo. Never thought I'd ever see anything like that. And now they tell me he's gonna be governor. Why, I remember Jeff when he wasn't nothing but a—Ho, I can't say that, either. He's paying me my wages now. Seems like there ain't a damn thing I *can* talk about."

Weber put down the coffee cup. "I've got to go."

"Already? You ain't even finished your coffee."

"It's good coffee, but I've got some riding to do tonight."

"Well, all right, but listen, do me a favor. Tell Fred to come hisself next payday. And tell him I need some sugar."

"I'm sorry," Weber said. "I won't be seeing Fred Case. You see, I don't work for Lobo."

"Then how come you're here? Thought you was ridin' herd nearby and just stopped in."

"No—I came to see you, that's all. And the dam." Weber nodded and started to leave. At the door he turned. "Think it's a good idea to let people come up—at night?"

"Huh? Why not? You come, didn't you?"

"Yes, but suppose I was someone who wanted to—damage the dam?"

"Why'd anyone want to do that?"

"I don't know that anyone does. I just thought I'd mention it."

Shallcross regarded Weber in open astonishment and Weber, nodding, walked off. He returned to the long flight of steps and, descending, found his horse and mounted.

Overhead, the pale, almost full moon was lighting up the range as Weber rode easily across Lobo. He wondered, as he rode, if the night riders had paid him a call.

The night riders, about the time Weber was riding back to his ranch, were out, all right, but there were only two of them and they were some distance from Weber's place.

They rode their horses up to Leo Blatnik's barn and there Paul Partridge dismounted. He took a Winchester from his saddle scabbard and looked up at Pete Rawlins, who had remained on his horse.

"I'm ready!"

Rawlins raised himself in his stirrups. "Blatnik!" he called. "Come outside. . . ."

There was movement inside the house, but the door did not open. The muffled voice of Leo Blatnik called out, "Who is it? What do you want?"

"Open up!" thundered Rawlins.

"It's the Sheriff," cried Paul Partridge. "You don't come out, we'll burn your damn house down."

There was silence inside the house. "Damn," swore Rawlins, "he's going to make us do just that."

Then the door opened. Blatnik, framed in the doorway, had a double-barreled shotgun in his hands. He never got to use it. Partridge took quick aim with the Winchester, pulled the trigger and working the lever with amazing speed, sent a second bullet through Blatnik before the farmer hit the ground.

"Let's go," he sang out, whirling back to his horse.

It was Helga Weber who found her brother. Going to his house the next morning for her periodic house cleaning, she found the body sprawled outside the kitchen door.

18

There had been some discussion as to whether Blatnik's body should remain in his own home until time for the burial, or be taken to his sister's home. Charles Weber suggested the latter course, but Helga had demurred.

"I am sure he would want to be in his own house."

So Blatnik lay now in a rough, unpainted coffin in the "front" room of his three-room shack. A couple of benches had been set up along the walls and the farmwomen sat on them and every hour or so knelt to pray for the soul of the dead man.

The men gathered in the kitchen. They talked in low tones and drank a few glasses of wine. They came early, some of them, and they remained late.

The kitchen was too small and knots of men gathered outside. Some of the women, later in the evening, prepared food and platters were taken around to the various groups outside the house.

It was nearing ten o'clock when Lily Alderton rode up on her filly and dismounted near the barn. A half dozen of the farmers were assembled nearby and they watched her as she dismounted and walked toward the house.

"What does *she* want here?" one of the men asked.

"Probably come to make sure he's dead," grunted a second man.

Charles Weber, who was one of the group, spoke up. "Mrs. Alderton is not like that. She's a good woman."

"Her husband's no friend of ours," one of the men growled.

Lily Alderton was aware that men who had been talking fell silent as she came up and passed them, but she continued on into the house, went through the kitchen and into the room where the women sat around the coffin.

Helga Weber got up as she came in. "Mrs. Alderton," she said, "it is nice of you to come."

"Your brother was a good man," Lily said.

She went to the coffin, looked into the dead face of the farmer, then knelt on the floor and said a silent prayer. When she got to her feet, Helga said, "Thank you for coming, Mrs. Alderton."

Lily gave her a wan smile and, nodding, started to leave. Helga went with her through the group of silent men in the kitchen and outside.

"Good night, Mrs. Weber," Lily said, then. "My horse is by the barn."

"I would like to talk to you, Mrs. Alderton," Helga said, "if you do not mind."

"Of course not."

They walked past one group of men, stopping about half-way to the barn.

"There has been talk, Mrs. Alderton," Helga Weber said, "perhaps too much talk; that my brother was killed because he would not support your husband."

Lily was startled. "That's ridiculous!"

"Of course. That is why I am telling you. I do not put any belief in such talk. Nobody would do such a—a horrible thing."

"Mrs. Weber," exclaimed Lily, "believe me, my husband is not that kind of man. I know—I have heard that the farmers in the valley would not support my husband. That is their concern. They are entitled to vote for whomever they wish. My husband is a cattleman, you are farmers. Your interests are not the same as ours. But that does not mean that we are enemies. In fact, I would like very much to be your friend."

"No," said Helga, "I am afraid that cannot be. There—there has been trouble already. My brother is dead even now. I have told you that I do not accuse your husband of this terrible thing, but—but *somebody* killed my brother. That I cannot forget."

"Whoever it was, Mrs. Weber," Lily said warmly, "will be punished. The law——"

"The law? What law?"

"Sheriff Moon, Mrs. Weber. It was he who came to the ranch this afternoon and told me about your brother. He was very much concerned and he told me he was going to swear in some extra deputies and leave no stone unturned——"

"Please, Mrs. Alderton," interrupted Helga, "do not talk about Sheriff Moon. He stood by the other day while a ruffian beat up my brother, beat him badly, for no reason whatsoever."

Lily reached out and gripped Helga Weber's arm. "I'm sorry, Mrs. Weber, I'm only making things worse. You've suffered a shock and I—I'm standing here arguing with you. I'll come to see you in a few days. We'll talk things over and"—She smiled wanly—"I'm sure we can be friends on *some* basis."

"Perhaps," said Helga dubiously.

Lily started to turn away, then stopped abruptly. Tom Weber stood a dozen feet away. How long he had been there she did not know. Helga also saw Weber and exclaimed softly, "Mrs. Alderton, is that not my husband's son?"

Lily nodded. "Yes."

"Will you introduce me? I—I want to talk to him."

Lily hesitated. "You're sure, Mrs. Weber? That you want to talk to him—now?"

"Yes. It—it is important."

"Very well then."

Lily moved toward Weber, Helga at her side. "Tom, I want to introduce you to—to your stepmother. Mrs. Weber, Tom Weber."

It was a poor introduction and Lily knew it. She walked away quickly, leaving Weber alone with Helga Weber. Weber regarded his father's second wife dispassionately.

"Ma'am," was all he said by way of acknowledging the introduction.

"This is very awkward," Helga said discomfited. "I—I have thought so many times of what I would say if we ever met, but now—now, none of it seems to fit."

"I don't think there's much to say," Weber said evenly. "If you will excuse me . . ."

"No—wait!" Helga said desperately. "There is *much* to say. Charles—your father—told me of his meeting with you at the picnic. He has been greatly hurt by what you said to him."

"Perhaps I shouldn't have spoken to him at all."

A shudder ran through Helga Weber. "It isn't right that a son should hate his father. It—it's unnatural."

"Is it, Mrs. Weber?"

"Mrs. Weber?" cried Helga. "Is *that* what you are going to call me?"

"What else am I to call you? Mother?"

"Now you are mocking me. Please—I do not want to quarrel. I—I cannot stand to see your father as he is. Broken, miserable. Because—because of the way you are treating him. . . ."

Charles Weber came toward them. He had seen them together from a distance, had waited a long moment before coming forward. He walked now stiffly erect, almost like an automaton. Weber saw him approaching, but Helga, for the moment, was not yet aware of him.

She said, "Please, Mr. Weber, come and see him. See him as he is today. Not—not as you remember him."

Charles Weber said, "I think it is time we go home."

Helga cried out in dismay. "Oh, not this way, Charlie! You can't go on, the two of you, living so close to one another, not speaking . . ."

"When my son gets ready to talk to me, I will listen," Charles Weber said quietly. Then as Helga began to sob, he put his arm about her shoulder.

Weber left them that way. He walked to his horse by the barn, mounted and rode off without looking back.

19

The Weber farmstead consisted of a four-room cottage, a small barn and a few outbuildings. There was no dog and Weber stood in the gloom of one of the outbuildings when his father and stepmother drove up in a buggy.

He moved behind the shed while his father unhitched the horse from the buggy and turned it loose in the small corral attached to the barn. Later, after Charles Weber had gone into the house, Weber came out of the gloom and moved closer to the house. The shade in the kitchen was up and through the window he could see his father, seated at a small oilcloth-covered table, elbows resting on the table, his face buried in his hands.

Helga was not in the room, but as Weber watched from outside, he saw her appear in the doorway of the kitchen and look at her husband. The latter did not seem to be aware of his wife and after a moment Helga turned and disappeared into another room.

Weber, outside, walked quietly away from the house, a quarter of a mile to where he had left his horse. He mounted and rode back to his own place—that had been deeded to him by his father.

Weber saw the light in his cabin while still some distance away, but since he had left it burning, he thought that the raiders had passed him by for this night. Then, when he rode closer to the ranch yard he was startled to see a horse standing nearby.

Tonight he had carried with him only his Frontier Model, thrust under the waistband of his trousers, butt concealed by his buttoned coat. It was in his hand in a flash, as he slid from his horse and landed lightly on the ground.

Bent low he made a swift half-circle of the cabin. Near the remnants of the barn he came to an abrupt halt. Someone was sitting on the doorstoop, silhouetted by the lighted lamp in the room behind.

Weber's enemies would not sit so openly in the door of his house and Weber relaxed a little as he moved forward. Then suddenly he recognized the person on his doorstoop and he quickly thrust his revolver under the waistband of his trousers.

Lily Alderton saw him approach and rose to her feet. "It took you quite awhile to get here."

Weber said, "Would you mind coming away from the light?"

"Not at all." She moved forward a few feet, then stopped. "I see, you're afraid someone will shoot at you from the dark."

"It's been done before. Leo Blatnik got it that way."

She came forward again, following him as he moved a few feet into heavier shadow made by some nearby trees. Finally he stopped and she halted a few feet away.

"I had to apologize," she said.

"For what?"

"The—the way I introduced you to Helga Weber."

In the gloom he made a gesture of dismissal. "It made no difference."

"I liked her," Lily said suddenly. "I've seen her once or twice, but this was the first time I ever spoke to her. She's a real woman, Tom." Then she added quickly, "Now that that's out of the way, I want to ask if you've reconsidered my offer of a job?"

"It's still no."

She exhaled wearily. "I was afraid so." She was silent a moment. "Fred Case said that at least a hundred more head of cattle disappeared last night."

"You've got a lot of riders," Weber said. "They must be blind not to see anyone making off with the cattle."

"Lobo's big. The men can't be everywhere."

"They don't have to be everywhere. Put them along the border between Lobo and Rawlins' place."

"I gave that order three days ago."

"And it hasn't helped any?"

"What Lobo needs," Lily said poignantly, "is a strong man!"

"What's the matter with Jeff?"

"He's away—I told you."

"Seems to me he's away a helluva long time, for a man who's being robbed blind. Unless he *wants* to be robbed!"

Lily exclaimed, "What made you say a thing like that?"

"Jeff doesn't give a damn for the ranch—or for Lobo. He'll be governor if it *costs* him Lobo. . . ."

"Lobo isn't his," Lily burst out. "It's mine."

"But *you* belong to him."

"I do not! I don't belong to him. I've never belonged. Not really. I should think *you* would know that——"

"Me?"

"You *must* know, Tom," she whispered. "You *must* know . . ." In the darkness her arms came up in a supplicating gesture.

Weber did not see, for he turned away from her and stepped out of the heavy gloom. A low moan came from Lily and he threw up his hand.

"Quiet!"

An electric shock shot through her and she started toward him, then she saw that his head was cocked to one side in a listening attitude.

"Someone's coming," he said in a low tone. "Two horses."

"Here?"

"They're on the road, coming from town."

"Will they stop here?"

"I don't know. More likely they'll shoot and run. Here—grab your horse and follow me."

He ran swiftly toward his own mount, caught it by the bridle reins, then turning, waited for Lily to bring her own horse back to him. When she did, he started quickly toward the woods to the townward side of the clearing.

The horses on the road were coming at a swift trot and it was questionable if Weber and Lily got into the woods before the other horses turned off and headed for Weber's cabin.

"Get in farther," Weber whispered to Lily as she stopped beside him.

"Who is it?" she asked in a low tone.

He was peering through the leafy network in front of him toward the cabin. He could make out the horses, saw that a rider was on one of them. The second man was going toward

70

the opened door. He stopped in the light from inside the cabin.

Then a voice came to Weber and Lily. "Weber," the voice called, "I want to talk to you."

It was Jeff Alderton, returned to Lobo.

"Don't!" Lily whispered. "Don't talk to him—now."

"Nothing Jeff Alderton can say would interest me," Weber replied grimly.

By the house, Alderton called again, "Come out, Weber!"

When there was no response, Alderton said something inaudible to the man on the horse, then started into the house. For an instant, the light inside the house was dimmed, then there was a crash of glass and flames shot up.

Alderton had thrown the lamp against a wall and set fire to the house.

Weber swore and raised his revolver. "Don't!" cried Lily poignantly. She reached out and struck down the revolver in Weber's hand.

Alderton came running out of the house. In the sudden flare-up of light, Weber now recognized the second man. It was Mike Denver.

He said savagely to Lily, "Am I supposed to stand here while the house burns?"

"I'll pay for it."

"Sure you'll pay," Weber said harshly. "Money settles everything."

"Please," she pleaded, "you can't do anything—not now— when I'm here. They'd think . . ."

She could not say it, but Weber knew that she was referring to her being with him at night, alone, on his place. Weber relaxed and watched the flames shoot out of the open door, through the windows. The shack was old and flimsy, as dry as tinder. It made a quick, fine blaze.

Denver and Alderton did not wait for the house to be completely consumed. After the fire had a good start, they rode off.

Lily climbed on her horse then. "I'm sorry," she said stiffly.

Weber watched her ride off and even thought of going with her, but he realized that she knew Lobo range better than he, that she would probably make a swift circuit around Alderton and Denver and reach Lobo headquarters before they arrived.

20

Lily arrived at Lobo ranch headquarters a good ten minutes before Jeff Alderton and Mike Denver. She had time to unsaddle her horse, hang the saddle on a corral rail and reach the house before she heard the hoofbeats of Alderton's and Denver's horses.

She remained on the veranda of the sprawling house, with the light from the windows behind her, as the men rode up. They dismounted and were approaching the house before Alderton saw his wife on the veranda.

"You're up late, my dear," he said cheerfully.

"I've just gotten home. I've been to a wake."

"A wake?" cried Mike Denver. "Now don't tell me you went to Blatnik's!"

"Any reason I shouldn't have gone?"

"Yes," snapped Jeff Alderton. "I don't want you to have anything to do with those people."

"They're sodbusters," chimed in Mike Denver.

"Mr. Denver," said Lily Alderton evenly, "I'm not interested in your opinions."

"Lily!" cried Alderton, aghast.

"And furthermore," Lily went on angrily, "I don't want you setting foot on Lobo again."

"Whoa now, Lily girl," exclaimed Mike Denver. "That's pretty strong talk."

"I meant it to be."

"Do you know what you're saying, Lily?" thundered Jeff Alderton.

"I know, Jeff," retorted Lily, "and as soon as Mr. Denver gets on his horse and leaves, I've some things to say to you . . ."

"I see," said Mike Denver with forced cheerfulness, "a little family spat. You don't want me here. I'll see you in town tomorrow. And maybe Lily'll be in a better mood by that time."

"I won't be," said Lily, "as far as *you're* concerned. . . ."

Mike Denver turned to his horse and mounted. He gave Alderton a half salute. "Take it easy, Jeff!"

He started off at a swift canter. Alderton, his face black

with fury, headed for Lily. She did not wait for him, however. Coolly, she turned her back on him, opened the door and stepped into the house.

The door slammed in Alderton's face, but he tore it open and burst into the living room after his wife.

"Now what's this all about?" he demanded savagely.

"Don't you know?" asked Lily. "Or didn't you think I would ever find out?"

"I don't know what you're talking about."

"I went to the bank today."

Jeff Alderton gave a start. "You go to the bank all the time," he snapped. "So do I." He sneered. "Now don't tell me I'm supposed to get your permission before I draw out a few dollars?"

"Is a hundred thousand a *few* dollars to you, Jeff?"

"You wanted to be a governor's wife," Alderton snapped.

"No," Lily said quickly, "I never wanted that. *You* wanted to be governor. I tried to dissuade you right from the start, but no, you had your heart set on it. I went along—but I'm not going along any further. I'm not sacrificing Lobo to your ambition."

"So that's it," snarled Alderton. "Sacrificing Lobo, eh? Lobo's *yours*, eh? That's what's been in your craw right along. You went into this marriage with that reservation. Everything *I* had was to be yours, but everything *you* had was to remain yours——"

"You twisted that around very nicely," Lily said coldly, "but it's no use, Jeff. I did a little investigating today. The last beef you sold was Lobo beef—all of it. None of it carried your brand. The money from it went into *our* joint account, but *you* drew it out. You even opened a separate account of your own——"

"I'll have Eads' hide for telling you that!"

"No, you won't. And another thing, while you're gallivanting around the state trying to be governor, Lobo is being robbed blind. I've lost forty thousand dollars' worth of beef and I blame you for that."

"Lobo!" shouted Alderton. "That's all you can talk about. I've heard nothing but Lobo—Lobo, for the last two years and I'm sick of it. I've had enough. . . ."

"So have I," said Lily and turning, left Alderton alone.

Jeff Alderton was awake with the first flush of dawn. For a while he lay in his bed, thinking over the quarrel with Lily the night before. It was not to his advantage to break with her at this particular point in the game. In fact, it could well lead to disaster, but the more he thought over the situation, the more indignant he became.

He would not make a complete break, but he would go to his own ranch for a few days. Lily was a proud woman. She would not want a report of their quarrel to get around. She would come to terms.

He dressed and, leaving the house, walked to the corral. He disliked saddling his own horse, but the cowboys were still asleep and he roped a horse and put a saddle on it. When he rode out of the corral, Fred Case was crossing the ranch yard from his own cabin, headed for the ranch office.

He stopped when he saw Jeff Alderton.

"I didn't know you were back," Case lied, having overheard most of the quarrel the night before from a nearby vantage point. "Some things you ought to know about."

"Ask my wife," Alderton snapped. "Lobo belongs to her, not me."

He turned his horse away and put it into a gallop.

Alderton followed the ranch road to the main highway that ran to Barkerville. By the time he turned into the road his self-pity had boiled up within him and he was seething. He stopped his horse, looked over his shoulder to the north, then turned his horse, put spurs to it. He covered the two and a half miles to the Weber ranch in just a few minutes and, riding in from the road, saw that his firing of the night before had been extremely successful.

What had been a house was no more than a few smoldering embers. Tom Weber, armed with a long stick, was poking about the ruins, hoping to find some food that was not burned beyond use.

He seemed to pay no attention to Jeff Alderton.

Alderton placed his hands on the saddle pommel and leaned forward over the neck of his mount. "So it finally

74

went up in smoke! Always surprised that father of yours never burned it down when he was boozing."

Weber made no reply and Alderton continued, "Well, there's nothing holding you here now. You haven't even got a place to sleep——"

"I'm not leaving," Weber snapped.

"Maybe that fire wasn't an accident," Alderton said truculently. "Maybe somebody *set* it."

"I know damn well somebody fired it."

"You need it any plainer than that? People don't want you here . . ."

"Don't crowd me!" Weber warned.

"And don't threaten me," snarled Alderton. "I licked you when we were kids and I can lick you again . . ."

Suddenly whirling, Weber threw the pole at Alderton. The latter threw up his hand just in time, took the edge of the pole on his forearm and, yelling with rage and pain, threw himself from his horse. He hit the ground and rushed at Weber.

Weber tried to step clear of the burnt wreckage, but could not quite make it before the fury of Alderton's assault reached him. He took a hard blow on the forehead that sent him rocking back. Following through with his lunge, Alderton's shoulder caught Weber on the chest and drove him over backward. Alderton himself sprawled over Weber.

One of his flailing hands touched a hot ember and he yelped and rolled over. That enabled Weber to get clear and he scrambled to his feet. He met Alderton, springing up, and smashed the rancher with a savage blow that puffed up Alderton's left eye in an instant.

Alderton let out a roar and threw himself once more at Weber. Only the insecure footing saved Weber then. Alderton's fist caught him on the point of the jaw, but the blow lacked force. Alderton crossed with a hard right to the stomach that bent Weber over.

He followed through with an uppercut that straightened up Weber and left him gasping.

Sensing victory, Alderton crowded forward, ignoring the smoldering, fire-blackened wreckage all around. He swarmed over Weber, swinging with rights and lefts. Weber, hurt, tried to cover up, but was unable to do so; when Alderton whaled away at his stomach, he brought down his guard and then Alderton's fists went up to his head, rocking him from one side to the other.

He gave way and the big rancher followed him. Then, suddenly, Weber stepped on a two-by-four burned almost through. The wood snapped and Weber fell sideward. Alderton, swinging at the same instant, could not stop his blow and, missing, was off balance. Weber, seeing his advantage, kicked out with both feet even as he landed heavily among the burnt wreckage.

His boots took Alderton in the side and spilled him, head first, among the blackened embers. Sputtering, his face and hair soot-blackened, Jeff Alderton climbed to his feet. Weber was up before him and, stepping in, slammed Alderton in the face with his right. He crossed with the left and rocked Alderton's head.

Alderton struck out defensively, but his fist merely grazed Weber. Setting himself firmly, Weber followed through with a hard right and a terrific left that tore a gasp from the big man. Alderton gave way.

It was Weber's turn to crowd now. He followed Alderton, raining blows at him. Alderton's arms went up; he tried to cover his face, but Weber sent a hard blow to the midriff and Alderton's hands went down, leaving a perfect opening for Weber.

He hit Alderton with everything he had and the jar of the blow sent pain shooting up Weber's arm to his shoulder.

Alderton crashed amid the ashes and embers, and for a moment lay completely still. Then a groan came from his lips and he moved. He struggled to a sitting position, looked up at Weber and shook his head.

"Times have changed," Weber said.

Alderton took a full thirty seconds to climb to his feet. He did not resume the fight. He stumbled through the wreckage into the clearing and found his horse. He mounted heavily and rode off.

Lily Alderton was having her breakfast when she chanced to look through the window of Lobo ranch house. She saw the incredibly dirty and sooty Jeff Alderton and knew instantly where he had been. She got to her feet as Alderton came into the house. But he did not even seem to see her.

He went straight to his room, slammed the door and threw himself upon his bed.

After Alderton's departure, Tom Weber walked across the clearing, through the clump of woods and down to the bank of Lobo River. He took off his clothes and standing in the shallow water, gave himself as good a scrubbing as he was able without soap, even using sand to get the blacking off his hands and face.

He examined his clothes. They were filthy from the fight in the burnt wreckage of his cabin. Yet he had no other clothing. The extra shirts and underwear he had had on arriving in Lobo Valley, along with the few newly purchased articles, had all gone up with the cabin.

He had to wear what he had, or get new clothing. Standing naked on the bank of the creek, he debated the subject. He could probably wash his shirt and Levi's, but he would have to wait for them to dry, or put them on wet.

The faint clop-clopping of horses' hooves decided him. Quickly he donned the sooty, grimy clothes and made his way back through the woods to the clearing.

Two riders were coming along from the west and they turned in from the road even as Weber stepped out into the clearing.

The riders were Paul Partridge and Pete Rawlins. They pulled up their horses and surveyed the ruins of the cabin with considerable pleasure.

"Playing with matches?" Partridge asked, as Weber came up.

"Yes," retorted Weber, "I thought I'd save you the trouble of coming around at night and setting it afire—like you did the barn."

"Whoa now, wait a minute," bristled Partridge, "you accusin' me of burnin' your barn?"

"I could accuse you of a lot more than that," snapped Weber.

Partridge slid from his horse to the ground, and advanced on Weber. "I told you last time we was here to get yourself a shootin' iron . . ."

"You're Paul Partridge," Weber said thinly, "the fastest gun in the country—against men without guns."

Partridge cried out and his hand snaked to his holster. It came up in a smooth, seemingly-without-effort movement, the Frontier Model in his fist cocked. Yet he held his fire.

"I've never killed a man without a gun," he cried passionately, "but damned if you don't tempt me."

"Did Leo Blatnik tempt you?" Weber flashed at him.

"He had a—" Partridge caught himself just in time. A wild look twisted his face and his head swiveled toward Pete Rawlins. The ranchman's face was black with fury.

"You've got a rough tongue," he shouted at Weber. "You shoot your mouth off, then you hide behind being unarmed."

He made a wild, sweeping gesture. "You'r: through here, Weber. Your house is gone, your barn is gone. There': nothing holding you and I want you off this place by sundown : mean that. Be here after the sun goes down tonight and damned if I don't turn Partridge loose on you, gun or no gun!"

He grabbed up the reins of his horse, half jerked the animal's head about. "Come on, Paul. You'll get your chance at him if he stays here."

Partridge was loath to leave, but, after fixing Weber with a look of the utmost hatred, he went to his horse and climbing aboard, followed his employer.

Weber went back through the woods, gathering up his revolver and the Winchester from their hiding place. He took off his shirt, got down on his knees and washed the shirt thoroughly in the cold flow of Lobo River. Afterward he hung the shirt on a nearby bush to dry, and took off his Levi's and underwear and washed them. He donned his wet Levi's, but hung up his underwear to dry.

An hour later he again took off his partly dried Levi's, found the underwear and shirt only slightly damp and put them on. He picked up the Frontier Model, spun the cylinder to make sure that it was properly loaded and then hesitated for a long moment, debating whether to carry it openly.

He finally decided against it and hid it along with the Winchester in a thick clump of brush near the river bank.

22

Her marriage to Jeff Alderton had not come as a sudden decision for Lily Barker. She had known him for years. They had mutual interests and as the owners of the two largest ranches in Lobo Valley, it was only natural that they saw much of each other. That Jeff was an ambitious man, she knew, but she did not hold that ambition against him.

In those first years when she returned to Lobo Valley she saw Jeff occasionally in Barkerville, at various functions and affairs in the valley. She thought him an arrogant, somewhat ruthless man, in those early days. Then, after his father passed on and Jeff came into full ownership of the ranch, she saw him only infrequently. She heard about him. He had inherited a large ranch, well stocked with several thousand head of cattle. The ending of the years of drought in Lobo Valley, the new prosperity that came to the area was a boon to Alderton as well as to all others in the valley. Jeff took full advantage of his opportunity. He kept his cattle sales to a minimum and his herds increased rapidly. He bought additional land and in a very few years his worth was said to be as great as that of Lily Barker, who had lopped off a large section of her ranch and reduced her herds considerably to raise the money to build Lobo Dam.

When his wealth equaled hers, or perhaps exceeded it, Alderton began to come again to Lobo. He came now in the role of suitor, or royalty calling upon royalty. Lily Barker was the only woman in the valley equal in position to him. An alliance, he hinted, would make them the richest family in the valley, perhaps in the state. Together they would control a vast cattle empire and from there on there was no barrier to their progress.

His talk was not pleasing to Lily. Yet he was frank and bold. He could be charming when he wanted. The memory of the young wolf hunter in Lobo Canyon had grown dimmer with the passing years. Longer and longer periods of time went by between casual mention of his name. Charlie Weber, no longer the drunkard of Barkerville, had got married again and become a farmer. He was lost among the many farmers who settled in the valley. No longer an object of derision, people forgot about Charlie Weber and the son who had lived with him until he could stand it no longer and then had lit out on his own.

A year went by and not one single person mentioned the name of Weber. Meanwhile, Jeff Alderton continued to press his suit and, without its ever having been announced, people began to take it for granted that Alderton and the owner of Lobo would unite one day. Jeff seemed to take it for granted. And so, in time, did Lily.

They were married.

Alderton moved to Lobo, took over the active management of the ranch. Lily was consulted less and less about Lobo affairs. As a result she had much leisure and found time heavy on her hands.

She began to learn things about Alderton that she had not known before. His ambition now became the paramount thing. Lobo, of which he began to talk as his, was but a steppingstone to bigger things. Lobo Valley was too small a theater.

79

Whether it was Denver who came to Alderton, or Alderton who went to Denver, Lily never knew. Denver began coming out to the ranch. Alderton, one day, made an apparently careless remark to Lily that people had suggested he run for Congress.

It was not an immediate thing and Lily threw no cold water on the suggestion. Alderton saw even more of Mike Denver and then one day he had told her that he had given up the idea of Congress. People had told him he would make an excellent governor. The state had not had a cattleman-governor in some years. The cattlemen wanted one of their own to represent them and give them certain legislation.

The thought of leaving Lobo and moving to the state capitol did not appeal to Lily, and she became a little alarmed. She did not object openly to Jeff about his decision, but she began to question him about it. In various ways she let him know that she preferred the life of the range to a life in the city.

Jeff was indifferent to her wishes. He began to campaign actively, began making trips to various parts of the state. A speech here, a meeting of an association there, a call upon a politician, a "man who controlled a bloc of votes." These things became Jeff Alderton's life.

This state of affairs had brought them now to the crisis, the turning point.

Last night they had quarreled. Seriously. She had learned things about her husband; he had betrayed her, he had stolen money from Lobo.

During the night after the quarrel, Lily did not close her eyes. She went to bed, but she did not sleep. She thought— thought of her marriage to Jeff Alderton. It had never been really good.

And then suddenly she sat up.

Had *she* changed?

Had the return of Tom Weber altered her opinion of her husband? Was she seeing him now with different eyes from a year ago? A week ago?

She had talked to Tom Weber, had been stung by the harshness of his words to her, the callous indifference to—to everything. He had actually repelled her.

And then, last night, she had stood in the woods with Weber and watched her husband set fire to Weber's house and she had stopped Weber from going out and fighting with her husband.

She had only delayed the fight.

Early this morning, Alderton had left the ranch. An hour later he returned, his face battered and bruised, filthy with soot and ashes. It was obvious where he had been, what he had done.

He was big and strong and she had once seen him beat a cowboy to a whimpering hulk. He had worked out his anger toward her on Weber. Alone, with no one to stop them, they had probably fought until Alderton had beaten Weber into insensibility.

Lily paced the veranda. She did not want to see Weber today. But the thought of his lying in the smoking ruins of his cabin that Alderton had burned himself, finally forced her to go toward the corral and order one of the hands to saddle her filly.

She rode the horse away from the ranch at an easy lope but soon she had the horse galloping swiftly toward the east.

She reached the Weber ranch at a full gallop, leaped from her horse and ran to the burnt wreckage, from which a wisp of smoke still curled up here and there.

She searched for Tom Weber, but quickly saw that he was not lying in the burned-out ruins. She turned away and ran lightly toward the woods from which she had watched with Weber last night.

She went all the way through the woods to the edge of Lobo River, turned back and after running a few yards stopped and called for him. There was no response, for Weber had started for Barkerville ten minutes before her arrival.

She even whistled, in the thought that his horse might be grazing somewhere nearby and would whicker a response or perhaps come trotting up.

Finally, she had to concede that Weber was not in the immediate vicinity.

She returned to the ranch, riding her heaving horse at a fast walk and only an occasional canter or trot. Cowboys were standing around the bunkhouse, loafing about the corral. Fred Case stood in the doorway of the ranch office.

He came toward her as she left her horse by the corral.

"I called in some of the hands," he said, "like you told me yesterday."

"Yes?" Lily said absently.

"Mister Jeff doesn't answer," Case said carefully. "After you rode off I went in and knocked on his door, but I guess he was sleeping. Or maybe he's sick."

"What is it you want to know?"

81

"The rustling. What do we do about it?"

Lily winced. She had almost forgotten one of the things that had concerned her so greatly the day before. "Of course," she exclaimed, "we've got to do something about it."

"It's from the graze north of the river," Case said. "We haven't had but one night rider there in the last two-three weeks. No one during the day."

"How many men do you suggest we put there?"

"Six-eight during the day. A dozen at night. Maybe fifteen."

"All right, do that, Fred."

Fred hesitated. "We got seven-eight men here I pulled in from the west graze. We got some fence to ride there in the bad country and we oughtn't to take any men away from the south graze—don't have enough there now."

Lily remembered. "The men Mr. Alderton transferred to—to his ranch, Fred. What about them."

He started to speak, hesitated and ended up by spreading his hands, palms upward. "I'll send for them if you give the order."

"Fred, if *you* can't talk to me, who can?"

"I told you yesterday, Miss Lily, I'm not a man who wants to make trouble between man and wife——"

"Any trouble that's made I'll make," Lily said sharply. "Get the men from Jeff's ranch. Everyone who's there now who was on the Lobo payroll—before Mr. Alderton came here."

"Very well, Miss Lily . . ."

"Lily!"

"Lily," Case said gruffly.

Lily smiled wanly. "Fred. Now, would you have one of the men saddle me a fresh horse? I want to go to Barkerville."

Lily had been gone from the ranch for ten minutes when Jeff Alderton, cleaned up, but his face puffed and bruised from his battle with Tom Weber, came out of the house. He started for the corral, where seven or eight cowboys were mounting.

The hands shot covert glances at Alderton, then suddenly the entire body galloped off. Alderton stopped, saw Fred Case coming out of the bunkhouse.

"What's going on here?" he demanded.

Case regarded him blandly. "I don't know what you mean."

Alderton stabbed a pointing hand at the cowboys galloping away. "Why were they just now leaving? Haven't you got any system around here, keeping the men loafing around all hours? They should have been out at their work hours ago."

"They were," replied Case, stung. "I brought them in."

"Why?"

"Miss Lily told me to."

"*Miss* Lily? My wife, *Mrs*. Alderton. . . ." Alderton half turned, glanced toward the house. "Where is she?"

"Gone off."

"Where?"

"I didn't ask her." Lily had volunteered the information to him, but it was true he had not asked her.

Alderton swore. "Damn it, Case, you're getting impertinent. I've noticed that before. Just because you've been here a few years doesn't entitle you to any extra benefits, old man. You've been shirking your work for quite a while now and I don't like it one damn bit. I pay a man a day's wage, I expect a day's work from him. That goes for you, as well as anyone around here——"

"Miss Lily pays me," blurted out Case. "It's her ranch."

"Oh," said Alderton, suddenly purring like a cat about to pounce on its prey, "so that's the way the wind blows today! You're cock-of-the-walk again, the big foreman of Lobo. And you probably heard that my wife and I had a little spat last night." His voice suddenly became hard and savage. "You're through here, Case. Understand? I'm firing you. Get your things and get off this ranch. Now!"

Fred Case was stunned. He stood for a moment staring at Jeff Alderton, his jaw slack. Then a shudder ran through him and he turned away. He walked toward the ranch office, his shoulders slumped, his back bent. He was a very old man.

23

Lily entered the bank and found Marshall Eads coming out of one of the tellers' cages. He came toward her at once.

"Could we talk—privately?" Lily asked.

Eads looked into her drawn face, nodded. "Come into the directors' room."

He led the way to the rear, into a small office, furnished simply with a table and several chairs. He closed the door.

"We will be alone here," he said.

Lily sat down at the table, her hands clasped tightly together. She stared at a Currier & Ives print on the wall, a New England winter scene. Eads looked down at her a moment or two, then moved quietly to a chair opposite Lily and seated himself.

"You've had it out with Jeff, I suppose," he said gently.

For a moment she did not react, then she nodded. "We're through, Uncle Marshall."

"That serious, eh?"

"We should never have married in the first place."

He shook his head. "I am not going to criticize you, Lily. Nor am I going to tell you that I never approved of your marriage in the first place. The right or the wrong of it isn't important. Your present situation *is* important, Lily . . ."

She looked up at him, saw his sober mien and a ripple of alarm shot through her. "What is my present situation, Uncle Marsh?"

"I'm not going to minimize it, Lily. It's precarious, to put it mildly. It's so serious that I feel I must break all the rules of banking and violate certain banking ethics. Mike Denver was in to see me this morning. He warned me against making any loans to Lobo."

Lily was jolted almost to her heels. "How can Mike Denver warn *you* against making loans?"

"He's a director of this bank, Lily. A stockholder. I don't control this bank, Lily. I haven't in years. Oh, in the old days the bank was entirely my own, but when we had the boom here, the boom *you* created, Lily, we made a lot of loans. And we had to make a great many more that we couldn't handle because of lack of capital. I had the bank incorporated, got in fresh capital. Jeff's father bought a bloc of stock, so did Mike Denver and a number of others. Mike Denver has quietly bought up a lot of that capital stock. He has almost as much as I have. With Jeff's stock, he can outvote me . . . throw me out of the bank. I didn't know myself until this morning, that to all intents and purposes, Mike Denver is in control of the Barkerville State Bank. . . ."

"I'm sorry, Uncle Marsh. I know how badly you must feel . . ."

"It's all right, Lily. Don't worry about *my* problems. Yours are more pressing. I know what it costs to run Lobo and I know that you haven't enough money right now to meet next month's payroll. . . . Not unless you sell off a great many

84

head of cattle. And you know better than I that this is not the time of the year to ship cattle."

"That's the main reason I came in to see you, Uncle Marsh," said Lily tautly. "We—we're losing cattle." She stopped, her forehead creasing into deep furrows. "We've lost a thousand head or more, this past week, and I—it is hard to say this, Uncle Marsh, but I believe Jeff *let* those cattle be stolen. . . ."

Marshall Eads stared at her.

Lily Alderton returned to Lobo. She went through the house and found it empty. The door of Jeff's room was open. She went inside and looked in his closets. His clothing was still there.

She left the house and walked to the office. Fred Case was not in it and she assumed that he had saddled up and gone off with the men, for there wasn't a single cowboy at the ranch at the moment.

In fact, aside from Lily, there were only two people on the ranch, Juanita, the Mexican woman who cleaned and cooked for Lily and Jeff, and Doc, a Chinese who cooked for the cowboys in a cook shack off to one side of the bunkhouse.

24

The funeral services for Leo Blatnik were held in the little white painted church that the Bohemian farmers had built a few years ago. Father Novak, who was of their own nationality, read the services and then the mortal remains of Blatnik were carried to the little cemetery behind the church.

Virtually every farmer in Lobo Valley attended the funeral. A half-dozen businessmen came out from Barkerville, but when the funeral was over they got into their buggies and buckboards and went off.

The farmers lingered behind and somehow, without any prearranged plan, the women found themselves gathered in the churchyard, while the men assembled in a corner of the cemetery. There was some idle talk for a few minutes, then a man named Kazumplik brought out the thought in the minds of many of the farmers.

"Leo was a good man, but he's gone now and we've got to pick someone else to be our leader."

"How about you?" one of the men asked. "You went to high school back in Illinois."

Kazumplik shook his head. "I am a married man, with four children. They are too small yet to work. I do not have the time."

Another man said, "I think we are going about this wrong. We cannot say so-and-so shall be the leader. That is as good as putting a price on a man's head. They killed Leo—they'll kill the next leader we choose."

Kazumplik exclaimed, "I did not refuse because I am afraid. I do not have the time and I—I am not a leader. We need a man who is not married."

Several pairs of eyes singled out a man named Kapek, a strapping tawny-haired man in his middle thirties. The man promptly shook his head.

"I will fight any man with my fists, but I am not a gun-fighter. These people will stop at nothing. We have already learned that."

Charlie Weber, who was at the edge of the gathering, suddenly said, "Hire a gunfighter. That's what Pete Rawlins did."

"How do you go about such a thing?" one man asked. "Where do you find these gunfighters?"

"You hang around the saloons," Webber said harshly, "that's the kind of talk you hear in saloons. A gunfighter in Wyoming shoots down a man, you hear it here and everywhere else inside of a week or two."

The man Kazumplik regarded Weber thoughtfully. "We are farmers, all of us, even you, Charlie, but you are something else. You are a cattleman. Once you owned most of this valley——"

"That was a long time ago."

"The cattlemen still remember you. The point I am getting at, you *think* like a cattleman."

"I think like a farmer. I've got my forty acres like the rest of you——"

"That is true," Kazumplik continued, "and it is also true that Helga, your wife, was Leo Blatnik's sister."

A murmur ran through the crowd of farmers. Then Kazumplik held up his hand for silence. "You must be our leader, Charlie."

A general murmur of approval went up.

Driving home from the cemetery in the heavy farm wagon that was Weber's only vehicle, Weber sat hunched forward, his face frowning in heavy thought. Helga sat quietly beside him, now and then giving him a quick glance. Neither spoke until the wagon was turning into the lane that led to the farmstead. Then Helga said, "They have accepted you as one of us."

Weber shook his head. "We can't win, Helga. We may have the right of it, but our people are not fighters. Blood's going to be spilled and it's going to be our people that lose it. I'm afraid of it."

"No, Charlie, I do not think you are afraid. You will do what has to be done. Perhaps you will not succeed in what you try to do, but whether you win or lose, I do not think you are afraid."

Reaching his farm, Charlie Weber unhitched the team, put the horses into the barn and rubbed them down. He gave them hay, then exclaimed angrily and went to the house.

Helga had taken off her things, changed into a house dress and was in the kitchen, preparing a simple lunch. Weber came in, went through the kitchen into their bedroom, where a trunk stood against the wall.

He raised the lid of the trunk, lifted out the tray and dug into the old clothing in the lower part of the trunk. At the very bottom he found what he sought, a worn holster and cartridge belt, wrapped about a Frontier Model revolver. He took out the gun, saw that is was loaded and strapped the belt about his waist.

He left the bedroom and crossed through the kitchen for the yard. Helga pushed the coffee pot to the rear of the stove and went to the kitchen window. She saw her husband leading the team he had only minutes before stabled out of the barn to the farm wagon.

She waited until he had harnessed the team and then took off her apron and went outside. Weber was climbing into the wagon.

"You will be careful," she said.

"I won't pick a fight," Weber replied, "but I'm going to tell Mike Denver a few things——"

"Denver?"

"Rawlins doesn't take a deep breath without Mike's permission. It may have been Rawlins, or one of his gunfighters who killed Leo, but you can be sure they did so only because Mike ordered it." He picked up the lines, then looked steadily at Helga. "I didn't want this job, Helga, but if I've got to do it, I've got to do it."

"I know."

He gave her an awkward half salute and drove out of the farmyard. Helga Weber stood outside and watched the wagon until it left the lane and turned into the road a quarter mile away.

Then she finally turned and walked back into the house, a woman who had shed tears for her brother that morning and now could shed none for her husband.

25

Two men got off the northbound train. One was in his middle twenties, the other a few years older. The older one was named Ord and the younger one used the name of Pendleton, which was not his real name, but it had a nice sound to it and the young man liked it.

Paul Partridge, who had met Ord somewhere, moved up from the depot.

"Ord," he said.

The man named Ord regarded Partridge carefully; it had been several years since he had seen him and he wanted to make sure that he was talking to the right man. He finally nodded. "Partridge, how's things?"

"Warming up," said Partridge cheerfully. He looked at the second man. "You're Pendleton?"

Young Pendleton shrugged. "What've you got here, range war?"

"More or less," replied Partridge.

"Any competition?" Pendleton asked.

"Sodbusters. You'll be ashamed to take the money."

Both of the gunmen brightened. "I hope the grub's good," said Ord. "That Mexican food never agreed with me."

"We've got some horses up the street," said Partridge, "and we'll pick up the boss. His name's Rawlins." He hesitated. "He isn't really the boss, but he pays the wages."

Young Pendleton shrugged. "Oh, one of those deals. We never get to know Mr. Big. Who is he, the banker?"

Paetridge shook his head.

Weber got down from his farm wagon in front of Denver's real estate office and was ducking under the hitchrail when Pete Rawlins came out. He stopped when he saw Weber.

"How's the turnips?" he asked leeringly.

"Terrible," retorted Weber, "some wet-behind-the-ears cowboy cut my fences and turned their steers into the turnip patch."

He continued on into the real estate office. Inside, he saw that the clerk was not in the outer office and pushed open the door of Mike Denver's room.

"Well, well," said Mike Denver from behind his desk.

"You offered me a deal the other day," Weber said.

"Now why would I offer *you* anything?" asked Denver.

"You wanted me to swing the farmers' votes."

Denver shook his head. "You must be drinking again, Charlie. I never talked to you about any votes."

The door opened behind Weber and Rawlins came in. "Just thought I'd stop in," he said, "unless you're talking private."

"Nothing private, Pete," said Denver. "In fact, I'm glad you dropped in. Mr. Weber here's making some strange talk and I may need a witness." He grunted. "He's got some idea I'm in the vote-buying business."

"He must be drunk, Mike!"

"That's just what I said. I thought you were on the water wagon, Charlie."

"I'm taking this," Weber said tightly, "because I'm trying to avoid trouble. I'm ready to make that deal you wanted."

Denver became serious. "You taking over for Leo Blatnik?"

"I'm not here on my own."

Denver nodded. "I rather thought you'd be their next leader. You really have become a sodbuster, Charlie. Biggest ranch owner in the state once and now a mealymouthed sodbuster."

"You can have the votes," Weber said, restraining himself with an effort.

"At how much a vote?"

"Nothing. Not one red cent. All you've got to do is tell your brother-in-law here to get rid of his gunslingers and let us alone."

"Gunslingers?" asked Denver mockingly. "Have you got gunslingers working for you, Pete?"

"I've got some *cowhands* who carry guns. The only reason they carry them is because Weber's clodhoppers have been taking potshots at them. And you might as well know right now that I've given them orders to shoot back the next time anyone shoots at them. Pass that word along, Weber, to your farmer friends."

"You've got some dirty scheme up your sleeve, Denver," said Weber, ignoring Pete Rawlins. "I don't know what it is, but I'm warning you, don't crowd us too far. We don't have any gunfighters but we've got a lot of men. More than you can raise by a good number——"

"First bribery," said Denver, "then threats."

Weber whirled away from the politician and whipped open the door. He stalked out. In Denver's office, Rawlins looked inquiringly at his brother-in-law. Denver nodded. Rawlins went out.

Paul Partridge and the newly imported gunmen were in front of Denver's office when Weber came out and went to his wagon. Rawlins came out and said something to Partridge. He continued on, crossing the street, as Partridge stepped up to Weber's wagon.

"Hey, farmer," Partridge accosted Weber, "I hear you been makin' threats against me."

Weber stared at the gunman and his stomach suddenly seemed to turn over. "I don't want any trouble," he said inanely.

"You're the man makin' trouble," Partridge said nastily. "Just because you're an old man you think you can say anything you like about anybody and get away with it."

Weber turned his back on Partridge to climb into the wagon. Partridge grabbed his shoulder and whirled him around. "I'm talkin' to you," he snarled.

Weber, jerked off balance, threw out his hands instinctively. One clawed at Partridge's chest and the gunfighter, retaliating savagely, slammed Weber back against the wagon.

"That does it!" he cried. "Reach . . . !"

Weber, hurt by being hurled against the wagon body, seemed to shrink. "No!" he whispered, "no . . . !"

"I'll count to three," Partridge went on remorselessly. "One . . . !"

Tom Weber, riding in from the west, pulled up his horse in the middle of the street.

"Two!" said Partridge, his voice rising. "Three . . . !"

Charlie Weber's palsied hands shot into the air, over his shoulders. Partridge's hands streaked down to his holster, came up with his revolver in his hand.

He did not fire. There were too many people on the street

watching. It was too obvious that Charlie Weber had made no resistance, now had his hands in the air. As raw as he was, there was one thing Partridge could not do—kill a man whose hands were raised.

Yet he had received his orders from Pete Rawlins. He could not back down. He took a quick step toward Charlie Weber, his gun raised high.

"You chicken-livered old coot," he raged, "you wanted to fight so damn bad, now fight . . ."

"No, no!" whispered Charlie Weber.

Tom Weber had turned his horse in from the middle of the street. He would reach the tie rail only feet from his father and Paul Partridge. Partridge's newly imported gunfighters moved forward to block him off.

Partridge's revolver came down, caught Charlie Weber on the side of the face, laying open the skin of his cheekbone.

"I'll pistol whip you within an inch of your life," the gunfighter continued savagely, "I'll make you wish you *had* drawn . . ."

The gun came back, raked the other side of Weber's face. Weber cried out, fell to his knees. Partridge, pivoting to get at him again, was suddenly faced by Tom Weber on his horse.

"You!" he said thickly. "His yellow-livered son. You're going to get some of the same."

He sent a quick look at his two gunfighters, saw they were conveniently close and moved on Tom Weber.

Tom Weber raised his hands shoulder height, threw his left leg over his mount's neck and slid to the ground. Partridge was forced to back up, step around the horse to get at Tom Weber again.

"You've been in my hair ever since I first set eyes on you," he snarled. "I'm sick of the sight of Webers——"

"Three to one odds," said Tom Weber suddenly. "That's just about right. Especially if the one's an old man."

"Hey!" exclaimed young Pendleton. "Listen to who's talking . . ." He started moving forward and Tom Weber suddenly smashed him a terrific blow in the face. In almost the same movement, Weber pivoted completely around, struck Paul Partridge's gun arm with the edge of his hand. The blow was so hard the gun was knocked from Partridge's hand and went spinning. Weber reached the end of his pivot, came back like a coiled spring and his left fist smacked against Partridge's nose. He felt the cartilege crumple under his knuckles

91

and, turning around again with the force of the blow, found himself facing Ord, the third killer.

Ord was in a crouch, his hand hovering over the butt of his gun. He was at a loss as to what to do. He had not been briefed about the Webers. He had seen Partridge attack an old man and turn on another man without a gun. He did not know what the consequences of such acts would be. He was a stranger in Barkerville and wherever he had been previously it had been against the rules to do such things.

You could shoot a man from ambush, you could gun one down in the dead of night, but you didn't do those things in broad daylight, with a dozen or more witnesses around.

Ord backed away from Tom Weber. "Not my fight," he muttered.

Tom Weber turned away from him. He walked back to Paul Partridge, who was on his feet, his hands clawing at his face, blinded from the smashed nose and the power of Tom Weber's blow.

"I'll kill you," he was screaming, "I'll cut you to pieces and rip out your blasted guts."

Coldly merciless, Weber hit him in the stomach. The blow bent Partridge forward, gasping. Weber brought up a terrific uppercut that caught Partridge under the jaw and smashed him back against the Weber wagon. Partridge hit the wagon with a crash, recoiled and fell on the ground on his face.

Tom Weber came face to face then with his father, who was struggling to his feet, blood streaming from his wounds.

For one terrible moment, Tom Webber looked at his father. A shudder ran through his body—and then he turned away!

He had not gone to his father's aid, had not stepped in because of pity. He had fought Partridge and the young gunfighter only because they had attacked him; it had been nothing more than self-defense.

Weber stepped back to his horse, put his foot in a stirrup, preparatory to mounting. Sheriff Moon came running up, his revolver in his fist.

"Hold on there, Weber!" he cried. "You're under arrest. I saw what you did——"

"Get out of the way, Sheriff," Weber said through bared teeth.

"No, you don't," Moon shrieked. "I've got the drop on you."

Weber brought his foot back to the ground, started for the Sheriff. Moon backed away. "Don't you come at me," he babbled. "Stop where you are, or by heaven . . ."

Mike Denver stepped out of his office at Moon's elbow. He said sharply, "Let it go, Moon!"

That was all Sheriff Moon needed. He turned, took a quick jump and, passing Denver, went into the real estate office.

26

Juanita came into the ranch office where Lily was poring over the tally books. "You eat supper now, Señora?"

Lily flexed her arms and shoulder muscles, stiffened from bending over a desk for two hours. "Yes," she said, "I'm not making much headway here, anyway."

Juanita bobbed her head, even though she did not understand. "I have nice supper ready."

"I'll be right in."

Juanita, however, did not go. "Señor Al'erton eat with you?" she finally asked.

That reminded Lily of the ordeal she still had to endure. "No," she said, then added quickly, "I mean, yes, you can set the table for him, but I think I'll eat in my room. Or, you can bring me something here. It doesn't make any difference."

Juanita, assuming the prerogative of long service, asked cheerfully, "You and Señor Al'erton have fight?"

Lily winced. "I guess you might call it that."

"Good. Fight sometimes ver' good for husband and wife. I bring you supper here."

She flounced out of the office and Lily, her thoughts brought back to the immediate present, got up and strolled to the door. Three or four cowboys had returned from their work and were loafing about near the bunkhouse. Lily became aware then that the sun was about to sink below the horizon in the west and knew that it was late.

She called to one of the cowboys. "Billy!"

The man came swiftly toward her. "Ma'am?"

"Have you seen Fred Case?"

"Why, no, ma'am, he was here when we rode off to work this mornin'. Ain't seen him since."

"Have you seen my husband?"

"He was talkin' to Fred this mornin' when we went off."

Lily turned away from the cowboy and went back into the

93

office. She had scarcely entered when she heard the pounding of galloping hooves. Going to the door, she winced as she saw Jeff riding into the ranch yard. He pulled up his mount, sprang to the ground and called to one of the hands to take care of the horse. His tone was more arrogant than ever and Lily wondered why she had never been aware of it before.

He started for the ranch house, glanced toward the office and caught a glimpse of Lily moving away from the door. He changed his course abruptly and came toward the office.

Lily retreated to Fred Case's desk. Boots crunched the hard-packed earth outside the office, then Jeff entered.

"Some things you and I have got to have out," he said abruptly, "if this marriage is going to continue——"

"It isn't!"

"Don't crowd me too far, Lily," Alderton said angrily. "I'm willing to overlook a lot, but there are certain things I won't concede."

Lily seated herself in Case's chair. "Anything you propose is going to be predicated upon one condition, that you give back to Lobo what you took from Lobo."

"What the devil are you talking about?"

"The money you drew from the bank for your political adventure. Every cent of it, Jeff."

He started to make an angry gesture, then stopped it in mid-air. "I thought our marriage was a partnership," he said stiffly, "but if that's the way you feel about it, all right. You'll get back what I spent, over and above the actual Lobo expenses. Anything else?"

"A thousand head of Lobo cattle have disappeared . . ."

"You don't know that."

"You told me yourself that rustlers were stealing cattle."

"I never mentioned any figure like a thousand. A few head maybe . . ."

"I've been going over the tally books."

"Fred Case is senile. If he ever knew how to keep a tally book he forgot it along with his memory. That's the chief reason I fired him——"

"You fired Fred?" Lily cried, aghast.

"I sent him packing this morning."

She sprang to her feet. "How dared you! Fred was my father's foreman before I was born."

"Every man on this ranch carries his load. I won't have a deadhead on the place."

"*You* won't have?" Lily said hotly. "You have no right to give orders on this ranch. Lobo is mine."

94

"Keep it, then!" snarled Alderton. "Keep it and be damned to you."

"There's nothing more to talk about," Lily said coldy.

Jeff cursed himself inwardly. His violent temper had momentarily got the best of him, as it had the evening before. Lily had not yet plumbed the depths of his perfidy—and he could not risk her going into things too deeply. Not at this stage.

He *needed* her. He had to retain the old way for a while yet. And if it meant crawling . . .

He said with a tremendous effort, "We shouldn't quarrel this way, Lily."

"I'm not quarreling."

"All right, I am. I apologize."

"It's a little too late for an apology."

"Do you want me to get down on my knees?" he cried.

"It wouldn't do any good, Jeff. I know what you've done, how much you've stolen from Lobo—"

"Stolen? When we got married we merged our ranches, our money. We pooled everything——"

"Did we?"

"Of course. All right, perhaps I should have consulted you more. But since I was running things——"

"I don't ever recall giving you permission to run Lobo."

It was necessary for Alderton again to make a tremendous effort to restrain himself. He wanted to smash the beautiful face in front of him. He wanted to . . .

He said hoarsely, "How much can you humiliate me, Lily?"

"You wanted to have it out, Jeff," Lily said tonelessly. "All right, we'll have it out. I went to the bank today. I know what you've done."

"Eads had no right to tell you."

"You stripped Lobo of everything. You took Lobo's income and put it into your personal account and now your fine friend, Mike Denver, had put on the pressure——"

"What?"

"Denver controls the bank. Or didn't you know that? He's forbidden Marshall Eads to make any loans to Lobo. In order to continue operations on this ranch, I've got to sell off stock. And with the rustling that's been going on, I don't know what——"

"You've *tried* to borrow from the bank?"

"No, but Denver anticipated that I would. He seemed to know that I would have to."

Jeff Alderton's face was a picture of puzzled anxiety. His previous concern about his relationship with Lily was gone for the moment.

"I saw Denver this afternoon," he said. "He didn't say a word about . . ." His words trailed off and he turned abruptly and strode out of the ranch office.

Puzzled by the sudden change in him, Lily got up from the desk and went to the office door. She saw Alderton striding toward the corrals and a few moments later she saw him come out astride a fresh horse. He put spurs to it and was off in a rush of clattering hooves.

Lily watched him out of sight, her brain a welter of wild speculation. She was still standing there when Juanita came shuffling up, carrying a tray.

"Señor Al'erton come back for supper?" she asked.

"I don't know," Lily said.

27

Mike Denver entered his Lobo Saloon and stopped just inside the door. He surveyed the narrow room in the manner of a liege lord looking over his domain. A man at the bar saw him and called out, "Evenin', Mr. Denver."

"Hello, Jenner," responded Denver genially, "How's the wife?"

"Just fine, Mr. Denver, fine as silk!"

Denver moved forward and a half-dozen others greeted him. Denver signaled to the head bartender. "One for everybody, Jules. On the house."

A roar went up at that and repaid Denver for the four or five dollars that the round of drinks would cost him. Only one man did not join in the general approval: Marshall Eads, who stood at the end of the bar nursing a glass of beer.

Denver said to him, "Want to talk to you, Eads."

"Good," said Eads, "I've been waiting for you. . . ."

Denver went to the stairs and climbed up to the balcony. He was a little annoyed when he reached the top to note that Eads had paused to finish his beer before following.

Eads went slowly up the stairs and, when he reached the head of them, found Denver already ensconced behind his desk.

"Mike," Eads began, "there's something I've got to settle with you——"

Denver held up a hand. He had things of his own to talk about and his own affairs came first. "Rawlins is shipping some cattle," he said, "about two thousand head. He wants fifty thousand against the shipment——"

"As soon as he produces the bill of lading."

"No," said Denver, "he won't be shipping for another week or so. He needs the money now."

"We can't give him the money until we have the bill of lading. The amount is too big unless it's secured."

"My word's the security, Marshall."

"Very well, if you'll stop in at the bank in the morning, and sign the note, I'll credit Rawlins' account with the fifty thousand."

"Sign what note?"

"For Rawlins. His signature isn't worth fifty thousand, but yours is."

"You heard me wrong, Marshall. I said my word was the security. I didn't say I'd sign a note."

"But it's not good without a signature."

"I just told you it *was* good."

"Mike," said Eads, "there are rules about banking procedure. Laws——"

"I haven't the time to learn them now. Just give Rawlins the money and don't bother me with the details." He leaned back in his swivel chair. "Now what was it you wanted to talk about?"

"It doesn't matter," Eads said shortly. He started to turn away. Denver came forward in the swivel chair. "Just a minute, Eads!"

"Yes?"

"I understand the bank's holding a lot of paper on these sodbusters."

"We have perhaps forty to forty-five mortgages, yes."

"Close them out."

Eads gasped. "What!"

"I said, foreclose on the mortgages."

"That's impossible," ejaculated Eads. "Virtually every one of the mortgages is amply secured. The people behind them are——"

"Sodbusters," snorted Denver. "We can do without them. This is cattle country and we're better off without these piddling little sodbusters making trouble."

"But *you* brought them in, Mike. *You* sold them the land."

Denver shrugged indifferently. "Man makes a mistake now and then."

"You've made one right now, Mike," said Eads tautly. "You've gone just a little too far. You think you've got enough votes to kick me out of the bank, you go ahead and do it. Call your stockholders' meeting for tomorrow. Vote your stock——"

"A showdown? You'll lose, Eads."

"Then I'll lose, but I'll be damned if I'll be a party to your dirty schemes. . . ."

"Very good, Eads, you've said your piece. Tomorrow, then!"

"Just one thing. I'm going to have the satisfaction of telling you what I think of you." He told Denver and the wily politician's smile froze on his face.

When he was through Eads clumped down the stairs and out of the saloon. Denver, his face red, took a key out of his pocket and unlocked the center drawer of his desk. He pulled out a sheet of paper on which were written the names of the stockholders of the Barkerville State Bank and the amount of the stock owned by each.

Some of the names were checked and Denver, taking up a pencil, made a list of the checked names, with the figures after them. He totaled the figures.

"I'm safe by a hundred shares," he muttered, "even if that damn fool, Alderton, loses his wife's shares."

He had scarcely muttered the thought than the owner of a hundred shares entered the saloon and headed directly for the balcony stairs. Denver was still studying the list of shareholders when Jeff Alderton appeared before him.

"Jeff!" exclaimed Denver, startled a little. "I was just thinking about you."

"Good," snapped Alderton, "because I've been thinking about you. All the way from Lobo. Lily tells me you've taken over the bank."

"You two still at it?" grunted Denver. "Thought you'd made up by now."

"We're not making up."

"Think that's wise, Jeff? Right now before election——"

"Don't get me off the subject," Alderton said hotly. "There're some things we're going to have out and we'll take them up one at a time."

"Sure, sure, whatever you say. I'm a man who believes in laying all the cards on the table." Denver had never in his life laid his cards on the table.

"Item one—have you taken over the bank?"

"I've got the votes to do it, if I want to," said Denver, thinking even then of Alderton's one hundred shares with a par value of a hundred dollars a share.

"There isn't much you haven't got your fingers into."

Denver shrugged expansively. "That's no surprise for you."

"It shouldn't be, I guess, but why did you have to spring the bank business *now* of all times?"

"Why, it seemed like a good time, Jeff. How's it bothering you if you've broken with Lily? I should think it would be in your favor . . ."

"It's one of the things that caused the break," said Alderton angrily. "You know how much I've spent on the campaign. I'm strapped for money."

"I know, Jeff, but Lily went into the bank and found out that you'd been tapping Lobo. She was going to cut you off, anyway, so I figured the best thing I could do would be to make it a little tough on her."

"You made it tough on me, damn tough."

"Let's see," said Denver. "You own a few shares of bank stock yourself, don't you?"

"A hundred."

"I might take them off your hands, just to help you out."

The carelessness of Denver's tone created a sudden suspicion in Alderton. "At how much?"

"Forty, all right, fifty dollars a share."

"Par's a hundred."

"They're not worth a hundred the way things have been going with the bank." Denver exhaled heavily. "You may as well know; I've got to let Eads go. He hasn't been running things properly. Made a lot of bad loans. Fifty dollars a share is more than the stock's worth, but to help you out, I'll say sixty, Jeff."

"A hundred! The stock's always paid a dividend."

"Won't this year. All right, hang onto the stock, Jeff. I only thought . . ." He shrugged. "What else is bothering you?"

"Lily knows about the rustling. It's got to stop."

"Fine, I never liked that business anyway. It was just to help you."

"Help me!" Alderton suddenly exploded. "Help me, damn it, Mike, you've helped me so goddam much that you've just about ruined me."

"*You* wanted to be governor, Jeff, not me."

"I wish I'd never thought of it," groaned Alderton. "A year ago I was a happy man. I had the biggest ranch in the state, plenty of money in the bank, a wife. Today I'm on the verge of bankruptcy. That damn governorship has cost me everything."

Denver chuckled expansively. "A fight with his wife sure plays hell with a man, don't it? Get drunk, Jeff, go downstairs and get yourself a snootful. Then go to the hotel and sleep it off. In the morning things'll look better. Lily'll have had another night to think things over and you can go out there tomorrow and make your peace."

"I doubt it," said Alderton. "We went pretty far tonight. I'm not going to return to Lobo."

"All right, go to your own place. Lily'll come around after a while. Especially after you're elected governor."

"*If* I'm elected!"

"That's no way to think, Jeff. You'll make it, all right. One more swing around the state——"

"One more?" cried Alderton. "I can't afford it."

"You can't afford not to, my boy. I've been getting reports from all over. You're running neck and neck with the Old Man and a little more here and there'll do it."

"How much?" asked Alderton desperately. "How much more do I have to pour into the rathole?"

"Very little. Twenty, thirty thousand at the most."

"I haven't got the money, Mike."

"The bank'll lend it to you. Of course, you'll have to sign a paper on your own ranch, but that's just a formality. Stop in tomorrow sometime and I'll fix it up." He suddenly frowned. "That is, *if* I'm running the bank. Eads is forcing a showdown. Wants a stockholders' meeting to see if I have enough votes to give me control."

"Do you have the votes?"

"I think so. Just about. Of course Lily'll probably vote her thousand shares against me now, but I think I'm all right without it. Just to be on the safe side, you'd better give me your proxy for the hundred shares you own . . ."

He pulled out a drawer of the desk, rummaged a bit and brought out a printed form. "Here, just sign this, in case. . . ."

Alderton clutching at straws, suddenly drew back. "Wait a minute, Mike, let's talk about those shares. You made me an offer a minute ago. I didn't like the offer. Don't you think they're worth a little more?"

"They won't be worth half what I offered you if Eads stays in control of the bank."

100

"Mmm," mused Alderton, "maybe Eads would like to buy my shares?"

Denver leaned back in his swivel chair. "Maybe he would, but do you think you want to sell to him? Will Eads elect you governor?"

"I don't see what that's got to do with this? The two are entirely separate. You're always talking business, Mike. You say never let your right hand know what your left is doing. All right, I think you need my bank shares. You can have them—for the right price."

Denver stabbed a forefinger at Alderton. "I'm warning you, Jeff, you're out of line."

"Thirty thousand!" Alderton said suddenly. "Enough to pay for the last swing around the circuit."

Only the slight flaring of Denver's nostrils revealed the politician's real thoughts. He drummed his fingers on the desk before him, suddenly broke into a smile.

"I guess I underestimated you, Jeff," he said. "You've got more guts than I gave you credit for." He nodded. "You win. Thirty thousand it is—and no hard feelings."

"And no hard feelings," agreed Alderton in vast relief.

Denver pulled out his center drawer and took out a checkbook. He picked up a pen and swiftly wrote out a check. Then he handed the pen to Alderton. "Now if you'll just sign this stock transfer . . ." He slipped the "proxy" form under Alderton's hand.

Alderton looked at the sheet and grunted. "You said this was a proxy to *vote* the stock."

Denver shrugged. "For talking purposes. I figured all along to buy. It's a stock transfer. Sign it and take your check."

Alderton hesitated, then signed the transfer. But instead of handing it to Denver, he picked it up. "I just thought of something, Mike. You'll be running the bank tomorrow. You could stop payment on this check."

"I could," said Denver thinly, "but do you think I would?"

"No," said Alderton coolly, "but I'll tell you what. I'll bring this stock transfer to the bank tomorrow morning and you can meet me there and give me the thirty thousand—in cash."

Denver tried to control his face muscles from twitching, but did not quite succeed. He said, with some effort, "If that's the way you want it, Jeff."

"I like the feel of cash."

Denver forced a smile to his lips. "You're learning, Jeff.

Business is business. I like you the better for it. Now let's go down and have a drink and then I'll see you tomorrow."

"I've a long ride ahead of me. I think I'll skip the drink . . ."

"Nonsense. We made a bargain. Let's seal it with a drink . . ."

Denver got up and taking Alderton's arm, led him to the stairs. They descended and stepped to the bar, some of the customers making room for them.

"Amos," Denver said to one of the bartenders, "a drink for Mr. Alderton and myself. The *private* bottle."

Amos, starting to reach for a bottle of whiskey, turned back and looked sharply at his employer. Denver fixed him with a stony look but made a quick covert signal with the hand that was away from Alderton.

The bartender stooped below the bar, got some glasses, taking a rather longer time than usual for such a simple job, then setting the glasses carefully before the two men, got a bottle from a top shelf. He uncorked it and filled the two glasses.

Denver picked up his glass. "Victory next month, Governor!"

Alderton shook his head, picked up his glass and raised it. "I hope so," he said, and downed his whiskey in a single gulp. Denver stepped away from the bar then.

"Tomorrow at ten!"

"At the bank," said Alderton and turning left the saloon.

Denver looked casually at Amos and found the man staring at him. He said, "I'm going into the back room and lie down for a while. I don't want to be disturbed."

"Of course not, Mr. Denver," replied Amos.

Denver walked easily to a door at the rear, opened it and stepped inside. He struck a match, found a lamp and lighted it. Then he turned to the door and shot a bolt.

He moved swiftly to a dresser, pulled out a drawer and took from it a revolver. Next he stooped to the floor and picked up a lantern. Shaking it to make sure that it contained enough kerosene, he went to a door at the rear, unlocked it and stepped out into the alley behind the saloon.

There was a small stable a dozen feet behind the saloon and going to it, Denver went inside and in the dark saddled one of two horses. He led it out of the barn, mounted and rode down the alley to the cross street.

He turned left to the main street of Barkerville and,

reaching it, turned north; the road Alderton would take to ride out to his own ranch, or to Lobo beyond.

The chloral hydrate knockout drops that Amos the bartender had put into Alderton's glass would normally take effect in two or three minutes. For a person walking or riding, the time would be a little longer. Five minutes.

Alderton's spiteful character saved his life. Leaving Denver's saloon, he crossed to the hitchrail, untied his horse and was about to mount when he saw Marshall Eads standing on the sidewalk just a few feet away. Eads had been there ever since leaving Denver.

The banker had defied Denver, but even as he made the defy he had known that it was an empty one. He stood now in the darkness thinking about his impending defeat and its tragic consequences.

Sight of Eads stirred up the smoldering anger in Alderton. He turned away from his horse and stepped up to Eads. "Mr. Eads," he said mockingly, "you did me a dirty trick when you told my wife that I'd transferred some money from the joint account to my own. Well, I just now repaid that little favor. . . ."

"I'm sure you did," said Eads glumly, "since you've come out of Denver's place."

"I just sold him my bank stock." A sudden spasm of pain gripped Alderton in the pit of his stomach. He gasped, but managed to continue, "That hundred shares gives him enough votes to throw you out of your—damn—bank."

The second spasm of pain caused Alderton to grip at his stomach. He groaned aloud and Eads suddenly peered into his face. "What's wrong?" he exclaimed.

"My stomach," gasped Alderton. "I—I'm sick . . ." He suddenly doubled over and fell to the ground at Ead's feet.

Alarmed, the banker dropped to his knees beside Alderton. He saw that Alderton was unconscious although moaning and stirring feebly. He turned him over and a folded sheet of paper sticking out of Alderton's breast pocket brushed his hand. He took the paper between two fingers, drew it out and held it up into a shaft of light that came from the saloon. He started to read, exclaimed softly, then refolded the paper and thrust it into his own pocket.

He got to his feet, looked down at Alderton, then turned and was about to go into the saloon. He decided against that, however, and turning to the left walked quickly to a store. The front door was locked, but Eads saw a light burning in a

103

rear room and rattled the door and knocked on it with his knuckles.

A man appeared inside the store, came forward and recognizing Eads through the window, unlocked the door.

"Martin," Eads said to the storekeeper, "Jeff Alderton's lying out there unconscious and I want to bring him in."

"Of course," agreed the storekeeper readily.

He went with Eads and between them the two men carried the unconscious Alderton into the store and to the room at the rear. As they deposited him on Martin's own cot, the latter got a whiff of Alderton's breath.

"He's drunk!"

Eads shook his head. "I don't think so. He's had a drink from Mike Denver's private bottle."

"Denver? Alderton? Why, they're thick as thieves."

"Thieves fall out sometimes."

28

Mike Denver spent a full two hours on the road, riding up and down with a lighted lantern, seeking Jeff Alderton's unconscious figure that should be lying somewhere along the road. He finally gave up the searching, cursing Amos the bartender, who had apparently failed him.

Tom Weber left his horse at the end of the lane that led to Charlie Weber's farmstead, climbed through a pole fence, and walked along the edge of a wheat field to within a hundred feet of the Weber home. There he left the field and entered the farmyard, circling around behind the barn.

Finally, he came along the south side of the barn and, standing in the shadow, looked toward the kitchen of the house some fifty feet away. The light was on inside and Charlie Weber sat at the table. Even at the distance, Tom Weber could see the heavy padding of bandage on both sides of his father's face where the gun of Paul Partridge had laid open the skin.

Helga Weber sat across the table from Charlie Weber. She was leaning forward, talking earnestly to her husband, who replied only now and then briefly.

From where he stood Tom Weber could see every detail of

the kitchen. It was plainly furnished with an oilcloth-covered table, four chairs, two for possible guests, a large wood-burning range, a sewing machine, a rocking chair and an open cupboard in which were stacked dishes and utensils. Everything seemed in order, neatly arranged. Helga was an excellent housekeeper.

Yet neither Charlie Weber nor his wife had learned from the death of Helga's brother. They sat in the kitchen with shades raised, in full view of any intruder who might come up in the darkness. A stone could be thrown from the shelter of the barn and break the kitchen window. A bullet . . . it would take a poor marksman to miss at the distance.

So Tom Weber thought as he stood in the shadow of the barn and watched the scene inside the house.

The moon was rising in the sky and there were patches in the open spaces where the light revealed objects about the farmyard. Only in the shadows was there darkness.

After Weber had been watching the house for some fifteen or twenty minutes, his father got up from the table and went into the bedroom. A light showed from there for a few minutes, then went out, but Charlie Weber did not return to the kitchen. Apparently he had gone to bed.

Helga busied herself with a basket of darning. She worked a half hour or more, then put away her work and carried the lamp from the kitchen into the bedroom. In a few moments the thread of light from the bedroom winked out and the Weber house was in complete darkness.

Tom Weber remained by the barn, however. It was not more than ten o'clock, the hour when night riders would be apt to start out on their missions. He finally left the barn after another half hour, returning to the wheat field and to his horse. He remained at the head of the lane near his horse for a full hour, standing by the fence for part of the time and the rest of the time sitting in the corner of the wheat field.

It was after twelve-thirty when he finally mounted his horse and rode off. Even then he did not follow the secondary road to the main east and west road that ran past his place. He cut across the Rawlins range until he reached the back end of his own 320 acres.

He was nearing the site of his burned-out buildings when it occurred to him that there was really no object in lingering in that area. There was nothing left of his house and barn, no shelter of any kind. He was just as well off sleeping in the woods.

He started to turn the horse off to the left, to ride down to the woods that bordered Lobo River, when the animal pricked up its ears. The long years of the kind of life Tom Weber had led had given him an instinct about such things. He pulled up the horse instantly and, leaning forward in the saddle, patted the animal's neck.

There was another horse not too far away. Since it was unlikely that it would be a stray it was obvious to Weber that a human was somewhere near.

He dismounted and faced the general area of the ranch yard.

A voice came out of the night, "Tom?"

His relief was so quick that he actually winced. Then he walked forward, leading his horse.

It was a moment or two before he saw Lily's face. She came out from the shadow of a tree nearby.

"This is getting to be a habit," she said as she saw him approaching.

"I wouldn't say it was a good one," he replied. "Of course, there's nothing left to burn so I guess it doesn't make much difference."

"I've been here for hours," she said. "At least it seems that long. Where've you been?"

He made no reply to that. "Don't count on finding me here again."

"Why not? You've got to . . ." She was about to say "sleep," then realized the absurdity of it, as Weber had himself a few minutes ago. If a man had to sleep under the stars, it really didn't make any difference where he stretched out.

She said, instead, "I want you to come to Lobo, Tom."

"Haven't you seen Jeff today?" he asked mockingly. "Or did you think he got those lumps on his face by riding into a tree?" He grunted. "For that matter, I've a few myself."

"The reason I'm here tonight," Lily said evenly, "is that Jeff and I have broken up."

His chin came up and he became alert, although in the semidarkness she could not see the look in his eyes.

She continued, "I *need* you, Tom."

"I told you yesterday," he said, "I'd be no good ramrodding Lobo——"

"I'm not offering you a foreman's job now." Lily was glad of the darkness so he could not see her face.

He shook his head. "I'm not interested in any job, as foreman or otherwise."

"I'm not offering you a *job*, Tom!" Lily cried poignantly. "Look at me!"

He took a quick forward step and peered into her face. She was standing in the moonlight, her body taut, half on her toes. A shock rippled through him, jolted him.

"No," he said abruptly.

She moved toward him. A hand reached out, touched him lightly.

"Tom," she half whispered.

He tried to speak, was compelled to clear his throat. "It's too late, too late by eleven years."

"Is it? *Is* it too late?"

The hand that touched him so lightly moved, found his arm and gripped it.

And then everything exploded in Tom Weber. He reached out, seized her and crushed her to him. His mouth found hers and kissed her savagely. He could feel the tremor that ran through her and then her arms were about him, gripping him. All the years of thinking about him, all the years of waiting broke the dam that she had built up within her.

Then as suddenly as he had seized her, he shoved her away violently. He took a quick step back.

"No!" he snarled. "It's too late for that . . ."

"Tom," she sobbed, aghast. "What is it? What *is* it?"

"You wrote a letter to a man," he said savagely. "You wrote to a man named Fargo . . . you wanted him to come and do some dirty work for you. . . ."

"Uncle Marsh told you!" she exclaimed. "He shouldn't have, but . . ." She floundered. "I don't know why he told you and I—I don't see how that makes any difference. . . ."

"Eads didn't mail the letter. He *gave* it to me. Don't you understand? He didn't *have* to mail it."

He saw her strained face in the moonlight, saw a sudden tremor run through it. A gasp was torn from her. "You—you're Tom Fargo!"

"I've been Tom Fargo for eleven years. I'm the gunfighter you sent for."

She took a backward step and stared at him. Her tongue came out, moistened her lips and even then it was a moment before she could speak. "You—you're Tom Fargo," she repeated then inanely.

"Tom Fargo, gunfighter. Killer for hire." A low, harsh humorless laugh came from him. "Still want me as foreman of Lobo?"

She said, too numb to think of what she was saying, "Perhaps Lobo needs a man like you."

"And Lobo's owner? Does *she* need a man like Tom

Fargo?" He took a quick step toward her, half raising his hand to point at her. She retreated instinctively and he stopped, dropping his hand.

"See? You shrunk back from me. Oh, don't worry, it doesn't bother me. It hasn't in a long, long time. I've seen women cross the street so they wouldn't have to pass me. Children run when they see me."

"That's terrible!" she cried. "I—I think I'm beginning to understand. Something I couldn't grasp until now. The—the bitterness in you——"

"Bitterness?" he laughed hollowly. "What have I got to be bitter about? I came back to the home that I hadn't seen in a long time and I found my father, a man who had been nothing but a drunken bum, a respected citizen of the community. Of course he may not live for very long, but he'll die knowing that he—he atoned for his past."

"You *are* hard," she said, her voice becoming toneless. "You've built up such a wall about your emotions that you can't break through—not for more than a moment, at least. But I know, Tom, *I* know."

"You know what?"

"I know," she said, "all that I've thought about you, *you've* thought about me. All that I've felt . . ."

"Ah, no," he said, "you're wrong. You're not even close. You've lived here, a good life, you never had to go hungry, you never had to fight for your life. You never had to—kill someone!"

"Don't, Tom, you're torturing yourself."

"Love," he said, "what's love? An emotion, that's all. And one of the lesser ones. It doesn't begin to compare with hate."

"Hate me, then!"

"I think," he said wearily, "we've covered it."

She looked at him, across the few feet that separated them. A touch had broken him down, had brought him across that short distance. Could she do it again?

There was a pain, a terrible hurt within her. She knew that his hand, his touch would soothe it, but she also knew that the moment had passed, that she could not a second time reach out to him. He would have to do it this time.

He didn't.

They stood there for moments, long moments in the moonlight, near the dead embers of what had once been his home. They had embraced and for a moment revealed themselves. Then almost as quickly as had come the surrender, the walls had gone up once more.

The tortured silence could not last. It was Lily who broke it. She said, "I think I'll ride home."

He did not speak, made no sign to stop her and she walked to her horse and mounted. Without looking back at him she started off.

He moved, then. "Wait!" he called. "You wrote me a letter. You sent for Tom Fargo. . . ."

She stopped her horse, turned around. He went on, "My gun's for hire. You're not the only one that wants it. The reason I came back to Lobo Valley—I had a letter from Pete Rawlins."

"Rawlins?" she cried. "*He* sent for you?"

"He made me an offer—a hundred a month and a bonus of a thousand dollars at the end of six months. I haven't accepted his offer. I'm open for a better one."

A cry was torn from her. "All right, I'll double it!"

"Mrs. Alderton," he said thinly, "you've hired yourself a gunfighter!"

"Get on your horse then," she said, almost hysterical. "Come along."

"Oh, no," he said, "you've hired me, but I have to do the job in my own way. You'll see me now and then, but not too often. I've been in this trade a long time and I've learned my job. Nobody knows where Tom Fargo is when he's working. He won't be where you expect him to be and he'll be where he isn't expected. Go home and sleep. Tom Fargo's working for you."

She started to say something, then suddenly choked and, whirling her horse, sent it off at a full gallop.

29

Tom Weber remained where he was until the hoofbeats of Lily's horse were faint and then faded out altogether. Finally, he turned and went back to his own horse. He stood beside it a moment, then, exclaiming softly, vaulted into the saddle.

He sent the animal forward, toward the road and crossed into Lobo territory. He rode steadily for ten minutes at a stiff pace. Suddenly he jerked the horse's head and turned it northward.

He had no special plan in mind. The past hour had been

109

one of the most tumultuous of his life and he knew that he could not sleep, could not even rest until he had tired himself physically.

As he rode along the range he was only casually aware of grazing cattle and he had traveled northward for two or three miles before his subconscious began to nag at him. He stopped his horse. What was it that was nagging at him?

There was little to see in the moonlight. The land was flat, treeless for several miles in all directions. There were no night herders in sight, he had passed none. Was it the absence of the night herders? Possibly. No, the scarcity of the steers. This was supposedly Lobo's best grazing land. It should have had hundreds of steers, perhaps not grazing this late at night, but certainly clumps of cattle that had bedded down.

He had passed not more than a dozen head so far. Yet— there was the dull sound of cattle movement. Weber climbed down from his horse and stretching out, put his ear to the ground.

He heard it then, the heavy pounding of many cloven hooves on the earth not too far away. A large herd moving.

He remounted his horse, turned it eastward, by north. He touched his heels lightly to the horse's flanks and it began to move faster, picking up its walking gait, then going into an easy lope. A mile of grassland was quickly traveled and Weber could not only hear the moving herd, but could smell the dust that had been raised by it.

There was a slight rise in the ground ahead and the herd was apparently on the other side, going downhill.

He was nearing the crest of the rise when a voice came to him, the words unintelligible. He pulled up his horse abruptly, dismounted and turning the animal so that it traveled obliquely with Weber walking on the near side.

He reached the top of the rise. Less than a quarter of a mile ahead was a compact mass of moving cattle. The herd was heading east by north and it was being driven easily by several riders who were traveling along the rear and sides of the herd.

There were at least three men at the rear of the herd driving the animals along in a steady, although leisurely, fashion. From the fact that there was almost no shouting or hurrying of the animals it was obvious that the herders were trying to move the herd as quietly as possible.

The size of the herd was too great, of course, to muffle all sound but certainly the herders were restraining themselves from the normal shouting and cursing that went with the movement of a compact herd of cattle.

Weber started to move downhill in the wake of the moving herd, suddenly changed his mind. Riding back until he crested the rise to the south, he sent his horse into a steady run that ate up the distance.

It was about three miles before he reached the main road. He turned into it, headed north and now pushed his tiring horse into a really hard gallop. He covered perhaps three miles along the road when he estimated that he was due west of the Rawlins ranch headquarters. He pulled up his horse, gave it a five minute rest, then continued on another mile.

He halted again, dismounted and cocked his head to one side, listening. The herd was approaching and would cross the road not too far from where he stood.

He moved his horse off the road onto the edge of the Lobo graze and leaning against the animal felt its side heaving from the run.

He patted the horse's flank, sniffed the air and thought that he smelled dust. The herd was drawing near.

A steer lowed and then Weber saw the dark mass of the moving herd.

Weber drew the Winchester from under the saddle strap, levered a shell into the chamber and waited. The herd, it seemed to him, was being driven somewhat faster than when he had been in the wake of it. It was about to leave Lobo land, cross the road and go onto Rawlins property.

He mounted his horse, then aiming the rifle carelessly in the general direction of the herd, the muzzle raised sufficiently to clear any of the cattle, he pulled the trigger.

The report of the rifle was startlingly loud and the bullet whined off into the night air. Quickly he levered a second cartridge into the chamber, fired again, then fired the rifle as quickly as he was able to, emptying it completely.

There were yells by the herd, flashes of fire as guns were discharged in Weber's general direction.

Weber, the instant he had emptied the rifle, was off, not down the road, but across it into Rawlins' land. He rode straight ahead, for a mile or more, then pulled up his horse and listened for pursuit.

There was none.

He rode on again, still heading east and after fifteen minutes of steady riding, crested a hill and looked down upon the sprawling buildings of the Rawlins ranch.

There was a light on in the bunkhouse, one in one of the

111

barns and two or three windows of the ranch house were lit up.

He refilled the Winchester, levered a bullet into the chamber, then fired, taking careful aim at one of the lighted windows of the house. He turned his horse then and sent it away from the Rawlins ranch.

30

Helga Weber watched her husband toy with his breakfast. She saw that he ate less than two spoonsful of the oatmeal and only one strip of the crisp bacon. His eggs he did not touch at all. She made no comment, but waited until he had stopped pretending to eat and then cleared the table.

"Charlie," she said then, "if you can spare the team I would like to drive over to the Novaks'. I promised Anna that I would come and see her today."

"Somebody's sick?" he asked.

Helga hesitated. It was not in her to tell a direct lie, but she did not wish to be questioned. She said, "Anna wants me to help her with a dress. She cannot understand the pattern."

"Will you be back by dinner?"

"I think so."

"I would like the horses this afternoon."

"Very well, I will tell Anna I must be back."

He got up from the table and went out to the barn. Helga busied herself with a few things in the kitchen, then got a light coat and put it on. She went outside and found that Charlie had harnessed the team.

She climbed up on the wagon and started into the lane that led to the road a quarter of a mile away. Weber watched her a moment from the yard, then went into the house.

He sat down again at the kitchen table, then suddenly got up and went to the bedroom. From here he could see down the lane, to its end. The Novaks lived east of them, yet Helga, even as he watched, reached the end of the lane and turned left, or west.

"She shouldn't," Weber said aloud.

Reaching the road, Helga clucked to the horses, slapped their rumps with the lines and coaxed them into an ambling run. The wagon bounced and jolted along the rough road.

112

It was a mile and a half to the Barkerville road and when Helga reached it she turned north. After about two miles she reached the northernmost bridge across Lobo River and just beyond she looked for the old Weber house.

She blinked her eyes when she did not see it, then inhaled sharply when a second glance revealed the blackened remains of the cabin. The barn, too, she noted, had been burned recently.

She turned the wagon in toward the burned ruins and pulled up. Seated on the wagon seat she searched the area in all directions. There was no sign of Tom Weber.

"Tom," she suddenly called. "Tom Weber!"

There was no reply, but Helga, looking off to the right, thought that she saw movement among the trees. She stood up in the wagon, calling again. "Tom!" Then she cupped her hands about her mouth. "Tom Weber!"

She seated herself and clasped her hands in her lap. She waited two minutes, three.

Tom Weber came out of the patch of woods, walked easily toward the farm wagon. Helga was aware of his approach, but waited until he was only a dozen feet away. Then she said, "I want to thank you for what you did yesterday."

"I did nothing," Weber said.

"You saved his life. They would have killed him."

"He can't fight them," Weber said. "They're professional killers."

"I know," she said. "I have heard." Then: "What is it they want? We are not hurting them. We—we are farmers, working people."

"You're in the way," Weber said. "Mike Denver doesn't want you around."

"But Mr. Denver is the man who sold us the land, the man who brought us all here."

"He's changed his mind, or maybe that was part of his over-all scheme. He needed the money you paid him for the land. Mike's got a twisted brain. He doesn't figure things out like most people."

Helga made a quick gesture toward the burned buildings. "They—they did this?"

Weber hesitated, then nodded.

She said, "Our home is yours, Tom. . . ."

He looked at her sharply and she continued, "You have no roof, you cannot live like an animal without shelter."

"I'm used to it."

"But it is not right. Not when your father's house is so near, when we have plenty of room."

Weber shook his head. "My father and I chose our paths a long time ago. His went one way and mine another."

"Tom," Helga said earnestly, "your father has told me everything. He—he did not spare himself. But the man who is my husband today is not the man who was your father when you went away. He is a good man. He works hard and—he does not drink."

Weber nodded soberly. "I am not the same man who left here eleven years ago."

"You've both changed, then, and there is nothing to keep you apart."

"Isn't there?"

A frown came to Helga Weber's face. "You—you mean because your father married me?"

"No," Weber said. "I hold you no grudge, Mrs. Weber. How could I when I don't even know you . . . ?"

"That is bothering you. That you don't know me. Perhaps that is why I—I came to talk to you today. To get to know you better. Charlie does not even know I am here." Her voice became low, almost a whisper. "Tom . . . come to our home today!"

"I can't," he exclaimed.

Her bosom rose and fell as she drew a deep breath and exhaled. "I cannot say more than I have said." She picked up the lines, then looked at him steadily. "Is there—any message you want me to give to your father? Anything you want to say to him?"

He shook his head. "Just to you. Draw your shades at night."

She looked at him puzzled, then exclaimed suddenly. "Because someone might shoot . . . ?"

He nodded.

She worried her lower lip with her teeth, then suddenly bobbed her head as she decided something in her mind. She clucked to the horses and they started forward. She turned the wagon in a sharp circle, but as she was about to drive off, she pulled up the team.

"How do you know our shades have not been drawn?"

Weber shook his head, turned and walked back toward the woods. Helga watched him a moment, then a faint smile played over her mouth and she continued on out of the farmstead toward the road.

31

It was eleven years since Tom Weber had visited the head-quarters of Lobo. Sam Barker had still been alive then. There were improvements, he noted. A wing had been built onto the ranch house, the office building had been added, as had the cookhouse and dining room for the hands.

Under Sam Barker, the hands had eaten in the ranch house. There had been only one cook then, and Sam had eaten the same food as everyone else on the ranch.

It was an hour after breakfast and seven or eight hands were loafing about the ranch yard; that, too, Weber would not have seen in the old days. Barker ran Lobo with a minimum of cowboys and the men worked from daybreak until dark and even after dark when it was necessary.

Weber did not know, of course, that Fred Case was no longer at the ranch and, even though Lily had told him the night before that she had broken with Jeff Alderton, she had not gone into details. He did not know, therefore, that Alderton also had left the ranch and that there was no one now to give orders to the men. No one except Lily, and she was just sitting down to breakfast after a restless few hours of sleep.

He dismounted near the main house, threw the reins over his horse's head and walked to the veranda. He knocked loudly on the door.

Inside the house, Lily called to Juanita, "See who that is."

Juanita came to the door and looked inquiringly at Weber.

"Mrs. Alderton?" Weber said briefly.

"Señora Al'er . . ." began Juanita, then her face broke. "But it is the young Señor Tomas! It is a long time since you have come to this ranch!"

Weber nodded soberly. "How are you, Juanita?"

"Ah, you remember Juanita." Juanita whirled and called, "Señora, it is Señor Weber. . . ."

Lily left the table and strode to the living room, into which Juanita was ushering Weber.

"You came!" she exclaimed. "You were serious, then, about—about coming to work here?"

"I was never more serious in my life," Weber replied. "In

115

fact, I worked for you last night after you left. You lost about a thousand head of stock——"

"Oh, no!" wailed Lily. "Not again!"

"It's all right, I know where they went and we'll charge them against Pete Rawlins' account." He looked beyond her toward the dining room. "I'm sorry, Mrs. Alderton, I have no food at my place and since I'm working for you . . ."

"Of course. Please—I was just having breakfast. Join me."

"I can eat with the hands."

"Don't be absurd! Juanita, breakfast for Mr. Weber."

Delightedly, Juanita made for the kitchen. Weber, ill at ease, followed Lily to the dining room.

"You're sure it was Rawlins?" Lily asked as she poured coffee for Weber.

He nodded. "I gave them something to think about. And there'll be some more today. I would like a fresh horse, the fastest you have on the place. It may be important."

"That'll be Midnight. He's coal black and the fastest horse we've had since I've been on Lobo. The only trouble is he's hard to handle and not broken too well."

"He sounds like just what I need." He inclined his head toward the ranch yard. "There's a bunch of men loafing around."

She winced. "Jeff fired Fred Case yesterday and I guess there's no one to tell them what to do. I'll have to do it unless . . ." She looked at him inquiringly.

He shook his head. "I didn't hire on for that job."

Juanita came padding out of the kitchen with a platter of pancakes and a mound of scrambled eggs. She set them down on the table. "I get bacon in minute. Eat, Señor Tomas."

She hurried out again and Weber started to eat. Lily watched him, noting that he was ravenously hungry. She did not know that he hadn't eaten since the afternoon before in Barkerville.

He looked up suddenly and she rose to her feet. "I'll have Midnight roped and saddled."

She left the room and Weber devoted himself to the food, doing complete justice to it, to the delight of Juanita who hovered nearby.

He was drinking a second cup of coffee when Lily returned.

"Where are you riding?" she asked.

He shook his head. "No questions, remember?"

She frowned. "I know, but—well, I have to go to town and I thought if you were going in that direction I'd ride with you."

116

"No," he said, "I ride alone." He started for the door, then stopped. "Don't go to Barkerville today."

"Why not? I've some business to take care of."

"Let it go," he said gruffly, and went out.

The black was saddled and tied to the corral beside the bunkhouse. Only two men were still hanging around. The others had saddled and were headed off in various directions. Both of the men watched Weber mount and waited expectantly as Midnight started to do his stuff. A savage raking of the black's flanks with Weber's boot heels, a kick in the rump and a tight short grip on the reins quickly subdued the black, however, and Weber turned him away. One of the cowboys nodded. "He can ride a little."

Weber rode away from the ranch in a northerly direction, but out of sight of the ranch buildings he changed his course and soon cut the ranch road to the main highway.

32

Marshall Eads was standing in the doorway of the bank when Mike Denver came out of his saloon a few doors away and came toward the bank.

"It's almost ten," Denver said as he came up. "Are the stockholders here yet?"

"They're not coming," replied Eads easily. "I sent word to them that there wasn't going to be a meeting."

"Then you can just send word again that there *is* going to be a meeting. Or better yet, to make sure they get the messages, *I'll* send them myself."

"You'll just waste your time, Mike," Eads said. He took a folded sheet of paper from his pocket, unfolded it and held it up for Denver to read, although out of sudden reaching distance.

Denver took a bare glance at the paper. He grunted. "So you got to Alderton . . . !"

"He got to me. As a matter of fact, I picked him up last night. Right outside your saloon. Seems your bartender gave him a Mickey Finn. He had a nice sleep, but about six o'clock this morning he woke up and in addition to feeling very bad in general, he seemed to have a slight hate for his former partner, Mike Denver. That's why he gave me this stock proxy to vote."

"Well," said Denver philosophically, "I guess our Mr. Alderton doesn't care to be governor. A pity after all the money he's spent." He smiled wolfishly. "And you, Mr. Eads, I guess you'll be running your little bank a while longer."

"And I won't be making any unsecured loans, Mr. Denver. You might tell your brother-in-law."

"I will."

Denver turned away. He had put on a bold front, but he was seething inwardly. He walked back to his saloon, had two stiff drinks, something unusual for him as he seldom took a drink before noon.

Then he left the saloon and crossed to the real estate office.

About ten minutes later, Rawlins rode in Barkerville with the gunfighter, Ord, at his side. He went directly to Mike Denver's real estate office. He found his brother-in-law seated at his desk, a scowl on his face.

"Hey," said Rawlins, "you don't look so good."

"I've had a little setback."

"Well, I've got something to cheer you up. We got close to eleven hundred head of prime beef last night."

Denver barely nodded acknowledgment. "Who'd you bring with you?"

"New man. Says his name is Ord. Why?"

"I've got a job for him."

"Who this time? Charlie Weber?"

"Not yet. I may not have to bother with him and his bunch of clodhoppers." He drew a deep breath. "Alderton."

Rawlins blinked. "I thought he was in with us."

"Not any more."

Rawlins' forehead creased in a frown. "Alderton's a big man. Not just here. You took him around the state, gave him a build-up. He's made friends——"

"They're *my* friends first, Pete."

"Just the same, he's a candidate for governor. Can you kill a man like that without having the state law down on you? Or the Federal?"

"Let them come. They'll investigate and what will they find out? That Jeff Alderton's closest friend was Mike Denver, who spent a hundred and fifty thousand trying to put Alderton into the state capitol. And who will they find are Alderton's enemies in Lobo Valley? A bunch of farmers. Alderton had trouble with them, a farmer was killed—the leader. So"—Denver shrugged—"the farmers retaliated."

118

The frown did not disappear from Rawlins' forehead. "It isn't good enough, Mike. Oh, it's all right for a starter, but once investigators come in here they're going to do a lot of snooping around. There's the widow Alderton——"

"She broke with her husband. They've separated. Maybe she had it in for him. How do I know? The marshals may even decide *she* could have killed him. As a matter of fact, Jeff milked her bank account and she's got plenty to be mad about."

"And two thousand head of Lobo cattle, Mike? We moved a thousand last night. They're on my ranch getting their brands altered right now."

Denver regarded his brother-in-law blandly a moment, then he got to his feet and went to the wall map of Lobo Valley. "I think it's time I explained the plan to you, Pete."

"You don't have to. You said you were after the whole thing. I believe you."

"But you don't know *how* I've planned it. What I've had in mind, right from the start, ever since I had the survey made, when I brought in the farmers. Look, here's Lobo, the key to the whole thing. Rather, Lobo's water. The Barker girl put up the dam here. That's fine. It changed the valley from a desert to the best grazing land in the state. What this map doesn't show is the contour of the land, the elevation at various points. I'll get to that in a minute. Right now, watch my finger as I follow Lobo River. Here it runs almost due east through the upper part of Lobo Ranch. But here, where does the river go when it finally leaves Lobo Ranch?"

"It cuts across a corner of the Weber fellow's piddling layout."

"Exactly. That's why I had you put that man Hopkins on his place. Now I'll point out what I meant by contour of the land. The front end of Weber's place is twenty feet higher than the rear. In other words, there's a slope *away* from the Barkerville road. A little dam put right here on Weber's little corner would turn the river completely. The water would spill away over Weber's place and down to——"

"My ranch!" cried Rawlins.

"Exactly. The river would probably cut a new channel, but even if it didn't, it would never cut across this wedge of your land here, or the corner of the farmers' lands—or go back onto Lobo and then down to Alderton's. . . . In other words, if we cut the river at Weber's place here, there's no water for Alderton, Sampson or Quayle. Their ranches wouldn't be worth two bits. They'd *have* to sell."

"Be damned," swore Rawlins. "You really had it figured out." He scowled. "But what if the Lobo people didn't like your cutting the water below them. What if *they* decided to keep the water gates closed on the dam, or cut it before it got to Weber's place? What then? The water'd go spreading out over Lobo, but nobody else'd get any—not me, or *anyone* else."

"That," said Denver, "is the weak spot. That's why I got the idea of sending Alderton to the state capitol."

"How does that solve your problem? He'd still own Lobo."

"You're not thinking deep, Pete. The whole scheme depends on *me* owning Lobo. If I own Lobo, I shut off the water. Inside of a year the farmers are starved out and Alderton's begging me to give him a few dollars for his ranch. Same for Sampson and Quayle. When I own the valley, I turn the water on again—and you got any idea how much I'm worth by then? A million acres of the best graze in the country and about a hundred thousand head of prime beef, most of which I've picked up for a dollar or two a head."

Rawlins stared at his brother-in-law as he unfolded his insidious scheme. When Denver concluded he shook his head. "I got to hand it to you, Mike, you think big."

"I've had to, Pete, I've had to. I started with a cheap saloon. I nursed it along. I watched others act big, and all the time I knew that they were working for me. In the end, I'd get what they'd built up. The fourflusher, Alderton, I listened to his drivel for years. I catered to him, flattered him. I put the governor's bug in his ear and I drew him along until he got in so deep that he couldn't back down. He *had* to steal from his wife, which I figured was just about what he'd do. Hell, I would even have let him become governor, if he hadn't gotten too big for his britches."

"What about the woman? Isn't it going to complicate things with Alderton dead?"

"I want complications. Lobo's in her name, but I've got a mortgage on Alderton's place. The estate doesn't have the cash to meet it, so I attach Lobo. She'll claim I can't do that, but it'll go into court. In the meantime, she hasn't got a dollar, not even enough to meet this month's payroll. I won't let her sell off any stock. She's got to come to me."

Rawlins shook his head in admiration. "Damn you, Mike, I'm glad you're my brother-in-law! I'd hate to have you looking at me from the other side."

"Keep thinking about that."

33

Weber rode into Barkerville on the prancing black Midnight and tied the animal to the rail in front of the hardware store. He went into the store. The proprietor stepped up behind the counter at which Weber stopped.

Weber drew his Frontier Model from the waistband of his Levi's. "I want to get a holster for this, but I'd rather not have a new one."

The man looked at him quizzically. "I got a old one, kinda worn."

"Could I see it?"

The hardware man stooped below the counter and rummaged about for a moment. He came up with a black leather cartridge belt to which was attached a low-slung holster. Leather thongs dangled from the end of the holster.

Weber took the belt and buckled it about his waist. Stooping, he tied the thongs about his thigh. He slipped his revolver into the holster, adjusted his belt, then made a smooth, quick movement. The revolver appeared in his hand.

The hardware man watched thoughtfully. "Maybe I ought to tell you that belonged to a fella come through here a couple of years ago. Fancied himself as a gunfighter. I gave the Sheriff two dollars for the holster after they buried him."

Weber took five dollars from his pocket and laid it on the counter. "That do?"

"Yes, sir! And how about some shells?"

Weber bought a box and filled the loops of the cartridge belt. Then he left the store.

He was moving toward the black, tied to the rail, when Marshall Eads hailed him.

"Tom!"

Weber turned and waited for Eads to come up. "I've got to talk to you, Tom."

"Later, Mr. Eads."

"This is important. It's about the bank and Lily—" He stopped, his eyes on Weber's newly purchased holster. "You're wearing a gun!"

"I answered the letter you gave to Tom Fargo. I've taken the job."

121

Eads gasped. "No, Tom!" he said hoarsely. "You can't . . ."

Weber's eyes flickered across the street. Rawlins was coming out of Mike Denver's office. Weber nodded abruptly to Eads. "Man I've got to see. . . ."

"Wait, Tom . . . !" cried Marshall Eads. Weber paid no attention. He started diagonally across the street.

Pete Rawlins, moving toward their horses with Ord, the gunfighter, came to an abrupt halt.

"Making your report to your brother-in-law, Rawlins?" Weber asked loudly.

Rawlins gave him an angry scowl. "What the devil are you talking about?"

"Why, you know, the raid you made last night on Lobo. How many head did you rustle?"

"Damn you, Weber!" shouted Rawlins. "You're going too far."

"I went a little far last night following your boys, then heading them off and scaring the life out of them." Weber chuckled wickedly. "Bet I scared hell out of *you* when I put that bullet through your window——"

"You!" cried Rawlins. "You had the nerve to do that?"

"Why not? Your gunfighters were out with the herd, weren't they?" Weber looked cheerfully at Ord. "Partridge and the others sleeping late today . . . ?"

"Weber," cried Rawlins, "you're a dead man . . . !"

"Am I, Rawlins? What about it, Ord?"

A shudder ran through Ord. "Wait a minute, Rawlins. I've seen this man before. I wasn't sure yesterday when he wasn't wearin' a gun, but now——"

"Tell him, Ord," cried Weber mockingly.

"Kill him," screamed Rawlins.

Ord looked as if he was about to become ill. He shook his head slowly. "This man is Tom Fargo, boss. I'm sure of it."

"Tom Fargo!" roared Rawlins. Then the full significance of the name struck him. "Fargo . . ." His roar became a croak and his head swiveled wildly toward the door of Denver's real estate office, where Denver was standing. "Mike!" he yelled. "He's Tom Fargo!"

Denver had already heard Ord. Rawlins' confirmation was unnecessary. He backed away, suddenly whirled and ran back into his office.

Rawlins, deserted by his brother-in-law, went completely to pieces. "I'm not going to fight you, Fargo," he babbled. "You're a killer——"

"So are you, Rawlins," taunted Weber, "only you do your

122

shooting from the dark—and you pick on farmers. I'm no farmer and I'm facing you and I'm calling you out to your face. You're a sneaking thief. You've been hiding behind your brother-in-law, rustling Lobo's beef——"

"Hold on, Fargo," the gunfighter, Ord, suddenly said. "I don't want to fight you, but I'm working for him and——"

"Earn your pay, then!"

A jolting shock ran through the body of Ord, the gunfighter. This was his way of life. He was a hired killer and it was his job to face other killers. He had heard of Tom Fargo for years, had vast respect for his reputation and he was not at all sure that he could beat Fargo to the draw, but he was being challenged and if he wanted to remain a gunfighter he could not back down.

He was alert, every instinct in him alive to the menace before him. It was to be a split second thing, he knew. Any advantage he could gain might be the difference between life and death.

Pete Rawlins gave him the advantage. Rawlins, hysterical, suddenly cried out in sheer terror. Ord's hand streaked for his gun. He had a shade the head start on Tom Weber, but Weber's gun was out of his holster while Ord was still pulling on his own. And as Ord's gun cleared the leather, Weber's barked spitefully. The bullet hit Ord high in the chest, half spun him around.

Weber's eyes did not remain on Ord to see the gunfighter fall. A sixth sense told him that the sudden climax would break Rawlins' hysteria. He was right; Rawlins, prodded beyond endurance, guessing that perhaps Weber's attention would remain on Ord, went wildly for his gun.

He never even drew it from the holster. Weber, whirling, sent a bullet crashing through Rawlins' head. Rawlins fell as though struck by an ax.

Weber looked from the fallen Rawlins to Ord, then shifted to the door of Denver's office. His gun still in his hand, he started swiftly for the open door. He strode through, crossed the small anteroom in a single bound and burst into Denver's private office.

He was too late. An open window showed him how Mike Denver had fled, the instant he had heard the name of Tom Fargo.

Weber slipped his gun back into his newly purchased holster, turned and left Denver's real estate office. A crowd was forming in the middle of the street. At the head was Marshall Eads, leaning over Pete Rawlins' body.

123

"Tom," he exclaimed as Weber reappeared. "You—you've killed him . . ."

"He was a rustler and a murderer," snapped Weber. "He killed Leo Blatnik from ambush." His voice suddenly rose ringingly, "Tell Mike Denver that Tom Fargo's working for Lobo. Tell him also that I've got a bullet waiting for him as soon as he dares to come within range of me."

It was a boast and a taunt and Weber made it deliberately. He wanted the people about him to hear it. It would spread like wildfire through Barkerville, through Lobo Valley.

He started for his horse across the street, people giving way on both sides, forming a lane for him to walk through. He reached the black, untied the slipknot, turned the animal and mounted. He was about to turn away when Marshall Eads came running toward him.

"Go out to Lobo, Tom," Eads called. "I'll meet you there."

Weber hesitated, then nodded and wheeled his horse. He eased his tight grip on the reins and the black took off down the street at terrific speed.

34

Having fled his office by a rear window, Mike Denver didn't stop running until he reached the courthouse. Even there he scuttled through the corridor to the rear and into the Sheriff's office.

He burst in on the deputy who sat with his feet up on the Sheriff's desk, reading his inevitable dime novel.

"There's a killer after me," Denver cried. "He's just killed a man outside my office, maybe two."

"I didn't hear no shots," said the deputy carelessly.

"You weren't listening," snapped Denver. "You've had your nose buried in that book." He shot the bolt in the door and stepped to the gunrack. "Where's the key to this?"

The deputy finally put down his book. "Now, Mr. Denver, there's no need for that. . . ."

The doorknob was rattled from the outside and a fist pounded on the door. "Open up!" cried a voice outside the door.

Mike Denver tore at the gunrack. "The key," he cried. "Hurry up, he's after me, I tell you———"

"That's the Sheriff," the deputy said easily.

"Bloss, you fool," came the voice of the Sheriff through the door. "Open up . . . !"

The deputy crossed to the door and shot back the bolt. Sheriff Moon started into the room. "What the devil." Then he saw Denver and stopped short. "Mr. Denver, there's been a killing up the street. Two——"

"I know," said Denver, relieved. "I—I saw. . . ."

"One of them's your brother-in-law."

Denver nodded unhappily. "I saw him go down." He suddenly reached out and clutched the Sheriff's shirt front. "Tom Fargo!" he exclaimed. "*He* killed Rawlins——"

"I know," said the Sheriff.

The deputy came alert. "Tom Fargo? You say Fargo's in Barkerville?"

"We had him here the other day," said the Sheriff unhappily. "Tom Weber."

The deputy whistled softly. "Tom Weber's Tom Fargo?"

"You've got to get him," cried Denver. "It's your duty, Sheriff."

"I can't draw a gun on Tom Fargo," protested Moon. "I'm no gunfighter."

"Me, neither," chimed in the deputy promptly.

"Look, you two," said Mike Denver angrily, "you've had it easy enough all this time. Arresting a few drunks, pushing around farmers and cowboys. All right, I don't expect you to go up against Fargo alone. But you're going to get him one way or another. If you're afraid to face him alone, swear in some extra deputies."

"Volunteers?" asked Moon glumly. "Who'll go against a man like Fargo?"

"Rawlins' men," exclaimed Denver. "Partridge, that man Hopkins and—and another man that came in yesterday. I forget his name. And the rest of Rawlins' crew—he's had ten-twelve men out there. They've been drawing good pay for a long time. It's time they did something to earn it."

"Mr. Denver," said the Sheriff, "I can't deputize men like Partridge and—and those others. They're hired gunfighters as much as Tom Fargo."

"With one exception," snapped Denver. "They're on my side. Fargo isn't. All right, that's it. I want Fargo. I want his body brought into Barkerville by this time tomorrow, or you can be damn sure there'll be a new Sheriff here the day after."

"The people elected me Sheriff," protested Moon.

"I'm the people, you oaf," snarled Denver. "*I* elected you

125

Sheriff. There isn't a man in this county, or Barkerville, for that matter, who holds office, who wasn't elected because I *let* him be elected. You know that as well as any of them—and you know what'll happen to you if you cross me. I'll not only take that tin star from your chest, but I'll have you thrown in this jail. Malfeasance of office, shortage of funds. You name it, Moon, and I'll prove it in Judge Tompkins' court. Do you believe me?"

Moon believed it. He had protested Denver's orders only because of his aversion to performing them. He said wearily, "All right, Mr. Denver, I'll raise a posse. We'll bring Fargo in, dead or alive——"

"Dead! Not alive. I want him dead."

"You'll have him the way you want him." The Sheriff took a key from his pocket and unlocked the gunrack. He handed a Winchester to the deputy, took down a double-barreled shotgun for himself.

"Let's go," he said bitterly to the deputy. "Let's earn that money Mr. Denver's been paying us."

A diabolic gleam came into Paul Partridge's eyes as he listened to the Sheriff. "I knew there was something wrong about him the first time I saw him. That was before I hit this town, back on the railroad. I'd seen him years ago in Cheyenne, or maybe it was Ogallala. It was on the tip of my tongue to call him by name, but he fooled me. He wasn't wearing a gun and he looked like a hobo. And then he told me this was his home town. . . ." He smacked his lips. "Tom Fargo, eh?"

"I'd like to take a shot at him myself," snarled Honsinger, one of Rawlins' young gunfighters.

Toward noon, Jeff Alderton essayed a small drink of brandy and felt the better for it. After a while he took a larger drink and it seemed to him that the agony in his stomach that he had felt ever since awakening that morning was just about gone.

He soaked his head in cold water, dried himself and thought he would have some breakfast. It went very well and Alderton then decided that he would go to Barkerville and have the showdown with Mike Denver.

He strapped on a cartridge belt and revolver, and walked out to the bunkhouse. Things had been slack on Alderton's home ranch for sometime and there were eight or nine cowhands loafing about, several of them playing poker for matches.

"Men," Alderton said as he entered the bunkhouse, "I want six of you to ride into Barkerville with me—with guns. There might not be any trouble, but there might. That's why I'm asking for volunteers."

He looked around the circle of faces. Several of the men tried to avoid his eyes. Alderton said angrily, "There's ten dollars apiece for the six men."

"Well," said a young cowboy, no more than eighteen, "ten dollars is a lot of money . . ."

"I'll take a piece of that," volunteered a second man.

The promise of the money got him the six volunteers, and ten minutes later Alderton and his men were riding swiftly for Barkerville.

Even though the Sheriff and his deputy had gone out to recruit a posse from Rawlins' gunfighters with the intention of taking the trail of Tom Fargo, Mike Denver no longer felt safe in his real estate office and had moved to his saloon. He sat behind his desk on the balcony, a revolver on the desk and a shotgun leaning against the wall behind him. His bartenders down below were armed.

Even then, alarm streaked through Denver, when he looked down from his perch and saw Jeff Alderton and six of his cowboys come into the saloon. Alderton looked around, saw Denver upstairs and gestured to the bar. "Have a drink, boys, but don't get drunk just yet."

He climbed the stairs to the balcony. Denver picked up the revolver from his desk and kept it on his lap out of sight. As Alderton reached the balcony level Denver said, "That old boyhood friend of yours turned out to be a wolf. He's just killed Pete Rawlins and one of Pete's gunslingers. . . ."

Alderton, his mind on himself, said, "I'm not interested in any old boyhood—" Then he stopped. "What'd you say?"

"Weber," exclaimed Denver. "Tom Weber—he's Tom Fargo, the famous gunfighter."

Alderton was rocked. "Be damned! And you say he killed Rawlins?"

"Less than an hour ago. But brace yourself, there's more. He's working for your wife."

Alderton gasped. "You're lying, Denver. I don't know what your game is, but——"

"Hold it," snapped Denver. He came away from the desk and stepped to the railing. "Amos," he called down, "what happened out on the street a while ago?"

Amos looked up, wincing as he saw Jeff Alderton. "Tom Fargo killed Pete Rawlins and one of his boys."

Denver turned back to Alderton. "Well?"

For a moment Alderton stared at Mike Denver, then he exclaimed, "So that's it! She had a crush on him when she was a girl. She never got over it and since he's returned——"

"She's been seeing him," Denver said. "That's obvious."

"I played right into her hands," groaned Alderton. "I left her alone to go on that damned trip. She met him over at his father's. I remember now the night I came back, she got to the ranch just ahead of us. She was with him then."

Denver shrugged. "Look, Jeff, about our little trouble last night——"

"You slipped a Mickey in my drink," snapped Alderton. "You were going to steal that damn stock transfer."

"All right, what of it? You were holding me up." He waved it away. "You got even with me by giving the proxy to Eads. But you were cutting off your own nose at the same time. I'll admit I shouldn't have done to you what I did—but neither should *you* have tried that fast one. We'll forget it now. We've *got* to forget it. We're in big trouble unless——" He lowered his voice and talked for two solid minutes without Alderton interrupting him once. At the end of that time, Alderton said explosively, "No!" but Denver continued to talk and Alderton continued to listen.

35

Weber kept crowding the black all the way to Lobo, and the animal was beginning to heave when he finally dismounted by the Lobo corral and tied him to one of the poles.

As he strode toward the ranch house he sent a quick look around and noted that there wasn't a single cowboy on the place. Lily had apparently sent them off to various jobs.

She saw him from the house and, as he neared it, she opened the door and came out. The first thing she saw on him was the holster tied down to his thigh. A frown creased her smooth forehead.

"Yes," he said grimly, "I tried to force a showdown, but Denver wouldn't stand still."

"You—you fought him?"

Weber shrugged. "Rawlins and one of his gunslingers"—He paused—"they're dead."

She had half expected some such statement from him, but when it came she recoiled. Weber said harshly, "You can't hire gunfighters without someone getting hurt."

"*You* killed two men?"

"They had the advantage and the breaks. Don't shed any tears over Rawlins. He's robbed you blind and he killed Leo Blatnik in cold blood. Maybe he didn't do the actual shooting himself, but he directed it. On orders from Mike Denver." He gestured toward the bunkhouses and corrals. "You sent all the men out."

"There were two things to be done. Since I have no foreman——"

He nodded. "I know, but things are going to be popping. I forced the showdown and Mike Denver's got to play his hole card. I don't know what it is, but it'll be something unexpected—and drastic." He frowned. "How far is that husband of yours likely to go? You know him better than anyone else."

She looked at him worriedly. "This is terrible, that I should have to say things about a man to whom I am married." She drew in a quick breath and expelled it. "I'm afraid he'll go all the way."

"I rather thought he would. I think you ought to keep some people around here. Let the work go for a day or two. I told Marshall Eads I'd be here, but it's too risky. They could cut me off."

"The men Jeff sent over to his ranch haven't come back. I told Fred Case to call them in, but I guess Jeff fired him before he could do it. There aren't more than eight or ten men on Lobo altogether—and none here right now. Except the cook."

"Can he ride a horse?"

"I've never seen him——"

Juanita, who had been standing just inside the door, popped out. "I ride horse, Señor Weber. I ride him good."

Weber turned from Juanita and looked inquiringly at Lily. Lily Anderton frowned. "What do you want her to do?"

"Get the men back. Or at least find one of them and have him go after the others. The Lobo men at Alderton's, too. You may need every one of them before this is over."

"I'll ride to Jeff's ranch myself."

"No!" he exclaimed. "Somebody's got to be here as they come in, tell them what to do—get them to stay here. Some of them may want to run out if they hear there's danger."

129

He turned away and strode back to his horse. Juanita dashed into the house to change to some clothing in which she could ride.

Mounting, Weber rode the black back to Lily Alderton by the house.

"I mean that, about staying here!"

She started to make a protest, but he kneed his horse and it started off at a swift run.

Weber had been gone from Lobo a half hour and Juanita, almost twenty minutes, when Lily, seated on the veranda of the house, became aware of a dust cloud on the road leading to Barkerville. She got to her feet, stepped out into the open and shading her eyes, studied the approaching dust cloud. She soon made out that it was a group of riders coming swiftly toward the ranch.

She ran into the house and caught up a Winchester she had moved into the living room. Pumping a cartridge into the chamber she again stepped out of the house.

The cavalcade of riders was only a couple of hundred yards from the house now. It was composed of six men and when she recognized Sheriff Moon at the head, Lily exhaled in relief. The relief vanished in a moment, however, when she saw that one of the men was Paul Partridge and another Hopkins, the man who had squatted for a time on the Weber ranch.

She stepped back to the door, ready to spring inside if it was necessary, and waited for the horsemen to sweep up. They halted in a flurry of dust only yards from the veranda. Sheriff Moon and Paul Partridge dismounted and the others promptly dispersed, two of them heading for the bunkhouses and the other pair riding around behind the house.

"Ma'am," said Sheriff Moon, "I have a warrant for the arrest of one Tom Weber, alias Tom Fargo, and we have reason to believe that he may be here."

"He isn't," snapped Lily.

"If he is, he's a dead goose," Partridge sang out.

"Mrs. Alderton," the Sheriff continued, "Weber's wanted for murder and I must warn you that that's a serious charge——"

"A man named Leo Blatnik was killed the other day," Lily said coldly. "Have you made any attempt to find the man who murdered *him?*"

Paul Partridge chuckled. "Salty, eh? Well, that's all right, I like my women a little rough."

Lily gave him a contemptuous glance and returned her attention to the Sheriff. Moon came forward. "I'll have to take a look. . . ."

Lily brought the muzzle of the Winchester around. "You'll not step foot into this house!"

"Ma'am," exclaimed the Sheriff, "I told you I had a warrant. You try to stop me, you're liable to get arrested yourself. In fact, I'm not too sure I shouldn't do it anyway. Weber announced in town, after killing Mr. Rawlins and Ord, that he was in your employ. That may make you accessory before the fact——"

"It sure does, lady," chimed in Paul Partridge.

The two men who had ridden toward the bunkhouse came galloping back. "No one there," one of them called.

Lily's eyes went instinctively away from the Sheriff. Moon, seeing his opportunity, lunged for the gun in her hand. She saw the grab, however, sprang back and again swiveled the gun toward Moon. But the moment's distraction was her undoing. As she swiveled from one object to another, Paul Partridge sprang in.

She saw him too late, tried to bring back the gun, but wasn't in time. Partridge's hand closed about the barrel. He yanked—and Lily's hand pulled the trigger. The bullet and the blast missed Partridge by less than an inch, scorching his shirt.

He tore the rifle from Lily's hand, half pivoted, and his hand came up and struck Lily's face. It was an openhanded blow, but it was hard and it knocked Lily against the wall.

"Damn little wildcat," he snarled.

"I warned you, Mrs. Alderton," Sheriff Moon said.

36

Kazumplik, the Bohemian farmer, saw the activity by the river at the corner of Tom Weber's ranch as he rode past on his way to Barkerville, but so many things had been happening around Weber's place of late that he thought it best to mind his own affairs and continue on. However, as he rode along, he kept thinking about it and wondered about certain things he had seen.

He was halfway to Barkerville when he suddenly exclaimed aloud and, turning his horse in the road, put it into a heavy gallop, unsuited for his work horse.

Fifteen minutes later he pulled up the heaving horse by the bridge and dismounted. The work he had observed was going on less than two hundred yards from the bridge, but some of the activity was concealed by a bend in the river.

Kazumplik left his horse by the bridge and climbing down to the river's edge made his way along the bank. As he approached the work area he became aware that a half-dozen teams were working away at the riverbank, two of the teams pulling plows, the others dragging scrapers generally used in road grading work. In addition seven or eight workmen were ahead of the horses, digging with spades.

In all, there were fifteen or twenty men engaged in the work. And there were a half dozen or more who were not working, but stood around in strategic spots. All of these latter were armed, Kazumplik noted.

The full significance of the work suddenly dawned on Kazumplik and he exclaimed aloud, "They're trying to turn the river!"

Mike Denver, accompanied by a man carrying a rifle, stepped out of a clump of woods between the workers and Kazumplik.

"Mr. Denver!" cried Kazumplik.

"Kazumik, or Kazumplik, or whatever the hell your name is," rumbled Denver, "you're trespassing on private property."

"But so are you," cried Kazumplik. "This land belongs to Mr. Weber."

"Weber's an outlaw, wanted for murder," retorted Denver. "His property's been confiscated. Although there's some question that he's really owned this place for some years. A matter of back taxes——"

"But what are you doing, Mr. Denver?" cried the farmer.

"What does it look like to you?"

"I don't know," replied the bewildered Kazumplik. "It—it looks like you are turning the river."

"Well, well," said Denver, "you're smarter than I figured you for. You're right, we're turning the river back into its *old* channel. . . ."

"Old channel?" echoed Kazumplik.

"That's right. I found some old maps that show this river went off to the west and north here in the old days. That's it's proper channel and all we're doing now is putting the river back in its rightful course."

"But you—you are taking the water away from—from the east."

"From you sodbusters," agreed Denver cheerfully. "And the rest of the valley, too."

"How can you do that?"

"How? Why, you're watching how right now. And I think you've seen just about enough, too. Suppose you run along now and spread the word among your fellow sodbusters. Tell them that they're such fine farmers they're going to get a wonderful opportunity to prove it—by farming without water."

Kazumplik stared at Denver in utter astonishment. The gunman beside Denver took a forward step.

"Beat it," he ordered.

Kazumplik retreated a few steps. "You cannot do this, Mr. Denver," he wailed.

"We *are* doing it," snapped Denver. "Go tell your friends. And don't forget to tell them that there are some guns here, quite a lot of guns. And we've got the law behind us. Don't forget *that*, Kazumplik."

Kazumplik turned and stumbled away, heading for the road and his horse.

Charlie Weber was in his field not too far from his house, feeling ripening stalks of wheat here and there to determine whether the kernels were hard enough, when he heard approaching horses, walked to the edge of the field and saw Kazumplik, Novak and another Bohemian named Nanovic coming toward him.

He climbed through the rail fence.

"Charlie," Novak announced as the three men came up, "we have learned something terrible."

An involuntary shudder ran through Weber. "Yes?"

"They are turning the river at your son's ranch," exclaimed Kazumplik.

Relief flooded through Weber and for a moment he was unaware of what Kazumplik was saying, for he had been expecting to hear that his son was dead.

". . . He warned me that they had the law behind them and that they would shoot anyone who tried to stop them," Kazumplik went on.

"What?"

"Denver's behind it," exclaimed Kazumplik. "It's his way of getting even. He wants to ruin us."

"He's doing it," agreed Novak gloomily. "Without water, we're done for. . . ."

"Now wait a minute," cut in Weber. "Let me get this straight. You say Mike Denver's down at—at my son's ranch turning the river away from here?"

"That's right, Charlie."

"But he can't do that!"

"He says he can," declared Kazumplik. "Something about some old maps that show the river used to turn north there, instead of east, like now. Says he has a right to put the river back into the *old* channel——"

"Be damned," swore Weber. "I was one of the first two men in Lobo Valley and that river *always* ran like it does now—when there was water in it."

The farmers facing Weber regarded him eagerly; they were clutching at straws. "Can we make him stop, then?" Novak asked.

Weber hesitated. "You say Denver's out there in full force? Guns?"

Kazumplik nodded. "And he said the law was behind them."

Weber made an impatient gesture. "Denver's the law. He owns every judge and politician in this area. I guess he can make any law he damned well wants and his puppets will back him up." He shook his head. "I had a feeling Mike was up to something dirty, but this is a little more than I expected." He frowned. "By turning the river across Tom's place he carries the water onto Rawlins' ranch——"

"Rawlins is dead," interrupted Novak, then winced.

Weber looked at him sharply. "Since when?"

"This morning," replied Novak. "I—I was in Barkerville when it happened . . ."

Something in Novak's attitude made Weber suspicious. "Who killed him?"

Novak exchanged quick glances with the others; it was obvious that the three had already discussed the matter on their way to see Weber.

Kazumplik exhaled heavily. "You'll hear it anyway, Charlie, you may as well have it from us. It was your son who killed Rawlins."

Weber stared at the three men. "How? How did he do it?"

Novak dropped his eyes from Weber's. "I was in a store. I—I saw part of it and the rest they told me. It seems he came into town and saw Rawlins and this other man, someone named Ord, coming out of Denver's. He—Tom—went over to them and began to call them names. Then this other man drew a gun. Tom killed him—and then shot Pete Rawlins."

"He killed them both? And they were armed?"

"Oh, yes. In fact, they, the people who were close and saw what happened, said that the man Ord drew his gun first. And Rawlins, too. . . ."

"And Tom beat them both?" Weber looked sharply at Novak. "You're holding something back!"

Novak nodded. "There was talk—your son was supposed to have said it himself—that he's really a famous gunfighter—somebody they call Fargo——"

"Fargo!" A low cry was torn from Weber's throat. "So that's it! All these years that he's been away. . . ."

He closed his eyes tightly for a moment, then passed a hand before his face. "I'm sorry," he said, opening his eyes. "We were talking about the river being turned . . ."

"We were also talking about your son," Nanovic said gruffly. "He's Mike Denver's deadly enemy and we thought maybe—well, we're Denver's enemies too."

"No!" exploded Charlie Weber. "If my son is who you say he is, if he's killed two men in cold blood, I want no part of him. If he's a murderer he must pay the penalty for his crimes——"

"But it wasn't murder, Charlie," protested Kazumplik. "They—the people in town—say he shot in self-defense."

Weber shook his head stubbornly. "Gentlemen, I must admit I did not have the slightest suspicion that my—my son was this notorious Tom Fargo. I had not heard from him in eleven years, but I have heard of Fargo. I get some newspapers and magazines and through the years I have read stories of gunfighters, yes, I have even heard of this man Paul Partridge—and I have heard of Tom Fargo. It is not self-defense when a man like that kills someone. It is murder, plain murder . . . !"

"But your brother-in-law Leo was killed in cold blood, probably by this same Partridge you mentioned."

"Two wrongs do not make a right. My son is wrong. I do not wish to talk about him."

"And Denver!" exclaimed Kazumplik. "Is *he* wrong—or right?"

Weber hesitated. Denver was a crook from way back; no one knew that better than Charles Weber himself. He knew, too, that everything that had happened in the past, that was happening now, was the outcome of some long range, insidious scheme of Denver's. Yet could Weber encourage these farmers to resist Denver?

Denver had the might and would fight with every available weapon. He was callous and merciless, Weber knew. He would not stop at anything, as witness the murder of Leo Blatnik, the assault upon Weber himself.

Blood would be shed, and Weber was afraid that most of it would be the blood of these men, people like Kazumplik, Novak and Nanovic.

He said heavily, "I cannot advise you. I do not know what to tell you. . . ."

"But we're being ruined," cried Novak. "We *can't* let the river be turned!"

"I do not see how you can stop it," said Weber, "without a fight."

"Then we'll fight," said Kazumplik grimly. "There are a good many of us and we'll make Denver sorry he ever started this."

Weber shook his head. "All of you know that Jeff Alderton and Mike Denver are partners. It should be obvious that if Denver turns the river he will also be hurting Alderton's ranch to the east and south. That can only mean he's turning the river with Alderton's consent. And Alderton, as you probably know, has perhaps sixty to seventy men working on his ranches, men used to firearms. Denver himself can hire as many men as he wants in Barkerville—or bring them in from the outside. He can get those men deputized, which means that if you fight them you're fighting the law. . . ."

The three farmers exchanged worried glances. "What can we do then?" asked Kazumplik.

"Nothing."

Novak groaned. "Maybe we need to do just what Tom Fargo did. Go right to the heart of the trouble." A sudden gleam came into his eyes. "Mike Denver's the trouble. If we get rid of him, we stop everything. . . ."

Kazumplik caught his meaning. "You're suggesting *we* hire Tom—I mean, a professional gunfighter?"

"Why not?" snapped Novak. "Somebody suggested that the other day at Leo's funeral. I'm thinking it's the thing we've got to do."

"I'll have no part of it," said Charlie Weber.

More than a dozen farmers had gathered at Kazumplik's farm by dusk and they continued to come as the Bohemians discussed their impending doom. The talk was loud and an-

136

gry, and again and again the name "Weber" and "Fargo" were thrown out. Always there were protests, but always too there was approbation.

While the meeting was going on at Kazumplik's, Charlie Weber sat in his kitchen, staring at the pattern on the oil-cloth-covered table. He had eaten scarcely a mouthful of his dinner.

As it grew dark in the little room, Helga lit the table lamp, but before doing so she went to the kitchen window and drew the shade carefully to the sill. "Tom told me to do this," she said.

Her words did not penetrate Weber's brain for a while, but he finally looked up.

"You said something about Tom?"

"When I saw him this morning he told me we ought to keep the shades drawn at night."

"Why should he tell you that?" asked Weber. "How did he know that we *weren't* drawing them?"

"Because he has been coming here at night. He's been standing outside for hours at a time, watching, guarding the house."

Charlie Weber stared at his wife in amazement. "He told you that?"

"Of course not. When I asked him how he knew about the window shades he would not reply. But I've looked—his footprints are out there by the barn."

Weber got up suddenly and crossing the room, took a lantern from a hook on the wall. He raised the chimney and striking a match applied it to the wick. When he turned Helga had the door open. "I will show you."

They both went out to the barn. Weber got down on his knees at the edge and for a long moment studied the ground. Finally he rose to his feet.

"I think," he said, "I will drive the team over to Kazumplik's."

37

Mike Denver had grown soft from years of town life and when the sun began to dip toward the horizon he said to Jeff Alderton, "No use you and me staying here at night."

"It's twelve miles to Barkerville, nine to my own ranch," said Alderton.

"But only four-five to Lobo," suggested Denver.

"You'd go there knowing Weber—Fargo's working for my wife?"

Denver grinned. "I forgot to tell you. About an hour ago, a fellow came along here. One of my late brother-in-law's boys. He said the Sheriff and his posse had been camped out at Lobo since midafternoon. They figured our friend Weber's liable to show up there and if he does they want to collect the reward."

"What reward?"

"The two thousand I said I'd give to the man who put a bullet into Weber, and the hundred apiece that goes to every man who's there at the time Weber gets it and has a hand in it."

Alderton grunted. "So *that's* why you're brave enough to ride over to Lobo. . . ."

"Before it gets dark!"

At Lobo headquarters, Sheriff Moon was in full control. Nominally, at least, for Paul Partridge was giving the orders to the possemen, who were spread out about the house, the ranch yard and bunkhouses. Juanita had done her job and had found a cowboy to pass the word on to others to come in to ranch headquarters. Juanita herself returned in midafternoon and soon afterward two cowboys came loping in.

They were promptly disarmed by possemen and relegated to the bunkhouse. Another Lobo rider came in a few minutes later. Faced by Paul Partridge, he bristled and refused to surrender his gun. Callously, Partridge sent a bullet through the cowboy's upper arm.

The other cowboys, as they came in, were herded into the bunkhouse. Two possemen, armed with revolvers and rifles guarded the bunkhouse, one in front and the other in the rear.

All through the afternoon Lily Alderton had refused to go into the house. It had been thoroughly ransacked by the Sheriff, his deputy, Bloss and Partridge, but Lily remained outside, seated on the veranda where she could see the Barkerville road and anyone who came along it.

No one came.

Until now, as dusk was falling swiftly over the rangeland. Four horsemen appeared in the distance, riding swiftly toward the ranch. Lily became alert and as the horsemen neared she got up from her chair and stepped out to the ground.

Paul Partridge, who was watching from the middle of the ranch yard, sent her a look. "Relax," he said, "it's only your husband—and the boss."

The four horsemen pulled up near the corral; they were Alderton, Denver and two of Alderton's cowboys, brought along as bodyguards. Sheriff Moon and Partridge joined the newcomers by the corrals and there was a considerable discussion there before Alderton, Denver and the Sheriff crossed to the house.

"Good evening, my dear," Alderton said mockingly. "You're looking very well."

"She's lookin', all right," chuckled Paul Partridge. "She's been sittin' there all afternoon, *lookin'*—who for, I dunno."

"Her old beau," Alderton said nastily. "Tom Weber, alias Tom Fargo, the outlaw."

38

Tom Weber had spent most of the afternoon in the vicinity of Lobo Dam and had even spent an hour or so sitting on a rocky slope some half mile from the dam, watching it.

The place had a fascination for him. He had roamed this area as a boy, in his late teens had hunted loboes in the canyon, now converted into a lake. It had been there, not too far from where he now sat, that he had had that fateful encounter with Lily Barker which had changed the entire course of his life, which had driven him from Lobo Valley to become a gunman.

Once or twice as he sat there, he saw the tiny figure of the caretaker walking across the dam and back again to his little shack and once even he had caught a flash of sunlight on a metallic object. A rifle perhaps.

Late in the afternoon, Weber finally left the vicinity of the dam. The black horse had rested and grazed, and Weber sent him swiftly across the lush Lobo range for a distance of four or five miles. By that time the sun was beginning to set in the west and Weber became more cautious.

He had headed for Lobo, but there was an uneasiness in him. The ranch headquarters was the focal point of his strategy, but at the same time it was the weak spot. Lily Alderton was there.

He was a mile from the ranch when he stopped and sat on the black for a long moment, looking through the darkness. There was a pinpoint of light that indicated the ranch house, but Weber did not like it. There should have been more lights. Lights in the bunkhouse, two or three in the ranch house.

He finally dismounted and taking down the cowboy's rope from the saddle pommel tied a short hobble on the black's front legs, to the snorting disgust of the horse. He was ruthless, however, and after hobbling the horse, turned in the general direction of the ranch and began to walk swiftly across the level ground.

He approached to within a quarter of a mile, then began to reconnoiter the ranch, making a half-circle around it and finally approaching again, but this time from the east.

Two hundred yards from the ranch house he got down to his hands and knees and moving forward in that position, advanced to within a hundred yards of the ranch house.

He studied the ranch buildings. There was a single light in the house and a smaller, fainter one in the bunkhouse, the latter a lantern. It was somewhere between eight-thirty and nine o'clock in the evening, and while cowboys go to bed early, this was a little too early. There should have been some activity in and around the bunkhouse, if not in the main house.

After a few minutes he became aware of something. There were horses in the yard, several of them tied to the corral poles. Normally the horses would have been inside the corral.

Weber knew then that there were strangers at the ranch and strangers could only mean enemies. He turned and crawled away from the ranch until he was at a safe enough distance to come to his feet.

He located his horse without too much difficulty and, unhobbling it, led it from some distance to the north before he mounted.

An hour later, having again hobbled his horse at a safe distance, Weber repeated a similar advance upon his own ranch. If a posse was staked out at Lobo headquarters, it was quite likely that anyone seeking him would have men near his own place.

He found out very quickly that his suspicions were correct. The faint twanging of a mandolin came to his ears and with the direction of the music as a guide he was able to locate the camp down by the riverbank.

He spent an hour reconnoitering it, had a narrow escape from discovery by an armed sentinel and worked his way back to his horse staked out on Lobo land.

He knew then that he had been on the right track all of the time. The rustling, the political maneuvering of Mike Denver, the carefully nurtured "feud" between ranchers and farmers was all part of Denver's vast over-all scheme to win, by conquest, Lobo Valley.

From the moment of Weber's return to Lobo Valley someone had been after his tiny ranch. First Alderton, then Rawlins and Denver. And even earlier, Tate Hopkins, a hireling of Rawlins, had squatted on the place.

The farmers began to gather as early as two o'clock in the morning. Some came on foot, some rode horses and still others drove up in buckboards and farm wagons. By three o'clock more than thirty had assembled and were drinking hot coffee prepared by a number of women who had come to Kazumplik's farm with their husbands. By three-thirty a force of more than fifty had gathered. A few more farmers straggled in later, and at ten minutes to four the men moved out of the Kazumplik farm. They numbered fifty-eight and were led by Charlie Weber riding a borrowed horse. His own team was drawing his farm wagon in which rode a half-dozen men.

Dawn was breaking when the cavalcade turned right in the Barkerville road and halted along the frontage of the old Weber ranch.

No attempt had been made for stealth and the noise of the approaching farmers had been heard by the men in the river-turning camp long before the horses, men and wagons had been sighted.

Charlie Weber, flanked by Kazumplik, Novak and two other farmers, stepped away from the main body on the road. They crossed onto Weber land and stopped.

"Hello, the camp!" Weber called.

For a moment there was no response although Weber himself heard the clicking of a rifle bolt somewhere in the woods ahead of him. Then a voice called out:

"What do you want?"

"This is Charles Weber," replied Weber. "I want to talk to Mike Denver."

"He ain't here," came the prompt reply from the woods.

"We've got fifty-eight men here," Weber said, "all of us have got guns. We're coming in if Denver doesn't come forward. . . ."

There was another brief silence. Evidently there was some discussion in the woods. Then a new voice spoke up, "We're telling you the truth, Mister. Denver isn't here."

"Do you want us to come in?" Weber called.

"No," came the prompt reply, "we're not going to let you come in. There aren't fifty-eight of us, but we've got quite a few guns of our own and we've got our orders. You come closer we fight."

Weber turned to his lieutenants. "Well?"

"We came prepared to fight," said Kazumplik.

"Novak?" asked Weber.

"We settled everything last night!"

Weber nodded. He started to turn away, to go back to the main body when the voice from the woods suddenly called out, "We'll fight if we have to, but we'd rather not. Denver's at Lobo Ranch. Him and Alderton both."

Weber stopped. "What do you think?" he asked his friends.

"Damned if I don't think he's telling the truth," said Kazumplik. "Trust Denver to go where he's got a soft bed to sleep in."

A brief discussion ensued with the opinion being that the river-turning men had probably spoken the truth. At any rate, only an hour or two of time would be lost against a certain loss of life.

The farmers turned off the Barkerville road onto Lobo territory. Across the road, at a safe distance, a half-dozen men with horses were posted to cut off any possible messengers that might try to get to the ranch ahead of the farmers and if necessary to fight a rearguard action.

The main cavalcade moved on in the early dawn toward Lobo.

Mike Denver and Jeff Alderton were having breakfast, served by a sullen Juanita, when a man came bursting into the house. "There's a whole passel of people coming!" he cried. "A reg'lar army . . . !"

Denver and Alderton slammed away from the table and hurried outside. Paul Partridge and a group of possemen were already looking down the road at the approaching "army."

"Must be a hundred of them," ejaculated Tate Hopkins.

"Uh-uh, half," said Paul Partridge.

"Too many for us," Alderton said quickly. "Let's go . . . !"

"Hold on," Denver said tautly. "It might be better to fight them here than in the open." He looked at Partridge. "What do you say?"

"Farmers," said Partridge cheerfully. "Fire a gun at them and they'll scatter." He drew his revolver, but Denver hastily threw out a detaining hand.

"Wait!" He sent a quick look around the ranch yard. "We've got twelve-fourteen men here, fighters all of them. And we've got shelter. I think we can stand them off. Long enough——"

"Long enough for what?" cried Alderton.

"Play Number Three."

Alderton gave him a dubious scowl. "What are you talking about?"

"Do you think I haven't foreseen this?" grunted Denver. "I didn't work out this scheme yesterday, or the day before. I planned it a long, long time ago. I covered every possible angle. If one thing went wrong I was prepared for an alternative. Well, just about everything has gone wrong up to now, but I've still got the old ace-in-the-hole. Plan Number Three."

He caught Alderton's eye and walked off, out of earshot of Partridge and the others. Alderton followed. Denver began to talk earnestly and Partridge from a distance watched with growing distaste. "Some scheme to save his own hide, I'll bet," he said cynically to Honsinger, the young gunfighter.

"Hell," said Honsinger, "who wants to be an old man?"

"You'll never be one, that's for sure," Tate Hopkins said sourly. He shook his head. "I don't think I care for this setup at all. Look—they're spreading out. They're going to surround the place and move in from all sides. We won't have a chance. . . ."

Denver, watching out of the corner of one eye as he talked to Alderton, also saw the circling maneuver and came abruptly back to Partridge and the others.

"Partridge," he said, "I want you and a couple of the boys to get horses and make a run for it. We'll hold them here."

"Well, now," said Partridge mockingly, "that's doggone nice of you, Mr. Denver."

"Don't be a fool," snapped Denver. "I haven't got time. I want you to ride to the camp by the river, down at Weber's ranch. They've got some dynamite. You're to pile it into a wagon and then drive the wagon to"—He licked his lips with the tip of his tongue—"to Lobo Dam——"

"That's all," said Partridge nodding, "get past this young

army, ride like hell for five-ten miles, get a bunch of dynamite and drive it across rough country ten-twelve miles, with farmers taking potshots at me—and the dynamite—all the way. I do this because I like the way you part your hair——"

"You do it for *this*," snapped Denver. He reached into his breast pocket and whisked out a wallet. He skinned out a half-inch stack of currency—all hundreds.

"It'll take two men," he continued. "No, better make it three. Five hundred apiece right now, and a thousand apiece when the dam blows."

"Oh, we blow up the dam, too?"

"That's the easiest part of the job. There's no one there but an old caretaker. He can't see a hundred feet beyond his nose."

Paul Partridge took the stack of bills from Denver's hand. "Well, kid?" he said to Honsinger.

"That's a lot of money," Honsinger said.

"Hopkins?" Partridge asked.

Hopkins sent a worried glance at the encircling farmers. "Damned if I like it, but I can use the money. Come on. . . ."

The three men headed for the corrals in a rush, mounted and, whooping, sent their horses galloping off to the west.

"Two and a half hours," Denver said to Alderton. "Maybe three."

"Can we hold them that long?"

"We don't have to hold them that long. Only long enough for Partridge to get the dynamite and get a good head start for the dam."

39

Charlie Weber, at the head of the encircling column, was aware of the three riders leaving Lobo and spurred his horse forward to try to intercept them. Several of the farmers followed him, but their mounts were work horses, slow and clumsy. The last of the trio escaped the circle by more than a hundred feet.

Novak sent a rifle shot after them.

"They're going for help," exclaimed Kazumplik. "The men at the river camp . . ."

"I don't know," said Weber worriedly. "None of those men were Mike Denver. If he's here and staying behind, he's got something up his sleeve." He nodded suddenly. "Let's find out."

He reached into his hip pocket and drew out a clean white handkerchief. Tying it to the muzzle of his rifle, he nodded to his companions and rode toward the ranch.

In the lee of the ranch house, Denver and Alderton saw the handkerchief on Weber's gun. "He wants a truce," Alderton exclaimed.

"That's fine," Denver said with huge satisfaction, "we'll kill some time."

He stepped out into the open. Alderton hesitated, then followed, first sending a quick glance around the ranch yard and noting the men at strategic spots.

He was catching up with Denver when the house door banged and Lily came dashing out.

"Mr. Weber!" Lily called at the top of her voice.

Alderton whirled. "Get back in the house, you fool!"

He started for her. Lily dodged off to the right, started past Denver, to run toward the approaching farmers. Deputy Sheriff Bloss, hiding at the edge of the house, suddenly stepped out and thrust his foot in the path of Lily. She was too late to see the obstruction, tripped over the deputy's foot and crashed to the hard earth.

Alderton dashed up, caught Lily's arm and jerked her to her feet. Lily, half stunned by the fall, struggled to get free of her husband, but he caught her up bodily and strode to the house.

Denver moved forward to meet Weber, Kazumplik and Novak.

The three farmers rode up to within fifty feet of Denver before he raised his hand. "That's far enough. I can hear you from here."

"You've seen our men," Weber began. "You know we've got enough to take this ranch."

"Maybe," said Denver cheerfully, "and maybe not, but I want to call your attention to the fact that this is a legally constituted posse, headed by the legal Sheriff of this county. Any overt act, by any member of your group, and you're all equally responsible."

"Don't talk to me about law, Denver," growled Weber. "What you're doing down at my son's place is illegal."

"Since when are *you* a lawyer, Weber?" mocked Denver. "Have you been down to the courthouse lately and looked up

145

the records? Your son's ranch, as you call it, was sold for taxes seven years ago——"

"That's not true. The taxes were paid."

"Did *you* pay them?"

Weber had not paid them, but Marshall Eads had told him years ago that the property was still in Tom's name.

"And by the way," continued Denver, "is that fine son of yours with you? If he is, the Sheriff has a warrant for his arrest. Murder. Double murder. If you're protecting him——"

"Tom's not with us," snapped Weber.

"Charlie!" Kazumplik said suddenly. "We're playing his game—talking. He's stalling for time. Those men who rode off——"

"I know," said Weber. He turned his horse abruptly and started off, back to the line of farmers. His friends trotted at his side.

A half dozen of the farmers came forward to meet the trio as they returned. "Do we fight?" one of them called out.

"We fight," replied Kazumplik.

"I'm not so sure," said Weber. "I didn't like Denver's attitude one bit. He's too cocky and you hit it on the nose when you said that we were playing his game by talking. He *wanted* us to talk."

He looked off to the east. "Perhaps we made a mistake coming here."

"You think Denver wanted to *draw* us here?" asked Novak. "So they could finish the job down by the river?"

"I know that riverbank," Weber said worriedly. "It'll take them more then the few hours they worked on it yesterday. Unless"—he frowned heavily—"unless they use dynamite. . . ."

"That's it!" cried Kazumplik. "Those men—Denver sent them down to the river to tell them to blast away while he held us here. Damn it, we've got to go after them."

"Wait a minute," Weber said. "Let's not be hasty. I've known Mike Denver a long time. I—I even worked for him once. I saw the man every day and I saw him sit there and scheme. He was like a spider, the most devious man I ever saw. Never anything direct or open and shut. Always the plot, the trick somewhere. What he's doing now is just a bit too open and aboveboard. He'd got a crew down there digging away at the riverbank to turn the river. We can see that and understand it. But is it the *real* thing—the ultimate goal he's got in that crooked mind of his?"

"What else could he be scheming?" demanded Kazumplik.

"He's out to ruin us and the best way of doing it is turning that river."

"Yes, but is that *all* he's interested in—ruining the farmers? I think Denver's got a bigger scheme than that in the back of his head. I think he wants *all* of Lobo Valley." He turned and looked off to the north and west, in the direction of Lobo Dam.

40

Tom Weber did not sleep at all that night. He rode Lobo range and now and then stopped his horse and sat on the ground for a while. Once he even hobbled the horse and stretched out for an hour, but he did not sleep.

He had an oppressive feeling of impending disaster. He expected that the coming day would see the culmination of events in Lobo Valley, but he knew too that blood would be shed on this day. It could well be his own.

Long a fatalist, the thought of meeting his fate in this place and this day somehow made him apprehensive. He was not ready. There were things to be done—things that needed doing badly. Things he had done wrong in the last few days.

He was not satisfied.

Dawn found Weber in sight of Lobo Dam and when he saw the little cabin atop the dam he was reminded that he had eaten nothing since late morning of the day before, more than twenty hours.

The country was open for several miles in every direction except beyond the dam, and from that direction no one could come upon him unexpectedly.

He shook out the reins and kneed the black. The horse responded and Weber was soon at the foot of the dam.

He found a heavy stick of wood, drove it into the ground and staked out the horse on the cowboy's lasso, which would give it some thirty feet of grazing area.

He ran quickly toward the cement stairs that led up to the dam and began to mount them. He was halfway up when a voice suddenly called down to him, "That's far enough!"

Weber stopped and looked upward. The caretaker stood at the head of the stairs, a rifle pointing down at Weber.

Weber called up, "I was here to see you the other night."

"Yep, you sure was," replied the caretaker. "I had no business to let you up here then and I sure ain't goin' to let you now. You get down, Mister, and climb atop that horse of yours and hightail it out of here."

Weber groaned. He had counted on getting some food from the old man. He took a downward step and then a second man came running out of the caretaker's shack. "Tom Weber!" a voice called down to him.

Weber craned his neck and looked up again. The man who had just called to him was someone he knew, someone from the long-ago past. Fred Case, foreman of Lobo!

"Mr. Case," he cried, "I've been looking all over Lobo for you."

"I been here all the time," Case said. "I came here right after Miss Lily's no-good husband fired me."

Weber started quickly up the stairs and the caretaker did not again try to prevent his advance. He reached the top of the dam and went toward Case, hand outstretched.

The old-timer shook his hand warmly. "What's happening at the ranch, Tom?" he asked fearfully.

"Plenty."

"Lily's all right?"

"She was yesterday afternoon," Weber hesitated. "I'm not so sure now. I returned last night and the place seemed to be staked out with—with men who weren't Lobo men."

"What's going on? What's behind everything—the rustling, Alderton firing me . . . ?"

"I think Alderton and Denver are planning to take over the entire valley," Weber said soberly. "I came here because I've a feeling that there's going to be trouble—here. . . ."

"Here?" cried the caretaker. "What kind of trouble?"

"This dam is the key to Lobo Valley," Weber said. "I left here during the big drought eleven years ago. I still remember what Lobo Valley looked like then."

"I remember too," said Fred Case. "This dam has made all the difference in the world. Without it the valley'd be a desert."

"Maybe that's what Denver wants," suggested Weber. "A desert. You can buy desert land cheap—and then if you build a new dam . . ."

Fred Case whistled softly.

Partridge, Honsinger and Hopkins eluded the six men comprising the rearguard of the farmers without too much trouble. When they saw them lined up at intervals they made a sharp turn and putting their horses into a gallop, crossed the Barkerville Road and rode on to the Weber ranch. Once on it, they cut eastward and were soon galloping down on the camp by the river.

A man with a rifle challenged them, but they were passed through to a man named Newman, who seemed to be in charge in the absence of Mike Denver and Jeff Alderton.

Partridge told them what was wanted.

"We were getting ready to blast here," Newman said. "Another hour and we'd have been ready."

"You'll have to hold your boom-boom," Partridge retorted. "Pile the stuff on a wagon."

There were six large boxes of dynamite.

Hopkins suddenly said, "Who's going to drive?"

"You," replied Partridge cheerfully.

"Be damned if I will. The wagon hits a bump and you won't find anything of the driver but his teeth. . . ."

Honsinger, always so brash, regarded the dynamite dourly. "I never was much for driving a wagon."

"Neither was I," Partridge retorted, "but somebody's got to drive it." He thought for a moment. "We can draw straws."

"Wait a minute," Hopkins said suddenly. "We all got five hundred apiece. Why don't we hire one of these people to drive for us?"

The idea appealed to both Honsinger and Partridge, and they had a quick huddle. Then Partridge accosted Newman. "Look here, we need a driver for this wagon. There might be some trouble and me and the boys can't drive and fight at the same time. There's a hundred dollars for the driver."

Newman frowned. "A hundred? For two hundred I'd drive it myself. . . ."

"Two hundred it is!"

Newman gulped, but drew a deep breath. "All right, give me the money."

"When we get to the dam."

"I may never reach it."

"In that case, the money's blown to hell. No use wasting money like that. . . ."

"The money now," said Newman angrily, "or you can go to hell."

Partridge went back to the other gunfighters and collected money from them. He returned and thrust the bills into Newman's hands. "Start rolling."

Newman climbed into the light wagon, picked up the lines and started off heading northward across the length of the

149

Weber ranch. Partridge, Honsinger and Hopkins mounted their horses and cut directly across the ranch to the road, riding out in full sight of the six farmers, who were spread out in the distance.

They started toward them in a clump, saw the farmers assemble and come toward them. The three gunfighters swerved to the left and led the farmers in that direction. Then, when the farmers realized they were leaving their post and began to lag, the gunfighters suddenly wheeled their horses and headed northward.

By that time the dynamite wagon had crossed the Barkerville Road and was rolling swiftly along the road in the direction of Lobo ranch headquarters.

The three gunfighters got together in a tight group and rode for a hundred yards or so, then, suddenly wheeling their horses, opened fire on the farmers. The latter promptly scattered, but assembling after a few moments began to return the fire of the gunfighters. The gunfighters promptly turned and rode off again.

The six farmers did not pursue. They had been left behind as a rear guard; they had not been told about any wagons that might attempt to run the gantlet.

The dynamite wagon, with the three gunfighters keeping behind it at a safe distance, continued along the Lobo road for two miles or more, then the driver left the road and took a northwesterly direction toward Lobo River, which would in turn lead him to the dam, between five and six miles from Lobo headquarters and perhaps nine or ten miles from the Weber ranch.

Charlie Weber had left Kazumplik and Novak in charge of the farmers at Lobo. They were to continue the encircling of the ranch, but were not to provoke a general fight unless the forces at the ranch tried to break out—or insisted on a fight, which Weber thought unlikely.

Weber and four of the younger farmers were mounted on the best available horses and were trotting across Lobo range in the direction of Lobo Dam.

They were two miles from the ranch when one of the men raised a shout. Weber pulled up his horse, turned and less than a half-mile away saw a wagon coming out of a shallow swale. The wagon was going at a stiff clip, north by west.

"I think that's it," Weber said.

He turned his horse and started toward the wagon, riding in an oblique direction to cut the wagon's path. He had gone no more than a hundred yards, with the farmers following, when three riders came out of the same swale that had disgorged the wagon.

The riders saw the farmers and dashed forward. "Pull up!" roared Weber, drawing his own mount to an abrupt halt.

The farmers milled around. Weber, waiting for the attackers to come within range, suddenly grasped the tactics.

"After the wagon," he shouted and kicked his horse into action.

As the farmers started, the gunfighters opened fire. The range was too great for accurate revolver shooting, but bullets began to sing about Weber and his friends. They continued on, however, and the gunfighters suddenly broke and headed after the wagon.

They distanced the pursuing farmers on slower horses, but the slow horses were still faster than the team drawing the wagon and it was apparent that the farmers would soon catch up with the wagon.

41

Tom Weber was finishing his coffee in the little shack on top of Lobo Dam when the caretaker came running into the cabin. "Lookit this!"

Weber, with Case at his heels, pounded out of the shack. Down below, a quarter of a mile away, a light wagon was rolling toward the dam. Behind and to the right, three horsemen were following and beyond them, four horsemen. As Weber looked he saw puffs of smoke coming from the guns of the foremost horsemen and after a moment he heard the faint banging of revolvers.

"What do you make of it?" exclaimed Fred Case.

Weber suddenly pointed at the wagon. "There's dynamite in that wagon."

"Dynamite!" cried the caretaker.

"Denver's ace-in-the-hole," said Weber grimly. "They're going to blow up this dam——"

"But those fellows are shootin' at each other . . . !"

"The first bunch are protecting the wagon," Weber said, "the second group are trying to get it."

He turned to the caretaker. "Give me your rifle." The care-

151

taker, without question, ran into the shack. He returned in an instant with his rifle.

Weber grabbed the gun from his hand and, kneeling, sighted along the barrel. He was shooting downhill and the range was still far, but he wanted to stop the wagon before it came too close to the dam.

He squeezed the trigger, looked down into the valley. He had overshot.

He fired again more carefully.

Down on the ground the three gunfighters had heard the firing of Weber's rifle. They whirled, saw the men silhouetted on the rim of the dam. Almost as if by command all three men sprang to the ground and, dropping down, began to fire at the men on the dam.

Atop the dam, the caretaker cried out and pitched forward into space. Weber, about to fire, looked down as the caretaker's body turned over and hit the ground almost eighty feet below.

"They've got rifles!" cried Fred Case, who was armed only with a revolver.

Weber also had a rifle and he now took careful aim at the wagon, hurtling toward the dam. About to squeeze the trigger he suddenly winced. The wagon was too close. The force of a great explosion could conceivably damage the sluice gates.

Exclaiming angrily, Weber shifted his aim to the three gunfighters on the ground. They made small targets, but . . .

A bullet whined past Weber, missing him by inches only. He squeezed the trigger. One of the gunfighters—Hopkins—seemed to rise up from the ground, then throw himself forward again.

A bullet kicked up dirt at Weber's knee. He pumped a fresh cartridge into the chamber, heard Fred Case suddenly gasp. The old foreman was hit and he was toppling forward. Weber, lunging for him, barely caught the old man. Case, although old, was fairly heavy and the momentum of his fall upset Weber. He had to fight to keep from being overbalanced himself, and in the struggle the rifle slipped from his grasp.

Weber hauled the old man back to safety, laid him down on the top of the earthen dam and then reached for his rifle. It was gone!

It had fallen off the dam.

Weber sprang to his feet and started running toward the end of the dam, toward the steps that led down to the valley floor. A bullet whizzed by him.

Down on the ground Charlie Weber and the three farmers were pushing their horses as hard as they could. The distraction offered by the men atop the dam was working greatly in their favor.

The farmers closed the distance rapidly, were within two hundred yards of the gunfighters when Partridge and Honsinger became aware of their danger and stopped firing at Tom Weber, who had reached the cement stairs.

They squirmed about and to their horror saw the four determined farmers bearing down on them. Honsinger fired a quick rifle shot at the men, then threw aside his rifle and whipped out his revolver.

He was at his best with the revolver. He swept the gun up and scarcely aiming fired two, three quick shots.

A horse screamed, broke in its stride and pitched forward to the ground, turning a complete somersault. Partridge also fired one last rifle bullet, taking aim. He yelped aloud as the man he had aimed at toppled from the saddle. He tried to pump another cartridge into the chamber, found the rifle was empty and threw it aside. He, too, went for his revolver.

"Come on, you clodhoppers!" he screamed. "Come on . . . !"

The two remaining farmers had come too close now to retreat. They were forced to come on and were meat for the two gunfighters at the closed distance.

Honsinger brought down Charlie Weber himself, and Partridge, springing to his feet, toppled the last man off his horse.

The two gunfighters had no time to celebrate their victory, however. Whirling, they saw Tom Weber taking the cement stairs two and three at a time. He was nearly to the bottom. If Partridge and Honsinger could get him before he reached the ground . . .

They started running forward, toward the cement stairs. Behind them, wounded Charlie Weber fought to his knees, to his feet. He had lost his rifle and carried no revolver, but thirty feet away lay Tate Hopkins, a huddled lump. A rifle lay near his hand. Charlie Weber focused his eyes on it and staggered toward it.

It was Newman, the driver of the fateful dynamite wagon, who saw Weber. He had reached the dam, was pulling up his horses. He wanted desperately to get away from the wagon.

Jumping to the ground, he saw Charlie Weber reach the dead figure of Tate Hopkins, stoop with an effort and scoop up the rifle.

Newman cried hoarsely, thinking Weber was going to

shoot at him—miss and hit the dynamite in the wagon. He went for his gun, threw a wild shot at Charlie Weber.

Partridge, running ahead of Honsinger, toward Tom Weber, was jolted to a halt by the shot from the unexpected direction. He whirled, saw Weber and, crying out, sent a snap shot at the old farmer. Weber recoiled from the bullet, dropped to his knees and raised Hopkin's rifle.

Ten feet from the ground, Tom Weber came to an abrupt halt on the steps. His tortured eyes shot past the approaching Honsinger, past Paul Partridge and on to his father a hundred yards away.

Honsinger skidded to a halt, fired at Tom Weber.

The bullet hit concrete just above Weber's head. Weber threw up his revolver, fired, and Honsinger on the ground below cried out and spun about.

Partridge fired a second time at Charlie Weber, knew that he scored. His face twisting into a terrible sneer, he turned—to face Tom Weber.

Weber's gun was dangling at his side. He called out, "All right, Partridge!"

Partridge snapped up his gun, fired faster than he had ever fired in his life.

Weber's gun exploded a fraction of a second before Partridge's.

Partridge went over backward, hit the ground and did not move.

Weber came down the steps, ran past the dead Honsinger, the dead Partridge and on to his father.

Charlie Weber lay on his back. His eyes were open, but there was already a bloody froth on his lips. His mouth worked horribly as he tried to talk. "T-Tom," he choked out finally.

"I'm here," Weber said simply.

"Son!" said Charlie Weber.

The froth on his mouth burst, a shudder ran through Charlie Weber and he was dead. Weber remained on his knees for a long moment, then got to his feet. He was aware of movement not too far away, but he did not turn in that direction.

He continued to look down at his father. Finally his lips moved and a whispered word came from them, "Dad. . . ."

Newman, the driver of the wagon, came up, his hands held above his shoulders. "I didn't have any part in this," he babbled. "I—I was only hired to drive the wagon."

Weber turned to him. "Go away," he said wearily.

154

Weber rode the black, Midnight, to the line of farmers that surrounded Lobo. He was recognized from a distance and men came to meet him, among them Kazumplik and Novak. They saw the bleakness of his face, but they had to know. Kazumplik said: "Your father . . . ?"

"Dead," said Weber.

A murmur ran up through the crowd. Weber, without even pausing, continued to ride. Men gave way before him. He passed through the encircling line of farmers, rode up to Lobo.

They saw him coming from Lobo and they saw also the farmers behind him. Mike Denver stepped out from the Lobo ranch house, into the ranchyard. He signaled to Sheriff Moon who was by the corrals.

Moon hesitated, but when Denver gestured to him a second time he moved out reluctantly. Denver looked over his shoulder. "Jeff," he called toward the house.

Alderton appeared in the doorway, a rifle in his hand, looked past Denver and stopped. He brought the rifle up to his shoulder.

Behind Alderton, Lily Barker Alderton let out a scream. She rushed forward, struck at her husband with her clenched fist—just as Alderton pulled the trigger.

The bullet intended for Tom Weber was diverted—enough to hit Mike Denver in the back.

The politician-schemer fell forward to his knees, then to the palms of his hands. He started to twist himself around. He fell to a sitting position and, with the blood welling out of his back, found the face of Jeff Alderton standing in the open doorway.

"You!" he said thickly. "You stupid, blundering . . ." His hands clawed at his coat pocket, went in and came out with a shot-barreled, nickel-plated revolver. He raised it before him, squinted along the short barrel.

Alderton, aghast for the moment at having struck Denver instead of his enemy, Tom Weber, made a sudden forward spring. He levered a cartridge into the chamber, thrust out his rifle—and fired.

The blast of the rifle drowned out the bark of the little revolver, but did not silence the third shot that was fired after the double report.

Weber's revolver.

Alderton pitched forward, shuddered and lay still. Lily Barker, rushing out of the house, went past the body of her husband, not even glancing at it. She continued on past Mike

155

Denver, lying on his back, staring sightlessly at the sky over Lobo that he had coveted so greatly in his life, and went on to meet Tom Weber, who had a gun in his hand.

No one ever told her later whose bullet had killed Jeff Alderton—Mike Denver's or Tom Weber's.

42

The carnage was over. The farmers returned to their farms and buried their dead. Weber attended the funeral of his father in the cemetery behind the little Bohemian church. Lily Alderton, newly widowed, was at the funeral and when it was over she went to where Weber was about to mount the black Lobo horse that he was still using.

"You'll be riding, Tom?" she asked quietly.

"No," he said bluntly, "I'm through riding. I've got a ranch here and——"

"A ranch without a house."

"I'll build a house."

"I've got a house," she said.

"He shook his head. "It's *your* house!"

"It's too big for me. Lobo's too big, Tom. I can't run it. Fred Case is old and he's crippled. He may never be able to ride a horse again. I need you, Tom."

"You hired me for some work. I did the job for you. . . ."

"I want to hire you again—as foreman."

He looked over her head, toward Helga Weber, who was dressed in black and walking from the grave that held all of her hopes—and all of her heart.

"If I take the job," Weber said harshly, "will you let Helga come to Lobo?"

"Where else should she go? Lobo's her home—from now on." Lily looked up at him, into the bleakness of his face that was somehow softening. "Isn't it . . ." she asked quietly.

He nodded—and suddenly reaching out touched her arm. It was just a light touch, but it was the second time in the past week that he had touched Lily Barker.

It would not be the last, she knew.